A Market for Murder

REBECCA TOPE

Allison & Busby Limited
12 Fitzroy Mews
London W1T 6DW
www.allisonandbusby.com

Hardcover first published in Great Britain in 2003
This paperback edition published in 2011.

Copyright © 2003 by Rebecca Tope

The moral right of the author has been asserted.

*All characters and events in this publication,
other than those clearly in the public domain,
are fictitious and any resemblance to actual persons,
living or dead, is purely coincidental.*

All rights reserved. No part of this publication may be reproduced,
stored in a retrieval system, or transmitted, in any form or by
any means without the prior written permission of the publisher,
nor be otherwise circulated in any form of binding or cover
other than that in which it is published and without a similar
condition being imposed on the subsequent buyer.

A CIP catalogue record for this book is available from
the British Library.

10 9 8 7 6 5

ISBN 978-0-7490-0894-9

Typeset in 10.75/14 pt Sabon by
Allison & Busby Ltd.

The paper used for this Allison & Busby publication
has been produced from trees that have been legally sourced
from well-managed and credibly certified forests.

Printed and bound in the UK by
CPI Group (UK) Ltd, Croydon, CR0 4YY

*This book is dedicated to librarians
everywhere, with thanks*

CHARACTER LIST

At Peaceful Repose Burial Ground, North Staverton
KAREN SLOCOMBE

DREW SLOCOMBE

STEPHANIE and TIMMY – their children

MAGGS BEACON

DEN COOPER – former police detective, partner to Maggs

GERALDINE BEECH – organiser of the Food Chain and farmers' markets

The Stallholders
PETER GRAFTON – fruit juices

SALLY DABB – pickles

HILARY HENDERSON – honey and jams

MAGGIE WITHINGTON – bread

JOE RICHARDS – organic meat

OSWALD KELLY – ostrich meat

Others
JULIE GRAFTON – wife of Peter

DELLA GRAY – resident of North Staverton. Karen's friend, sharing childcare

BILL GRAY – Della's husband

FINIAN and TODD – their children

MARY THOMAS – friend of Geraldine Beech and Hilary Henderson

ARCHIE DABB – Sally's husband

ROBIN DABB – Sally's son

CHAPTER ONE

Stephanie's enthusiasm was all the more irritating for being so normal. Four years old, attracted to the sugars and colourings and froth of foods on offer, who could blame her for getting so excited?

'It's rubbish, Steph,' Karen repeated. 'Hardly any of it's real food.' She glared at the rows of brightly coloured yoghurts and Fruit Corners. 'Nothing but artificial junk.'

Her daughter pouted. 'Why did we come then?' she wanted to know.

Good question, Karen silently acknowledged. 'Because we have to get some tinned stuff. Beans and things,' she said feebly. And dishonestly. She didn't know, now, why she'd ventured back into SuperFare after almost a year of buying exclusively from village shops and local markets. Curiosity, probably. And something darker and deeper than that. The huge space, full of dazzling light, violent chaotic colours, jangly music and thronging shoppers – it was where people went. Had she perhaps been missing something by so determinedly avoiding it? She looked around her at the faces: most of them concentrated totally on the shelves surrounding them. Their eyes were narrowed, their mouths tight. It didn't strike Karen as an enjoyable process. There was something dogged and inhuman about these consumers doing their weekly food shop. Or so she liked to think.

She hoped she wouldn't meet anybody she knew. Recently, she'd become more and more outspoken on the iniquities of supermarkets. It would look like hypocrisy to be caught here now. Like a professed atheist turning up in church.

'Can we get some Coco Pops?' Stephanie asked. 'And those – what are they?' The child was pointing at a row of bright yellow bottles, containing some sort of pseudo milk drink.

'No,' Karen said vaguely. Then more firmly, 'No, darling. I'm sorry. I know it all looks wonderful. But it's nearly all rubbish, I promise you. The meat's tasteless, the fruit comes from the other side of the world, everything's processed and flavoured with chemicals. It's all travelled thousands of miles and been sitting in fridges and freezers for weeks.'

'Mummy!' Stephanie planted herself firmly in front of her mother.

Karen looked down at the child and smiled. 'I know,' she agreed. 'I'm being mean, aren't I. Look, it was a big mistake coming here. Let's just go, OK. Before they suck our souls out. This place is full of badness. The demons of commercialism are lurking behind the soft drinks, waiting to corrupt us.' She twisted her face and clawed her hands in illustration.

Stephanie giggled doubtfully and indicated the trolley containing two tins of baked beans and a jar of pickled beetroot, tilting her head to one side.

'Let's just leave it,' Karen whispered, rolling her eyes. 'Come on. We can go to the swings and slides on the way home.'

They almost ran back to the clanging jostling ranks of checkouts, where Karen paused. There was no way out other than through a gap between conveyor-belts, every one of which had a cluster of people waiting to pay for their goods. It was heresy to approach without a basket or a trolley. Already they were attracting glances.

Karen took a breath. 'Excuse me,' she said loudly. 'My little girl's going to be sick. Can you let us out quickly please.'

The obstructing shoppers parted like the Red Sea before Moses, and seconds later they were in the car park.

'Mummy!' Stephanie breathed, eyes wide with horrified delight. 'You told a lie!'

Before she could defend herself, Karen became aware of a familiar face close by: a woman with thick grey hair and dark eyebrows. 'Hello,' she said, without thinking. 'Fancy meeting you here!' The dark eyes probed mother and daughter, frowning slightly as if sensing something odd. Karen reproached herself. If she hadn't said anything, the woman probably wouldn't have noticed her. Now Mary Thomas, good friend of Geraldine Beech, would know she, Karen, had been to a supermarket.

'Oh – hello,' responded the woman distractedly. 'Are you coming or going?'

'Going,' Karen said.

'We didn't buy anything,' Stephanie explained capably. 'I felt sick, so we came out again.'

'Poor you,' Mary Thomas sympathised. 'Are you all right now?'

'Yes. I'm all right now.'

Afterwards, Karen couldn't say for certain whether it was the sight or sound or smell that struck her first, but it was the smell that remained with her. The hot, sharp, smoky reek that came billowing at them from one of the

10

big plate glass windows of the supermarket.

'Mummy!' Stephanie shrieked, her voice lost in the booming, crashing, screaming noise. Karen wrapped her arms around the child, bending over her, without thought. But she didn't hide her face and she didn't close her eyes. She watched the glass as it rained down on the tarmac, less than ten yards away; the shadowy faces and bodies inside the shop; the frozen men and women dotted around the car park; all staring in amazement at the new hole in their beloved cathedral of consumerism.

Drew couldn't stop shaking. Even the next day, his hands trembled and his heart outperformed itself. After the fifth repetition of 'You could have been killed' Karen ordered him to stop it.

'But we weren't,' she chided him. 'Neither was anybody else, come to that. Get a sense of proportion, you idiot.'

An old man had been sitting close to the abandoned carrier bag containing an explosive device, and was accordingly on life support in hospital. A young man and a middle-aged woman had both sustained unpleasant injuries inflicted by shards of metal from the window frame; others had been shocked. But the greatest impact had been taken by the window itself, which had obligingly exploded outwards onto an empty stretch of car park, causing no further damage.

The small town buzzed with the story of the supermarket bomb. The police appeared to be stunned and bemused, devoting their efforts to minute forensic examinations of the scene. Why in the world, they pondered, should anybody want to blow up SuperFare? Everybody *loved* the place. It sold loaves of sliced bread for 18p, baked beans for 16p and fifty-nine different sorts of breakfast cereal. Nobody had ever suggested that it was a bad employer. Indeed, it had recently donated a handsome sum towards a local scheme to give disabled children a better life. 'Must have been a nutcase' was the comfortable conclusion.

'Small explosion, nobody killed,' summarised Maggs carelessly to Drew in the office. 'If Karen and Steph hadn't been there, you wouldn't have given it a second thought.'

'I think I would,' he argued mildly. 'It's not exactly a regular occurrence around here. Somebody must have felt pretty strongly to have done that.'

'Maybe they meant it for their mother-in-law, and left it in the supermarket by mistake.'

Drew managed a laugh. 'Maybe they did,' he said.

Karen had not admitted to Drew quite how shaken she'd been by the incident. Not merely because Stephanie had needed more reassurance and attention than she'd expected, but because an attack on a supermarket was uncomfortably close to home. Over the past year, she had become increasingly involved in growing vegetables and fruit for sale, and participating in promotional and educational initiatives on behalf of locally produced food. She knew a number of people who loathed supermarkets and everything they stood for. And, it quickly turned out, everyone knew where she stood on the matter, too.

The Monday after the bomb, two police officers visited Karen at home. 'Mrs Slocombe? We understand that you were at the scene of the explosion at SuperFare on Saturday afternoon. Would you be kind enough to answer a few questions for us?'

Silently, Karen assured herself that it was mere routine. She had given her name and address to the police when they appeared minutes after the bomb exploded, and had been told there'd probably be some sort of follow-up. That's all it would be. She nodded, with a faint smile, and ushered them in.

They weren't particularly probing. They had a routine set of questions, noting down the answers with little sign of intelligent interest. 'Do you know anybody who might have a reason to want to attack the supermarket?' was the only one that seemed at all likely to lead to any sort of increased understanding on their part. It was also the only question that gave Karen some difficulty.

'Well . . .' she began, wondering how little she could get away with revealing. 'Um . . . I do know some people who advocate local food production. You know – they worry about food miles and exploitation of producers . . .'

She'd lost them. The phrases she'd used were part of daily discourse in the circles she mixed in, but they were clearly impenetrable jargon to these two young men. The one with the question sheet held his pen suspended over the paper. 'You mean a sort of pressure group?' he asked eventually, with a frown.

'Yes, that's right,' she nodded. 'You know – the people who run the farmers' markets, and all that.'

Relief suffused his features. 'Oh, yes. Mrs Beech and her friends. She's a school governor where my boys go.'

That was all right then, Karen realised wryly. Geraldine Beech was a dynamo who threw herself into a wide range of community activities, most notably a collective dedicated to local food production, known as the Food Chain. She was a friend to everyone, it seemed, including the police. The fact that she regularly made impassioned public speeches against the evils of supermarkets had evidently escaped their attention.

'One last question – did you see anybody you knew in the supermarket?'

Watching him, Karen realised that this was not on his crib sheet. He'd come up with it all by himself, which rather increased her respect for him, as well as her sense of unease.

'Just Mary,' she responded. 'In the car park. Didn't she give you her details?' She couldn't recall whether or not Mary had still been there when the police arrived. The man cocked an eyebrow at her.

'Mary?' he prompted.

'Oh, sorry. Mary Thomas. She lives at Cherry Blossoms, in Ferngate. You know where I mean?' She took a moment to note his blank expression. In former times, there'd have been a local bobby who wouldn't have needed any more than the name to be completely up to speed. Like they'd been when she'd mentioned Geraldine. Mary, it seemed, was rather less prominent, and Karen had to elaborate: 'That big house with a stone wall around it, right in the middle of the village. Anyway, I'm sure she'll have reported to you on the day, the same as I did.'

'Her name isn't here,' the policeman said. 'Which means she didn't make herself known to the officer at the time.' He wrote down the name and address she'd supplied. Karen found herself feeling mildly anxious at having given Mary away, before reminding herself that this feeling automatically accompanied any passing of information to the police. It seemed like a built-in gut reaction, no matter how innocent everybody might be.

The policemen left then, without enquiring as to whether she or Stephanie had suffered any aftershocks or post-traumatic symptoms. Not their problem, she assumed, with a flicker of resentment.

Den Cooper came to collect Maggs from work, as was his habit since they'd set up home together in the neighbouring village of South Staverton, three miles away. No longer a Detective Sergeant, he had found a modest job with the local Social Services, while he tried to decide what to do with the rest of his life. Karen kept him supplied with vegetables, and somehow he and Maggs managed to pay their rent and run a car. Maggs was now a full partner with Drew in his Peaceful Repose Burial Service, taking a share of all profits – but despite a steady increase in business, it was still a very modest income for them both.

Den and Maggs found themselves surrounded by people – including Drew and Karen – who had more or less dropped out of the consumer society. Instead of competing for the biggest car and most luxurious home furnishings, it had very much gone the other way. There was a contest, albeit unacknowledged, to see who could exist on the smallest income, and with most ecological virtue. This approach seemed to have spread rapidly amongst the local inhabitants, so that barter and mutual help were almost the norm. Everybody recycled as much as they could and helped each other with maintenance work. They gave each other lifts to save on fuel, and organised working parties to tackle large communal tasks. It felt like a big enjoyable game to most of the participants, with a dramatically snowballing effect as more and more ideas floated up on how they could enhance this 'alternative' lifestyle. Even Maggs, cynical child of her age as she was in many ways, quickly became one of the greatest enthusiasts.

And yet nobody quite knew where all this had started. Drew's natural burial service had been a factor, slowly establishing itself as a popular alternative to the sterile, formulaic cremations that had been threatening to become the only option. For a wide range of people the allure of the open field, on its gentle slope with a burgeoning assortment of young trees marking the graves, ensured that they brought their custom to Drew when their parents and spouses died. From a rocky beginning, where one funeral a week had been a distant goal, he and Maggs had somehow held on until three years later they were regularly conducting four or five interments each week. The eight-acre field, in theory capable of accommodating three or four thousand graves, was still far from full. But Drew had never intended to fill it as densely as a municipal cemetery, and had allowed his customers to choose favoured spots, so that it was now dotted with saplings and rough-hewn boulders, indicating burials right across the available land. Keeping track of precisely which plot contained which individual was one of Maggs's main tasks, and she performed it with total conscientiousness.

Karen's interest in growing vegetables had arisen even more casually. There had been a half-acre section of land between the house and the burial ground, which most people would have put to lawn with perhaps a few shrubs and borders. While there was some lawn remaining, with a climbing frame and swing for the children, most of it was now devoted to potatoes, beans, sprouts and a lot more. A substantial surplus had coincided with the launch of a local farmers' market and she had taken a stall from the outset. As the whole initiative staggered from tiny beginnings to an increasingly popular source of locally grown fresh food, Karen had found herself more and more involved.

But it was a jerky process, rife with setbacks and frustrations. Almost every stage of the business was obstructed by Government guidelines and Health and Safety Regulations. Labelling, packaging, traceability and storage were all potential sources of trouble. Many a time Karen threatened to drop the whole thing, but the charismatic Geraldine Beech always prevailed on her to stick with it.

'Don't you wish you were still a cop?' Drew teased his friend, as he prepared to close the office for the day. 'All this excitement over the bomb must make you miss it.'

Cooper blew out his long lean cheeks in scorn. 'No way,' he objected. 'It'll be all down to forensics, anyway. Whoever left that bag will be well away by now.'

'Karen was there,' Drew said, trying to keep his tone mild. 'And Steph.'

Cooper did a double take. Suddenly it was a lot less funny. 'What? Karen doesn't go to supermarkets.'

Drew smiled ruefully. 'That's right. She doesn't. But on Saturday she did. Even she doesn't seem to really know why.'

Maggs had already gone to the car, parked just outside the gate. She tooted the horn now, summoning Den. 'Gotta go,' he grinned. 'Her Ladyship won't wait.'

'You have to be firm with her,' the undertaker advised, for the hundredth time. The relationship between Maggs and Den, now approaching its first anniversary, had not always run smooth. Most people winced at the punishment the tall mild-tempered man took with apparent equanimity. He even seemed to like it.

'See you then,' he threw back over his shoulder, as he trotted down the path from Drew's office. Karen came to the front door of the adjacent cottage and waved, but Den didn't see her.

'He's in a hurry,' she called to Drew, as the elderly Fiat pulled away.

Drew locked the office door, and hopped over the low fence dividing his work premises from his home. 'Maggs waits for no one,' he said. 'Why – did you want to talk to him?'

'Sort of. Did he say anything about the supermarket bomb?'

'Only that he was glad it didn't concern him.'

'You saw the police here, I suppose?' She looked him in the eye, and he realised she was perturbed.

'No.' He frowned. 'When?'

'Damn it, Drew. You must have seen their car. They parked it across the gateway. They asked me a whole lot of questions, because I was there at the time of the bomb. Whether I'd seen anyone I knew.' She chipped irritably at a fingernail, staring unseeingly at it, waiting for her husband's response.

'So which is the bit that bothers you?' he asked mildly.

'Oh, I don't know. It felt scary, that's all. I mean – supermarkets are a sensitive subject around here. They didn't seem to understand that, and I didn't want to be the one to explain it to them.'

He pulled her to him, and rubbed gently between her shoulder blades. 'Nobody expects you to,' he chided. 'You're still in a state of shock, that's all. They should have been more careful than to come blundering in less than two days after it happened. I bet they never asked how Steph was, either.'

Karen shook her head. 'No, they didn't,' she pouted.

'Then they don't deserve your help. Let them work it out for themselves. You've got enough to worry about.'

She wriggled away from him, making an exaggerated expression of anger at the blundering police.

'Yes, I have, haven't I,' she agreed.

CHAPTER TWO

Three towns in the area provided venues for farmers' markets, with Bradbourne hosting theirs every other Tuesday. Seven stallholders presented themselves this week, arriving before eight o'clock and setting up their displays. Geraldine Beech was, as always, at hand, fielding questions, complaints, disruptions and disasters. The area designated for the stalls was not ideal: Bradbourne had an old town centre with narrow streets. Its Market Hall was firmly under the control of the mainstream traders, selling picture frames, sweets, books and Taiwanese toys. No way would the 'organic brigade' be permitted access to those portals. They therefore clustered at the widest part of the main street, down at one end where there was a sort of square. Unfortunately the square was bordered by shops selling meat, vegetables and bread. The competition with the farmers was all too obvious, and all too full of animosity.

Lukewarm support from the Town Council had provided 'no parking' cones, and very little else. Once the local shopkeepers had realised this, they blithely disregarded the cones and parked their vehicles obstructively on the square. Geraldine Beech, undaunted, arranged the stalls between and beside the cars and vans, blocking them in on occasion. By the time everything was set up and the first shoppers drifting up, tempers were frayed and emotions running high.

Oswald Kelly, who kept ostriches and sold their meat, and was therefore inevitably known to all as 'Oswald-the-ostriches', always made a big production about his 'tasters'. Small crumbs of warm meat were provided for would-be customers. He had to keep a heater going all morning, powered by a small generator which made a large noise. Stallholders on either side complained they couldn't hear their own customers over the racket, and the Council inspector clearly didn't like it either, when he did his rounds. Oswald made helpless deprecating gestures, but did nothing to reduce the nuisance. Tall and thin, a big white apron wrapped around himself, he presented a gloomy demeanour, despite the somewhat ludicrous ostrich feather that he wore in his white chef's hat. 'Don't worry,' he said, from time to time. 'I'll soon be out of business at this rate.' Ostrich meat sold slowly.

Maggie Withington sold bread, and did a roaring trade. There was never enough, and by ten o'clock she had usually sold out, and was impatient to pack up and go home. But she couldn't because she was always blocked in, and to dismantle her stall and take it all home would leave a gaping hole that Geraldine would not permit. So she counted her profits, tucked it all away safely and then went off to stroll around town and get herself a cup of coffee.

Geraldine had her undoubted favourites. Karen Slocombe was one of them. Quiet but friendly, reliable and good-natured, she caused very little trouble. She was also interesting to talk to. It generally happened that the two would slope off to a side street coffee shop in the middle of the morning and spend a pleasant twenty minutes in companionable gossip.

The gossip this week was mainly about a developing romance between two other members of Geraldine's favoured list. Peter Grafton and Sally Dabb were both married, and seemed to be complacently convinced that nobody had noticed a thing. Their stalls were side by side, and they often had to be shouted at by customers before they would disengage from their intense conversations. Peter's fruit juices and Sally's pickles were dependable stalwarts of the market, neither presenting any competition to other stalls – which was probably why everyone seemed to like them.

Over coffee with Karen, Geraldine chuckled tolerantly, having commented on the increasing intimacy between the two. 'Have you ever seen Sally's husband?' she asked.

Karen shook her head. 'I don't think so. He doesn't come to any of our meetings, does he?'

Geraldine gripped her mug of coffee with a strong brown hand, and tossed her grey-blonde curls dismissively. 'Doesn't want to get involved. He's an electrician; about five foot five – at least two inches shorter than Sally, with nasty thin hair and a strong Birmingham accent. When you compare him to Peter . . . well, who can blame her?'

Karen's smile was queasy. 'It just seems – well, so . . .' she stuttered. '*Blatant*, I suppose.'

Geraldine patted her hand maternally. 'When you get to my age, you learn to live and let live.'

For the hundredth time, Karen wondered exactly how old Geraldine was. It bothered her that she couldn't find an answer to such a simple question. The woman had no children, no husband, not even any parents as far as anyone knew. She just *was*. Her face was weathered, but could have been a battered fifty as easily as a mobile sixty-five. And for some reason, Karen had never felt able to ask outright. It felt like a secret that Geraldine seemed anxious to preserve, which struck Karen as silly, but insurmountable.

Using a phrase like 'when you get to my age' was pure provocation, and Karen sighed impatiently. 'But Sally's got that little boy,' she objected crossly. 'Doesn't she know what a risk she's taking? It can't possibly have a happy ending, can it?'

Geraldine shrugged. 'Who can say? It might turn out to be best for everyone.'

Karen felt even angrier. 'Of course it won't. Peter's got a perfectly nice wife. How long's he been married – five years? It's all wrong. So many hurt feelings.'

'Hey, don't get in a state about it. I'm not even sure they've, er, *acted* on it, yet, anyhow. It could just be a harmless flirtation.' Geraldine kneaded her own neck absently. Karen watched in fascination, noting that there was scarcely any spare flesh under the woman's chin. No 'wattles' as Americans called them.

The conversation turned to the price of greens and organic beef. Karen knew herself to be a heretic when it came to matters organic.

She refused to pay the high prices charged by the producers of meat or milk with the magic label, unable to convince herself that they were justified. The myths surrounding meat production irritated her more and more, as she talked to local farmers and understood more of their problems. But she had learnt to keep quiet on the subject in the presence of Geraldine and most of the others. She still didn't have enough hard facts to sustain an argument, and was loathe to place herself in purdah on account of her opinions.

Feelings ran high when it came to chemical fertilisers, antibiotics and pesticides, and her moral credit was healthy, thanks to Drew and his natural burials. If it was possible for a funeral to be organic, then Drew's were. Karen's garden produce was fresh and healthy, with judicious daubs of mud on the carrots and swedes to authenticate them. When questioned, she would openly admit to an occasional dressing of commercial fertiliser, but denied ever using toxic pesticides. Nobody had yet made the connection between the presence of dead human beings just the other side of the fence and the exuberant growth of her crops. Not that there *was* any direct connection, Karen would have insisted – it was just a rather disconcerting thought.

There were those amongst the market stallholders who wouldn't dream of poisoning their systems with coffee, or tea or alcohol. Karen, who had actually been known to buy the concentrated caffeine drinks designed to keep drivers awake on tedious motorways, openly rebelled at such extremes. And yet she liked these people. She respected their principles and the air of something like purity that hovered around them. Perhaps that was why she felt so uneasy about the affair between Peter and Sally being conducted right under her nose.

Back at her post for the final hour or so of the morning, she threw herself animatedly into the task of selling everything on her stall. Spring greens, early lettuce, broad beans, and radishes were the only varieties she had on offer, May being a lean month, harvest-wise. The lettuces were already starting to look tired, despite only having been pulled that morning. The cool weather should have kept them fresh for a while longer, she thought crossly, the image of the bright green and apparently eternally crisp offerings in the supermarket entering her mind unbidden.

She knew many of her customers by sight if not name. Scarcely any of them were under thirty-five and most were well over fifty. There were very few men of any age. This was largely due to it being a weekday morning, of course. It was only to be expected that 'housewives' would make up the great majority of shoppers. But people worked in offices in many of the buildings close at hand.

They could, if they chose, run out for ten minutes to buy some fresh local provisions, instead of calling in at the supermarket on the way home. There was cheese, meat, bread, vegetables, pickles, jams, honey and fruit juice all available. Apart from milk, this range seemed to Karen to cover everything they might need for their evening meal. And yet almost nobody would consider making the market their sole source of food for the day.

She'd raged about it to Drew and Geraldine and even poor old Den, many a time, until they were all tired of hearing her. 'You're doing your best to change it,' Drew assured her. 'But if the market's only there once a fortnight, how can you expect people to remember? You're asking them to change their routine, one day in fourteen. It's against human nature, Kaz. Surely you can see that?'

The fact that she *could* see it only made the whole thing more frustrating.

Hilary Henderson, who sold honey and homemade jam, strolled across, as she often did, for a chat. 'Doing OK?' she asked.

Karen indicated her almost-bare stall. 'Fine,' she nodded. 'How about you?'

'Only one jar of last year's honey left. I had four hundred in September. They'll all have to wait a while now, until the next lot's taken off.'

'How many hives have you got now?'

'Seven. I just got a new one.'

'It must be a lot of work. And all that jam-making as well.'

Hilary laughed, her mouth unselfconsciously wide, despite some blackened and crooked teeth. She was a broad woman with well-developed muscles, who made no concessions to social niceties. She had wiry black hairs growing from her chin and bushy black eyebrows. Unlike Geraldine, she made no bones about the rapid approach of her sixtieth birthday. Mother of five children, wife of a farmer, she was outspoken, sociable and disconcertingly intelligent. Her small brown eyes, almost lost in a network of wrinkles, saw everything that went on. Keeping seven hives in full production was just one of her innumerable occupations.

'No more work than you're doing,' she said, with her comfortable Devon tones. 'Don't tell me you're a slouch, Mrs Slocombe, because I wouldn't believe you. Look round you – Sally, Geraldine, Maggie – they all work a twelve-hour day in one way or another. 'Tis the way women are. Nothing surprising to it. Work or die, seems to me. What else is there to life?'

Karen regularly found herself wishing she knew Hilary better; that they had time for longer chats over drinks or even a meal once in a while. There was a sense of suppressed emotion about her – something hot, like rage, though tempered by a lucid intelligence and genuine friendliness. At meetings, Hilary Henderson always made passionate speeches about the obstructive Town Council and the timidity of the food producers. She had no time for regulations, shrugging off the edicts about labelling and precise weighing that she and her husband were supposed to adhere to.

Being one of Hilary's pets was not always comfortable, but it was infinitely better than being on her blacklist. For some reason Oswald-the-ostriches was in this latter category. Hilary was constantly casting bitter and contemptuous glances his way, and losing no opportunity to ridicule him and his product. His noisy generator only fuelled her dislike, and more than once she had sabotaged it by throwing a blanket over it, or disconnecting a vital piece of its workings.

Karen gazed around at the whole untidy scene, wondering as she often did just what she was doing there. It felt, if she was honest, like a pointless exercise. She didn't make any serious money at it; she didn't change anybody's habits or opinions; she liked the people well enough, but didn't really *care* about them. It had meant she had to enter into an inflexible childminding arrangement with a neighbour, which she and Stephanie, if not two-year-old Timmy, found irksome at times.

But she knew she'd carry on. Telling Geraldine otherwise was too daunting a prospect. Suddenly, she caught the eye of Peter Grafton, over the ranks of bottled apple juice that hadn't appeared to sell too well this morning. He, like her, seemed to be scanning the whole market, and Karen had the impression that although their eyes had met, he hadn't fully registered her identity. He seemed distracted, almost afraid, in those few seconds of connection. Afterwards, Karen strained repeatedly to recapture the precise look on his face.

Because as she watched, something awful happened to Peter Grafton's throat. He was wearing an open-necked shirt, jaunty as always. Before he could clap a frantic hand to the place, blood spurted. Some sort of stick was incomprehensibly fixed right through his neck. Nobody else had noticed. Everything continued as before, in the clatter of Oswald's generator and the rumble of traffic. Karen screamed. Then she turned to look behind her, where the pavement was thinly occupied, with a hedge behind it, the public lavatories and a pedestrian walkway to the town's main car park beyond that. There was nothing to see: just a slowly increasing stillness as everyone very gradually reacted to events. When she turned back again, Peter was gone, too. Karen began to think she must be in a dream.

Then the turmoil started. Not the panicked general expression of fear and confusion that there'd been after the supermarket bomb. This was acute and personal distress. And there was a word contained in it. *'Peter!'* it howled, at the highest achievable pitch. Karen pushed around her stall towards the spot.

Sally Dabb was kneeling over Peter's prostrate form. Shoppers and stallholders coagulated into ranks of helpless observation. Then one of them shoved forward, throwing herself down beside the bleeding victim. Sally continued to scream, but no one else seemed moved to join in. Strange how unafraid we all are, thought Karen, simultaneously noting that she was in fact very much afraid. She had been watching as Peter received some sort of bolt or arrow through his vulnerable throat. She could feel the skin of her back contracting at the thought that the same thing could at any moment happen to her.

The newcomer straightened, after a quick inspection. 'He's dead, I think,' she said.

In the street, only yards away, traffic continued to flow, albeit slowly, as the drivers understood that there was something going on. Karen was rooted where she stood, unable to think of anything constructive she might do. The aftermath of the supermarket bomb superimposed itself on her awareness, until she wasn't sure where she was, or what was happening. *At least Stephanie's not here* she thought. This wasn't as bad as Saturday had been. She'd coped then, and she'd cope now.

Unlike at the supermarket, the police seemed to take an age to arrive. The crowd grew bigger; nobody appeared to be in charge, not even Geraldine. Sally had stopped screaming and simply sat on the ground, legs curled beneath her, holding Peter Grafton's hand. Every few seconds she would raise her head and look round at all the faces, eyes wide.

The woman who had broken ranks and pronounced Peter's death was Mary Thomas, Karen slowly realised, with no sense of significance. Mary Thomas was out and about a lot – asking her usual brisk questions, pushing her face into yours, as if waiting to snatch up your replies before they were half out of your mouth. She was wealthy, intelligent, highly competent and intrusive. You'd expect it to be Mary Thomas who stepped forward at a time like this.

Suddenly the whole scene began to disintegrate. An ambulance appeared, closely followed by a police car. People were moved back but asked not to disappear. With an efficiency that greatly redeemed the police force in Karen's eyes, they collected names and addresses and eye witness statements. Nobody moved Peter's body, and the thought suddenly came to Karen that he probably wanted to be buried in Drew's field. At least, that's what he *would* have wanted, if he'd been able to express a preference.

But Drew couldn't have him yet – not by a long way. The ambulance men were shaking their heads, and explaining to Sally, still clinging to the dead hand, that it wasn't a job for them. Peter would have to be taken to the mortuary at the Royal Victoria Hospital, once the police had finished examining the scene.

The police had initially assumed that Sally was Mrs Grafton, and it took them some time to ascertain that not only was she 'just a good friend' but that the real Mrs Grafton was presumed to be somewhere in Yorkshire, because her father was in hospital there and she'd gone up some days ago to be close to him.

It emerged that Karen was the only person who had seen the impact of the bolt, which was by this time confusedly understood to have been fired from a crossbow. The word *crossbow* was circulating through the crowd, to universally raised eyebrows and rounded mouths. Karen was asked to describe exactly where Peter had been standing and precisely which way he'd been facing. The missile had approached him from in front. He had been facing Karen; therefore the bowman must have been somewhere in Karen's direction. Behind her, she concluded, after a moment's consideration.

She and the police officers scanned the scene behind her stall. They carefully noted the clump of trees on the right, the public lavatories behind the tidy little hedge, the pedestrian route to the car park – little more than an alleyway – and then, on the left, a bank and a cycle shop, both with residential flats on the first floor. The windows of these flats overlooked the site of the market. 'I didn't see anybody running off.' She frowned at the man questioning her. 'It can't have been an accident, can it?' she concluded. Reconstructing the exact angles was almost impossible. The bolt could have come from a surprisingly wide arc, it seemed. Peter could have turned slightly at the critical moment. And, of course, nobody had examined the body very attentively yet. Undertakers would have to come and transport him to the mortuary before that happened. The police surgeon, expected at any moment, would merely confirm sudden and suspicious death. A photographer would capture angles and environs, distances and debris.

The market stallholders were anxious to take

down their stands and go home, shaken and sickened by what had happened, but the police wouldn't let them. Everything had to be left exactly as it was, so the Scenes of Crime people could make their measurements and search for significant clues. Geraldine Beech dithered uncharacteristically. 'How long will that take?' she asked.

'Best part of the day,' came the laconic reply.

Karen's gaze kept returning to the inert covered length of Peter Grafton, dead on the ground in a sea of blood, trying to make sense of the attack on him. The bolt must have severed an artery; but he had died too quickly for loss of blood to be the cause. Perhaps his spinal cord had been in the path of the missile, or maybe the appalling trauma was in itself enough to close down vital functions. In any case, he hadn't had much time to suffer; for that, she tried to persuade herself, they should all be thankful.

It seemed indecent to leave him there so long. Sally Dabb had been led away, weeping now, but still wide-eyed.

Suddenly, into the picture walked Den Cooper, a head taller than anyone else present, his long stride and calm manner giving him a natural air of authority. 'Karen?' he said, looking round. 'What the hell's happened?'

'Peter Grafton's been shot. He's dead. I saw it.'

And something all of a sudden clicked. She saw it reflected in Den's eyes. 'They won't think it's something to do with me, will they?' she gasped. 'After the supermarket on Saturday as well?'

'They'll have noted it,' he said neutrally.

'And Mary – Mary Thomas was there, too. And here,' she babbled disjointedly. 'Where is she?' Karen slowly looked at the people still lingering in the vicinity. 'She's gone.' She ran a hand through her hair. 'They told everybody to stay, but she's gone. Why are *you* here?' she demanded.

'I saw the squad car, and the tape. Old habit made me curious. I'm supposed to be somewhere in a minute.' He glanced at his watch. 'There's an old man that nobody's seen for a week or so. They wanted me to go along, when they break down the door. I always seem to get that job.'

Karen grimaced sympathetically. 'It's all happening, isn't it. Even in sleepy little Bradbourne.'

'Right,' he sighed. 'But a shooting's well out of character. A *street* shooting, anyhow.'

'Actually, it wasn't a gun,' she elaborated. 'It looks as though it was a crossbow.'

'Good God,' said Den. 'I hate those things. I always think anyone keeping a crossbow must be a bit twisted.'

They were standing outside the police tape,

close to the shop owned by the butcher who took exception to the farmers' market. 'Me too,' Karen agreed. Jumbled thoughts skirled through her head.

She turned to gaze at the window of the butcher's shop: could *he* have done it, from his own doorway? Maddened to the point of murder by the competition and the disruption? But why *Peter*? Much better to shoot Oswald, if you didn't want people selling meat, or Joe Richards, with his expensive organic Aberdeen Angus beef.

'Did you know the chap?' Den was speaking softly, as if aware that it was not his place to be asking the questions.

'Peter? Yes, a bit. He was one of the originals, like me.'

Den cocked his head sideways. 'Original whats?'

'Stallholders. He did the apple juice. Not just apple – pear, apricot, blackcurrant, as well. Lovely stuff.'

'Right.' Den stopped her. 'I thought . . .'

'What?'

'I'm not sure. I didn't think he'd be a market trader.' He scratched the slight groove between his eyes. 'Why didn't I?'

'I have no idea.' Karen let irritation season her words. A headache had taken hold, jabbing sharply on one side of her brow. 'Look, I'm going home. I can't take any more of this now. When are they going to move that body?' Her voice was growing shrill.

'Hey, hey. Don't get in a state. The undertaker's men will be here any minute now, and take him off to the mortuary. They had to wait for the photographer and the police doctor and the SOCO people. What time did it happen, anyway?'

'Oh, I don't know. Elevenish, I suppose. Maybe ten past.'

'Well, it's only half past now. They haven't been hanging about.'

'Half past? Half past *eleven*?' She stared at him. 'It can't be.'

He smiled his understanding. 'Time can do funny things,' he said.

Drew sat down heavily, as the full import of Karen's story sank in. 'I don't believe it,' he said, untruthfully. She was hardly going to make something like that up.

'It's true,' she assured him. 'Peter Grafton, the apple juice man, was shot dead in the middle of Bradbourne farmers' market, and I saw the whole thing.'

'Thank God you didn't have the kids with you this time,' he said thoughtlessly.

'This time?' she echoed. 'You think I

deliberately make a habit of being there when people are trying to kill each other?'

'Of course not. Don't be stupid. It's just a coincidence.'

'I know that. What else could it be?' She fixed him with a savage glare. 'And it's not just me, anyhow. Mary Thomas was there both times.'

'Oh?'

'But she's got more sense than me. She managed to make herself scarce before the police showed up – both times. There's only my word for it that she was at the supermarket.' She stopped for a second's reflection, before adding, 'Unless she had someone in the car with her.'

Drew took a deep breath. 'Well, I just hope this is the end of it,' he said. 'My nerves won't stand much more.'

'Den was there this morning,' she offered, in a calmer voice. 'Just happened to be passing. Maybe that's all it was with Mary. Bradbourne's a small place, after all.'

'True,' Drew agreed, before the phone rang and Karen left him to it.

Childcare had been a difficulty for Drew and Karen when Stephanie was small, but the gradual emergence of a genuine community structure in the cluster of local villages had provided a solution. Karen left both children with Della Gray, another North Staverton mum, on Tuesdays and Fridays, in return for having Della's Finian and Todd on Mondays and Thursdays. No money changed hands, and the kids remained the best of friends – or so their mothers liked to believe. 'Why isn't everyone doing it like this?' Karen wondered, over and over. 'Instead of all that hassle with day nurseries and minders?'

'Because most people work full-time, and this sort of set-up wouldn't solve the problem,' Maggs told her crisply. Much of what Maggs said carried a subtext of *Surely you already know the answer to that!*

'Yes, but they could work part-time, which suits most people better anyway,' Karen had argued weakly. Arguing with Maggs was seldom a good idea.

'Round here, maybe,' the girl nodded. 'But this isn't typical.' And then she'd lost interest, leaving Karen to finish the debate in her own head.

Collecting Stephanie and Timmy from Della's was one of her favourite moments. She would walk the mile through the village, and out the far side, into a quiet lane where her friend lived. It was rare for a vehicle to pass her on the walk. North Staverton was on a road that led to nowhere but a few farms before eventually looping south-westwards to the main road. Even the main road wasn't as busy as it used to be, with the M5 attracting much of the traffic, a few miles to the south.

North Staverton had a large farm in the middle, a church and a pub. Cottages and farmhouses dotted the perimeter and a row of four connected houses dating back two hundred years formed the core of the village. Opposite them were two larger detached houses with generous front gardens. In recent years, three more homes had been built on pockets of available land, with very little opposition from the existing inhabitants. The Slocombes' house had been the property of Drew's great-aunt, who had left it to his mother on her death. His mother's generous refusal to take rent from him and Karen was the single factor that had enabled him to set up his burial ground and concentrate on establishing it as a business. The eager involvement of Maggs Beacon, a mixed-race eighteen-year-old who had done work experience at the undertaker where Drew had been a bearer and coffin-maker, clinched the whole matter. She had worked for peanuts for two years, at the end of which time Drew fulfilled his promise to make her an equal partner in the operation he founded.

The walk took Karen around the edge of the yard of Staverton Farm, where a hundred or more Dairy Shorthorns stood about after being milked.

The cows always made her pause, if only for the welcome relief from the ubiquitous black-and-white Holsteins and Friesians on other farms. These were all shades of red-brown, some with mottling, some with the richest deep mahogany coats. Two collies would always come to greet her, their feet muddy, ears and tails often spiked with bits of hay. Once in a while Mrs Westlake would come out for a brief word, between her tasks of feeding calves or shepherding cows back to their night-time quarters.

Today, it was evident that the farmer's wife had been watching out for Karen. She came trotting across the yard, wiping her hands on the faded dungarees she always seemed to wear.

'Heard you was there when that chap was shot,' she opened, without ceremony.

'That's right,' Karen said. 'It was dreadful.'

'The apple juice man, from over to Lower Huntley, they say.'

Karen nodded.

'And no one saw who shot 'un? Proper strange, must have been.' She spoke breathlessly, as if the words had been straining to emerge for some time.

'I still haven't really come to terms with it,' said Karen, knowing this was quite the wrong thing to say. Mrs Westlake would prefer gory details, emotion, drama. 'Coming to terms' with something would mean very little to her.

'Why'd somebody do that, then?' the woman pressed on, as if Karen could obviously answer this question if she chose to.

'I have no idea,' said Karen flatly. 'I must go. The kids'll be waiting for me.'

Della's house was big and airy, with all the doors thrown open. Karen heard voices in the garden at the back, and went to watch for a moment, unobserved, as the children played.

Stephanie was at a remove from the three boys, her back to Karen. She was sitting on the lawn, pulling violently at tufts of grass. Her movements were jerky, and her head hung down. It was a picture of an unhappy sulking child; a picture that Stephanie very seldom presented. Her nature was to address difficult feelings, to express anger or hurt with no prevarication. Sulking was not her style at all.

Without conscious thought, Karen crossed the garden to her daughter. 'Hey, Steph? What's the matter?'

The child whirled round, the look on her face an unsettling mixture of guilt and fear. 'Mummy,' she said, her voice full of relief. 'Timmy's got a bad knee.'

'Oh? How did that happen?'

'I don't know,' Stephanie said with heavy

emphasis. Karen knew she was lying, and had no idea how she ought to react.

'I'll ask him then, shall I? Where's Della?'

'Here I am!' sang a cheery voice. 'Are you early, or are we late?'

'I don't think I'm early.' Karen examined Della's face, hoping for some explanation for Stephanie's odd behaviour. 'Have they been all right?'

'Fine. Timmy's got a bruise on his knee – did he tell you? I've an awful feeling that Finian did it. Timmy's being very loyal, saying it was just an accident. I didn't like to argue with him. I'm afraid Finian's getting very bossy these days. He likes to pull rank, being the eldest. Is he like that with you?'

'A bit,' Karen said. 'I think he's ready for school.' She should know – she had been a primary school teacher until motherhood persuaded her to abandon it.

'Roll on September, then,' laughed Della.

'What have you done today?' Karen turned her attention back to Stephanie.

The little girl shrugged clumsily. 'We went to the shops – sort of. Played in the garden. Della did scrambled eggs.'

'Your favourite! Lucky you.'

'Mmm.'

When Della made no mention of the shooting,

46

Karen assumed she knew nothing about it. With four under-fives swirling around her all day, there'd be little time for keeping up with local news.

Timmy edged up to her, looking tired and grubby. He wrapped an arm around her legs and leant against her.

'I hear you've got a bad knee?' Karen said and rolled up the leg of his trousers for a look. A purple bruise covered the whole of his kneecap.

'Oh, Tim! That looks very sore,' she said. 'Does it still hurt?'

The child nodded solemnly. 'When I walk,' he modified.

'Did you put anything on it?' Karen asked Della, fighting to keep the accusation out of her voice.

'What? Oh, no. Sorry. I didn't think it was anything. It wasn't bleeding. Kids bruise easily, don't they.'

'Where did it happen? Did he fall on it, or did it get kicked?'

'I don't know, to be honest. He was out here and I was in the house. He was very brave about it.'

Karen looked to her daughter for assistance. 'Steph? Did you see what happened?'

Stephanie cast a quick glance at Finian. 'He fell over,' she said.

47

Karen closed her eyes for a moment. Was it possible that a child of four could be suspected not only of bullying, but of arranging for his crime to be covered up? That Finian had somehow exhorted Stephanie to lie about the incident? She'd seen it a thousand times in children of eight and nine during her career as a teacher; but under fives were always so transparent. Or was Stephanie herself protecting Finian for some reason? Had *Stephanie* pushed Timmy? Did it matter?

'Well, never mind,' she asserted. 'Lucky we've got the buggy. You won't have to walk at all,' she told Timmy. 'And when we get home I'll put some ointment on it, and it'll feel better.' In the morning, the whole leg would probably be stiff, she thought. He might even have a cracked patella. Drew was going to make such a fuss about it. Drew had once been a nurse and clucked over his children's health abominably.

She shouldn't blame Della, she told herself. Kids had skirmishes all the time. It was just that Finian was four and a half, and Timmy was still some way short of three, and small for his age. If this sort of thing was going to happen, Karen would be forced to reconsider the arrangement with Della. Especially as the woman seemed so unconcerned.

'You haven't heard what happened today,

then?' she said, as she fitted Timmy into the buggy and Della handed her the bulky bag of assorted possessions.

'No – what?'

'Peter Grafton – you might not know him – was shot this morning, in Bradbourne. At the farmers' market.'

Karen sensed Stephanie tensing beside her, and wished she hadn't said anything. Della's reaction only made it worse.

'Peter?' she squealed. 'You're joking. Of course I know Peter. He was my first boyfriend. He used to work with Bill, until just a little while ago. Nobody would want to shoot Peter. How badly hurt is he?'

Karen tried to indicate with a meaningful look that it was a bad idea to upset the children. In vain. Della was pressing her palms to her cheeks, in unmistakable distress. Karen could see no alternative to finishing the story now. 'Well, actually,' she tilted her head away from Stephanie, somehow hoping the child couldn't see or hear her if she did that, 'actually, it was – well, fatal.'

'Oh, God!' The sensible capable Della suddenly became a limp string puppet, her legs folding up beneath her.

'You can say that again,' Karen muttered, her arms impossibly full of frightened children.

CHAPTER THREE

Maggs was quick to form the same conclusion as Karen had. 'The Grafton chap's sure to be buried here, isn't he?' she said to Drew. 'Organic to his toenails, from what I hear.'

'Don't count chickens,' he advised her. 'Whatever it'll be, we won't know for days yet.'

'Yeah, yeah,' she dismissed. 'But *eventually;* and think how much publicity there's going to be. "Murder Victim's Funeral in Natural Burial Field". Great stuff. There'll probably be media.'

'So we'd better get cracking on some grass cutting, hadn't we? The paths are awful.'

'Den said he'd have a go at it on Saturday, if you like. He loves cutting grass. Says it reminds him of hayfields. I'm not sure when he's ever been in hayfields, but it's probably best not to ask.'

'We'll have to work out an action plan. Where people won't be allowed to go – that sort of thing. We don't want cameramen trampling on the new graves.' He stopped himself abruptly. 'Listen to me – running ahead. It's your fault.'

'Naturally,' she dimpled.

The afternoon was sunny, and the office door stood open, facing the lane and gateway. Long shadows were dappling the small front lawn and the parking area inside the gate.

'Karen's a long time getting back from Della's,' Drew observed. 'It must be gone five.'

'And your supper's going to be late, is it?' she taunted him. 'Maybe you should go and get it started. Give her a nice surprise.'

'I don't know what we're having,' he said helplessly.

The phone rang at his elbow, and he picked it up. 'What?' he said after a minute spent listening in silence, puzzlement outweighing alarm. 'Is she OK? Have you phoned Bill? Oh, all right. Give me three minutes and I'll be there.'

Maggs raised her eyebrows.

'Della's fainted, and Karen can't leave her – or her kids. She wants me to go and collect ours, and she'll wait there until someone can take over.'

Accustomed as they both were to sudden summons to jump in the van and drive to scenes of death and despair, Maggs and Drew

51

fell into a smoothly choreographed sequence.

'OK,' Maggs nodded. 'Den'll be here soon, anyway, but I won't leave till you get back. You might need another vehicle, if Bill's held up. Did Karen call an ambulance?'

'No, no. It's not that bad. Just shock. Della knows Peter Grafton, apparently.'

'Course she does. They all know each other around here.'

Drew jigged impatiently. 'Well, anyway – she passed out when Karen told her he'd been killed.'

Maggs's eyebrows took another leap skywards. 'Oh-ho!' she breathed. 'Fancy that.'

Drew was halfway down the path, and missed the innuendo. His concern was all for his children, Stephanie especially. He didn't want her witnessing a prostrate woman, and the trauma of such an unexpected collapse. Not after Saturday, not with Karen already in a state of tension. He urgently wanted to remove her from further shocks, and restore normal life as quickly as he could.

Della was sitting up on the grass in her back garden when he arrived. Karen was kneeling beside her, one arm around her shoulders, the other outstretched as a sort of barrier between Della and the children. Finian and Todd were standing as close as they could, watching their mother's face. Todd was sucking his thumb, Finian simply watching, his features expressionless. Stephanie and Timmy were slightly further away, and turned quickly to greet their father. 'Della fainted,' Stephanie announced. 'But she's all right.'

'I hurted my knee,' Timmy muttered, evidently worried that he'd been upstaged.

'Is she all right?' Drew asked Karen, his gaze on Della.

'I think so. She wasn't out for long. It was just a couple of minutes of chaos, but we've calmed down now. You go, and I'll walk back as soon as I can. Bill's on his way home. I phoned him. Poor chap, he sounded really worried. Watch out for Timmy's knee. It's got a nasty bruise.'

Maggs and Den were standing beside their car when Drew got back with the children. Their faces were filled with expressive questions, but neither spoke. Drew got out of the van and paused a moment, savouring as always the strange asymmetry that the couple presented. Den so tall and pale and careful; Maggs round and black and impulsive. That they loved each other was beyond question, but Drew still couldn't feel confident that their relationship would last. Den had a past, and was almost ten years older than Maggs. Drew's business partner's attention was very much on the job and her career, despite her unconcealed passion for Cooper. Peaceful Repose Funerals had grown, much as she'd predicted, and could become something very much bigger with substantial levels of commitment and investment. Could the one-time police detective, now seemingly so aimless and shadowy, keep up with her in the coming years? Drew doubted it. Karen went further. 'Not a chance,' she said, whenever they discussed it.

'No need to hang about,' Drew told the couple. 'It's nothing much. Karen's coping and I'll get these two started on their supper.'

'What happened exactly?' Den asked, narrowing one eye as if suspecting some sort of obfuscation.

'Della fainted, that's all.'

'She's probably pregnant again,' said Maggs, with a certain sourness. People who kept having babies did not earn her wholehearted approval.

'Very likely,' said Drew with an understanding smile.

'She fainted because Mummy said the man was shot,' Stephanie said shrilly. 'The Peter man.'

Den scanned all the faces before him. 'That's interesting,' he said.

'I thought so,' Maggs agreed, reaching for his hand. 'I wasn't serious about her being pregnant.' Too late, she realised that the suggestion made in front of Stephanie had probably been unwise. The saying about small pitchers and large ears came to mind.

Stephanie was clearly undiverted. 'What's pregnant?' she demanded. 'Is it having babies?'

Nobody answered her. Maggs and Den began to move towards their car.

'I hurted my knee,' said Timmy, quite loudly.

'OK,' Drew assured him. 'I'll look at it as soon as we're indoors.'

Maggs and Den took their leave. 'What's for supper?' she asked him as they drove home.

'Lamb chops. I got them at the farmers' market this morning.'

'Oh? The same farmers' market where the Grafton bloke got killed?'

'The same. Though before it happened. I popped out early on, when they were first setting up.'

'Your office isn't that close to where they have the market,' she noted. 'Didn't they mind you bunking off?'

'Hardly anybody was in. They work funny hours, that lot.'

'You knew about the shooting then?'

'Only missed it by a few minutes.'

'No, no,' she protested. 'This isn't making sense. Karen said it was after eleven . . .'

'I went back. Sort of.'

'Explain.'

He went through his morning in detail. An early visit to the market to buy the chops; a couple of hours in the Social Services office, discussing two or three cases being presented in court; leaving to go to the house of the old man, noticing an unusual clustering of people and vehicles at the far end of the High Street, where the market was; the encounter with Karen.

'I get it,' Maggs nodded, at the end. 'Small place, Bradbourne. You'd be bound to notice something was up.'

'Only because I've been trained to it,' he said.

'And once a cop, always a nosy parker,' she jibed.

'Maybe so.'

'You didn't see a person carrying a crossbow running away then?'

'No such luck. Karen's the only proper witness, as far as anyone knows. Which is very odd, given there were so many people at the scene. Karen was watching Grafton when he took the hit. It's important to know where the killer was at the time – which side of the street and so forth.'

'Why?'

'Because then we could eliminate some people.'

'We?'

'Sorry. I meant they.'

'But whoever it was got away. It's too late, surely, to worry about where they were standing. Even if forensics work out the angle and distance, they won't have a complete picture of where everybody was. Besides, it sounds as if they must have been in a car, or inside one of the buildings. If they'd been standing in full view in the street, loads of people would have noticed. Unless the crossbow was disguised as an umbrella or something.' Maggs's flights of fancy were getting under way, as always.

'Er – I suppose . . .' he stammered.

'There's all sorts of possibilities, and most of them are unprovable. Seems to me it's hopeless,' she summed up cheerfully. 'You'll need to get Drew and Karen onto it. Drew does this sort of thing quite well. And we think we'll get the funeral. Grafton's sure to have wanted something natural.'

'Probably,' Den agreed vaguely. 'And I know there's not much prospect of forensics doing any good. But it's all there is to go on.'

'Bollocks!' she scoffed. 'People don't just shoot people at random in Bradbourne. It'll be all down to motive. And murder weapon. They'll have to find the crossbow. That should help. Wake up, Denzy. You're slipping. Been too long away from the job.'

He turned to look at her, the car slowing as he gave her words some thought.

'Don't call me Denzy,' he said.

'Sorry.'

'Anyway, I'm finished with the police,' he said heavily. 'This is nothing to do with me. Or you.'

'Oh, I'm not so sure about that,' she flashed back at him.

Karen and Drew were surprised when their doorbell rang later that evening. Drew opened the door to meet Geraldine Beech on his step. 'Sorry,' she said. 'Can I come in? Is Karen here?'

'She's just getting the kids to bed. They've had rather a hectic day, and it's taking a while to settle them.' He stepped aside to let her in. He knew her only slightly, through Karen, and was uncertain as to how to approach her. He needn't have worried. She followed him into the living room and dropped unceremoniously into a chair. She was wearing baggy trousers which stopped well short of her ankles. Her legs seemed very long as she stretched them out before her.

'You get on, if you're busy,' she said. 'I'll wait for Karen. I don't mind if she's a while. I need to have a bit of a think, anyway.'

'Can I get you a drink?'

'Coffee would be great, if it's not a bother. Black, no sugar. Thanks.'

Drew disliked people who wanted black coffee. It made instant seem so churlish somehow. They'd obviously really prefer thick dark espresso, made in a proper machine and stronger than any instant could manage to be. But he did his best, piling two large spoonfuls into the medium-sized mug, and hoping it was black enough for her. When he took it through, she seemed to have forgotten her injunction to him to get on with what he was doing.

'It seems ages ago now,' she said with a tightening of her features. 'This morning, I mean. Karen and I went for coffee together, just before it happened. We were talking about him.'

Drew slipped effortlessly into his undertaker mode. 'How well did you know him?' he murmured.

'Oh – fairly, I suppose. We went to a lot of meetings together. He was always rather an ally of mine. We got on famously. I admired the way he worked so hard, building the juice-making up from nothing. He was quite an asset. We need people like him. He's a big loss.'

'It's going to be a huge shock for everyone.' He spoke with authority, the platitude emerging as a piece of hard information. 'A sudden death takes people in funny ways. On one level, we all adjust amazingly quickly. We absorb that basic fact of the death without too much difficulty. But the trauma goes on for a long time, and takes all sorts of different forms. I must admit I'm a bit worried about Karen. She actually saw it happen, as I suppose you know.'

'What?' Geraldine pressed a hand across her nose and mouth, compressing her nostrils for so many seconds that Drew wondered when the next breath would happen. Eventually she inhaled noisily through her fingers. 'What do you mean?' she mumbled.

'She saw him as the bolt hit. It's not something you'd ever choose to witness. She's going to have that picture in her head for a long time.'

The woman frowned, her gaze fixed on a patch of wall across the room. 'Did she see where it came from?' she asked.

'Well, no. Obviously not, if she was watching Peter. It doesn't sound as if anybody saw who did it. He must have been in a car, or one of the buildings, presumably. Must have tucked the weapon inside a coat and just walked casually away, I suppose. Though I think a crossbow's quite a big thing. I'm not sure I've ever seen one close to. Have you?'

'Poor little Sally was in a bad state,' Geraldine changed the subject after a perfunctory shake of her head.

'Yes, she must have been.' Drew nodded, not at all sure what he thought about that side of the story. Karen hadn't mentioned it before today, and it had taken a poor second place to the primary fact of the shooting. Only now did it strike him that this was a glaringly obvious motive for the murder. 'Was her husband around this morning?' he asked slowly.

'No, no. He's working up near Gloucester on a big new block of flats, doing the electrics. Doesn't get back till eight most evenings. He's always landing some contract like that. Can't be bothered with the small domestic stuff these days.'

'So he doesn't know?'

'About Sally and Peter? I doubt it. Or he didn't until today. That could all have changed by now, I suppose.'

'Secrets usually leak out when a person dies,' Drew observed, from yet more personal experience.

'Indeed,' she said, inattentively. She was staring at the wall again. Drew began to feel she was hard work, and he'd much rather be reading the paper or watching television than struggling to make conversation with this woman he barely knew.

'Karen shouldn't be long now,' he said. 'I'll go and see if I can take over.'

'Oh, I'm sorry,' she burst out. 'I know I'm not very good company. It's just . . .'

'That's all right,' he soothed. 'Let me go and find Karen.' He scurried out of the room in relief.

Karen was just settling down to read to the children. Drew almost snatched the book. 'Here, I'll do that,' he said. 'You've got a visitor. Didn't you hear the doorbell?'

'Ages ago,' she said vaguely. 'Who is it?'

'Your Mrs Beech. Seems in a bit of a state.'

'What does she want?'

'Search me. Something about Peter Grafton, I assume. Go on – she doesn't seem to want to talk to me.'

Stephanie and Timmy grumbled a bit when he started the story. 'We've had that page,' his daughter informed him, leaning over from the upper bunk bed. 'Read the part where the sword won't come out.'

The book was a simplified story about the young King Arthur, which both children unaccountably adored, despite its plodding language. Drew knew it by heart, and disliked it with a passion. But he dutifully read them a full three pages before putting it down and telling them it was time to go to sleep. It still surprised him when they obeyed this command. They would both snuggle into their pillows, Timmy's thumb would go into his mouth, and Stephanie's faded pink bear would go under her chin, and they were away, just like that. It seemed miraculous. Dimming the light from the doorway, he whispered, 'Night, night, then,' and left them to it.

Karen had not expected a visit from Geraldine, and was even more taken aback when the woman got up from the chair and rushed to meet her as she entered the room.

'Karen, you have to listen carefully to what I'm going to tell you,' she said urgently, gripping the younger woman's shoulders, pushing her face up close. 'It's terribly important.'

'Wh-what is it?' Karen managed, putting her hands up to fend off the onslaught.

'You mustn't say anything about Mary,' came the incomprehensible reply.

Karen simply stared at her.

'You know – Mary Thomas.'

'What about her?' Karen felt thick-headed and stupid.

'You mustn't say anything about her being there this morning. You haven't, have you?'

'Well, yes,' Karen admitted. 'I told Den and Drew, actually. But loads of people must have seen her, anyway. It won't just be me. She was the one who said Peter was dead.'

'Yes, yes, I know that.' Geraldine backed away, chewing viciously at her own lower lip. 'But we don't want it broadcast. I mean – she's a bit worried about the publicity.' She paused, breathing heavily. 'It sounds more sinister than it is. I'm not putting it very well.' She put a hand to the back of her neck and flipped at some of the wispy curls she found there.

Karen watched in bemusement. 'No, you're not,' she said bluntly. 'I have no idea what you're talking about.'

'Never mind, then. I expect I'm being very silly. This has all come as an awful shock. Poor Peter.' She tweaked her hair again, before adding, 'Oh, and listen – before I forget, we're having a meeting on Thursday evening, at my place. All the stallholders. That's one reason I've come to see you.'

Karen tried to clear her head. 'I expect I can get to the meeting. It'll be good to see everybody. But I don't follow all this stuff about Mary. Why does it have to be kept quiet? Quiet from who?'

'The police, mainly. Did you say anything to the police?'

'No.' Karen wondered why she felt so defensive. 'No, I didn't. They didn't ask who was there. It was a whole *crowd* of people, after all.'

'Exactly. And probably not many people know Mary by name, anyway.'

'I told them she was at the supermarket, though. I gave them her address,' Karen remembered.

Now it was Geraldine's turn to look bewildered. 'Supermarket?'

'When the bomb went off, on Saturday.'

'Oh, no,' Geraldine said emphatically. 'Mary was most definitely not there then. You must have been mistaken. Got her muddled up with someone else. She can't possibly have been.'

'Well, she was. I spoke to her. I was speaking to her when the bomb went off. As plain as I'm speaking to you now.'

'And you told the police?'

'I did, yes. They wanted to know if I'd recognised anybody when I was there.'

'If Mary was there, then she's a fool,' Geraldine murmured to herself. 'What're we going to do now?'

'You'll have to explain this to me. It's beginning to sound as if you and Mary are involved in something I wouldn't like.'

Geraldine said nothing, which gave Karen time to straighten her thoughts.

'Do you mean you know who put that bomb there?' She heard – and felt – again the blast, the breaking glass, the fear for her small daughter, and sensed a mounting rage.

'Of course I don't. At least . . .'

'It wasn't Mary,' Karen supplied with a brief laugh. 'But there's obviously something going on. Aren't you going to tell me?'

'Truly, there's nothing to tell. It's only the usual stuff – the Food Chain business. Mary and Hilary and I have been passionate about changing people's shopping habits for years now. And the rest of it. It's all been going so well – this is absolutely the last thing we needed. And we don't want the police to start thinking we're activists or anything of that sort. Not when there's so much of that going on.'

'You mean protests against GM crops? Tearing up the maize? Have you been involved in that?'

It was a delicate question, which had occurred to Karen before. A large group of hooded protesters had uprooted a ten-acre field of experimental maize, a few miles south of Bradbourne, only two weeks earlier. They'd succeeded in evading the police, and everyone in the area had their suspicions as to who might have taken part. Suspicions, however, which largely remained unspoken, since the vast majority of the population wholeheartedly endorsed the action.

Karen expected a wagging finger, at the very least, for daring to mention it, but Geraldine's expression was oddly soft and pleading.

'Not that, no. This is something you'd approve of if you knew about it. And we really do need Mary to be kept out of the limelight, if at all possible. With any luck, the police won't bother to follow up what you told them about Saturday. They've got Peter's murder to worry about now, after all. The bomb's going to be old news.' She seemed to be speaking more to herself than to Karen.

'Except they're quite likely to connect the two,' Karen said, half hoping to startle the woman with this remark.

'No, no. They're not bright enough for that,' Geraldine dismissed.

'You mean there *is* a connection?' Karen demanded. Geraldine looked at her with a scornful little smile. 'Of course there is,' she said.

CHAPTER FOUR

'I'm going to go and see Mary,' Karen announced to Drew for the third time. 'She'll be able to explain it to me.'

'Leave it alone,' he warned her tiredly. 'It sounds to me as if you're far better off staying right out of it all. There's something very nasty going on. And I doubt very much if the Thomas woman would tell you anything anyway.'

Karen huffed out a long breath of frustration. 'I know she was in those protests against live exports,' she recalled. 'And there've been other things. She's an *activist*.' She stressed the word portentously.

'What if she is? Aren't we all, round here, in one way or another? Trying to change the world, make people see sense. Me, you, Maggs – all of us.'

'Not Den,' Karen couldn't resist. 'Den's avoided all that sort of thing.'

'Not really,' Drew defended Cooper, as he always did. 'He's not afraid to get his hands dirty, and see if he can do his bit for justice, like the rest of us. Why are you always so down on him?'

'I'm not,' she snapped. 'I just don't see what you and Maggs obviously do. I think he's wasting his time, when he could be making so much more of himself, that's all.'

'You sound like his mother.'

'We don't know his mother.'

'No, I mean, you're saying the sort of things a mother would say. How did we get onto this, anyway? I've got to open the office. Maggs isn't here yet. We've got Miss Lincoln at two, and the grave's not dug yet.'

When he and Maggs had started out on Peaceful Repose, they'd had a gravedigger working with them. When he had left, in a certain amount of disgrace, they'd persuaded themselves that they could do without a replacement. Drew would dig the graves. Unlike those in churchyards and municipal cemeteries, his were barely four feet deep, and the ground was generally soft. It took a surprisingly short length of time. But when it was raining, like today, he rather regretted his failure to delegate the job.

Maggs arrived two minutes after he opened up the office, very apologetic. 'The car wouldn't start,' she explained. 'It doesn't like wet weather.'

'You've still got the bike, haven't you?' Maggs had been renowned locally as being the girl on the motorbike, until she met Den and started to travel by car instead.

'The bike?' She blinked. 'Yes – but it's not taxed any more. Maybe I'll use it again this summer, though.' She turned wistful. 'I liked the bike.'

'It had its uses,' Drew agreed. 'But I suppose people grow out of things.'

'I haven't *grown out of* it. I just like to ride with Den now. We talk in the car. It's nice.'

'I'm sure it is,' he said, trying to placate her.

'Miss Lincoln at two, then,' she went on briskly. 'Better get digging. I've marked the spot.'

'So I see. What're you doing today?'

'Chasing up the late payers. Chasing up the printers about those leaflets. Maybe phoning Gary to see if there's any word from the mortuary on the Grafton bloke . . .'

'Too soon for that,' Drew interrupted her. 'Much too soon. And insensitive, probably. We have to wait till the wife or someone calls us.'

'No, Drew.' She was firm. 'We might let him

slip through our fingers if we don't stake our claim. We know he'd want to be buried here, but maybe he never said anything to his wife. If I call Gary, and he says something to Stanley while they're doing the post-mortem, it'll all help to sow the seed. Stanley'll be seeing the family as soon as they've finished. It could be any time now, come to that.'

Post-mortems mostly took place in the early morning, and even a murder victim was unlikely to have necessitated the summoning of the pathologist from his normal afternoon routine the previous day. Particularly since the cause of death in this instance was hardly a topic for much deliberation. Anyone could see that the severance of the man's windpipe and cervical vertebrae, along with the carotid artery for good measure, would lead to rapid death.

Gary was the mortuary attendant at the Royal Victoria Hospital, and Stanley the Coroner's Officer – liaising between police and the dead person's family. An inquest would be quickly opened, and then adjourned, pending further police enquiries into what exactly happened to the unfortunate Peter Grafton.

Drew had some years of experience of this routine, and the individuals involved. The delicate business of contacting specific undertakers at the time of a sudden death was fraught with competition and ill feeling. Three years earlier, the main Bradbourne funeral director, run by a certain Daphne Plant, had sold out to the multinational conglomerate known as SCI, and had accordingly become a very slick operation. Since Plant & Son retained the same name, many ordinary citizens had failed to notice the change of ownership – although Drew and Maggs wasted no opportunity to publicise it. Plants would almost certainly have been called to remove the body from the market square, and take it to the mortuary, the previous day. This would give them an automatic prior claim to handling the funeral, since the family would be directed to them by default. The fact that this was very unlikely to have met with Peter Grafton's wishes was something that could not be relied on to guarantee the funeral came to Peaceful Repose. Not unless the grieving widow could somehow be alerted to the freedom she had to choose a different undertaker.

'It would be better if we could get Karen to speak to someone who knows the family,' Drew went on. 'It would look more . . . casual.'

'No it wouldn't,' Maggs argued, changing her original position. 'It would look transparently sneaky. How do we know what the chap's wishes were, anyway? Who says?'

'Well . . . he's sort of one of us,' said Drew lamely. 'He believed in our sort of thing.'

'Lots of people still think cremation's the organically correct way of doing things,' Maggs reminded him.

'True,' he concurred gloomily.

Den's restlessness increased as the morning wore on. Knowing there was a murder investigation being conducted just outside his place of work was distracting. Most ex-police officers found their way into private security companies, or occupations of that sort. Some did actually become private detectives, although Den had never encountered such a person. Driven by a vague but insistent desire to 'work with people' and to utilise his hard-won skills, the local Social Services office had seemed an obvious point of call.

The people there had been friendly, and cooperative up to a point, but the rigours of the bureaucracy involved in hiring new personnel meant that for a long time, Den had still not been employed in any officially recognised capacity. He was entered as an 'anomaly' in the files, paid as a special one-off payment every month, and given a handful of vaguely defined tasks to perform. The acute sensitivity to the potential for abuse of clients did ensure that references were sought and taken up with immense care, but that accomplished, Den Cooper was instantly assimilated as one of the 'support team', albeit untrained and therefore poorly paid.

He had quickly discovered that things only happened if he pushed for them, and that it would have been quite feasible to sit in a corner all day, doing almost nothing, and nobody would have felt it incumbent upon them to notice.

As it was, he developed a strategy of simply putting himself forward for whatever needed to be done. The workforce was overwhelmingly female, a fact that worked in his favour. Regarded as steady, strong, experienced and willing, he tagged along on any procedure that threatened to be unpredictable or particularly untidy. After ten months, someone in personnel showed extraordinary inventiveness by labelling his job as 'pre-police assessor'.

'That means, you get to work out whether the case needs to be referred to the police, or whether you think we can handle it ourselves. Very useful,' the woman had explained to him.

With a proper job description, he was transferred to the permanent payroll, given a rise and his own telephone extension. Apart from that, he carried on exactly as before.

Sometimes he wondered what in the world he thought he was doing. How could this pretence of a job be preferable to the structure and challenge of the police? As a Detective Sergeant he'd been required to use his brain far more than now. He'd had to collect evidence, conduct interviews, get to know people as intimately as he could, particularly on long investigations. Now he was just a sort of dogsbody, in an artificially created job, surrounded by people who were even more stressed and defensive than the police officers had been.

'I'll have to get out soon,' he said to Maggs, every week or so. 'I'm just wasting my life like this.'

'Something'll come along,' she always told him comfortably. 'Just keep your eyes open, and don't dismiss anything too quickly.'

Bradbourne was a quiet town, ringed by quiet villages. The rocky beginnings of the twenty-first century had brought the area its share of trauma, and a collective sense of slowly rebuilding lives and value systems. Not only had foot and mouth disease swept through much of the county, but disconcerting numbers of multi-ethnic asylum seekers had been billeted in small towns not far distant. This gave rise to flurries of resistance amongst people who had hitherto regarded themselves as tolerant and liberal. Burglaries were automatically blamed on the strange newcomers, as well as a free-floating conviction that they were mostly Muslims intent on destroying the western world. The Social Services department had been closely involved in much of this, and Den had seen at first hand the wretched experiences of many of the refugees. He tried his best to imagine how it must be for them, and developed a profound admiration for their persistence and stoicism in the face of the cold British reception they encountered, which must have come as such a shock; such a grim disappointment. Contrary to Karen's assessment of him, Den was every bit as committed to the task of changing society as she was; he just couldn't entirely convince himself that the best way to do it was by growing lettuces and selling them in fashionable little markets.

There had not been a murder in the region since Den had left the police. Not one, in almost a year. And murders had been Den Cooper's special interest. Reading the local paper, with the stories of traffic casualties and suicides and alcohol-related violence, he had not missed his former job at all. Not until now.

Now there was a murder investigation going on, just outside the door – and Den wanted to be part of it.

Karen was equally restless in her own way. Wednesday was the day she and Della each looked after her own children. But after the crisis of the previous evening, Karen wondered whether she ought to offer to have Finian and Todd. Timmy's knee was still bruised, but seemed to be working normally, and wasn't particularly painful, so that could hardly be used as an excuse for a quiet day. The important thing, she realised, was that she was in search of an excuse. She didn't want Della's boys in her house, and she wasn't altogether sure why. It wasn't simply the suspicion that Finian had kicked Timmy's knee: it had as much to do with Stephanie's manner the previous afternoon. The child definitely had something worrying her, and Karen wanted time with her, in the hope of discovering what it could be.

The most likely explanation was the supermarket bomb, of course, and Karen tried to talk to Stephanie about it.

It wasn't easy. 'Did you have any dreams last night?' she asked. Stephanie merely shook her head.

She tried an even more oblique approach. 'Would you like to come with me to the shops this afternoon?'

'What shops?' Stephanie demanded.

'Oh, the fruit place in Bradbourne, maybe. And the cheese shop.'

'Can I get out of the car?'

Karen blinked. 'Of course you can. I never leave you in the car, do I?' The remark was puzzling, until the explanation dawned on her that Stephanie might associate car parks with the bomb. After all, they'd been standing among shoppers' vehicles when the explosion had happened. So when Karen mentioned shopping, Stephanie had thought this meant being left in a town car park. It made a certain sense, Karen supposed.

'Maybe we won't go, anyway. The weather's not very nice for going out.'

It was raining, which meant she couldn't easily spend an hour or two in the garden, with the kids playing nearby. That in itself was frustrating, with May such a busy month. And despite Drew's clear opposition, she still very much wanted to go and see Mary Thomas and get to the bottom of the mysterious remarks made by Geraldine Beech. Mary was reasonably good with children, and would probably have no objection to Karen paying a visit accompanied by Stephanie and Timmy. She had always made a big thing of having an open house, welcoming callers announced or otherwise. Karen had concluded that the woman was lonely, rattling around in that great mansion all on her own, since she'd been widowed some years before. There were seven bedrooms, three bathrooms, and a maze of cold under-furnished downstairs rooms. On the few occasions that Karen had dropped in with the kids, they'd absolutely loved it, given permission to explore at will.

Peering out of the window at the burial field behind the house, Karen assessed the prospects for the weather. The sky appeared to be lightening, she thought, and the rain turning more to a misty drizzle. Darn it, she'd go, whether Drew liked it or not.

Despite their financial hardships in the early days of Peaceful Repose, Karen had always insisted on retaining a car of her own. When she was teaching, it had been a necessity, and since giving up the job, she'd made sure she retained the mobility she felt she was due.

'Tell you what,' she said to Stephanie, just after lunch, 'why don't we go visiting?'

Stephanie frowned thoughtfully. 'Visiting?' she echoed.

'A nice lady – Mary's her name. You saw her at the . . .' She stopped herself just in time. What folly *that* would have been, to remind the child about those seconds before the bomb blast, when Mary Thomas had been talking to them in the supermarket car park. Damn it, thought Karen – there doesn't seem to be any safe topic to talk about any more. And what if Stephanie recognised Mary and had hysterics because of the association? Well, she'd have to take that risk. There were limits to the levels of avoidance you could sustain.

* * *

Mary Thomas's house was the dominant feature of Ferngate village, as Karen had explained to the police on Monday. Its name of Cherry Blossoms was amply vindicated by the presence of a large old orchard full of fruit trees, many of them fruiting cherries. The blossom was just finishing now, the petals making a dense sea of white and pale brown beneath the trees.

'Stay here a minute,' Karen told the children, although they had little choice, strapped as they were into their seats in the back of the car. 'I'll just see if she's in.'

'Don't!' said Stephanie urgently. 'Don't leave us.'

'Bang, bang,' said Timmy happily and irrelevantly. Stephanie punched him.

'Hey!' Karen warned her. 'Look, I'm just going to the door – there. You can see it easily.'

The front door was imposing, with a porch almost worthy of a church and a clanging bell to be handled with authority if it was to attract attention from the bowels of the house. Nothing happened for a full two minutes after Karen had done her worst with it. She was turning to leave when a voice called from a distant point away to the left, where the orchard was.

Mary Thomas came quickly towards her, wading through high grass and fallen blossom. She wore a long skirt, which made her seem old-fashioned and eccentric. Not a flowing Indian cotton skirt, but a heavy straight one, too warm for the time of year and entirely wrong for a rainy day. It did not, however, appear to encumber her progress.

'Hello?' she said, from the wrought-iron gate that separated her front garden from the orchard. 'What can I do for you?' The tone was cool, the expression unsmiling. Karen thought again what a distinctive face it was: the eyes so deeply sunk that it seemed they'd have difficulty in seeing out from beneath the thick brows.

'Well . . .' Karen felt suddenly self-conscious. 'I brought the kids. Um, you did say, any time we fancied a change of scene . . .' It was true: Mary Thomas had definitely given an open-ended invitation to call in. But that had been nearly a year ago.

'Did I? Well, yes, maybe I did. I'm sorry Mrs Slocombe, but it isn't really a very good day for it. I'm trying to get the raspberry canes in, and I see the peach tree is threatening to blow over again. It keeps coming away from the wall. You know how it is.' She didn't seem to care whether Karen knew or not; she was clearly not going to be diverted from her plans.

'Oh. Right. Sorry to have bothered you then.' Karen backed away, trying not to feel offended. She might have succeeded if it hadn't been for the *Mrs Slocombe*. That had been uncalled for, surely. They'd had plenty of companionable chats in the village shop, in recent months, in addition to Karen's occasional visits.

'Oh!' she remembered, turning back. 'I wanted to ask you . . .' But the woman had already covered a considerable distance and was apparently no longer even aware of her visitor. With gritted teeth, Karen accepted defeat. Getting back into the car, she threw a glance at the children.

'Can we get out, Mummy?' Stephanie asked carefully.

'Sorry, pet, no. We're going home again. But the rain's stopping, look. There's a bit of blue sky – see?' She neglected to mention that they wouldn't be able to play outside until Miss Lincoln's funeral was over. Drew had stipulated that there should be no chirruping children in the garden while a burial was taking place just beyond the fence. 'It's not good for them, or the mourners,' he'd insisted. 'Sorry, but that's final.' Karen sometimes thought he'd got that part of things badly wrong. She wanted her children to feel natural about funerals and death, to regard it as just another part of their normal experience. But now was not the moment to worry about that.

She sat in the driving seat for a moment,

wrestling with her emotions after the encounter she had just undergone. Not only offence but a kind of humiliation was seething within her. And, threading through all that, there was a strong sense of something amiss. Mary Thomas had not been quick enough to suppress the flash of anxiety that crossed her face when she recognised Karen. Nor the flurried movement of one hand, plunging deep into the pocket of that ridiculous skirt.

Drew and Maggs need not have worried about getting the Grafton funeral. At three on Wednesday afternoon, as the last of the handful of mourners for Miss Lincoln were departing, Drew took a phone call.

'Is that the natural burial place?' came a subdued voice. Drew recognised the tones of a person in shock. 'That's right,' he said. 'Can I help you?'

'This is Julie Grafton.'

'Oh, yes. Hello. I'm very sorry about your husband.' Drew was practised at pitching the condolences at the precise point between gushingly overdone sympathy and callously single-minded attention to the practicalities. The aim, basically, was to avoid eliciting the onset of tears. Undertakers were there to deal with the disposal of the body, and although there were ways and ways of doing this, the essential purpose remained.

'Yes, well, he'd have wanted to be buried in your . . . place. He knew your wife.'

'Indeed.' Drew refrained from mentioning Karen's close involvement with Mr Grafton's death. 'Has the Coroner's Officer seen you?' he asked.

'He telephoned me a little while ago. I told him I wanted you to do the funeral. He said you'd understand the procedure – that we couldn't make any firm arrangements for some time yet.'

'They'll have to open an inquest,' Drew agreed. 'And that isn't likely to be for a few days yet. There is a police investigation to be taken into consideration, of course. It's all very difficult for you, I know.'

'It hasn't really sunk in yet,' she confided, and although Drew understood that this was partly true, he also knew that people adapted with astonishing speed to a new and unexpected situation. Even being told that your perfectly fit young husband had been murdered in a small country town was a piece of information the average woman could get to grips with within twenty-four hours or so.

'I was in Yorkshire, you know – when it happened,' she went on. 'I had to be with my father. He's very ill, you see. My mother's at her wits' end with it all.'

'That must have made things difficult.'

'I feel as if I have to be in two places at once. And we daren't tell Dad what's happened to Peter. It would probably be the final straw.'

Drew suppressed the urge to tell her otherwise; to force his own view upon her: that it was always better to tell the whole truth. It wasn't his place to tell people how to manage their own families. Poor woman, he thought. Sounds as if she'll have another funeral to go to before long.

'So, we have to be patient, until the Coroner's Officer lets us know when the inquest is opened and then adjourned,' Drew said. 'It probably won't be too long. When it's to be a burial, rather than a cremation, the rules are more relaxed. They'll very likely release the body to us within a few days, and we can have the funeral whenever we like after that. I just need you to understand that we can't fix a date yet.'

'No, I didn't expect to.' Her voice was softly musical, a slight Devon accent giving it a friendly, almost intimate, resonance. But Drew was never again going to be seduced into getting too emotionally close to a client. That had happened once, and once was more than enough.

Having noted some necessary details – full

name, address, age – he left it that Julie Grafton would come and see him when notification came through that the body was being released. 'Phone me any time if there's anything you'd like to know,' he offered.

His sympathy for her was genuine as he put the phone down. Not only had her husband just been killed, but the gossip about his relationship with Sally Dabb was sure to be flying around the neighbourhood at that very moment. When a person died, their secrets instantly became common currency, despite injunctions about not speaking ill of the dead. It seemed to be a simple matter of the person no longer being there to keep the lid tightly closed on facts that were generally private. And in the case of a sudden death, this was even more true. Emails went undeleted, diaries undestroyed. Letters, jottings, even observed behaviour, all acquired greater significance when their author or object was no longer present.

Unless, Drew supposed, there was a wholesale and determined conspiracy to maintain the silence. If Sally Dabb behaved herself, and if there were no letters or emails or recorded phone messages, then perhaps the secret was safe. He found himself hoping this was the case.

CHAPTER FIVE

Karen's heart spasmed uncomfortably at the sight of the same two police officers on the doorstep again, that evening. She let them in unwillingly, then kept them standing in the hall, with the excuse that her husband and daughter were engaged finishing a jigsaw in the final few minutes before Stephanie went to bed. 'I don't want my daughter disturbed by your visit,' she said firmly.

'Mrs Slocombe, I expect you know why we're here,' said the heavier of the two. A man with very little neck and the largest ears Karen had ever seen. His colleague was hardly slim, either, but seemed rather more in proportion.

'I assume it's about Peter Grafton,' she said.

'That's right. We'd just like to run through

the sequence of events with you again. And perhaps go back a bit further in time than in your statement yesterday.' He produced a sheet of paper and consulted it. 'That is, before you went for coffee with Mrs Beech. How was Mr Grafton behaving at that time?'

'He was . . . he seemed quite relaxed. Happy, even. Chatting, and so forth.' She found it tremendously difficult to avoid mentioning Sally Dabb, and wondered why she was bothering, anyway.

'Who was he chatting to?' came the next inevitable question. So much for discretion, Karen thought.

'Well, mainly to Sally, I suppose. Her stall was next to his.'

'Sally?'

'Mrs Dabb. She sells pickles.'

'Ah, yes. The lady who was so upset, according to most of our witnesses.'

'Anybody would be upset,' Karen affirmed. 'Blood everywhere and the whole thing so completely unexpected.'

'Did you notice anybody watching him, earlier in the day?'

Karen shook her head. 'I was too busy for anything like that. And it was crowded. I wouldn't have been able to see anybody beyond the row of customers at his stall.'

'He sold apple juice, is that right?' The burly officer seemed to have a clear logic in his own head, directing the course of his questions, but Karen wasn't following it very well.

'Apple, peach, raspberry, blackcurrant,' she ticked them off on her fingers. 'And combinations, of course. Whatever he could find, really. I mean, he made it all himself, from local fruits. It must have been hard work . . .' she tailed off.

'Yes, we've seen his premises,' interrupted the slighter man. 'Very impressive.'

'Is it?' Karen spoke without thinking.

'You've never been there?'

She shook her head again. 'No. I've never had reason to. I suppose it must be interesting.'

'We thought it was quite hi-tech,' the same man confided. 'Considering everything's supposed to be so natural and small scale and so forth. He doesn't exactly squeeze the juice out by hand.'

'Didn't, Ricky – didn't,' the larger man corrected him.

'Didn't,' his colleague nodded. 'There's even a machine for putting the foil tops on the bottles.'

Karen shrugged. Peter Grafton's juicing arrangements hadn't concerned her when he was alive, and were even less relevant now he was dead.

'Anyway,' pressed the big man, more urgently, 'we'd like you to have a think about what we've been asking you. And then we'd like you to drop into the Incident Room in Bradbourne tomorrow and let us have anything you've remembered.'

'Incident Room?' Karen frowned.

'It's in the Town Hall. The *old* Town Hall. Because the police station's been moved to Garnstone, and it isn't convenient for our purposes.'

'Ah,' Karen nodded, as if she understood. The old Town Hall in Bradbourne was a strange square building, used for jumble sales and one-off sales of oriental carpets or remaindered books. It was indeed convenient, however, for the scene of Peter Grafton's murder, being about twenty yards away.

'So you'll be there? Tomorrow morning?'

'Well, it'll be difficult. I've got four small children here tomorrow.'

'Oh dear,' came the unsympathetic response. 'Well, I'm afraid this is important.'

'So I'll bring them all with me, shall I? And you'll find a friendly police officer to take charge of them while I answer questions?'

'If necessary,' he said stiffly.

'Well, I'll try,' she said. 'But I don't think I'll remember anything. I'm sure I've told you everything I saw.'

'We can take you outside and get you to run through the angles and things, as well,' the policeman added, with a certain vagueness. 'It would be helpful.'

The smaller man spoke suddenly. 'Is there any connection, do you think, with the supermarket bomb?' he said, as if the idea had dropped into his head from the sky. 'Last time we were here, we were asking about that.'

'Connection?' Karen echoed. 'Like what?'

'Well, Mrs Slocombe,' said the heavier man, 'for a start, you seem to have been at the scene of both incidents. Don't you?'

No sooner had she shut the door on the policemen than Drew appeared from the living room, with Stephanie close behind. 'All clear?' he asked.

Karen wished he'd been slightly earlier, so she could have slammed the front door. It would have alerted him to her mood. Instead she merely nodded.

'You kept them out here all that time?' he marvelled. 'Poor blokes.'

'You knew who they were then?'

'I saw the car outside. Thought I should keep a low profile, as they say. It's made Steph awfully late for bed though.'

'Drew, it was horrible,' Karen burst out. 'Stop making it sound as if the vicar just dropped by.' She watched him bite back a quip about vicars, before adding, 'And I've got to go to their Incident

Room tomorrow morning. With all the kids.'

'You can't. It'll be bedlam. And you can't get them all into the car.'

'So I'll leave them here for you to watch, shall I?'

He frowned.

'How long will you be?'

'An hour or so, I imagine. Don't worry – I can ask Della. She probably isn't doing anything.'

Drew glanced down at the little girl at his side. 'Well, I'll do bedtime then, shall I? I'll be down again in a bit.' And he led Stephanie upstairs, where her little brother was almost certainly already fast asleep.

When he came down again, Karen was on the sofa with a brimming glass of white wine. 'I need this,' she said, as his eyebrows rose. 'You can get yourself one too, if you want.'

When he'd settled in an armchair at right angles to her, without any wine of his own, he leant his head back and gazed at the ceiling. 'Mrs Grafton phoned today,' he said. 'I haven't had a chance to tell you. We've got the funeral.'

'Congratulations,' she said, half sincerely. 'When?'

'Don't know yet. Still lots to do.'

Karen laughed abruptly, a harsh sound without humour. 'Maybe they think I killed him, to bring you some business.'

'What?'

'Why do I seem to be slap bang in the middle of it all, that's what I want to know? It's horrible, having the police pestering me, and Geraldine making scary hints, and Mary telling me to get lost. I feel as if I'm falling down a long dark hole, and every day takes me deeper. It's got nothing to do with me, and yet I'm reminded of it at every turn.'

'What exactly is *it*?'

'That's the trouble – I don't know. It must have something to do with the farmers' markets, or the Food Chain people, I suppose. Something's been going on that I must have missed out on. There's a meeting tomorrow evening; I suppose I'll find out a bit more then.'

'Assuming you want to,' he murmured.

'Oh yes, Drew,' she said with feeling. 'After having my little girl almost blown up, I do most definitely want to.'

Karen was distracted and short-tempered even before Della arrived with her boys on Thursday morning, ten minutes earlier than usual. Karen had phoned her, and asked if she could stay at Karen's with all four, while Karen went to do her duty as a police witness.

The reply had been unenthusiastic. 'Well, try not to be long,' Della had said. 'I've got plans for the day.'

When she turned up, she seemed to have forgotten all about her fainting fit of two days earlier. 'Sorry I'm a bit ahead of myself,' she breezed. 'I thought you could get this police stuff over with quickly and let me get going.'

'Oh?' Karen was unsure what to make of this.

'I thought I'd go to Taunton and find some things for the summer. Is there anything you want?'

'Like what?' Karen had a bizarre vision of Della buying a swimsuit or pair of shorts on her behalf.

'Oh, I don't know.' Della waved a careless hand.

'So you're quite recovered then?' Karen asked coolly. 'After Tuesday?'

'Gosh – sorry. I should have thanked you, shouldn't I. It seems ages ago now. I was back to normal right away. It wasn't like me at all. I suppose it was just the shock.' She eyed Karen accusingly. 'You did tell it rather, well, *baldly.*'

'We're doing the funeral,' Karen said, watching the other woman for a response.

It was less than gratifying. 'Oh. Right. I imagine you would be. They'll have a church service first, will they?' One of Drew's long-term plans, initially resisted but eventually agreed to because of Maggs's persistent nagging, was to erect a small chapel of his own, in a corner of the field, for funeral services.

Until then, they either used the village church, or held the whole funeral at the graveside.

'I have no idea,' Karen admitted. 'It won't be for a while yet.'

'Poor Peter,' Della murmured, with a sigh that looked contrived to Karen. 'Well, off you go. We'll be fine here. Stephanie can show me where things are.' She paused. 'It'll mean you owe me an hour or so sometime, won't it?'

Karen knew the question was fair, that this sort of arrangement only worked if everything was kept strictly level, turn for turn about, but she still resented the remark. It wasn't *her* fault there'd been a murder before her very eyes.

'Fine,' she replied, wondering just why she felt so frosty.

There was no sign of the two policemen from the previous evening at the Town Hall when she went in. There were people sitting at four or five tables, with computer monitors in front of them and telephones at their elbows. Cables ran carelessly in all directions, and there was a big white flip chart on an easel in the middle of the room. It was strange and intimidating. Nobody came forward to meet her as she stood gazing around. Eventually she noticed a desk close by, with a hand-written card saying 'Public' on it. There was nobody sitting behind it.

'Hello?' she said, addressing a woman wearing headphones at the next desk along.

The woman lifted one earpiece away from her head, and looked up enquiringly.

'I'm supposed to be helping you,' Karen said awkwardly.

'Sir!' called the woman, across the room to a man in plain clothes. When he finally reacted, the woman dipped her chin at Karen and replaced her headphones.

The man was holding a sheaf of papers, and seemed to be thinking deeply about them. He came slowly towards Karen.

'Morning, madam,' he said. 'I'm Detective Inspector Hemsley. How can I help?'

'I was asked to come in this morning. I'm Karen Slocombe. It isn't very convenient, actually . . .'

'Oh, well, thank you very much, then,' he said blankly. 'Slocombe?'

'Yes, I saw the bolt hit Peter. I saw what it did to his throat. They thought I might be useful, or so they said.' Her voice was rising, and she was strongly tempted just to turn and walk out again.

'Oh, yes – Mrs *Slocombe,*' he repeated, as if she'd deliberately mispronounced her own name to mislead him. 'That'll be Doug's department. Doug!' he shouted.

A man in uniform detached himself from

another desk and came to join them. 'This is Mrs Slocombe, the lady who saw the shooting. Can you take her to the scene and see if she can remember anything more? Take Helen with you. Thank you, madam, for coming like this. We really do appreciate it.'

The whole thing was a fiasco, Karen had already realised. She stood in the empty square where she thought her stall must have been, facing the marked spot where Peter had fallen. 'So the bolt can only have come from *there*,' Doug said hopefully, waving an arm towards the bank and the public loos.

'Not necessarily,' argued Helen, a tall fair-haired girl with a bored expression.

'Actually,' said Karen, slipping into primary-teacher mode, 'unless you can reconstruct it with total accuracy, and measure the precise angle of the bolt in his neck . . .' she savoured Doug's quickly suppressed wince, '. . . then it's going to be pretty difficult to pinpoint where he was. But now I'm here again, I think it's most likely to have been in there.' She pointed at the low brick-built edifice that was Bradbourne's oldest public convenience. It had its back to the street, with a small area of grass and a low hedge separating it from the pavement. Its entrances opened onto the car park, which was approached by an alleyway leading from the town centre. There were narrow windows, with frosted glass.

'What – in the loos?' Doug was clearly unconvinced.

'It makes sense,' she persisted. 'Why don't you go and have a look? See if you can find footprints on the toilet seats. See if the windows are easy to open.'

'Thank you, madam,' said Helen with an irony too heavy for maximum effect. 'We have already done that, naturally.'

'Oh, good. That's all right then,' approved Karen. 'Do you think I could go now?'

Helen scanned the area behind Karen. 'There are several other scenarios,' she pointed out. 'A shop and a bank, each with an upper floor. We've interviewed the people living in those flats already. And the trees are thick enough for someone to hide in. More shrubs than trees, really.' She nodded towards the cluster of greenery to the right of the toilets. A mid-sized sycamore was accompanied by a buddleia and an overgrown privet. Shade cast by the tree made the bushes a credible hiding place – just.

'Hmmm,' said Karen. 'Perhaps he was in a car?'

'Not much chance of a car driving through when there was a market on.' Helen gave Karen an enquiring look. 'Did cars drive around behind your stall?'

'No,' Karen said. 'Definitely not. There wouldn't be a way through. But the alleyway would make a good escape route on foot.'

'Risky,' said Helen. 'Too many people coming and going. And it wouldn't be easy to hide a crossbow.'

'What about parked cars?' Doug managed to get a word in. 'Someone might have been lying on the back seat, or kneeling on the floor, and fired out of a window.'

'It's a thought,' said Karen, feeling weary. 'There were a few cars about. The local shopkeepers try to obstruct us by putting their cars just where we want to set up the stalls. Geraldine won't let that stop her, though. We just box them in.'

'So a person could have been hiding in one of the cars?'

'I imagine so,' Karen agreed. 'Do you know what the range was? I mean, how far away must the killer have been?'

Doug spoke with authority. 'Not more than thirty yards or so. Crossbows are fairly difficult to aim, unless you're an expert.'

'How do you know this wasn't an expert?'

'We've been through all the members of the local club, and they've all got very good alibis. There are only eight of them. It's not a very popular activity these days.'

'But a person can still be an expert, without belonging to a club,' Karen objected. 'Surely the range is a lot more than that?' She squinted across the square, and up the whole length of the High Street, trying to imagine herself aiming a crossbow. 'Don't they have telescopic sights and things, as well?'

Helen gave a warning cough and Doug flushed. 'We can't discuss this in any further detail,' he said stiffly.

'Well, I hope I've been of some help,' Karen said, in another attempt to excuse herself. 'It's all very bizarre. Surely somebody *must* have seen who did it.'

Helen nodded. 'That suggests it was someone above suspicion,' she remarked. 'Someone you all just took for granted. When they popped the crossbow into a bag and strolled away, nobody would even have noticed.'

'What a nasty thought,' Karen replied shakily.

Den observed the Incident Room set up in the old Town Hall, as he walked from the car park to the office on Thursday morning. He knew the signs: the police cars parked outside, the human traffic in and out of the big open door, carrying boxes and various pieces of equipment. And the television crew on the pavement with a reporter speaking to camera. Den sidled closer to listen.

'Less than forty-eight hours ago, a shocking killing took place only a few yards from here, in the peaceful market town of Bradbourne,' chirped the pretty young woman, by way of introduction. 'Detective Inspector Danny Hemsley, who is in charge of the investigation, has promised to give us a few words . . .' she turned towards the Town Hall, and sure enough, there was Danny, Den's old comrade from when they'd worked together in West Devon, appearing right on cue. 'Thank you, Inspector, for giving us your time. Now, could you update us on how it's going?'

Danny faced the camera, looking flushed and apprehensive. 'Well, as you know, a Mr Peter Grafton was killed here on Tuesday morning. We have ascertained that the weapon used was a crossbow. This is unusual, and not many people are in possession of such an item.' He paused, and let his gaze wander. Too late, Den tried to step out of his line of sight. Recognition dawned in Danny's eyes. But the reporter returned him to the matter in hand.

'So you'd like the public to assist?' she prompted.

'Yes. Yes, indeed. If anybody knows of anybody with a crossbow, we'd obviously be very pleased to hear about it. You can call us here at the Incident Room, anonymously if preferred. This was a cold-blooded killing of a young man, and it's up to the whole community to apprehend the killer.' His voice was gaining volume and confidence, just as the reporter must have received a signal to wind things up.

'Thank you, Inspector,' she purred, before turning back to camera herself. 'So there we have the latest news. The police are following up this particular kind of weapon, as well as asking the general public to bring them any information they can. This Incident Room—' she gestured behind her, '—has been set up in Bradbourne's old Town Hall, and will be manned twenty-four hours a day. The telephone number will appear on your screen in a moment. This is Gail Hollywell, BBC South West News.'

Hemsley did not return immediately to his desk. Instead he stepped out of camera range, straight towards Den, who had known he would.

'Cooper,' came the curt greeting. 'Not seen you for a while.' The Inspector had taken Den's resignation from the Force badly. For a while he treated it as a personal insult, cold-shouldering his colleague at every opportunity.

'First murder in this part of Devon since I left,' Den remarked.

'S'pose it must be. Missing us now, then? Now it's getting exciting again?'

'It feels odd,' Den admitted. 'Especially as I'm on the spot.'

'Say again?'

'I work just round the corner there,' he pointed. 'And I know the woman who saw the killing. My girlfriend works with her husband. It feels . . . local.'

'Like last time,' Hemsley said, eyes narrowed.

'Time before last, actually. And that was quite a while ago now.'

'Back in the good old Okehampton days,' the Inspector added, his tone a notch lighter.

'You're liking it over here then?' Den asked. 'I didn't know they'd moved you. Where're you based now?'

'Tiverton. Much bigger outfit altogether. They didn't move me – I put in for a transfer. The marriage came apart . . .' A ripple of misery crossed his face. 'Same old story, eh.'

'I'm sorry,' Den said, meaning it. He'd only met Mrs Hemsley two or three times, not enough to judge her or the marriage. But it was a curse that lay on the majority of police officers, which only made it worse somehow, when the break-ups happened. It was, if he was honest with himself, one big reason for his own defection. Rightly or wrongly, he'd attributed his lack of success with women to the demands of his work.

'Anyhow, tell me more about your involvement

here. With this Grafton thing, I mean. Have you got anything that might be useful?'

Den's heart leapt a little at the invitation. It couldn't have worked out better if he'd planned every move. 'Well,' he began, 'I might have a bit of background for you.'

Drew and Maggs ate a snack lunch together in the Peaceful Repose office, as usual. It was a tradition that seemed to increase in importance with every month that passed. Maggs brought her own sandwiches from home, and Drew made his before work, sometimes with Karen hovering at his shoulder telling him he ought not to cut the cheese so thick, or put so much mayonnaise on the lettuce. The result was an escalating competition between Maggs and Drew as to who could produce the most flavoursome and original meal, at the lowest cost.

'It's not fair – you've got all the raw materials just there for the taking,' Maggs complained.

'You can have anything you like from the garden, you know that.'

'Yeah, but I don't know what Karen wants to take to market. I don't like to just help myself.'

'You refuse to get to grips with the system,' he said. 'It's simple enough. I don't understand your problem.'

'Honestly, Drew, I can never remember which box is which. Neither can Den. And that's another thing – I'm never sure whether he's already taken something. It's embarrassing.'

'All down to communication,' Drew chewed comfortably, resisting any temptation to take the repetitive conversation further. It wasn't his business, anyway, which partly explained why it never really worked. Without Drew as liaison between Karen and the other two, the unease would continue.

'This avocado's very good,' she remarked. 'With lemon and basil and a smear of garlic. Try some.' She broke off a corner and proffered it. Drew took it delicately.

'Not bad,' he approved. 'But I think my nut paté with sliced radish and Little Gem lettuce beats it.' He held out a reciprocal mouthful.

'Is the nut paté home made?'

'Yes, but not by Karen. Someone at the farmers' market does it.'

'What sort of nuts?'

'Cob, I think. Picked in the wild, I'm sure.'

'It can get silly,' Maggs said, not for the first time. 'We're turning into food faddists.'

'Too late. It happened years ago. We just didn't notice at first.'

'I definitely prefer the avocado,' she decided. 'Now, what's on for this afternoon?'

'Not a lot. I did think that journalist from the *Farmers' Weekly* might show up, but nobody's phoned.'

'Didn't they do us last year?'

'No, that was some other farming magazine. This sounds a bigger item, with costings and so forth. I'm not sure how much I should tell them, actually.'

'Our prices aren't secret.'

'No, but it might be a mistake to spell out just what cardboard coffins or willow baskets cost. Some of the others in the business like to keep all that rather close to their chests.'

'Especially the traditional lot, who just dabble in ecological funerals as a sideline. Their charges are extortionate. I think we should expose them. It'd be a public service.'

'I know.' Drew licked his fingers, and rubbed them on his trousers. 'But it'd be a distraction. The point isn't really money, is it?'

'Some people think it is. Some of these farmers think it'd be an easy option, and would make much more profit from their land than growing corn or hay or something.'

'Well, I'll be as straight as I can. In any case, they might not show up. Something more interesting probably came along instead.'

Maggs opened her mouth, insistent as always on having the final word, when someone knocked on the office door. The two partners looked at each other in surprise. Normally the sound of a car arriving gave them plenty of warning of an impending visitation. This time, there'd been no engine noise.

Maggs opened the door, obscuring the person outside with her body, so that Drew couldn't see anything. 'Yes?' The tone of her voice revealed that she didn't recognise the visitor.

'Oh, hello,' came a breathy voice. 'Sorry. This is the right place isn't it? The natural cemetery, or whatever you call it. I did see the sign . . .'

'Come in,' Maggs invited. 'And tell us how we can help you.'

Drew remained in his chair, behind the desk, hurriedly folding the paper bag that had contained his sandwich. An apple still sat on the desk. He watched as a woman came into the room, ahead of Maggs, who closed the door before following her. Drew could see that she was intrigued.

And no wonder. The newcomer's hair was unbrushed and tangled; her face streaked with multi-coloured marks; her eyes bloodshot and her clothes ill-assorted. She looked like a refugee from a battle zone – or a wife fleeing from severe domestic violence.

Drew got up. If this was a newly bereaved daughter or wife or mother, she had certainly been taking the death badly. And if she wasn't newly bereaved, why in the world would she come to an undertaker's office?

'So there you have it,' Sally Dabb concluded, fifteen minutes later, looking worriedly from Drew to Maggs and back again. 'I know I shouldn't have come, by rights. It's Julie's place, not mine. I *know* that. I just wanted to make sure . . . well, I've told you already, haven't I? Do you believe me?'

Maggs pressed even closer, from her position only inches away. She had been alternately rubbing the upper arm and patting the hand of the distressed woman, as the story tumbled out. 'Of course we do,' she said.

'It isn't really any of our business,' Drew mumbled, still trying to work out his own role in the matter. 'Mrs Grafton has already contacted us. It's all in hand.'

Maggs glared at him and sighed. 'Drew, you haven't been listening. Sally isn't worried about that.'

'No, no. I do understand,' he assured them both. 'And you have been through a terrible experience.'

Sally had made some token attempts to improve her appearance as she talked to Drew and Maggs. 'I must look dreadful,' she said. 'I didn't sleep a wink, and never even thought of brushing my hair this morning. I must have scared poor little Robin.'

'Robin?' Drew queried.

'My little boy. Archie had to take him to school for me. I was in too bad a state to drive.'

'But didn't you drive here?' Drew was disbelieving. 'Don't you live in Lumstone? That's five miles away.'

'I did, actually, though I almost decided to walk. Walking's good for thinking. I parked down the road, near Della Gray's house.'

'Drew,' Maggs checked him again. 'Never mind all that.' She turned to Sally. 'It's all right. You don't have to worry. We won't spread any false rumours.'

Sally sat back in her chair, and rubbed a finger beneath both eyes. 'Oh, thank you! I know it must have sounded rude, to accuse you of indiscretion. But I had to start somewhere. I had to make *someone* believe that Peter and I weren't having an affair.' She gazed earnestly at Maggs. 'You *do* believe me, don't you?'

'Yes,' said Maggs solemnly. 'We believe you.'

'You believed her then?' Drew said, when the visitor had gone. 'I could see you did.'

Maggs rubbed her cheek, consideringly. 'Yes,' she said firmly. 'I told her, and I'm telling you. I definitely believed her.'

CHAPTER SIX

'There's a bit more to it, though, isn't there?' Drew went on, having made coffee for himself and Maggs and answered the phone to a journalist wondering about Grafton's funeral. 'Hmmm?'

'This business between Julie Grafton and Sally Dabb. There's something I don't really get.'

'What? That two women can be friends?'

'That one is the wife, and one is a close friend of the same man. Everyone would assume they'd be bitter rivals,' he said.

'Not all women feel a need to fight over a man, you know. Maybe Julie's got a life of her own? And Sally's got a little boy. She might have lost interest in men, in the way you mean.'

'OK. But it still feels odd. Wasn't there something below the surface she wanted us to understand?'

'Drew – she wanted us to help her scotch the rumours, that's all. She wanted neutral, respectable people like us to take her side and treat her with proper esteem. She's probably right that if we do that, other people will follow. We should be flattered.'

'Maybe,' he agreed slowly. 'But I couldn't shake off the feeling that she was scared of something. That she had more to worry about than her reputation.'

'Of course she has. Her marriage, for a start. And don't forget . . .' she fixed her dark gaze on him, 'she was standing inches away from him when that bolt whacked through his neck. I think even I might be a bit scared after that.'

As she walked up the path to Geraldine Beech's house, Karen realised she'd been waiting impatiently for this meeting, ever since she'd been told of it. The number of cars parked untidily along the verge outside the house suggested that it was to be very well attended. If all the stallholders from all three farmers' markets showed up, there could be fourteen or fifteen people. Some brought their partners, too. She was conscious of an urgent need to exchange observations with those who'd been at Bradbourne on Tuesday, and to see if any more sense could be made of Peter Grafton's death.

The door was on the latch and she went straight in. A babble of conversation came from the living room, and she joined the group unselfconsciously, immediately catching the eye of Hilary Henderson. The jam-and-honey supplier patted a small area on the couch next to her, and Karen squeezed herself in. Geraldine had brought a motley assortment of chairs and stools into the room, and arranged them in a rough circle. She herself was perched on an incongruously high kitchen stool, almost in the fireplace, surveying the gathering like a Victorian schoolteacher.

Karen had apparently been the last to arrive. Glancing round the room, she met the eye first of Maggie Withington and then of Oswald Kelly, before encountering two women she knew less well, who only took stalls at other markets. The option existed to participate in one, two or three markets, which operated according to a complicated timetable through the month. Only Maggie, with her highly popular bread, availed herself of all three.

'Thank you all for coming,' Geraldine began, before Karen could finish assessing the turnout. 'I know it's quite a long drive for some of you, and I do appreciate you making the effort. Those of you who weren't at Bradbourne this week will have heard, of course, that our friend Peter was killed there. It's partly to give you a chance to talk about this dreadful event that I called this meeting.'

Sally Dabb wasn't present, Karen soon realised without surprise. Drew had described her visit to him and Maggs, and she'd been as interested as he was in the woman's intentions.

'Several of us have been questioned by the police, needless to say,' Geraldine went on. 'I don't suppose any of us have been involved with a murder enquiry before, and it isn't a very comfortable experience, I'm sure you'll agree.' She looked at Maggie and Hilary and Oswald, one by one, leaving Karen feeling she'd been deliberately left out. Could Geraldine be aware that Karen had indeed been involved in murder enquiries before?

'It's certainly a first for me,' Oswald agreed, trying to look calm about it. 'Poor old Peter; never did anybody any harm. Terrible thing to happen.'

Squashed onto the sofa beside her, Karen heard Hilary give a low *tut* of irritation.

Joe Richards, on a narrow spindly looking chair in a far corner, cleared his throat. 'We must all be suspects, don't you think?' he said quietly. Karen gazed at his unruly chestnut hair and threadbare clothes. He might charge the earth for his organic meat, but he never looked as if he had change for 50p about his person. She'd wondered, now and then, just what to make of Joe. On the face of it, he was the most charismatic of all the stallholders, in a romantic, tormented sort of way. Well under forty, with craggy features and abundant hair, he seemed to take the business of food production extremely seriously. He could talk fluently on the injustice of the system which made his prices seem artificially high, when in fact it was the supermarkets who sold meat for unfairly low sums. Karen had often been swayed, listening to him, only to think about it afterwards, and find a number of flaws in his argument. He was also said to be a cheat in a small way. Some of the more challenging regulations associated with organic status could be fudged, and Joe Richards fudged them, by all accounts.

But what he said now was a shock. 'No!' she said, impulsively. 'It couldn't have been one of us.'

Everybody looked at her. 'Why not?' Geraldine asked, as if she really wanted to know.

'Because.' Karen stopped to think. 'Well. I'm just sure it wasn't. I *saw* it.'

'You didn't see a person with a crossbow, did you?' Geraldine already knew the answer to that one.

'No,' Karen admitted. 'But it was someone in the street, behind my stall. I worked it out with the police this morning. They might have been hiding in the public lavatory. There are windows facing the right way.'

'Ladies or Gents?' asked Oswald with a snigger.

'Both,' said Karen.

'We shouldn't be discussing this,' Hilary Henderson said, rather loudly.

'That's right,' Joe endorsed, with uncomfortable emphasis. 'We'll be accused of influencing a material witness.'

Too late, thought Karen unhappily. Although she liked the loo theory, she'd already allowed a picture into her mind, where one of the stallholders had managed to fire the bolt from the shadowy shrubs, drop the weapon in the foliage, saunter back to their stall, and collect the crossbow later. Anybody apart from Sally Dabb could have done that, if they'd been bold enough. And so could any of the people in the street. The suspect list seemed hopelessly long to her at the moment.

The police were probably ahead of her. They'd be messing about with trajectories and measuring distances and angles of entry, mainly on the basis of what she'd told them, and the nature of Peter's wound. And, it hit her now, with a terrible pang, they must include her on their list of possible killers.

'This isn't really what I wanted to talk about this evening, anyway,' Geraldine went on. 'Obviously it's at the forefront of your minds, and we can't pretend it didn't happen, but there is another very urgent matter we need to discuss. Some of you won't have heard very much about it, and it was in order to ensure that you're all properly informed that I asked you to come.'

Karen watched Geraldine closely, suddenly aware that she was one of those still in ignorance. She had no idea what the woman was talking about, but it seemed reasonable to assume that it had a lot to do with the strange secretive utterances of Tuesday evening, when Geraldine had come to her house.

'Don't tell me SuperFare want to build a new outlet in one of the villages,' Maggie Withington said, with a forced laugh. Karen was disproportionately pleased to realise that Maggie too was unaware of the mystery.

Geraldine shook her head. Her untidy hair with the curly ends made her seem girlish. Her weathered skin was flushed a sort of salmon colour. 'No,' she said. 'That particular nightmare hasn't struck us yet.'

'Then what is it?' Karen demanded impatiently. 'What's all the mystery?'

'Patience,' murmured Hilary at her shoulder. 'Don't spoil her fun.'

The three people directly opposite Karen, on a row of kitchen chairs, all fixed their attention on Geraldine. A man and two women, none of them very well known to her, all betrayed inside knowledge, in their complacent expressions. 'They know!' Karen complained. 'Evan and Gillian and Freda – look, it's obvious.'

'Yes, they do,' Geraldine admitted. 'They're all directly affected. In fact it was Evan who first drew my attention to what was happening.' The man bowed his head in acknowledgement.

Karen mastered her tongue, and waited. Geraldine clearly needed to control the way the information was disclosed, and impetuous questions were not going to influence her in a favourable direction.

Maggie Withington had been bouncing on her seat for the past minute or two. 'It's about GMO, isn't it!' she said excitedly.

There was a silence for at least three heartbeats. Then Geraldine laughed. 'Well guessed, Maggie. Clever old you.'

Karen leant back, with a sense of anticlimax. Was that all? It wasn't even something new; there'd been genetically modified crops of corn popping up all over the country for years, as the scientists endeavoured to demonstrate that these crops had no effect on the surrounding environment.

'Where is it this time, then?' Maggie demanded. 'Where do we meet to grub it all out? I'm game. The idea stinks, however you look at it.'

'It's not corn this time,' Evan said.

'That's right,' Geraldine nodded. 'You haven't managed to guess the whole story. I doubt if anyone could. I only came across it by accident myself. I couldn't believe it, to begin with.'

'Come on, for heaven's sake,' Karen burst out. 'Stop being so circumspect.'

Geraldine pursed her lips. 'It's not that easy,' she reproved. 'There's a lot of implications we haven't properly explored. We really don't know quite how to tackle it.'

'Tell the press,' said Oswald. 'That's the way to do it. Feed them the worst-case scenario and let them have their heads. The whole population'll rise up and follow us then.' Karen looked at him with amusement. He was given to poetic turns of phrase that she often found entertaining.

'I agree that publicity would probably be good for us,' Geraldine said. 'But I do need to protect my sources, and without disclosing how I know about it, they might not listen.'

'So how *do* you know about it?' asked Maggie.

'A friend of a friend, who's been developing some of the computer software for the people involved. He suddenly realised what some of the data meant, and emailed it to my friend, and she phoned me about it.'

'Sounds very machiavellian,' remarked Hilary, who'd been uncharacteristically quiet so far. 'I still think you need much more proof before you take any action.'

'You know what it's all about then, do you?' Karen turned awkwardly to meet Hilary's eye.

'It concerns me,' Hilary said shortly. 'Anyone working with fruit needs to be worried.'

Karen scanned the room quickly. Evan produced apples and plums; Hilary her jams and honey; Gillian had a large holding that grew strawberries and currants.

'Not quite,' Geraldine corrected Hilary. 'Only really apples, as far as we know.'

'Peter Grafton made apple juice,' Karen said, with a sense of foreboding. 'And Sally uses a lot of apple in her pickles.'

'And I make apple jelly,' Hilary said. 'That's right.'

'OK,' Karen nodded. 'So we're talking about genetically modified apple trees, are we? And you're all worried that pollen from them will contaminate your own orchards. But wouldn't it take ages for these new trees to get going and produce fruit? And aren't apples already modified in every sort of way, with all that grafting and so forth? And there are all those hundreds of varieties to choose from. Why would they bother? What's the point?' She was into her stride now, knowing enough to ask sensible questions, but far from expert on the growing of fruit.

Geraldine answered carefully. 'We're not entirely sure about what they think they're doing, but you can bet it has money at its core.' Oswald snorted at the pun, which nobody else but Karen seemed to notice. She gave him a comradely giggle, to show she'd spotted it too. Geraldine made a show of forbearance, before continuing. 'There are various possibilities: getting them to fruit earlier, or for a longer season; slowing the rate of decay; forcing them to inter-pollinate more freely – it could be any of those, or something quite different. And actually, Karen, it only takes a couple of years for a tree to start bearing fruit.'

'And do we know *where* this is happening?'

'Not exactly.' Geraldine's expression was wary, and Karen didn't believe her. She remembered her visit to the suddenly inhospitable Mary Thomas in Ferngate.

'If I had to guess,' she said, 'it would be somewhere not a million miles from Ferngate.' She watched Geraldine closely for a reaction.

'Guess as much as you like, Miss Clever,' the woman responded sharply. 'This is too important to play games with.'

Karen refused to be crushed. 'So why are we here? What is this actually all about?'

'As I said, partly it's a chance to go over Peter's death, and air our feelings about that. However you look at it, it was a terrible thing to happen. Poor Julie – her life's never going to be the same again. And we gather that your husband's going to be doing the funeral, so that makes you even more closely involved in a way.'

'Closer than actually seeing it happen, you mean?' Karen grimaced sceptically. 'I don't think so.'

'Well, of course that's true. And it's all rather soon after the event, I realise now, for any considered reaction.'

Karen had a sense of the people in the room growing restless. Gillian and Freda, flanked on either side of Evan, had said scarcely a word between them. She thought Gillian sold ordinary vegetables, as well as soft fruit; she didn't know Freda's line of business at all. She doubted whether they'd known Peter Grafton very well.

'There's another reason, then,' Karen insisted. 'Something to do with this GM apple business. But instead of just telling it straight, you've been beating about the bush and making us guess. Me and Maggie and Oswald and Joe, anyhow. Everyone else seems to be in on the secret.'

'We don't grow apples, that's why,' said

Maggie. 'But we do live close to Ferngate, all four of us.'

'That's right,' Geraldine agreed. 'I'm sorry, Karen. It's so sensitive, you see. Nobody knows that we know about what's going on. And in spite of Oswald's suggestion, I don't think going to the press just yet would be wise. But it needs to be stopped. Everybody's very clear about that. I know you're not officially organic, but it would potentially affect your garden, too. And Joe feeds his animals food-stuff that he grows himself, which is guaranteed GM free. So does Oswald. We can't *afford* to let this go on.'

'But apples don't pollinate with my vegetables or Joe's corn,' Karen objected. 'And I'm not really close to Ferngate. What possible risk can there be?'

Hilary answered that, pushing herself forward on the sofa, and clasping her hands together. 'The insects!' she said forcefully. 'The pollinators. They *eat* the stuff, as well as pass it from plant to plant. It could have all sorts of ghastly effects on them. It could wipe them all out, or make them change their habits. The whole thing is so delicately interwoven, you see. Change one element, and it could all come unravelled.' She spoke with such zeal that Karen's heart rate sped up at the apocalyptic vision before her. She'd heard it before, many a time, but somehow never *felt* it like this. And yet, with her rational mind, she still doubted that there was anything to worry about. She still trusted the scientists not to be quite that crazy and irresponsible.

'We have to seek and destroy, in short,' Oswald put in, with evident relish. 'And if you're not with us, you must be against us.'

'Steady on, Ozzie,' Joe Richards protested from his spindly chair.

'He's right, though,' said Maggie bitterly. 'We're up against powerful forces here, remember. They're not going to just stand back and let us trash their life's work.'

'They're used to it,' Hilary said. 'Monsanto particularly.'

'Is this Monsanto, then?' Karen asked.

'Apparently not,' Geraldine said. 'Although it's hard to be sure. They hide behind a host of different names these days. Not that it matters, really. They're all as bad as each other. And with fickle public attention turned elsewhere, they think they can carry on just as they like.'

The meeting seemed to run out of steam at this point. Geraldine went off to make coffee, and conversation fragmented into twos and threes. Karen still wasn't sure she'd grasped the central purpose, although she'd certainly learnt a great deal. She was impatient to get home and share the disclosures with Drew.

But nobody seemed inclined to leave just yet. Hilary put a hand on her arm, as if sensing her wish to get home. 'It really does matter, you know,' she said.

'I'm sure it does.' Karen felt guilty at her own deficiency in zeal.

'It's too easy just to assume everything's going to be all right, you see. I was like that myself a few years ago, so I know how it is. You've got Drew and the kids to occupy you, and that wonderful garden you're making. It's always busy, with not much time for serious thought, let alone reading the reports that are coming out. But you *must*. We might not get a second chance.'

'I don't really understand what you're asking me to do,' Karen said.

Hilary glanced around the room, as if checking that nobody was listening. 'Divert attention,' she said in a whisper. 'The police have been questioning you. You've been unlucky – in the wrong place at the wrong time. Like it or not, your name is going to pop up again and again on their computers. They might ask you for opinions on Peter. Just mind what you say. We've put so much work into this community . . .' her voice rose, '. . . we can't bear for it all to get ruined now.'

Karen stared at Hilary's open country features. 'But it would never even have *occurred* to me before this evening that Peter was killed because of food politics.'

Hilary grinned. 'Well, we have been silly then, haven't we?'

Den suspected that Hemsley was disappointed with the information he'd provided. When it came down to it, all he'd been able to offer was that he knew Karen Slocombe, chief witness to the shooting of Peter Grafton. 'Is that it?' Hemsley had demanded, after the all-too-brief explanation. 'I thought you were going to give me something useful.'

Den shrugged. 'It could be useful,' he maintained. 'I'm well positioned to get more background for you. Karen doesn't much like the police. She's not going to put herself out to help you.'

'She likes you though, does she?'

They were meeting for the second time since Den had seen the Inspector giving his television interview. Taking an hour out from his Social Services tasks, Den had dropped into the Incident Room, in the hope of catching his friend. It was ten thirty on Friday morning.

Den paused at the question, bending his long head thoughtfully, staring at the formica table in front of him. 'She's not mad about me,' he admitted. 'It can be awkward sometimes. The four of us, all connected as we are. Drew gets caught up in the middle, and Karen feels left out. But so do I, on and off.'

Hemsley shook his head. 'I'm not with you,' he complained. 'Drew and Karen are married, right? And your girlfriend works for him?'

'Right. That's it, basically.'

'So there's plenty of scope for jealousy,' the Inspector noted shrewdly. 'All these pairings, all these high emotions when there's a messy funeral or one of the kids gets sick. D'you fancy her at all?'

'Who? Karen? No!' Den spoke robustly. 'Absolutely not.'

'OK. I shouldn't have asked that. It's just my experience that when you get these close foursomes, it very often ends up with everybody fancying everybody else. Just because it can all get so intimate and matey.'

'Your experience, eh?'

Hemsley nodded glumly. 'It happened to me – don't tell anyone this, mind,' he warned. 'My Ginnie had a fling with Paul, who was my best mate. It didn't last, but it did the marriage no favours at all. And it meant I lost my mate as well. I don't recommend it, my friend. Try not to let it happen – right?'

'There's not a lot I can do. Maggs isn't going to break off her partnership with Drew, whatever happens. I sometimes think she's more likely to break it off with me.'

'Career woman, eh?' Danny was sympathetic, shaking his head understandingly.

'In a way, except she earns hardly any money, and seems to spend most of her time mooching about between the graves. It's not exactly a dynamic enterprise. And she talks to Drew. She talks to him all the time, as far as I can see.'

'Dodgy,' the detective agreed. 'Bound to be a bond between them.'

'Danny, I'm not *jealous* of Drew. He's a great chap, and straight as they come. He and Maggs had worked together for two years when I met them. There's never been anything between them. That's not what I'm saying.'

'No. Right. Well.'

'Oh, forget it. Everything's fine. We're all happy. What got us onto this anyway?'

'Mrs Slocombe and the dead fruit juice man.'

'Fruit juice?' Den tilted his head thoughtfully. 'I didn't know which stall he had. Did he sell fruit juice?'

'To the exclusion of all else. Talk about weird jobs. Thought you knew all that.'

'I just knew he had a stall. I knew he couldn't be the meat man. At least.' He stared at Danny without really seeing him. 'I bought some lamb chops there, that morning, you know. But I didn't pay a lot of attention to any of the other stalls. Karen was off somewhere, and nobody seemed to know me, so I didn't stop to chat or anything.'

'Cooper, what's going on in that daft head of yours? You're sounding very strange.'

Den laughed. 'I'm beginning to feel like a policeman again, that's all. It's disorientating.'

'Well, don't let it worry you. I doubt you can help us on this one, after all. Especially since I see no sign of you using your detecting skills. They've all dried up and died, seems like. But if you wake up one morning and think you can explain to us just *why* somebody might take it on themselves to kill a man who sells fruit juice, then give me a call, OK?'

'OK,' Den sighed. 'Sorry I'm so useless.'

'Don't let it worry you,' Hemsley said again. 'Just pay for these coffees, will you? I don't think I can justify putting it on police expenses.'

CHAPTER SEVEN

It was Della's turn to have the kids again, and Karen continued to regard the arrangement with some ambivalence. She did have several urgent gardening jobs waiting for her, which required the absence of children. Earthing up celery; thinning out a variety of seedlings; digging a new stretch of ground ready for further crops. In total she had close to half an acre at her disposal, which was a very substantial plot. Over-ambitious, Drew had called it, which only made her more determined to utilise the entire area. Potatoes took up lots of space, and were low maintenance. Broad beans, large cabbages, courgettes and peas all liked plenty of room to spread themselves. And everything grew so prodigiously on new ground.

But as she dug, she found herself worrying about her children, particularly Stephanie. Since the supermarket bomb, the world had suddenly seemed a lot less safe, and she was uneasy with them out of her sight. Sternly, she admonished herself that nowhere on earth could be more secure than a remote Somerset village on a tiny road that led nowhere. Despite Della's disconcerting reaction on Tuesday, and Timmy's damaged knee, for which there had still been no proper explanation, she was essentially reliable. Until now, Karen had not felt the slightest pang of concern.

So she nudged her thoughts back to the meeting of the previous evening instead, with Drew's responses to consider as well. 'Gosh!' he'd said, when she'd splurged the central facts on her return home. 'Sounds as if they're seriously bothered.'

'I think they are,' she'd agreed.

'But, what're they planning to do? You didn't say you'd get involved, did you? Did they ask you to?'

She shrugged wordlessly. Despite her natural inclination to question any overblown assertions made by Geraldine and her friends, she was after all regarded as one of them. Of course she agreed with their basic aims and practices. She wanted the world to stop using supermarkets, for local communities to provide all their own needs, for giant lorries to stop transporting unrealistically shiny and uniform fruit and vegetables up and down the country. She knew with complete certainty that all this was the insane face of consumerism, which nobody could ever manage to defend rationally.

But genetically modified crops were a slightly different matter. She hesitated to leap unthinkingly onto that bandwagon, because there might actually be some lurking good sense in some of the things the scientists were doing. She couldn't name any, it was true, and the 'terminator gene' that so cynically and capitalistically prevented farmers from using seeds from their own crops for next year's planting was one of the grossest things she had ever heard of. But surely it was desirable for growing seasons to be extended, and for weeds to be kept to a minimum?

On the face of it, she had to acknowledge, it was absolute folly to plant these mutants out in the open country. So little was yet known about the way bees operated, while other insects were even less well understood. And the argument that little *would* ever be known without these experiments struck her as dangerous and unintelligent. She remembered her mother a few years ago saying how the older she got, the more apparent it became that the people in control were terrifyingly stupid. It was one of the things that forced themselves onto your awareness, as your life proceeded. Karen had found this observation lodging itself firmly in her mind. Still a mere thirty-two, she took note of the occasional experience which seemed to confirm the hypothesis. If it was true, then Geraldine and Hilary, both aged around sixty, had doubtless both become aware of it. Probably, Karen thought, she should listen to them, and trust to their superior wisdom.

Drew was interested, but no more than that. There was none of his usual eagerness to dive in and solve the mystery with Maggs as his sidekick. He might be doing Peter Grafton's funeral, but somehow that gave him little incentive to explore just who killed him and why. Karen, on the other hand, was a lot more concerned than previously. She had to be – she'd seen it happen. She'd witnessed the damage that occurs to a person when a crossbow bolt hits them in the throat. And she kept thinking she *must* have seen the killer, without understanding just what she was looking at. Someone who'd been walking nonchalantly away, or even standing still and watching events unfold. Who, she asked herself repeatedly, had been there in the High Street at the time?

The seven stallholders, counting herself and Peter; Geraldine Beech; at least a dozen shoppers within a few feet of the stalls and another dozen on the pavements beyond; and Mary Thomas.

The immediate mystery concerned Mary, to such a degree that Karen felt it couldn't possibly have been her who had killed Peter. If it had, then surely Geraldine wouldn't have drawn such attention to the woman by her melodramatic visitation on Tuesday evening. Except that Geraldine wouldn't have *known* Mary was the killer. Would she?

The obvious conclusion based on known facts was that Sally Dabb's husband had learnt of the presumed affair with Peter and conceived a murderously jealous passion. His alibi as reported by Geraldine – that he was at work miles away – might be false. Or he might have paid someone else to do it.

The strongest pull, the subject her thoughts persistently returned to, was this business of the GM crops. It concerned apples, and Grafton had produced apple juice. More than that, it seemed that his enterprise was a long way from the somewhat amateurish and unreliable production methods of all the others in the food group. Even Maggie's bread was baked in her own kitchen, albeit in two large industrial ovens that she'd bought secondhand with all her savings. Hilary's honey and jam were entirely home produced in time-honoured fashion. Oswald butchered his ostriches himself, mincing the meat and growing the herbs that went with it.

Giving herself a rest from turning the heavy soil, Karen leant on her spade for a moment. No wonder she was tired, she realised, looking about her: she'd just dug six whole rows without stopping. It only showed what your body could perform when your mind was actively engaged elsewhere.

'You look like Old Whatsisname – the gardener in *The Secret Garden,*' came a voice. 'All you need is some straw in your hair.'

'Hilary!' Karen was startled.

'Hi. Did I come at a bad time?' The woman had walked round the side of the house, at the opposite end to Drew's office. Karen's patch of land extended some distance beyond the side of the house, parallel to the road. Hilary had walked across the small lawn and was standing between rows of spring greens.

'Not really. I could make a cup of tea.'

'Sounds good to me.' The forced cheerfulness in her voice was unmistakable. It gave Karen cause for some anxiety, the more so as she remembered the whispered exchange of the previous evening.

'Don't worry,' Hilary reassured her, as she walked slowly over the garden to lead the way into the house. 'I didn't mean to alarm you. Nothing's happened since last night.'

'So what can I do for you?'

'Make the tea first. It's all rather delicate.'

Karen reminded herself of how she'd always liked Hilary Henderson. The woman had seemed dependable and balanced. She didn't care what people thought; she was strong and self-assured. They'd had innumerable chats during the farmers' markets, but Karen could not now remember anything they'd talked about.

The afternoon had clouded over, and it seemed a trifle chilly for sitting outside, so Karen led her visitor into the living room, a mug of tea in either hand. 'I've run out of biscuits, I'm afraid,' she said. 'I was going to make some this evening.'

Hilary waved this away as of no importance.

'Has Geraldine said anything to you about Mary Thomas?' Hilary started as soon as they were settled.

'Well, actually . . .' Karen began. 'She has, in a way.' Geraldine's injunction to avoid mentioning Mary's presence at the killing of Peter Grafton rang loudly in Karen's head. Who would she trust, if it came down to a choice – Geraldine or Hilary? She liked them both, and would hate to find them on opposite sides in any confrontation, but she owed more allegiance to Geraldine. She had given Karen her first market stall, had nursed her through the early stages, encouraged and instructed her. Geraldine was immersed in the whole business of food production and food politics. She was passionate on the subject and Karen had faith in her.

Hilary was in many ways out of the same mould, but she was much more of a dilettante. She not only kept bees and made jam; she kept sheep and spun their wool; she spoke fluent Russian and ran classes in it, whenever there was a demand. She was married to a farmer and had five grown up children. There was about Hilary an air of irresponsibility. If one endeavour didn't work, she'd turn unscathed to another. If people wanted something from her, she'd only give it if it required no great effort or sacrifice on her part. Karen liked her very much, but she would not have run to Hilary Henderson in a crisis. She could not imagine Hilary taking care of an elderly mother or ailing husband. She had the impression that her children had more or less run wild, looking after each other while their mother indulged some fleeting whim or other.

But, Karen acknowledged now, all this could be quite wrong.

And so Karen maintained her silence as to just what Geraldine had said about Mary Thomas. 'She said Mary didn't really know Peter,' she supplied weakly. 'Or something like that. I'd mentioned her for some reason, and that's all Geraldine said.'

Hilary put down her tea and examined Karen closely, her eyes fixed on the younger woman's face. 'Is that all?' she said disbelievingly. 'It can't have been.'

Karen shrugged. 'Well, I don't know Mary very well, and I've got no idea how friendly she and Geraldine are. Why should either of them talk to me about the other?'

'Because we all need each other, that's why.' Hilary's voice was low and intense. 'You need us, we need you, and everybody needs Mary Thomas.'

'But *why?*' Karen almost wailed. 'It all sounds so frightening. As if you know there's something horrible about to happen.'

'Wasn't the killing of Peter Grafton horrible enough for you?'

'Yes – of course, but you're not talking about that, are you? You're talking about some sort of fight, something illegal, something secret and dangerous.' She nibbled at a finger joint. 'I can see it on your face. There's something really nasty going on.'

Hilary leant back and sighed. 'That's right, Karen Slocombe. Something really nasty's going on. And we want you to help us stop it.'

Maggs and Den could never relax completely at the weekends, because Maggs was perpetually on call to rush off and help Drew remove a body from a hospice or nursing home. It happened infrequently, but they were usually expected to turn out when called, within two or three hours at most.

'What about when you go on holiday?' Den had demanded in disbelief when they'd first met.

'Haven't had one yet,' she shrugged.

'What – in two years? You're joking!'

'I can go away for the day, if I really want to, but it's a risk. Karen would have to go on the removal with Drew, which would mean finding someone to have the kids. And she wouldn't like doing it.'

'How often has that happened?'

'Never.' She grinned. 'I've only been away once, to London with my mum. I didn't enjoy it; I was too worried that they'd never cope without me. We actually only get called out like that about once every six weeks. Most people can wait till next morning, the way we do things. We still have to be ready to go. It's OK, you get used to it. You shouldn't let it bother you.'

'You're mad. You're wasting away your youth.'

'Yeah,' she sighed dramatically. 'Tragic, isn't it.'

On this particular weekend, Den felt a strong desire to get away. He'd been unsettled by the conversation with Hemsley, and was less than happy with himself as a result.

'Let's go to the sea or something,' he said. 'Take your mobile, so Drew can call you back if he needs to.'

'Not the sea,' she wriggled her shoulders. 'It's too cold. How about a B&B weekend on a farm somewhere?'

He blinked. 'A farm?'

'Something like that. Somewhere different.'

'But we're surrounded by farms here. That wouldn't *be* different.'

He examined her face closely. 'If you want a change we ought to go to Bristol or Plymouth or somewhere.'

She met his gaze, her big brown eyes serious. 'No, Den. You're not getting it. There's something about farms. Land. Animals. Something I've always missed out on. You've seen more of them than I have, but you've never actually *lived* on one, have you?'

He shook his head. 'What am I not getting?' he asked, with some foreboding.

'Well, it's just a little idea I had. It's probably stupid. We'd never raise the money, for a start. And everybody else seems to be getting out of farming. And I've got Drew to consider and everything. It's just—'

'Maggs Beacon. Are you trying to tell me you think we should go into *farming?*'

'Well, not exactly. Not milking cows or

anything. But don't you think it would be brilliant, to have our own bit of land? Some sheep maybe. You could work from home, find some sort of occupation, making things, I don't know. I want a *change,* Den. I hate it when every day's the same.'

'You wouldn't leave Peaceful Repose, would you? That'd be shattering for Drew.'

'No, but I think he needs a bit of a shakeup. He's got very slow and unambitious lately. Karen's the one with all the energy. She's got all these ideas, principles, projects. He used to be like that. Now he just sits about waiting for the phone to ring. It's *boring.'*

'So you're suggesting we go off to a farm somewhere and talk about this?'

'Right,' she said. 'Is that OK?'

'Course it is. Whatever makes you happy.'

'Den Cooper, I love you,' she shouted, flinging her arms round him, standing on tiptoe, but still only able to reach as far as his elbows. 'Bend down, so I can hug you properly.'

He obliged, his long arms wrapping around her, pulling her close, and lifting her off her feet.

Drew was indeed sitting beside the phone, that Saturday, when it rang in the living room. He hadn't been waiting for a call, though. He was helping Timmy with a wooden construction toy, the child perched on his lap and the pieces lined up on the arm of the sofa. For several seconds, he didn't have a hand free to reach over and grab the receiver.

'Oh, hello,' came a woman's voice. 'This is Julie Grafton again. Sorry to call at the weekend.'

'No problem,' Drew said, struggling to shift his little son onto the cushions beside him. Timmy stubbornly resisted. Before he could start protesting, Drew relaxed and let him stay where he was. 'How can I help?'

'I'd like to come and see you. Today.'

'Ah. Well, yes, that's fine. When exactly?'

'In about forty minutes? Is that too early?'

'No, that'll be all right. Although I've got my children here. I'd have to see you in the house, not the office. I'm in charge this morning.'

'It's not about the funeral,' she added. 'At least – not really.'

Drew almost laughed. 'Not about the funeral? What then?'

'I'll tell you when I see you. I don't mind about the kids. Except, do they have to be in the same room?'

He felt himself bristling with irritation, a sudden wash of it over-laying the polite concern he'd felt at first. 'We'll have to see,' was all he said to that.

She arrived in less than forty minutes, her face pale and flat as she got out of the car. Drew felt a return of his former pity for her, combined with curiosity and a slight sense of dread. He'd been here before, more than once. Distraught women, intent on explaining to him the reasons for their loved one's sudden death, throwing themselves on him for support, assistance, elucidation. If the dead person had been murdered, then Drew was the person they turned to. It was his fate, his destiny, now that his reputation as an amateur detective was so widespread. A reputation he really didn't feel he deserved, when he thought back over his erratic career. A succession of lucky accidents, stubborn argumentativeness, help from Maggs and Karen and a deplorable tendency to become emotionally involved with distraught women was mostly what it came down to.

He met her at the front door, putting out an arm to stop her coming in. 'We can go round the back, to the garden. I've got the kids playing out there, and we can probably get out of earshot, if we need to. I don't think they're likely to be interested, actually.'

'OK.' She seemed to be holding herself carefully, as if afraid that something would break or overflow if she moved suddenly.

He led her round the path at the side of the house, where Karen's garden, bigger every time he looked, stretched away to their right. Turning left, they found themselves in the smaller area, which was almost entirely lawn, strewn with playthings and featuring a climbing frame. Stephanie and Timmy were splashing their hands in a bowl of water, in a game that looked particularly mindless. They'd get cold before long, Drew realised, as the water soaked into their clothes. It wasn't a very warm day.

He sat himself and Julie Grafton on white plastic garden chairs, and encouraged her to speak. She needed very little urging.

'I've been thinking about who must have killed Peter,' she said breathlessly. 'At first I never even asked myself that. I couldn't get past the fact that he was dead. Do you understand?'

Drew nodded.

'But the police kept coming back with questions, and I had phone calls from the Food Chain people, and various friends, and they all kept on and on about who could have done it, until I woke up. I mean, now I really need to know. Obviously, I suppose. How could anybody *do* that? Just shoot him with no warning? It's . . . barbaric. Wicked. A *terrible* thing to do.'

Drew nodded again. 'Of course it is,' he agreed. 'There can be no excuse for that.'

'*Excuse!*' she echoed, her voice rising to a squeak. 'Of course there isn't.'

'I didn't mean—' He stopped. Something was nudging him, some perception that he'd almost missed. What was she really trying to say?

'Anyway,' she pressed on. 'I've been thinking about it. I lay awake all night, going over everybody he knew, everybody he'd ever annoyed or disagreed with. Racking my brains about crossbows, and whether I've ever seen one round here. Trying to find who might want to kill him.'

'And—?' he prompted.

'I couldn't think of any particular person, but it made me see things about Peter that I hadn't wanted to face up to before.'

Drew glanced at the children. They'd tipped the bowl over, and were mixing the water into the ground, turning a perfectly good patch of lawn into a quagmire. Well, he mentally shrugged to himself, it was only a very *small* quagmire, and he remembered very well how delicious the sensation of mud between the fingers could be.

'That's a good first step,' he said thoughtfully. 'I mean, not just for finding who killed him, but to get a clearer idea of who he was, what sort of marriage you had, that sort of thing.' He found it easy to talk like this, from his occasional work as a funeral officiant. He could home in on the reality behind the blank faces, venture into sensitive areas that would send most men

144

running. And he'd discovered that if people were ever going to tolerate this 'real' talk, it was at a time of great crisis. Some of their protective layers fell away and they could be addressed in terms that you'd never use in normal daily chit-chat.

'There was nothing wrong with our marriage,' she flashed. Drew waited passively.

'That's not what I mean,' she added more calmly. 'But he did have a life apart from me. Things I wasn't involved in. We thought it was healthy – you know, two well-rounded individuals choosing to be together, not because we were dependent, but because we loved each other.' She sniffed moistly, but there were no tears.

'So I think this killing was something to do with the apple juice,' she said. 'Because he wasn't actually organic, you see. Not that he pretended he was, but some of the others disapproved. They didn't like his using so much technology. And,' she took a deep breath, 'I've been out there, looking at his paperwork, talking to Patch.'

'Patch?'

'The boy who helps Peter. He's been trying to keep it going, bless him, even though he's only sixteen. He comes in after school. It couldn't all just *stop,* anyway.' She sighed. 'Patch had no idea what Peter was planning. At least, so he says . . .'

Drew waited. The story was clear enough without any need for further questions.

'He'd been approached by SuperFare,' she hurried the words out. 'They were interested in taking the juice, you see. I found several letters from them. They wanted him to expand, guarantee the right quantity, consistent quality, all that sort of thing.' She gave Drew a penetrating look. 'I knew nothing at all about it,' she said, and he felt her anger, despite it being under tight control.

'And how would you have reacted?'

'I'd have been disgusted,' she spat. 'It's a betrayal of everything he said he believed. Treachery. There really aren't the words for it. And if I think it's so terrible, there are others round here who'd feel even more strongly.' She chewed a corner of her mouth. 'Don't you think I might have discovered a motive for his murder?'

CHAPTER EIGHT

Drew couldn't wait for Karen to get back. He wasn't too sure where she'd gone; she'd rushed out of the house after breakfast muttering about Food Chain business and having to catch somebody. 'You're OK with the kids, aren't you?' she'd thrown over her shoulder.

'Yes,' he'd agreed. 'So long as we don't get a removal.'

'Pooh! You never get removals these days,' was her parting shot. The uncomfortable truth of this had put him in a sour mood for a good ten minutes.

She still hadn't got back at midday and he was beginning to think he ought to call her mobile and find out where she was. Except she never switched the darn thing on, and she wouldn't like him chasing after her, even if he got through. He found some salad things and threw them together for lunch, including a few pods of early peas that seemed ready to eat. He and Stephanie both preferred them uncooked, scattered amongst the tomatoes and radishes of the salad.

Julie Grafton's disclosures had made him realise he hadn't been keeping up with the activities of the Food Chain group. He helped Karen load the van when she had a stall, and arranged his own schedule so as to manage without the van, but that was about as far as it went. He didn't go to the meetings with her, barely knew Geraldine from Hilary, and nearly always experienced a stab of disappointment when she told him how much money she'd made.

The fact that the murdered man had been a stallholder at the market had made Drew more uneasy than he cared to admit to himself. Something was going on that he would rather his wife were not involved in. Something dangerous and incomprehensible. The bomb in the supermarket had been the first signal, one that shook him up badly. A murder only three days later did nothing for his peace of mind. Then there had been the odd evening visit from Geraldine Beech, and the sporadic comings and goings which he hadn't properly followed. Although he could see cars arriving at the house from the office window, he was often out in the burial field, or busy on the phone, too distracted to worry about his wife's activities. Whatever Karen did during the working day was her own business, and he seldom consciously tried to monitor her.

Suddenly Karen was there, bursting through the front door, her hair all untidy as if she'd been combing her fingers through it. 'Hey!' she said, coming to find him and the children in the kitchen. 'Guess what!'

He shook his head apprehensively. 'What?'

'The police have arrested Mary Thomas. I was there! It was amazing. She ran out into her orchard and they had to chase her. They think she planted the bomb in the supermarket. But – this is the really mad part – she swears blind she wasn't there. How can she say that when I *saw* her? I *spoke* to her. It's her word against mine.' She ran out of breath then, slumping onto one of the kitchen chairs, and running her fingers through her hair yet again.

'You were there? At her house?' Drew said. 'Why?'

Karen didn't answer. 'It's such a funny feeling. Someone telling an outright lie, like that. You know in films, where the main witness takes the police back to the place where she's seen some sort of clear evidence, but when they get there, it's all been repainted, and the doors moved and nothing remotely as she remembers? Like that. You doubt your own sanity. If it wasn't for Geraldine, I'd be thinking I'd dreamt the whole thing.'

'Kaz, calm down will you,' Drew urged her. 'We're having lunch.'

Stephanie and Timmy were both eyeing their mother uncertainly. 'Daddy picked some peas,' Stephanie said.

'What? Oh Drew, you didn't, did you? They won't be ready for at least another week.'

'Only a few. And they are ready. Just as we like them, eh, Steph?'

'They can't possibly be. But never mind now. Is there anything left for me?' She scanned the table. Part of a home-baked loaf remained, and a scattering of salad in the bottom of the bowl. 'Cheese?'

'Loads of cheese. Some of that coleslaw, too. In the fridge.'

She ate absentmindedly, obviously still reliving the events of the morning. Drew hustled the children out to the garden before returning to the conversation.

'They must be fairly sure, if they've really arrested her,' he remarked.

'I don't know. She didn't do herself any good by running away. God knows what she was thinking of. But it took them a few minutes to find her. She was in amongst her cherry trees.'

'Where were you?'

'Out in the road by then.'

'Can you tell me the whole thing again, slowly?'

'There isn't anything else, really. I went on a whim, because she'd been so off with me on Wednesday, and I couldn't let it rest. She didn't let me in, just kept me talking on the doorstep. Then when the police car showed up, she took one look and started galloping down the orchard, leaving me standing there. I felt a real fool.'

'Had you said anything about the supermarket to her?'

'Not really. I was just getting around to it.'

'But you heard what the police said to her?'

'Yes. I was out in the road, and they brought her right past me, to their car. They were saying they wanted to question her about the supermarket, and she gave me a most peculiar look and said right out that she hadn't been near the supermarket for months, and they'd never prove otherwise.'

'Gosh!'

Karen shuddered, clasping her arms tightly round herself. 'It was horrible, really. But the main thing is, I'm so terribly *cross* with her. How dare she tell such a lie!'

'Had it occurred to you that she might have a good reason?' he ventured. 'And that look she gave you, might it not have been something like "I know this is wrong of me, but please back me up"? Something like that?' He smiled boyishly. 'Just guessing, you understand. I don't even know the woman.'

'No, that didn't occur to me,' she admitted. 'I drove home full of visions of the police questioning me again, and thinking I was mad, or had some sinister reason for insisting she was there. It's very likely, you know. It's sure to be because of me that they nabbed her in the first place.'

'Do you think she did it? Planted the bomb, I mean?'

Karen paused and gulped. 'Drew, why haven't I thought of these questions for myself? I'm so stupid, honestly I am.'

'Not at all. You'd have got there in a while. But do you?'

She thought about it. 'It looked as if she'd only just got out of her car, when I bumped into her. But it was all rather confused. Steph and I were fooling about, almost running back to my car. I didn't take very much notice of what she was doing. But I suppose I don't think she did it. How could a sensible woman like that *possibly* do such a thing?'

'You were running?' Drew's mind seemed to change gear, flickering over all the different strands of the story. 'Did Mary see you running?'

'Probably. Why?'

'Let me run something past you,' he said. 'How about if Mary thinks *you* planted the bomb? So everything she did today, everything she says, is designed to throw them off the scent. Does that make sense?'

'No it doesn't. That's the sort of convolution that Maggs would have come up with. I had *Stephanie* with me, remember? Nobody plants bombs with their small daughter alongside. Anyway, Mary couldn't hope to protect me like that. The police know I was there; I presented myself like a good citizen. She could have kept quiet about the running, and still have told the truth about being there. And there's sure to be other people who saw us. For heaven's sake – nobody would suspect a woman with a little girl. We were just playing. Except . . .' She faltered. 'Except we hadn't actually *bought* anything. We just went in and came out again, pretending Steph was going to be sick. Bloody hell, I hope nobody remembers to report *that*.'

'On the face of it, it's rather a surprise they've opted for Mary,' Drew said grimly. 'If I'd been them, I'd have had you banged up long since.' He laughed, but the joke was too thin for any real humour.

Karen stopped trying to eat any lunch. 'This is actually quite scary,' she admitted.

It was with a sense of surrender that Drew accepted that he was from here on involved in the violence of the past week. As if to ratify this, as well as divert her fears into another channel, he told Karen about his conversation with Julie Grafton that morning: the fruit juice contract with SuperFare in particular.

She heard him out without much reaction. 'The police said something that fits with that,' she nodded, when he'd finished. 'That the juice production was much more hi-tech than they'd have expected. I wonder whether Geraldine knows anything about this?'

'Doesn't she do some kind of inspection before she lets people have one of her stalls?'

'She didn't do one on me. I doubt if she does. She'd take it on trust. And anyway, there are only a few rules. You have to make or grow the produce yourself, and live within 25 miles of the market. He qualified on both those.'

'Julie thinks it's a motive for killing him – the business with the supermarket contract.'

Karen shuddered again. 'Has it got to such a point as that?' She hugged herself tighter. 'I guess it has, if the bomb's anything to go by.' She remembered something else. 'And Geraldine told me, quite plainly, that the two things were connected. And I think she was saying the connection was Mary Thomas.'

'We're jumping to conclusions here,' he warned. 'Quite a few of these points have at least two interpretations.'

'Have they?' she said bleakly.

The phone rang, and there was a frantic scrummage while they searched for the walk-about receiver which hadn't been replaced on its cradle. 'Bloody thing,' Drew panted, finally locating it underneath the sofa. 'Hello?'

It was a nursing home, eighteen miles away. They had a body for removal, preferably by teatime. 'Are you sure you want me?' Drew asked, as he often did. Customers for his burial ground generally made themselves known to him before they died.

'"Drew Slocombe, Peaceful Repose Funerals". That's what it says here. Apparently a friend of hers is with you – if you see what I mean. Buried in your cemetery. She'd like to go alongside, if that's possible.'

'Who's the friend?'

The voice became more amicable. 'Now you're asking,' the woman said cheerfully. 'That's not the sort of thing I'd have a note of. It'll be in her will, I suppose.'

'I doubt if I can get to you by teatime. My assistant's away for the weekend, and it would take her quite a while to get back.' Inwardly he cringed at the thought of disturbing Maggs's romantic little holiday. Maggs in a sour mood was not something to be taken lightly.

'She's a tiny little lady. I would think you could manage her on your own, if you had to. I don't mind lending a hand if it comes to it.'

Drew had to think about that. It was unprecedented to do a removal unaccompanied. That had been drummed into him during his first job with Daphne Plant. Even when staff absences had stretched them to the limit, they always managed to find a second pair of hands.

'OK then,' he agreed. 'Thanks very much. I'll be on my way in a few minutes.'

'Don't get here before three, will you?' she said hurriedly. 'They'll still be in the recreation room till then, and we'd have to pass by that window.'

For the hundredth time, Drew allowed himself to wonder just what extravagant sensitivities ordained that inmates of a nursing home should not be permitted to observe the departure of one of their number. It smacked uncomfortably of *1984* and group manipulation. There one minute, disappeared the next. *Where's Hilda got to? Hilda? Oh, she isn't here any more.* Surely that couldn't be how they did it? They probably told some story about her passing away peacefully during the night, and the funeral flowers had been sent in everybody's name. No wonder so many of the poor old things spent their days in murky confusion. The normal rules of existence no longer applied once you got yourself institutionalised.

'Right,' he confirmed, glancing at his watch. It was only half past one. He wouldn't have to leave for another forty-five minutes or so.

Karen was hovering, listening to his side of the conversation. 'A removal?' she said. 'Who's going with you?'

'Nobody. She says I can manage on my own.'

'My God. What would Daphne say?'

'She'd throw a fit. Bugger Daphne.'

Karen made coffee. The children came back from the garden, dripping with mud and were cleaned off in the kitchen. Timmy, droopy from a hectic morning, went willingly to his bed for an afternoon nap. Stephanie embarked on a large colouring project on the kitchen table.

'Something just struck me,' Karen said, going back to Drew to finish her coffee. He pretended alarm, looking around her, craning to see the back of her head.

'Did it? Are you hurt?'

'Idiot. No, listen. You do realise that Julie might have done it, don't you? The cheated wife.

She might have heard things about Peter and Sally Dabb, and been murderously jealous. It does happen.'

'True,' he rubbed his chin while he thought about it. 'She said something. It wasn't so much the words, but the *tone*. Something about an excuse. It didn't fit properly. I hardly noticed, but it was like a tiny snag in a smooth surface. It made me think she might know *why* he was killed, if not who did it.'

'And then she told you all that about the supermarket contract and you thought that must be what she meant?'

'Right. Except it didn't feel as if that was really it. Hard to explain.'

'Well, we should remember the emotional stuff. Woman stuff. We can't just ignore the existence of Sally.'

'I wasn't suggesting we ignore her.' He glanced at his watch, wondering whether he should give the van a quick clean-out. Karen kept on talking.

'I know she told you and Maggs there was no truth in the stories about her and Peter. That doesn't actually make any difference, does it? If Julie believed it was true, that's enough. Or Sally's husband, of course.'

'Have they known each other forever?' Drew wondered. 'Did Julie and Sally go to school together and fight over him from the fifth form?'

'No, I don't think so. Della was reminiscing about schooldays a while ago. I was getting her to fill me in on the Food Chain people. I still feel like a newcomer sometimes, even after nearly four years. Anyway, if I remember rightly, Della and Sally knew each other, but Julie's an incomer like me. She's from Yorkshire, I think.'

Drew nodded. 'She has got a bit of an accent, now you mention it.'

'Oh, and she told me about the older generation, too. Della's mother's dead, but she was good friends with practically everyone around here. Hilary Henderson, Maggie, Mary Thomas – they all went to the Grammar School. Della's got one of those long photos with every single pupil on it. There were only about two hundred in the entire school.'

'Another world,' said Drew. 'I never see anyone I was at school with.'

'Me neither,' said Karen. 'Not that I'd want to, really.'

The removal went very satisfactorily. The woman at the nursing home turned out to be broad-shouldered and good-humoured. She insisted on giving him a cup of tea in her office before they did the deed. 'Give them time to settle down a bit,' she smiled. 'One or two pop back to the rec room for a magazine or their glasses or something.'

'Did you find the name of the friend?' he asked. His curiosity had become intense as he'd driven through the Saturday afternoon tourist traffic.

'Oh yes. I remembered. She used to talk about this woman quite a lot, a few years ago. You know how old people go back in time, and somehow get stuck?' Drew tilted his head, indicating uncertainty. 'Well, they do,' she assured him. 'Elsie's been with us for seven years, which is a lot more than usual. She's ninety-five. *Was* ninety-five, I should say, poor old love. The friend was someone she knew in her fifties, I think. A much younger woman. They were neighbours, and Elsie minded the little girls. Actually,' The woman leant forward confidingly across her desk 'I think there was a lot of very strong feeling between them. On Elsie's side, anyway. You should have seen her face when she talked about this Gwen . . .'

'Gwen?' Drew's heart lurched. 'You did say Gwen?'

'That's right. I see you know who we're talking about. I understand it was rather a celebrated burial. We had to do a bit of research, you see, when Elsie decided she wanted to be buried close to her.'

Drew knew there was only one Gwen buried in his field. And he had ample cause to remember her: she had been the very first body to be interred there. In fact the interment had happened before he'd even opened for business. And Gwen Absolon had been murdered.

'But surely she's got family? Or more recent friends?' He was stunned at the way the memories came flooding back. For several weeks, Gwen Absolon's name had been acutely significant to him; but that had been three years ago, and he'd hoped he'd forgotten it by now.

The woman shrugged. 'Evidently not. When we discovered your natural burial ground, and read all about it, she got very excited. I think she'd have wanted to go there regardless of Gwen. It fitted with her outlook, you see. Pity you never knew her. She was a splendid old lady.'

A new and awful idea struck Drew. 'The daughters. Gwen's daughters, I mean. Have they been in touch? Do they know Elsie's here?'

How would he cope if Genevieve Slater turned up again, after everything that had happened between them? And what – oh God, *what* would Maggs say?

The woman mercifully shook her head. 'We did write to one of them at an address in North Wales when Elsie was obviously failing, but never got a reply.'

'So, how did you find out where Gwen was buried?'

'The Internet, of course. You can find anybody these days. And Gwen was rather a celebrity, not very long ago. The papers were full of her. A search threw up loads of references, right away.'

They carried the defunct Elsie easily down the stairs and out through the back door to Drew's waiting van. Driving her back to North Staverton, he pondered on life's coincidences and the impossibility of remaining out of sight. Your lapses would always come back to haunt you. He had been mesmerised by Genevieve Slater, Gwen's daughter, allowing her to manipulate him and draw him into the unsavoury tangle that was her family life. Maggs had watched and warned, to no avail. The only good thing was that Karen had never been fully aware of what was going on. Pregnant with Timmy, at a point of crisis in her own life, she had let Drew work his own problems out.

Or so he had assumed.

CHAPTER NINE

'New customer?' Maggs stared at the small body in the cool room in astonishment. 'Who did the removal with you?'

'Nobody. The woman at the nursing home. She's so small, it wasn't a problem.'

'My God. What would Daphne say?'

'Bugger Daphne.'

'Right. Will you do it or shall we get Den onto it?'

'Don't be filthy.'

'So where's she going?'

Drew paused long enough for her to notice. She gave him a searching look. 'Tell me,' she demanded.

'It's a small world,' he began. 'It seems she has a friend buried here. A friend from nearly forty years ago. They lived next door, so now she wants to be buried alongside her, too.'

'Are you going to make me guess?'

'That's a good idea.'

'Drew!'

He sighed. 'Gwen Absolon. Remember her?'

Maggs clapped her hands like a small child, and crowed. 'I don't *believe* it. Really? What a hoot.'

Drew frowned and said nothing. He'd expected something like this.

'Is the hellion daughter coming? Does she still know this neighbour lady?'

'Apparently not, thank God. And I haven't had time to check that there's space next to that grave. I suppose there will be.'

'Course there is,' Maggs assured him. 'You've been steering clear of that bit of the field for three years now.'

'No I haven't. Or not for the reasons you think. I just didn't want people being ghoulish about it. Luckily most of them seem to have either forgotten the story or never heard it.'

'People have short memories.'

'Except for this Elsie Watkins. She hadn't seen Gwen since about 1960, but suddenly she has to be buried beside her.'

'What family is there?'

'There's a great-nephew in Dubai or

somewhere. He'll probably show up, if only to collect whatever goodies she's left him.'

'And pay for the funeral.'

'With any luck, that too,' Drew agreed.

With little more to be said on the subject, Drew asked Maggs about her weekend. She suddenly turned coy, and became busy with the morning post. 'It was fine,' she said. 'They let me have a go at milking the cows.'

'Gracious! On a three-legged stool in a straw-strewn cowshed?'

'Don't be stupid. It was very modern. There were lambs, too. Funny ones with long black ears. Blue-faced Leicesters, they're called.'

'I'm amazed.'

'What did you do, then, besides removing the Watkins woman?'

'Nothing, really. I had a visit from Mrs Grafton. That was interesting. And Karen was there when the police arrested Mary Thomas. And Della phoned this morning saying she didn't want Karen to have the boys until after lunch, so she's feeling a bit let down, I think. She'd got all geared up for some heavy duty glueing. Stephanie doesn't like doing that sort of thing without Finian.'

'The police arrested Mary Thomas?' Maggs repeated slowly. 'Is that the woman from Ferngate?'

'Right. She seems to be involved in something mysterious. Karen's got some rather wild ideas about it all.'

'I thought I was the one with the wild ideas.' Maggs pouted exaggeratedly.

'So did I.' This had all the signs of the last word, and Maggs took it as such. She went to the filing cabinet and extracted the detailed chart that showed precisely which grave was where. As expected, there was empty space on each side of Gwen Absolon's burial place.

Before she could point this out to Drew, the phone rang. He answered it, saying after a few seconds, 'Hello, Stanley. Haven't heard from you for a while . . . Oh, good. We'll be over for him tomorrow, then, all being well. Depends on the wife, of course. We can't keep him here more than a couple of days. I'll phone her, then. Right. Thanks very much. Bye.'

'They've released Peter Grafton,' Maggs summarised.

'Not quite. The inquest is this afternoon. Then, as likely as not, they'll let us have him.' Drew screwed up his nose, in a parody of disgust. 'You know something?' he said. 'We haven't had to deal with a body that's had a post-mortem – not since . . .'

'I know. Gwen Absolon,' Maggs supplied.

*　*　*

The new funeral, in addition to the large event that would accompany Peter Grafton's burial, seemed to send everything off balance. Drew couldn't help thinking about Genevieve, despite his stern admonitions to himself to stop it. Maggs appeared to find the whole thing both amusing and intriguing, and a side effect of this was a dramatically increased interest in the murder of Peter Grafton. It was as if the reminder of an earlier murder mystery had awakened something dormant in her.

'Den's been chatting to his old Inspector – man called Hemsley,' she told Drew. 'He thought he might be able to help with the market murder, seeing as how he was more or less there at the time.'

'And could he? Help, I mean?'

'Not really, except he knows Karen and she seems to be pretty much involved in the whole thing.'

'Den doesn't know Karen very well, though,' Drew pointed out. 'He doesn't know anything about the Food Chain stuff, or why anybody might have killed Grafton.'

'He soon realised that when Hemsley started asking questions. I think he was a bit sheepish about it. You know what it is, of course.'

'What?'

'He's missing the police. This is the first

murder he's come across since he left, and it's making him restless. He wants to be in there, like the old days.'

'Must be a bit strange,' Drew sympathised.

'Yeah, well, he should have known this would happen. Now I've got to try and distract him.'

'Oh?' Drew was careful to keep his face straight. Saucy innuendo between the two of them had always been kept to a minimum. It wasn't very difficult – Drew usually missed even the most obvious risqué jokes. Karen had pointed this out, years ago, saying she assumed it must go along with being an undertaker.

'No, no, I just prefer my gratification to come through actual contact, not through words and jokes,' he'd responded pompously.

This had changed slightly when Maggs moved in with Den. It evened up the balance; they were both now officially with sexual partners and could afford to relax their carefully platonic relationship. Even so, Drew still shied away from overtly prurient remarks.

'That's why we went away this weekend, to give him something else to think about,' she explained seriously. 'But now we're back, he's as bad as ever. Wants to come and talk to Karen, actually. See if he can spot anything significant in what she saw.'

'But . . .' Drew frowned. 'I'm not sure what she'll tell him.'

'I expect it'll be OK. He says he'll be very sensitive and low key about it. He's going to try and get here early this afternoon, and see if he can catch her. Don't say anything, will you,' she warned. 'It's up to him, if he wants to risk getting told off.'

'Actually, she might be quite cooperative,' Drew predicted. 'She's been having a few off-the-wall ideas about Mary Thomas, since Saturday, and might want to share them with a professional. She didn't really get very far with me. I tried to show an interest, but, somehow . . .'

'You're losing it, mate,' she told him blithely. 'Getting altogether too middle-aged you are, these days.'

'Middle-aged! I'm not even thirty-five yet.'

'So act it,' she said. 'Have a bit of fun, why don't you.'

Drew blinked, surprised at how much her words stung. 'Are you saying I'm getting dull?' he demanded. 'Me?'

'I expect it's only temporary,' she smiled.

'Just because I didn't go off for a romantic weekend rolling in the hay,' he grumbled. 'You wait. I'll show you.'

'I'll look forward to that.'

He went back to opening the post, and she put the map of the graves away carefully. The silence became more and more uncomfortable.

Maggs sighed noisily. 'Don't forget to phone Mrs Grafton then,' she said eventually.

'I'll wait until late this afternoon – after the inquest. Nothing's really certain until then.'

'OK.'

'We haven't been of much use to Sally Dabb, have we?' she said, a few minutes later. 'Nobody's asked me about her affair with Peter Grafton, at any rate.'

'Nor me,' he agreed. 'But it's early days, I suppose.'

'Will they catch who did it, do you think? Den can't see it. There aren't really enough bits of evidence. Unless they get some inside information. I suppose that's the way they usually solve crimes, when you think about it. They can't do much otherwise.' She was prattling, talking as much to herself as to Drew, as she copied Elsie Watkins' details into their record book.

'They might find the crossbow,' he said vaguely.

'Well, I really do think it's all very exciting,' she burst out, slamming the updated volume closed. 'There must be a connection between the farmers' market and SuperFare. I mean, it could be some kind of food politics, couldn't it? Somebody trying to stop something that could cost them money. Like – what if the supermarket was feeling threatened by the success of Karen's lot. They'd try some dirty tricks, wouldn't they?'

'They wouldn't have a chap shot, and they'd hardly blow their own place up with a bomb,' Drew pointed out. 'You don't really change, do you,' he added.

'What do you mean?'

'Same wild ideas, half-baked guesses, far-fetched conclusions.'

'But I'm quite often right, all the same,' she said, with a straight look. 'Aren't I?'

'You've been right once or twice,' he conceded. 'But usually for the wrong reasons.'

'Ha!' she snorted.

At four forty-five that Monday afternoon, Den Cooper and Della Gray met for the first time, with Karen and four children stirred in for good measure.

Della – tall and slim, with a long stride – had walked through the village, just as Karen habitually did in the other direction. It was a warm day, summer announcing itself deafeningly with birds and airliners working up to a crescendo. New bright green leaves thronged the hedgerows and livestock gorged on young fresh grass.

Den unfolded himself from the driving seat of his ageing Fiat, giving his legs the remedial shake he generally did after sitting in cramped conditions. Most conditions were cramped for him, being of abnormal height. He observed the young woman walking up the path to the Slocombes' cottage, and hesitated in his purpose.

He had fifteen minutes or more to fill, and hardly anything to lose. He even had his opening line rehearsed, in which he would ask Karen if she had any lettuces to spare, as well as enquiring as to the progress of the other vegetables.

He strode after the woman. 'Hello,' he greeted her. 'Come to see Karen?'

'I'm collecting my kids,' came the friendly reply. 'She has them every Monday. How about you?'

He looked into the clear eyes, enjoying the unusual sensation of a woman barely six inches shorter than himself. She had nice skin, he noted, and smelt of something natural like apples. 'My girlfriend works with Drew. I'm a bit early, so I thought I'd have a little chat with Karen.'

'Maggs? You're Maggs's partner? Funny I haven't seen you before. I'm Della.'

The name meant nothing. He smiled in acknowledgement of the introduction. 'Den,' he offered in return.

Before either of them could knock, Karen had pulled open the front door. Two small boys stood in front of her, making her bend awkwardly over their heads to get the door open. She moved them aside with deft and not entirely gentle movements of her feet and legs. 'Hey, you two! Get out of the way,' she scolded them.

The children scampered forward, to wrap themselves around Della's legs instead. 'Mummy!' they cried, in a parody of affection.

'Get off,' she said. 'We're not going for a few minutes yet.'

'Oh-h-h-h,' they whined in unison. 'I want my supper,' added the larger one.

'Have they been horrible?' Della asked Karen.

'No more than usual,' she smiled. 'Oh, hello, Den. Are you coming in?'

'I thought I might,' he said. 'I was hoping for a couple more lettuces if there are any.'

'Small ones,' she warned him. 'But fairly hearty. This weather should bring some more stuff on. Isn't it fabulous!'

Somehow they all got through the door and into the kitchen, including the children. Della sat down without invitation, and Karen filled the kettle. Den hovered uncomfortably. None of his planned conversation was going to happen at this rate.

Then Karen managed to move things on quite dramatically. 'You'll be wishing you could help with the murder investigation I expect,' she said to him, almost idly. 'It must feel a bit odd being out of it all.'

'Absolutely!' he agreed with fervour. 'I come over all peculiar every time I walk past the Town

Hall, knowing it's where they've got the Incident Room set up.'

'What are you talking about?' Della asked, her attention on little Todd.

'Den used to be in the CID. He worked on a few murders around here, before giving it all up. He's with Social Services now.' She flicked a bright look at Della, then an identical one at Den. 'Hey!' she added. 'Della used to know Peter Grafton. She was really upset when she heard he'd been killed – weren't you?' The image of the tall capable Della fainting returned to Karen, but she refrained from telling that part of the story.

'It was a shock,' Della admitted in a low voice.

Den remembered the previous Tuesday. 'Oh, that was you,' he said. 'You fainted, and Drew had to go and collect the children. Are you all right now?'

Della laughed. 'Oh yes. It was nothing. I was better about ten minutes later. Poor old Karen, she did panic a bit.'

Karen pressed her lips together and said nothing. Den cleared his throat uncomfortably and reverted to the earlier topic. 'I've had a word with the DI handling the investigation, actually,' he disclosed. 'I used to work with him. I told him I knew you, and one or two others who seem to be involved.'

'Who else do you know?' Karen frowned curiously up at him.

'Well, everybody knows Hilary Henderson and Geraldine Beech, I suppose. And Mary Thomas.'

'The three witches,' said Della. Then she clapped a hand over her mouth. 'Oops! That was a bit rude, wasn't it. Everyone calls them that, though.'

Den and Karen both looked at her. 'Do they?' Karen said. 'I've never heard it.'

'It's only that they're all such strong independent women, I suppose. And they make things happen. And they're all the same age, within a few weeks. They've known each other all their lives. Thick as thieves, as they say. If one of them coughs, the other two reach for the Fisherman's Friends.' Della laughed. 'They're amazing, really.'

Karen shook her head slowly. 'I had absolutely no idea it was like that,' she said. 'I've hardly seen them together, except Hilary and Geraldine at the markets, of course, but they never seem unduly pally.'

Della shrugged. 'You wouldn't expect them to be arm in arm. It isn't like that. More like sisters, in a way. They know each other's there in a crisis, and they probably go out for drinks together now and then. But they always know what's going on with the other two. And if someone upset one of them, the others would rally round like a shot.'

'Geraldine's nearly sixty, then, is she?' Karen felt an unreasonable surge of relief at finally finding an answer to that particular question.

'They're June, July and August, if I remember rightly. My mother was roughly the same, plus Maggie as well. In the same class at school, except for Geraldine. She went to a private school. Hilary's the oldest, then Mary, then Geraldine, I think. I remember they had a huge village party the summer they all hit forty. It was spectacular.'

Den and Karen exchanged glances. 'Village life,' he sighed. 'There's nothing like it.'

'Oh, well,' Della said, 'you incomers are never going to catch up with all the cross-currents. Everything connects, you see.'

'But nearly everyone's an incomer these days,' Karen objected.

'Not as many as you might think, actually.' Della smiled mysteriously. 'And there are some who leave and come back again, which muddies the waters a bit. Like Joe Richards, for a start.'

'What about him? I thought he'd always lived here.' But before Della could explain further, there was a howl from Todd; the kettle boiled; Den moved suddenly and his elbow caught a pot of chives perched on the worktop, sending it crashing to the floor; and Stephanie burst in with a scratched finger.

Mugs of tea and maternal sympathy filled the next ten minutes, and Den, having done his best to salvage the chives, realised he was about to be late for Maggs. He looked at Karen, his frustration clear. 'I wanted to have a word with you about last Tuesday,' he said.

'Don't worry, I'm going,' said Della, snatching the mug from her lip, as if her hand belonged to another person. 'See you tomorrow, Kaz. Come on, kids.'

In a whirl she was gone. 'Kaz?' Den echoed. 'I thought only Drew called you that.'

'Some people can't spare the time for two syllables,' she said, sounding cross.

'She seems quite nice,' he said tentatively. 'Good with kids.'

'She's all right. Steph and Timmy like her, which is the main thing. She ought to have been a primary teacher, really. She has plenty of good ideas. They learn a lot from her.'

'Listen . . .' Den urged her. 'This murder, they don't seem to be getting anywhere with it. Ironically, there aren't enough witnesses. Nobody actually *saw* anything, except you.'

'What's it got to do with you?' She said it gently, trying not to sound rude.

'Nothing, really. Except I met my old

colleague, Danny Hemsley, at the Incident Room, and got my interest up. Daft, I know. I've been out of the police for ages. It's just that murder . . . well . . .'

'You're as bad as Drew,' she sighed. 'Can't leave it alone.'

'It's the background that's puzzling them, Danny says. They don't get how the Food Chain network operates, and who does what. Basically, they don't understand anything that's even slightly alternative. I used to be just as bad. Even perfectly normal groups like the Quakers threw me, at one time.'

'Scary,' Karen nodded. 'They see sinister implications in anything they don't understand.'

'Right. So would you say there *are* any sinister implications in Geraldine and her food politics?'

Karen picked at a front tooth before answering. 'Well, there might be,' she said slowly. 'Actually, yes, there do seem to be. Den, I don't know whether I ought to tell you about it. I haven't said much to Drew. I don't know what good it would do to involve you. I mean – in what capacity are you asking?'

He rubbed a long-fingered hand down the plane of his cheek. 'Good question,' he said. 'Amateur sleuth, I suppose.'

She sighed. 'Join the club, then. Well, there's some talk about a new sort of GM experiment going on in this area. You know how strongly everybody feels about that sort of thing. It's to do with fruit trees, apparently. And Peter Grafton grew apples. But there's another angle, too. Not directly related, as far as I can tell. He was going to sign a contract to supply the supermarkets with juice. That's a real sell-out, in Geraldine's eyes. Like Daphne Plant selling to SCI. A betrayal. I don't think he'd have been allowed to get away with that.'

'But they wouldn't *kill* him for it, would they?'

She spread her hands. 'Somebody did kill him, Den. That's the big fact here, that we can't get round. Who knows why?'

'Find the *why* and you usually find the *who*,' he muttered.

'So I believe,' she nodded.

There came a sharp knock on the door, which then opened, and a voice shouted, 'Den! What's going on? You're late!'

'Coming,' he called back. 'What's the rush, anyway?' he added more quietly.

Maggs came into the room. 'I heard that,' she said. 'I've been sitting in the car for the past ten minutes.'

'Sorry. I wanted to talk to Karen. And we need a couple of lettuces. I'm doing a salad this evening. I got some eggs on the way.'

'Meat, Den. I want meat. We haven't had any for ages.'

'Aha! Well, I've got a surprise for you there. When I went in to Hendersons for the eggs, I got chatting and the upshot was that we've ordered half a pig, in return for fixing his barn roof.'

'But you don't know how to fix roofs.'

'Of course I do. It's obvious. You just nail down new sheets of corrugated iron, from the top of a long ladder.'

'Oh. You're OK with tops of long ladders, are you?'

'Perfectly OK,' he said bravely.

'Well, come on, then. Say bye bye to Karen and let's get home.'

'Bye bye Karen,' Den said.

CHAPTER TEN

Drew hadn't intended to talk about the new funeral over supper that evening, but somehow they were onto the subject before he knew it. 'Such a coincidence,' he marvelled, as much to himself as to his wife.

'What is?' she prompted.

Even then, his brain didn't properly engage. 'This new woman, from the nursing home. You know they said she had a friend buried here? Well, it's Gwen Absolon.'

'The woman who was murdered and dumped here before we opened?'

'The very one.'

Karen fell silent for so long that Drew eventually realised something was amiss. 'That was an awful time,' she said softly.

'We'd just discovered you were pregnant again,' he remembered.

'It wasn't that, Drew. I thought for a few days that I was losing you. I was terrified.'

He stared at her, his jaw slack. 'What? What do you mean?'

'That Genevieve. You were obsessed by her.'

He blustered desperately. 'No I wasn't! What a thing to say.'

'You didn't even try to hide it. You just thought I was so busy being pregnant I hadn't noticed. But I had, Drew. Is she going to come to this funeral?' Karen's eyes had grown suddenly large, the skin beneath them heavy.

'No, no. She's moved somewhere, miles away. My God, Kaz, why didn't you say something?'

'It was three years ago. The longer it went on, the less it mattered. I just packed the whole thing away. I don't often think about it now. But I'm learning, gradually, that nothing ever really goes away. We just carry a bigger and bigger bundle on our backs, the older we get.'

'Well, you can throw that particular bundle right out of the window,' he assured her. 'It's not worth thinking about.'

'Did you ever sleep with her?' The question came out with difficulty.

'No! Honestly, I swear, absolutely not. She was nine months pregnant, for God's sake.'

'Not the first time. When she wanted our house. I knew then that you fancied her.'

'That was just a flirtation. And she was trying to manipulate me, to get her husband the house he'd set his heart on. All her loyalties were towards him.'

'I know I'm being stupid,' she burst out. 'That only makes it all worse. Jealousy is so *demeaning*. It makes us do and think the most idiotic things. And it drives a wedge between people.'

He got up and stood behind her, wrapping his arms round her shoulders. 'Stop it, sweetheart. What can I say? I'm here. I love you. I've never touched another woman. I'm never going to. OK?' He bent down and nuzzled her neck. 'OK?'

'I know that, in my head. I trust you. Of course I do. But it happens so often. It seems as if *everybody* is being unfaithful. Why should we be different?'

'Because we're special. Because neither of us would do that to the kids. I was stupid and weak over Genevieve. I knew that even at the time. I embarrassed myself. Can we forget it now? Now we've cleared the air?'

'Probably,' she sighed. 'Sorry to be so wifey. I should never have said anything.'

'I'm glad you did. We shouldn't have secrets like that. They eat away at our foundations, like death watch beetles. They turn a marriage sour. Imagine if you'd gone on wondering for another twenty or thirty years! Wouldn't that be terrible!'

'Fairly normal, though, I would guess.' She rubbed her eyes, and turned to face him. '*Very* normal, if you can believe all the books and plays and things. They're always talking about ancient secrets finally coming out when the people are old.'

'Are they?' He was vague. 'Well, not for us. Put jealousy in the dustbin, where it belongs.'

'All right then,' she agreed. 'Now, it must be bathtime. Where are those kids?'

Maggs was frosty with Den on the drive home. 'What was all that about?' she asked again.

'It wasn't about anything, really. The murder, mainly. You've heard it all already. What's bothering you?'

'Oh, I don't know. I'm restless. It's probably hormones.'

Den did not fail to apprehend this buzzword. 'Really?' He looked at her quickly. 'As in female reproductive hormones?' The glint of excitement in his eye was impossible to ignore.

'Yes and no,' she said cautiously. 'The body's one thing, the mind quite another.'

'And what the hell does that mean?'

'It means I'm a healthy female of an age to reproduce. My body acts accordingly. But in my head, I do not want to cooperate. I don't want a baby. I have other plans entirely.'

'And this conflict puts you in a bad mood,' he summarised. 'Yes, I can see that. Understand, I mean. It sounds uncomfortable.'

'I can handle it,' she said stoutly. 'Don't let it worry you.'

'But the same sort of thing is going on for me,' he persisted. 'I've got hormones, too, you know.'

'Yes, but you've got a different conflict. You *want* babies, but you can't find a woman who'll cooperate. It's tough being a man.'

'At least we understand each other,' he said, feeling glum.

'So did you glean anything from Karen about the Grafton murder?' She changed the subject hurriedly.

'Sort of. There's some hush-hush project underway, to do with GM crops. She thinks Grafton could possibly have been involved.'

Maggs turned glittering black eyes on him. 'Wow! That's new news, isn't it? Does your friend Danny know about that?'

'I doubt it. Not unless the police have been asked to protect the site, wherever it is.'

'Do you know where it is? I might go and join

the riot myself. Is there a website or something?'

'I have no idea. Karen wasn't very sure, really.'

'She'd probably been ordered not to tell you. I'm surprised she said anything at all.'

'Well, I'm harmless these days,' he sighed. 'No longer one of the enemy.'

'Come on; it's not like that round here.'

'Maybe not. Anyway, I am fairly fired up now, about the whole business. I thought I might take a week off work. They'll probably let me, even though it's short notice.'

'Aren't you meant to apply in triplicate, ten months ahead?'

'Theoretically. But nobody really does.'

'Where will you start, Mr Detective?'

'Maybe we could have a go at the computer?'

'What computer? We haven't got a computer.'

'No, but when I cut Mrs Graham's hedge last year, she said I could use hers any time, in return. And seeing as how she's only next door, that should be quite easy and convenient.'

'Surfing the Net?' She grinned at him.

'Something like that. I'm not sure they call it that any more. It's time I got a bit more up to date on the subject, anyway. I feel as if I'm being left behind.'

'OK, give it a go. But no chat rooms, right? I

know what that can lead to. My mum's been having some bother in that department, ever since my dad got himself online. It's terrible, you know.'

'Don't tell me,' he groaned. 'What your dad gets up to is none of my business. Or yours, come to that.'

'I don't suppose you'll find anything, anyway,' she said. 'You'd be better off walking round the countryside using your own eyes and ears. Talk to people, have a look at what's growing in the fields.'

'You might be right,' he said.

'It's beginning to look like a team exercise,' she went on. 'All four of us trying to solve the mystery. We can't fail, really.' She paused. 'Are you going to tell your friend Danny everything we come up with?'

He gave that some thought. 'Why? Do you think I shouldn't? Are we in competition with the police?'

She dimpled. 'It's more fun that way.'

'Maggs, my angel, that's not a good attitude, as you very well know. You worked with the police when that little girl went missing, last year. I remember it well.' He gave her one of his soft looks, that she always thought of as *leans,* because he leant over her when he did it.

'Don't call me your angel,' she said. 'It sounds idiotic. And patronising.'

'It's meant sincerely,' he persisted. 'And you *have* been my angel. You rescued me from a lonely miserable existence.'

'I know I did. They say it's a mistake to take up with a man that nobody else wants. There has to be something wrong with him.'

Den sighed. 'That's true,' he said. 'I've got all the character defects you could wish for.'

'Nothing that can't be changed,' she said briskly.

Drew took a phone call at eleven that evening, notifying him of another death. 'You're happy to keep him with you overnight, are you?' he asked the new widow. She and her husband had been in to pre-arrange the burial, five months previously. It would be an easy funeral to conduct. She agreed that was not a problem, and he promised to collect the body next morning.

'Sad,' remarked Karen, half asleep beside him. 'Dying in May when the weather's so lovely and summer getting going.'

'May's often quite busy,' he told her. 'It's August when it goes quiet. Though you can never really predict.'

'Funeral on Friday? Or Thursday?'

'I'll have to try and keep him until Friday. We can't leave Grafton longer than Thursday.' He smacked himself on the forehead. 'I must be half asleep. We're collecting *him* tomorrow morning, first thing.'

'Can't you do them both in one journey?'

'I suppose we can. I'll have to put the shelf back in the van. Haven't used it for ages. I can't even remember where it is. We ought to have a shed for things like that.'

'There's nowhere to put a shed. We need all the space for garden and graves.'

'Maggs'll probably know where to find it. She probably knows how to fix it in the vehicle, too.'

'Early start then,' Karen said. 'Better get some sleep.'

Tuesday morning was a whirlwind of activity, compared to the usual pattern for Peaceful Repose. Some of the urgency was generated by Maggs arriving late – another breach of the usual scenario. Den had dropped her outside the gate and turned the car around with undisguised haste. He was just as obviously late for work.

'Come on,' Drew urged her from the office doorway. 'There's loads to do today.'

She moved heavily up the path, eyes unfocused, hair in a tangle. Drew knew without even thinking about it that she'd only recently climbed out of a warm connubial bed. And good luck to them, he told himself conscientiously. And it wasn't strictly connubial, either, he supposed, since they weren't actually married.

'Three bodies in the cool room at once!' She woke up slightly at this prospect. 'That's serious overcrowding.'

'Three graves to dig. Three families to keep happy. Three lots of paperwork. And we still don't know what two of them want, in any detail. Grafton's going to be church first, I should think.'

'Surely you asked the wife when she came to see you?'

He sucked his teeth for a moment. 'No, she didn't seem to want to talk about that.'

'Well, the vicar's not going to be too pleased if you don't fix it with him right away. He likes a bit more notice than that.'

'And he knows he won't get it with us. Damn it, this country's gone so sloppy over the timing of funerals . . .'

'Don't start that again,' she interrupted. 'Save your breath for these phone calls you're going to have to make.'

He looked at his watch. 'We should be at the Royal Vic by now. Gary's going to be fractious with us.'

'Calm down, Drew,' she ordered. 'This is not helping. You go and phone the vicar. I'll get the shelf thingy for the van. I know exactly where it is.'

'Where? Just for future reference.'

'Behind the cardboard coffins. I'd have thought that was obvious.'

'Right. Well, go on then.'

Suddenly everything fell into place, and by lunchtime all three funerals were arranged, with times, details of the ceremonies themselves, paperwork filled in and bodies safely stored in the cool room next to the office. There were several more tasks to be performed during the afternoon, such as ordering a special woven basket for Mr Lancaster, the most recent customer, but Drew felt he was in control again.

The willow baskets were an odd development, Drew sometimes thought. They were quite difficult to handle, and resembled nothing he'd ever come across in his browsing through the funeral customs of other societies. The only advantage he could see was that the body would quickly decompose, as air and water and underground organisms passed freely through the spaces in the weaving. The basket itself would not degrade very rapidly. But they looked quite nice, and a number of his clients requested them.

Peter Grafton's body was, as anticipated, not particularly pretty. Although it was near-miraculous the way a face and head could be restored after a post-mortem that involved removing the top of the skull and taking out the brain to be weighed and analysed, the throat and mouth closely inspected, there were additional problems in this case. The injury from the crossbow bolt was not the neat hole Drew had hoped for. The pathologist had cut it free, widening the wound considerably. Lower down, he was a mass of crude repair suturing, the assumption being that nobody was going to look beyond the head and face. As his temperature rose in the not-very-cool room, he became unavoidably malodorous.

'This isn't very good,' Drew worried to Maggs. 'What if Mrs Lancaster wants to come and see Mr?'

'Make her wait until Thursday afternoon. She had him with her all last night. I'd think she'd leave him be for a couple of days.'

'Thank goodness Elsie Watkins hasn't got any family. We can park her in the corner. This room isn't really big enough for three, is it?'

'It's OK. Nobody expects us to have four star facilities. That's the whole *point*, Drew. Sometimes I think you forget that.'

'You're right,' he laughed. 'As usual.'

Karen was having a busy day herself. Without the children she felt obliged to pack as much constructive activity into the day as she could.

There was another farmers' market due on Friday, and she was worried there'd be a shortage of produce to sell. Vigorous watering and weeding might just bring a few extra lettuces on by last thing Thursday, when she would pick them and pack them up ready for the early start the next day. Except, she suddenly realised, there was no certainty that the market would actually happen this week, thanks to Peter Grafton's funeral.

There were also other urgent matters on her mind, primary of which was Mary Thomas and her behaviour on Sunday. It infuriated Karen that her testimony should be so flatly contradicted, and despite Drew's interpretation, that there could be a good and important reason for it, she couldn't shake off her anger. Threading itself amongst the fury was a worry that she might have unwittingly got Mary into trouble by revealing her presence at the supermarket when the bomb went off.

She'd got through Monday, busy in the afternoon with four small children, without giving the matter much sustained thought, which only meant that now it came back in full force. She had to find out whether Mary was still being kept by the police. Surely that couldn't possibly be the case? They'd have had to have charged her by now, and the news of that would have got round by this time. She gave herself a rest from tending the vegetables and rang Geraldine Beech's number.

There was no reply on the home line, so Karen rummaged for the mobile number. Why are they always so difficult to remember, she asked herself irritably. Normally she had people's phone numbers firmly in her head.

Eventually, Geraldine answered. There was traffic noise in the background. 'Where are you?' Karen asked, before introducing herself.

'Who's that? Della? Is that you?'

'No, it's Karen. Can you hear me?'

'Perfectly. What do you want?'

'I wondered whether you'd heard what's happened to Mary. I was there on Sunday when the police came for her. It was all rather shocking in a way. I wondered.'

'There's nothing to worry about. She was only there an hour or two. They had no right to take her in like that. She'll probably sue them.'

'So she's all right, is she? I've been wanting to have a talk with her for ages now. Somehow I never seem to get the chance.'

'Leave it, Karen.' The voice was hard and cold. 'Why are you so intent on interfering?'

'I'm not!' Karen's heart was thundering. This wasn't at all like the Geraldine she thought she knew. 'I just—'

'Yes, yes, I'm sure your motives are pure. But

you've done enough damage already, blundering about. If we need you, we'll contact you, all right? I thought we had made that clear already.'

Karen felt ridiculously upset. She could feel tears gathering behind her nose. She swallowed. 'What about Friday?' she asked, trying to sound grown up and unscathed. 'Is the market still on?'

'Of course it is. Why wouldn't it be?' The organiser's tone was less abrasive now, despite the abrupt words.

'Because . . .' Karen's voice rose uncontrollably, 'because, you stupid woman, that's the day after Peter Grafton's funeral.'

'Calm down, for God's sake. Life has to go on. Nobody would expect us to abandon the routine like that. We can't just cancel the market. We'd lose credibility – and customers. Garnstone's tricky enough without any interruptions like that. I'll expect you to be there.'

'And Sally? Is she coming, too?'

'As far as I know, yes. She seems to be functioning fairly well. After all, she's not really in a position to display too much naked grief, is she?'

'Poor Sally,' said Karen softly.

'What?'

'Nothing. I'll see you on Friday then.' And she slammed down the receiver, her hands shaking.

CHAPTER ELEVEN

Den was another person with plenty to think about on the drive from North Staverton to Bradbourne. He and Maggs had scrambled out of bed, both knowing they'd be late for work, but neither much caring. The weekend away had taken their relationship a giant stride forward, and both were still glowing. They had even, in a very oblique and jokey fashion, mentioned marriage as something that could conceivably happen one day.

The idea of acquiring a farm had come out of nowhere, as far as Den could see. And it was completely crazy. Farms cost vastly more money than he and Maggs had earned in their combined lives so far. Unless they both found well paid professions instantly, he didn't see that there was the slightest chance of putting the idea into practice. And if they were both working fulltime, what would be the sense in having a farm anyway?

At least that had been his initial position. Maggs had clearly done some homework, and bombarded him with facts and figures about special loans, subsidies, grants, discounts all available to people wanting to act as 'stewards' of the land.

'They won't be called farmers for much longer,' she asserted. 'The whole thing's in a state of flux. It's all going to be very exciting.'

'But what about Drew?' he had asked, several times. 'It sounds as if you want to abandon Peaceful Repose.'

And she hadn't satisfactorily answered that. She'd frowned and changed the subject, scuffling a toe in the dry mud of the yard they were walking round at the time. All she would say was, 'I'm happy enough working with Drew, but there isn't enough for both of us to do. The quiet times drive me mad.'

He wasn't sure he believed in all these grants and subsidies that Maggs thought could make her dream feasible. Land was expensive, everyone knew that. When he was growing up, farmers had been the élite. Their children had all gone to private schools and they drove large ostentatious Discoveries and the like. Despite the past six or seven years when things had deteriorated so catastrophically for agriculture, he couldn't even begin to think of himself as belonging to that class of person. The idea was so new and strange, it made his mind go numb.

And yet, it wasn't as if he'd never known farm life. His first serious girlfriend had been a farmer's daughter, and he had spent time helping her with the animals. He had investigated two farm-based murders, which involved, among other things, some close experience of dairy cows. He was a country boy – so why the bewildered reaction?

Because, he concluded, there was a world of difference between living in a rural area, eating locally grown produce and listening to conversations about the weather, compared to getting onto a tractor and trying to plough a straight furrow. If Maggs had her way, Den would spend his weekends ditching, hedging, weeding, cutting grass for hay, applying for government subsidies, filling in a million forms and trying to justify the drastic change of lifestyle. No, no, he mentally shook his head. It just wasn't him. No way.

It was, though, undeniable that he was in a very unsatisfactory phase of his life, and something would have to change. He couldn't piddle about as a dogsbody for Social Services indefinitely. It was mildly interesting, but there was no sense of progress or even any feeling that he was significantly helping anybody. Better to apply for jobs with big charities, or get a more focused position as a probation officer or team leader, than what he was currently doing.

He'd known this point would come, but had tried to ignore it. He knew, too, what had precipitated it: the murder of Peter Grafton. Until then, he had managed to quell any stirrings of dissatisfaction. But he still couldn't work out whether the murder was in any way connected with Maggs's farm idea. The processes behind Maggs's thinking were almost always obscure to him – and he often thought they were to her, as well.

She phoned him during the morning, breathlessly, telling him how busy she and Drew were, all of a sudden. She sounded happy. 'Don't come for me at the usual time this evening,' she said. 'I'm going to have to stay a bit late. I'll call you when I'm ready to leave, OK?'

'No problem,' he said. 'I'll pop in and see if Danny's still around, when I finish here.'

'I hope he'll be pleased to see you,' she said cheerily.

Den hoped so too. He'd be a lot more welcome if he could provide some new information about the murder. It was unrealistic to assume that the police had missed the connection with genetic modification of plants, but maybe the snippet about the 'three witches' he'd gleaned from Karen's friend Della would count for something.

'Den? Are you with us?' He looked up, startled. Tony Gibson, the Chief, was frowning down at him, and had evidently been there for some time.

'Oh, sorry. I was thinking.'

'I won't ask you what about. I gather you were late this morning. And I can't help noticing your socks.'

Den's long legs, as always, stretched under the desk and protruded on the other side. People had routinely tripped over his feet until a new arrangement of the office furniture had been organised. He couldn't see his own socks without considerable effort. 'Are they odd?' he asked miserably.

'One blue, one brown,' Gibson confirmed.

'Maybe nobody will look,' Den said feebly.

'It isn't professional, is it? What would your Chief Superintendent have said?' Gibson harboured an undisguised resentment at Den's change of career, for reasons that were not too hard to ascertain. To an ambitious career man like himself, aiming for no less a post than the Head of Social Services, anybody casting doubt on the desirability of enterprise and ladder-climbing was understandably unsettling. Jibes such as this were commonplace, and Den was mostly successful in letting them fall harmlessly to the floor without retort.

'It's sloppy,' he agreed, swallowing the semi-automatic *sir*. People in this office never said *sir*.

'Well, don't let it happen again. Now, here's a job for you. Sounds quite interesting for once. More than you deserve, really.'

Den started to get up, genuinely keen to get out into the sunny streets of Bradbourne.

'Wait for it. Jenny'll come for you when she's ready. It's a family thing, by the sound of it. Kids of all ages. One of them hasn't been seen for weeks – and when it *was* last seen, it had bruises of a suspicious nature. The school called us yesterday, saying he's absent without any explanation.'

'So why wasn't he seen?' Den asked boldly.

'Not for want of trying, I can tell you. This'll be the fifth attempt. If it fails this time, we'll call for reinforcements. It's a boy, seven years old.'

Den didn't need to ask any more. Boys, rightly or wrongly, were not protected with such vigour as girls. And a child of seven, although vulnerable, was regarded as less urgent than an under-five. Seven-year-old boys could generally stand up for themselves, at least to some extent. This was the pragmatic state of affairs; far from ideal, but true just the same.

He and Jenny drove off to investigate the case, each trying to reassure the other that there was no need for much concern. 'People very seldom hurt their own kids,' Jenny said. 'It's more usually step-parents or someone a bit more removed.'

'Right,' Den agreed. 'Although . . .'

'Yeah. Sometimes it's the mother who bashes the brains out of a month-old baby. Or tortures it with cigarette burns. Some people are too sick to be allowed near their own children.' Jenny was thirty-one, fair-haired and nervy. To Den's eyes, she wasted a lot of time trying in vain to get organised. She lost files, left the office without important documents, and panicked easily. One of Den's regular tasks was to keep her calm and find things for her.

'I did try to see this little chap, you know.' She turned to him with a frown. 'I even got into the house and had a look for him. His mother said he was playing with his friends on the rec.'

'He probably was, then.'

'Well, I couldn't see him in the house. I mean – what're we supposed to *do*?' It was a familiar howl of frustration at the impossible role society was asking them all to play.

'We do what we can,' he said soothingly. 'It'll be OK.'

And, rather to his surprise, it was. The woman who answered the door to them was tidily dressed, not unduly defensive, and even came up with a smile.

'He's at school,' she said. 'Haven't you checked?'

'He was away yesterday,' Jenny said.

'Well, he's there today. I took him right into the classroom. He had a cold yesterday. Really, he's fine now.' She stood in the doorway, neither inviting them in nor obstructing their way. 'Go and see for yourselves. Though try not to make him feel an idiot in front of his mates. There's been enough of that already.'

Jenny was gracious. 'Well, sorry to bother you,' she said.

'It's no bother. I'm glad to see you're doing your job. But I've got nothing to hide, believe me. I can see it must have looked a bit odd, when he got those bruises, but Harry's not one for your register. I look after my kids, even if there are a lot of them.'

They went back to the car. 'Wasn't she a bit too good to be true?' Den queried.

'Maybe. We'll go to the school then, shall we?'

'Couldn't we just phone them? They ought to have let us know he was in today. If the teacher says he's OK, couldn't we leave it at that?'

Jenny chewed her lip. 'Gibson said I had to personally view him. Preferably without clothes on.'

'He knows that's out of order.' Den was indignant. 'You need a doctor for that.'

'Yeah, I know. He wasn't being serious. Let's go back, and phone the school, then.'

Jenny spoke to the child's teacher, and was assured that he was energetic, cheerful, noisy and clean. As far from an abused or neglected child as anyone could be, the woman said. The file was signed, closed and placed in Jenny's OUT basket.

It was one of many such inconsequential visits, which Den always found unsettling. Police work had often been the same, of course, which only made him feel more strongly that he'd dived into a cul de sac, and needed to find some direction for himself as a matter of urgency. At least he'd been paid a decent salary in the police.

All of which took Den up to within half an hour of his lunch break, with nothing accomplished, no sense of purpose or satisfaction, and a growing desire to get outside and do something to assist the investigation into Peter Grafton's murder. He came to a decision.

'Mr Gibson?' He put his head around the door to the boss's partitioned-off cubicle. 'Do you think I could have the rest of the day off? I can't see that I'm needed here at the moment. Actually, it might be as well to have the rest of the week. Would that be possible, do you think?'

'Paid or unpaid?' The man fixed him with an unresponsive stare.

'I do have some leave owing. I'd assumed it would be paid.'

'Supposed to give notice for that.'

'Yes, I know. But nobody else is away this week. It'd probably suit you better for me to be off now.'

'Don't tell me my job. Go on, then. But I'll expect you back here first thing Monday morning.'

'Right you are.' Again the ghostly *sir* hovered in the air.

He made directly for the Town Hall, where the fact that they were now a full week on from the murder was causing some concern. Den found Hemsley running his fingers through his thinning hair and shouting at a female Detective Constable. There was little sign of activity, and Den thought he detected signs that the Incident Room would shortly be dismantled and removed, leaving Bradbourne to resume its bric-a-brac markets and charity coffee mornings in peace.

'Den!' The Inspector's enthusiasm was born more of desperation than genuine pleasure. 'Got any breakthroughs for us?'

Den shook his head ruefully. 'Sorry,' he said.

'This is not good,' Hemsley grumbled. 'A man gets himself struck down in the open street, broad daylight, peaceful little market town, and nobody sees a thing. It's bizarre.'

'Whoever did it has to have been in one of the buildings,' Den said. 'Or possibly in a passing car. Has anybody thought of that?'

'We've *thought* of everything,' Danny said crossly. 'It's not *thinking* that's the issue. We need witnesses, proof, motive. We need the weapon. We need cooperation. We haven't got anything. And the longer it goes on, the more pointless it's all beginning to seem. We're just sitting here pretending to be busy. Even the press has lost interest.'

Den sighed sympathetically.

'So why are you here?' the Inspector asked.

'I thought I might help. I was bored. I've taken the rest of the week off.'

'And what help are you offering? I do have officers, you know. Paid and trained. You're not on the payroll, you're not covered for injury or misdemeanours. I can't give you any commissions of any sort.'

'But I know some of the people,' Den persisted. 'And I can talk to them informally without making them suspicious. Which I'm going to do, whatever you say. It cuts both ways, you know.'

Hemsley nodded his concurrence. 'Be my guest,' he said.

Den's eyebrows rose. 'Mellow!' he remarked. 'Is this the new Danny?'

'Maybe it is,' came the reply, with a small shrug.

'So I'll start with Mary Thomas, shall I?'

'Cooper,' Danny gave a weary warning, 'you don't work for me any more, remember. You can go along and chat to anybody you please, but don't so much as mention the police, or you'll be charged with impersonation. You're free to come and tell me anything you learn – or not. Just as you feel. If you impede our investigations, or compromise them in any way, you're in trouble. But – and this is between the two of us – we can't really do any worse than we are already. It's a total blank up to now. And you've just about got the sense not to smudge any prints or trample on anything forensics might find useful. Be my guest,' he said again. 'And enjoy yourself.'

'You took Mary Thomas in for questioning,' Den said carefully.

'Because she was at both scenes. Or was said to be. She denies being at the supermarket when it was bombed. She wouldn't tell us a bloody thing, to be honest. Clammed up like a professional. I felt very much like slapping her.'

'She was at the supermarket. Karen Slocombe

says so. That should be good enough for anyone.'

'Go and ask her about it then,' Hemsley invited. 'If you can find her.'

Den found her without difficulty in the cherry orchard. The fruit was forming in clusters on the boughs, and Den realised he'd never seen a serious crop of cherries before.

'Unusual,' he said, coming up to her quietly. 'What will you do with them?'

To her credit, she didn't jump, at least not visibly. She turned smoothly, every muscle under firm control.

'Good morning,' she said. 'Or is it afternoon?'

'I'm sorry to intrude like this,' he said with a smile. 'I'm a friend of Karen Slocombe's.'

If he'd expected that to elicit a notable response, he was disappointed.

'Indeed?' was all she said. Then she remained standing under the tree, simply waiting for what might come next. He observed her minutely. Medium height, slim, wearing the sort of clothes you'd expect on an older woman. A skirt that looked too thick for the warm season, and a tweedy sort of jerkin over a check shirt. She looked like someone off to the point-to-point, except that her feet were bare.

He hadn't noticed at first, in the long grass of the orchard. But now he could glimpse toes and ankles beneath the calf-length skirt and his entire impression changed. Here was a woman capable of anything. A woman without any respect for conventions, dangerous and unpredictable.

'You lied to the police,' he said calmly. 'Karen heard you.'

'Karen has it all wrong.'

'She thinks you're involved in some sort of secret activity, to do with food politics. GM crops, probably. You're thought to be part of the group that trashed the maize crop last month . . .'

'An eco-terrorist?' Her eyes twinkled at him. 'Isn't that what such people are called?'

'You tell me.'

'You haven't told me your name,' she accused him. 'That's not very polite, is it?'

'Oh, sorry. Den Cooper.' He still had to remember not to prefix his name with *Detective Sergeant*, and reach for his ID card.

'Well, Den Cooper, I really don't understand why you're here. You seem to want me to admit something, to make a confession to you. Can that be right?'

'It's right in a way. I'm not a messenger for Karen – she doesn't even know I'm here. But I want you to understand she's on the same side as you. She doesn't see why you and she seem to be opposed in some way. I think she's quite upset about it.'

'Ah! You're her protector. Sir Galahad. But hasn't she got a perfectly good husband for that sort of thing?'

'I'm not her protector. I want to know what's going on, for my own satisfaction.'

'And you think I'll tell you, just like that? I don't *know* you. You could be working for SuperFare itself, for all I know.'

'Well, I'm not. I'm just taking an interest, and trying to get to the bottom of what's been going on. I'd appreciate you telling me some of the background. What *is* food politics, anyway? It sounds daft, when you think about it. And I'm not working for SuperFare. I'm hardly working for anyone just now.'

She stared up at his face, as if trying to decide something. 'Are you by any chance trying to offer me your services?' she asked. 'Because that might be a different matter, if you are.'

'Why? Do you need somebody?'

'I do, as it happens. Come on in and have some soup while I tell you about it.'

Den realised afterwards that he ought to have known what was coming, at least in outline. A woman living alone, nudging sixty, with all her faculties, was inevitably going to have an eventful past. And that eventful past was very likely to impinge on the present and cause a variety of ripples. It was Den's experience that the explanation for most present crises lay in things that had happened decades earlier. He was aware that time scarcely mattered at all when it came to the passions that people generated between themselves. Emotional wounds never really healed, and if they were not aired and admitted, they slowly festered until something eventually had to give.

Mary Thomas told him a story that roughly fitted this view of things.

'I've lived in this area all my life,' she began, settling herself comfortably in the big wooden kitchen chair. They both had bowls of thick vegetable soup in front of them, and chunks of home-baked granary bread. 'It's funny how embarrassing it can be to admit that, sometimes. As if there's more virtue in moving around and living in a lot of different places. Makes a person sound dull, I suppose.'

Den smiled and waited.

'I married when I was thirty. He was a widower, quite a lot older than me, with three grown up children. We had twin boys.'

Den found himself looking round for signs of twin boys, despite knowing they must be adults by this time. The idea of twin boys appealed to him much more than he would have anticipated. 'Nice,' he said.

'Busy,' she corrected him. 'But they were bright

and funny and handsome. Not identical at all, by the way. But their father died when they were ten, which was not nice at all. He was fifty-five, which was far too young to die. He'd neglected to change the will he made when we were first married, which still left everything to his older children, and although I contested it, and did get this house, it was a meagre living for a while. I can see what you're thinking.' She aimed an accusing look at him. 'Why couldn't I go out and get myself a job?'

Den spread his hands in outraged innocence.

'Never mind. I did, as it happens, but my earnings were nothing to boast about. Anyway, I became expert at working the system, accepting whatever handouts various organisations might have available. And that included places at Christ's Hospital for the boys.'

'Christ's Hospital?'

'It's a boarding school in Sussex. They take boys – and girls now, I believe – with brains but not much money. They wear strange old-fashioned clothes, but it's an excellent place on the whole. It would all have been fine, except that I lost my sons in the process. They never really felt like mine after that. I went through a period of absolute rage against Michael for leaving his will the way it had been before the twins were born. I was sorry for myself and my boys, and I hated Georgina, Fergus and Ninian

– my stepchildren. Even though they were as pleasant as possible throughout, they clearly believed themselves entitled to the money, and never gave me anything beyond what they were forced to.' Den shook his head sympathetically.

'Anyway, they all dispersed, and I haven't spoken to any of them for ages now. They're not relevant. It's my own boys, Joshua and Humphrey, who concern me.'

Den began to wonder where all this was leading. Although she was speaking fast and the soup was still hot, he felt a flicker of impatience.

'Well, to cut to the main point, they, my sons, became very political in their senior school years. They both went to the LSE and took part in political rallies and campaigns and I don't know what.'

Ah! thought Den.

'Joshua gradually lost interest, after he graduated, but Humphrey has been getting more and more into it. He's been on all the big protests – and a lot of smaller ones. He's taught himself a mass of environmental science, been to America to see what's going on there, and is enormously committed. And he's taken me along with him, you might say.' She gave a rueful grin. 'It feels as if I've now got at least one of my sons back.'

'Joshua and Humphrey,' Den repeated, almost

reaching for a non-existent notebook to write down the names in.

'That's right. They're twenty-seven now, which is very hard to believe. Joshua lives in Leeds with a girlfriend. He's working in some little college that calls itself a University.' Her dismissiveness was awesome.

'And Humphrey?'

'He's based in London, but he travels all over. You never know where he might show up next. I've got very good at spotting him on the news. I knitted his balaclava, so I can always recognise him.'

If you can, so can the police, Den thought. 'So he's an eco-warrior, is he?'

'That's right.' Excitement glittered in her eyes. 'And he needs all the help he can get.'

Den remembered that she'd said she wanted his assistance. 'Oh no,' he said. 'Not me. You're not asking me to go and pull out genetically modified sweetcorn, are you?'

She laughed. 'Don't worry,' she assured him. 'Nothing like that. Though you ought not to condemn them for it until you understand the facts.'

'I do understand the facts,' he said crossly.

'Good. No, what we want from you, Den Cooper, friend of the estimable Slocombes, is *intelligence*. In both senses of the word. Ferret out the undercurrents for us: whether they're onto us; where they'll strike next – that sort of thing. But above all, I want you to persuade Karen to change her story about the supermarket. Tell her it's absolutely vital that she should stop saying I was there. Because I wasn't. That was not me. Karen was mistaken.' She slapped the table hard with each short sentence. So hard that Den very nearly believed her.

CHAPTER TWELVE

'You want me to *persuade* her?' he echoed. 'How am I meant to do that?'

'She's your friend, isn't she? Do it in whatever way you like.'

'We're not actually that close,' he began. 'I don't think.'

'Oh, well,' she shrugged. 'Don't get in a state about it.'

'If I could tell her there's a really good reason for changing her story, that might be different.' He tailed off again, as he realised this wasn't the case at all. 'No, it wouldn't,' he corrected himself. 'She's too honest for that.'

'All *right*,' she snapped. 'I get the message. Though I think you might be overestimating her a trifle. Nobody's above telling a few lies – even to the police.'

'True,' he smiled, hoping to appease her, before wondering just where that left him.

The soup finished, she produced two pots of homemade yoghurt, flavoured with something she said were her own cherries, frozen from last year. Den would never have guessed, but then he didn't think he'd tried frozen cherries before.

'Well, one final thing, and then I must let you get on,' she said. 'It's to do with my husband.'

Who was dead, Den recalled. He gave her a politely expectant expression.

'When he was married to his first wife, he worked at Porton Down. You know, where they do secret government scientific experiments. I always thought, actually, that he was somehow contaminated by some ghastly virus, which is why he died so young. But that's beside the point. He had a colleague there who became his best friend, and kept in touch right up to when Michael died. He still keeps in touch with me. He works in genetics now. Plant genetics.' She paused meaningfully. Den pushed out his lips to show he grasped the point. 'He has some very ambivalent feelings about the whole business,' she went on carefully.

'You mean he's a mole? A spy?'

'Something like that. He's very worried that

he'll be implicated in any direct action, if his association with me is ever traced. So we never do meet directly. We don't even email each other. We use go-betweens, you see.'

'Is this another job for me?'

'Clever boy!' She clapped her hands satirically.

'Let me think about it first,' he said. 'I'm not sure I like what I'd be getting into here. And it doesn't feel as if it's getting anybody any closer to sorting out who killed Peter Grafton.'

'Of course it is, you idiot,' she scoffed. 'Of course it bloody is.'

Maggs's mobile phone sang its little song at her, to indicate she had a text message. Drew widened his eyes in warning when he heard it. 'I thought you kept that thing switched off when you were at work,' he said.

'I do. It's only a text message.'

'But it played a tune. I *hate* them doing that. It's crass.'

'Drew, you are the most old-fashioned thirty-five-year-old in the world. What's the matter with you?'

'So you think it'd be OK if it did that in the middle of a funeral, do you? At the graveside, when we were having a minute's silent reflection?'

She sighed. 'No, of course not. I don't even take it out there with me. And I didn't mean to leave the sound on. It doesn't usually do that.' She peered at the tiny screen. 'It's Den. He's been to see Mary Thomas, and she has work for him.'

'What? Who?' Drew shook his head crossly. 'How can he say all that in thirty characters or whatever it is?'

'Ah! You're interested really, aren't you? You'd love to get into texting – go on, admit it.'

'Absolutely not. It's horrible. All those stupid abbreviations.'

'Well, don't get worked up about it. I'm switching it off, look. Satisfied?' She made a show of silencing the phone and putting it on a shelf. 'Just don't let me go home without it.'

'What is Den doing, exactly?' Drew went on to ask, risking Maggs's flicker of triumph at having his interest.

'I don't know. Last I heard, he was going to try and see his friend Danny again. I've no idea what's been going on since, except he's been talking to the Thomas woman.'

'Do you get the feeling we're not keeping up too well on this one?' he suggested.

'Hmm. I know what you mean. But we *are* keeping up, really,' she decided. 'We've got the victim's funeral, for heaven's sake. We've talked to his wife and his girlfriend. We're just following a different path . . .'

'Speaking of paths,' Drew interrupted, 'don't you think . . .'

'Drew Slocombe, if you say another word about those damned paths, I'll . . . I'll . . .'

'All right.' He put his hands up in surrender. 'But if anyone slips, or starts walking on somebody's grave, you'll be responsible.'

The paths in the burial ground were a constant worry to Drew. They were little more than mown strips between the complicated grid of burial plots, which were under Maggs's charge. They'd discussed laying decking or gravel or wood chippings, but always concluded that plain grass was best. After a busy spell, with several visitors, and a few burials, most of the paths were sufficiently well trodden to remain clearly visible, but with the lush spring grass and a few weeks of relative inactivity, Drew worried.

'Visitor!' Maggs announced. Her hearing seemed uncannily acute to Drew, who hadn't noticed a thing. When he looked out of the window he saw a red Citroën parked by the road gate, and a woman coming towards the office.

'It's Sally Dabb again,' he observed.

'So it is,' Maggs agreed.

'Must have come to view Grafton.'

'Very likely. And I thought we decided nobody

could see him until tomorrow. I haven't got him presentable yet.'

'I'll put her off if I can.'

'You won't be able to,' she said glumly.

Maggs was right about Sally's reason for turning up. She was calmer than on her first visit, but no easier to deal with.

'I've got to see him,' she urged. 'And I have something I want to put in with him. Just a letter – nothing you could object to. Is he in his coffin yet?'

'Well,' Drew said. 'The thing is . . .'

'He is *here*, isn't he?' she demanded.

'Oh, yes, he's here. But you have to understand . . . I mean, we're not like other undertakers. We haven't got the same facilities. And there are two other funerals this week, which is unusually busy for us.'

'So?'

'Well, it's a bit difficult to let you see him this afternoon.'

'Why?'

Drew clenched his jaw, badly tempted to give it to her straight, all about the post-mortem and the smell and the crowded cool room, and the unfinished, almost disrespectful, way Peter Grafton's body was simply plonked into the cardboard coffin. Worst of all, the fact that there was an uncoffined body currently lying on the floor, because the trolleys were both already occupied.

'Because it'll upset you,' he said.

'*Upset* me? Do you think I'm not already as upset as anybody can be?' She stared wildly at him, her eyes swimming. 'I was *there* when he died. I got his blood on me. I saw that bolt in his neck, heard the way he gurgled and gasped for air. I can't sleep, because every time I shut my eyes, I see it all over again.'

'OK,' Drew decided. 'Come on through.' She was right, of course. Nothing she saw now would be as bad as the experience she'd already had.

'But he's on the *floor!*' she shrieked. Maggs was in the room, trying her best to give Drew unobtrusively vicious glances.

'No, no, that isn't him,' said Maggs, washing her hands with strong green soap. 'But I know it looks bad. Can't be helped, I'm afraid. And it truly doesn't imply any lack of respect.'

Sally subsided, literally as well as emotionally. She drooped over the plain lidless coffin, and reached into it. 'Hi, Pete,' she whispered. 'What have they done to you, eh?'

She stroked his hair, which looked perfectly normal, but which Drew and Maggs knew hid a lot of crude stitching just below the surface. They both clenched their jaws with apprehension, watching her.

Sally looked up at them, her face completely serene. 'It's so strange, isn't it,' she murmured. 'It's him, and yet it absolutely isn't. He can't hear me or feel me. He doesn't care about anything at all. He's like a block of wood.' She lightly fingered the skin of the dead man's cheeks. 'Hard and cold. I loved him, you know, even though we never did anything to feel guilty about. He was a very loveable man.'

Drew realised he hadn't given much thought until then as to what Grafton had been like as a person. The various facts he'd gleaned from Karen and Julie, and now Sally hadn't added up to a complete personality. And nobody to date had described him as *loveable*.

'We were getting into a mess, weren't we Pete?' the woman went on, unselfconsciously. 'Are you glad to be out of it? Saved us a lot of damaged feelings later on, you could say. Fancy getting yourself *murdered*, though! We'd never expected that, had we?'

She leant over, one arm completely inside the coffin. It was a moving tableau, to Drew's eyes, but he could feel Maggs impatient and disapproving beside him. Aware of being surplus to requirements, he removed himself from the room, leaving his colleague to deal with the visitor as best she could.

'You'll get cold in here,' Maggs burst out, after a few minutes.

'It doesn't matter.'

'And – well – I need to get on, I'm afraid. Sorry.'

Sally Dabb did not take the hint. 'Don't mind me,' she said. 'I'm happy for you to carry on. It's rather nice in here, isn't it. You've got a lovely view of the field.' The cool room, comprising the end section of the single building that was the Slocombes' home and Drew's office, had a good-sized window overlooking the burial ground. Built of breeze blocks and painted a stark white, it contained aluminium trolleys, and a wall of deep shelves for the paraphernalia required for the disposal of bodies. Despite their simple alternative style of doing things, there was still a need for wrappings, and paddings and name labels and washing materials. Flat-packed cardboard coffins were bought in tens, and stacked on the bottom shelf. Even flat, they took up a lot of space. Maggs felt there was never enough room, and with three bodies and a visitor in there, it was difficult to move around. She sighed, and went back to brushing Mr Lancaster's hair.

'Has Julie been in to see him?' Sally suddenly asked. Maggs felt a further stab of disapproval. The question seemed to be lacking in taste.

'Well,' she began, the undertaker's natural reticence overtaking her. 'I think she said tomorrow.'

'It doesn't matter, you know,' Sally said, with a sad smile. 'Julie knew all about me and Peter. I mean, she knew we were great friends, and that we had something special. She didn't mind.' She looked at Maggs, recognising the frosty manner. 'We *weren't* lovers, as I keep telling you. It might have come to that, eventually – though I doubt it. We were just really good friends. You do believe me, don't you? You were so nice about it when I came here last week.'

'I believe you,' Maggs admitted. 'But it still sounds as if it was a bit of a mess.'

'It was getting complicated,' Sally admitted. 'In a whole lot of different ways.'

'That's obvious,' said Maggs.

'Why? What do you mean?'

'He got himself murdered, didn't he? And nobody seems to have any idea why. You can't really get more complicated than that, as far as I can see.'

Sally's wide lips curved in an involuntary smile. 'No,' she agreed. 'I suppose you can't.'

Both women acknowledged the moment of warmth; the intimacy that arises in the presence of a dead body. Maggs had felt it a hundred times before. The mere fact of being alive when the person lying there so cold between you was not, made for extraordinary alliances. A shared mystery, a shared relief; whatever it was, it had a persistent power.

Sally turned back to her drooping-over-the-coffin posture. 'It's tragic that he's dead, so young. He would have done all kinds of things.'

'It's a waste,' Maggs agreed with all sincerity.

'Will they catch who did it, do you think?'

'Bound to.' Maggs gave Sally a robust look. 'They won't rest until they do.'

'No,' said Sally vaguely.

Drew described the visit to Karen that evening, remembering how little consideration he'd given to the character of the deceased. 'What was he actually like?' he asked her. 'Maggs seems to think we've missed something.'

'Very good looking – you'll have worked that out for yourself. One of those really beautiful men, I suppose. Nice skin, thick hair, and a lovely voice. It had a kind of richness to it, that made you want to listen hard to anything he said. And he always met your eye when he was talking to you. And he smiled a lot.'

'This is all very superficial,' Drew objected. 'What about his *character*?'

Karen nibbled her lower lip thoughtfully. 'Pleasant. Sociable. Charming, even.' She heard her own words. 'I'm just saying the same things again, aren't I? The fact is, all I knew of him was that superficial charm. I've no idea where his real passions lay, or what he was thinking.'

Drew smiled. 'All the women seem to have adored him. Reminds me of Jim Lapsford.' Lapsford had been Drew's baptism of fire into the murky world of suspicious deaths and hastily prepared cremation papers. He and Karen had investigated the truth of Lapsford's death together.

'Oh, no,' she said emphatically. 'Not the least bit like Jim Lapsford.'

'But you were convinced he was having an affair with Sally Dabb. So he must have been rather more than pleasant towards her?'

She chewed the lip more frenziedly. 'No, not really. They laughed a lot together, and *touched* each other. Hands on shoulders, that sort of thing. Peter didn't do that with everybody. It was obvious how much she liked him. She gave him moony looks, all big eyes and girly smiles. And he liked that.'

'She told me and Maggs there was no sex going on between them, remember.'

'So you say. She wants you to be her PR people, and squash all the rumours about them.'

'Don't you believe her?'

Karen considered for a minute. 'I *did* believe her, when you told me what she'd said. I was absolutely on her side.'

'But now?'

'I don't know,' she admitted. 'She's obviously lost without him. If they weren't lovers, then they were very, very good friends. I don't see that it matters much whether or not they went to bed together.'

'It does though,' Drew assured her earnestly. 'It matters a lot.'

'Why?'

'I don't think I need to explain that to you, do I?' She met his gaze. 'I see what you mean,' she said.

Later, he had a very similar exchange with Maggs, when she described Sally's behaviour in the cool room. 'It makes them rather noble, keeping it all platonic,' she said. 'Don't you think?'

'It's nice not to have to disapprove,' he agreed. 'To credit her with a clear conscience. If you commit adultery, you cross a line and can never entirely claim the moral high ground.'

Maggs gave him a penetrating glance. 'Drew – are you talking about you and Genevieve Slater?'

He flushed, and shook his head, wishing he could tell her to mind her own business. 'No, not really. At least, perhaps I am a bit. I'm eternally relieved that we never . . .'

Maggs held up her hands. 'Sorry. Out of order,' she said. 'You should be saying all this to Karen, not me.'

'Precisely,' he said.

CHAPTER THIRTEEN

Den and Maggs also discussed Peter Grafton later that day, along very much the same lines. 'We don't have much idea of what he was really *like*,' Den complained. 'And now I've got myself into this weird business with Mary Thomas, it all feels like a diversion from the main issue.'

'Weird is right,' she said. 'You're being as bad as Drew, getting sucked into some woman's personal campaign. I thought you'd have had more sense.'

'She seems to know who killed Grafton,' he mused. 'Something about this bloke her husband used to work with. And a son who's deeply into environmental activism. But she wouldn't say anything more. I came away thinking the whole conversation had just been a sort of game to her. She was playing with me.'

'You said she had work for you,' Maggs prompted.

'Something and nothing,' he dismissed. 'I wouldn't touch it. I don't think she ever really thought I would. She's a very odd woman.' He shook himself like a dog. 'I felt as if I'd been dragged into something rather yucky.'

'But she must have been trying to tell you something,' Maggs said. 'She was making some kind of connection.'

'So why not just tell me straight?'

'Scared, probably. After all, she was taken in for questioning at the weekend. She wouldn't dare tell you anything that would incriminate her, after that.'

Den nodded grudgingly. 'That could be it,' he agreed. 'But the fact remains she didn't say anything useful.'

Maggs became brisk. 'Let's summarise,' she said. 'Suspects, alibis. Means, motives, opportunity. Isn't that the professional way to tackle it?'

He sighed.

'What's the matter?' She glared at him. 'Am I boring you?'

He reached for her, wrapping his long arms round her. 'Don't be stupid. I'm as involved as you are. But it's all muddled up with last weekend, and my job, and where-do-we-go-from-here. I can't concentrate on any one thing, because there are so many others waiting for my attention. Do you understand?'

'Perfectly,' she cooed, snuggling into his chest. 'You don't have to get in a state about it, you know. You can forget the whole thing. It's not your job any more. I think you keep forgetting that.'

'But . . .' he sighed again. 'I actually quite want to do my bit for justice. It's not OK to fire crossbow bolts through a chap's throat in broad daylight. I'd feel bad if I just dropped it.'

'Course you would. So let's get it sorted, and then we can think about some of those other things. Right?'

'Right.'

'Means, motive and opportunity. I love that list. It covers everything, doesn't it.'

'Yes and no,' he said cautiously. 'You hardly ever work out all three. It's just a rule of thumb, you know, not a formula for instant success.' He tried to suppress the tremor of recognition at the line Maggs was taking. His previous serious girlfriend, Lilah Beardon, had helped him with one or two murder investigations, and she, like Maggs, had dwelt obsessively on *means, motive and opportunity*. It seemed to appeal to women, for some reason.

'Well, the main person without an alibi is the wife,' said Maggs. 'She's got motive and opportunity. And I suppose anybody can get hold of a crossbow if they want to.'

'Sally Dabb's husband has motive, too,' he joined in. 'Assuming Grafton and Sally really were having an affair.'

'Whether they were or not, if people *thought* they were, that's enough to make their spouses want to commit murder.'

'And then there's the food politics stuff. That's where we need Karen. I still don't really understand what these people get so aereated about.'

'Well, all I know is Drew says that Karen says there's a big to-do about GM crops amongst the farmers' market people. And they both think that's at the bottom of this whole business.'

'Mary Thomas seemed to be saying something like that, as well.'

He frowned. 'She's really one of the chief suspects. Is she trying to divert me, do you think?'

'Does she think you're actually investigating the murder? I mean, does she know you used to be in the police, and that you've been seeing Danny lately?'

'I have no idea what she knows, what she thinks or what she wants. The woman's a complete mystery to me.'

Maggs sighed impatiently. 'Even though she talked to you about her intimate personal history for half an hour or more? You still don't know what she feels?'

'I didn't say feels. She said plenty about feelings. She resents her stepchildren – who are probably knocking forty by now; regrets sending her twins to boarding school; and insists it wasn't her that Karen saw at the supermarket.'

Maggs's head went up. 'What? What about the supermarket?'

'She says it wasn't her. Karen knows she's denying it. She was there when Mary was arrested, remember? They dragged her off amidst loud protestations that she'd never been near SuperFare. But Karen is absolutely certain she spoke to Mary Thomas only seconds before the bomb went off. It's the word of one against the other, and they're both unmovable.'

'Right,' said Maggs thoughtfully. 'Um . . . Den . . . do you think Karen's *definitely* the one we should believe? I mean, it's dreadful of me to say it, but she *was* there at both incidents. She does know all these organic people really well by now. That Geraldine Beech woman is a bosom buddy. She might have got pulled into something a bit nasty, to do with wrecking GM crops or something.'

Den shook his head. 'You think we're all getting into bad company, don't you,' he accused. 'Me with Mary, Drew with any woman that comes along,

Karen with the stallholders. We can't all be weak and gullible, can we? All except you, of course.'

'No need to be nasty,' she reproached. 'That's just the way it looks to me. And I am usually right, you know,' she added. 'You haven't really seen me in action up to now. Nothing much has happened since we got together.' She wriggled her shoulders in mock modesty. 'You still don't know all my hidden talents, you see.'

'Aha!' he pounced. 'I get it. You're *bored*. Nothing much has happened, eh? Just falling in love with the most handsome man in England, and having the best sex life there could possibly be. So now we've not only got to move to some god-forsaken farm, but you have to personally solve the murder of Peter Grafton all on your own. Just so you can feel as if something's happening.'

She didn't like his tone any more than she liked the words. A dark scowl turned her face into a mask of resentment. 'God-forsaken farm?' she echoed. 'Is that what you think?'

He pulled her to him again, sinking them in a tangled heap onto the cushions of their sofa. 'Come on, kiddo. We'd never manage a farm. It's a non-starter. Neither of us knows the first thing about animals or ploughing or digging out ditches. And we haven't the remotest chance of raising the cash for a place the size you're talking about. It's just way out of our league. Besides, you couldn't manage that as well as working with Drew, and I don't think you ought to even think of abandoning him. It's your *vocation*. You're brilliant at it.'

'Well, you were probably a brilliant policeman. It doesn't mean we have to stay doing the same thing forever.'

'Maggs, it won't be forever. Give it another three years, say. I know the money's not much good, but I thought we didn't mind that. We've got all we need.'

She picked at a fraying buttonhole on her cuff. 'It's years since I started working with Drew. I started just after Stephanie was born. It feels like forever, and then some. And look at my clothes. I could spend *hundreds* of pounds on new stuff. I haven't got any proper *shoes*.'

'But you'd have even less if we went with your farm idea.'

'Well, then I wouldn't *need* proper shoes, would I?'

'Drew should provide them for you. He should pay for them out of the business.'

Maggs merely sighed.

'Why do I feel this really isn't about Drew or your job at all?' he worried. 'What is it you're trying to tell me? Is it me? Are you fed up with *us*?'

She looked at him. 'It has got a bit samey,' she confessed. Then she pulled his head down to her chest, clutching at his hair fiercely. 'No, I didn't mean that. Don't panic, lover. I'm not saying anything scary. Us is fine. I *like* us better than anything. Honestly.'

He pulled away from her, almost losing his balance in the awkward tangle they'd become and tipping them both onto the floor. 'You would tell me?' he demanded. 'Wouldn't you?'

'Stop it,' she said. 'That isn't what I'm talking about at all. Don't be so paranoid.'

'Who can blame me?' he pouted. 'With my record with women. It's been a disaster up to now.'

'Sounds fairly normal to me. One serious relationship and a few casuals. Nothing to worry about, that I can see.'

'Maggs, can we get married?' The words were out before either of them had seen them coming. 'Do you think that would help, I mean?'

'Like – it would give me something to do, choosing the bridesmaids? Don't be stupid.' She punched him quite hard on the chest. 'What a bloody daft thing to come up with.'

He heaved himself upright, floundering horizontally for a moment, with her weight still mainly on him. 'Sorry,' he said.

'Oh, God, how did this happen? What would be the point of getting married? What difference would it make? It would just cost money, and nothing would change.'

'They say quite a lot changes, actually. Old-fashioned things have to be acknowledged, like commitment and families and sharing.'

'All much too old-fashioned for me,' she said lightly. Then, with a pretence at a wail, 'All I said was it would be nice to live on a farm.'

He didn't laugh, and she knew something had been damaged. He left the room, head hunched forward, a hand to the place where she'd punched him. She wished quite badly that she hadn't hit him. Somehow it gave him the moral high ground.

Karen was wearying somewhat of routine, too. Wednesday meant she and Della had their own children. It *always* meant that. There was a certain tedium to the predictability of it. Last week, she'd made that abortive visit to Mary Thomas and virtually had the door slammed in her face. This week she'd try again to do something different and interesting. The end of May was approaching; summer was in full swing and it was her duty to make the most of every day that was fine.

'What can I do with them today?' she wondered to Drew at breakfast. 'Something different.'

'Whatever you like, so long as it doesn't cost money,' he said unhelpfully.

'I could try and find out some more about Peter Grafton. This contract he's supposed to have had with the supermarket, for example.'

'How are you going to do that? With two small children in tow?'

'I don't know. I could go and see Julie, I suppose.'

'She's got the funeral tomorrow. She'll be busy.'

'I could help.'

'With Steph and Timmy? I doubt it.'

'Well, I'm not staying here all day. I want to get out somewhere.'

'You should find someone to go with you,' he advised. 'Another woman, I mean.'

'I could try Hilary, I suppose,' she said doubtfully.

'Isn't there anybody your own age? Apart from Della?'

'Sally Dabb, that's all. But I can't just phone her out of the blue and suggest we go out somewhere. I don't know her well enough.'

'You're saying you haven't got enough friends,' he accused.

'Maybe. It's the same as it's always been, though. I don't really do friends, do I?'

'Well,' he said, getting up and wiping toast crumbs from his chin, 'I'm afraid I've got loads to do. It's going to be really busy today. We'll probably get another removal, just when we'd find it almost impossible to cope.'

'You'd cope,' she said coolly.

CHAPTER FOURTEEN

In the end, Karen decided to go and see Hilary Henderson, although not without prior warning. 'Can I bring the kids round to play with your animals?' was the way she put it.

'You can try,' came the ready response. 'I'm not sure what the animals will make of it; they're not used to children.'

'Didn't yours used to play with them?'

'There are two answers to that,' laughed Hilary. 'First, none of the same creatures are here now. It's been ages since I had anyone under twelve. And second, they hardly ever went outside, apart from Justin. Typical of their generation, they just played with Game Boys and watched telly all day.'

Karen enjoyed a moment's complacency.

Her offspring actually liked being outdoors.

'So, it wouldn't be too much of a nuisance?'

'Not a bit. I can probably find you something useful to do. We never have enough pairs of hands around here.'

It took less than ten minutes to drive from North Staverton to the Hendersons' farm, despite having to drive onto the main road for a mile, and then off it again at the next turning. "Falderstoke" was proclaimed on the gateside nameplate, which was rusting and crooked, but somehow proud for all that. Hilary's husband's ancestors had lived there for centuries, by all accounts, in the white cob longhouse. Hilary's eldest son had arranged for a sliver from one of the huge oak beams in the roof to be carbon dated, with the barely credible result that the tree had been felled in the year 1212, give or take a decade.

All this Karen had gleaned in her brief chats with Hilary at the farmers' markets. It had sounded romantic and important, and quite worrying as to what the future might hold. Farmers everywhere were being forced to abandon their way of life, selling just such houses and letting their offspring take their chances in the real world of suburban estates and jobs with computer software. The thought of the Hendersons having to sell up was awful.

Karen had been here twice before, both times to Food Chain meetings. All she had seen of the house was a low-ceilinged kitchen and a large sitting room. She hoped today to get a better chance to explore.

The drive was bordered by large old trees – sycamore, beech, oak and ash which had clearly been there for ages. It was dignified and ancient, but not in the least intimidating. This was no stately home, or country mansion. The house, when it came into view, huddled in a shallow dip, with an untidy yard surrounding it.

'Why are we coming here?' asked Stephanie, gazing out of each car window in turn.

'It's a farm,' Karen told her. 'You can see the animals.'

'Will there be ponies? And rabbits?' the child asked.

'And croccy-diles!' added Timmy with complete certainty.

'Why?' Stephanie persisted.

'For a change. Because it'll broaden your horizons,' Karen snapped, opening the car door and getting out. Stephanie was mercifully silent, although steaming with resentment at her mother's unfair tactic in using language the child couldn't understand or argue with. Karen felt a stab of remorse. She had promised herself she would never do what she had just done. Not that she worried that Stephanie's feelings had been unduly bruised. As always, the child would inevitably win in the end.

There was no sign of Hilary or anybody else. Karen thought it unlikely that her friend would be in the house, unless she was making jam or dyeing wool in the kitchen. Whatever the weather, Hilary preferred to be outside.

'Hello!' came a loud voice from somewhere above them. 'Come and see my lambs.'

Karen located the speaker on a high bank where the ground rose steeply at one end of the house. Her head was just visible over a stone wall, which had been built aeons ago to prevent the higher ground from sliding across the track and into the house. A small field with tufty grass lay beyond the wall. Karen looked for a way up the bank.

'You can get round that way.' Hilary indicated a track that zigzagged upwards to a gate. Karen began to feel she was having an adventure before she'd even got out of the farmyard. Timmy would have to use his hands to scramble up the path, it was so steep.

'At least it's not muddy,' Hilary grinned, meeting them at the gate. She was carrying a good-sized lamb, which struggled resentfully in her arms. 'This is Toby,' Hilary said. 'He's the mandatory orphan lamb, which we vow not to rear every year. Sheer sentiment, every time.'

The animal was almost too strong for her, but she gripped it tightly, and leant down to allow the children to pet it. Timmy eyed it with dislike. 'Croccy-dile,' he said irritably.

Stephanie politely fingered the bouclé curls of the lamb's coat, and then gently pulled one ear. 'Hello, lamb,' she said.

'Has it been a good year for them?' Karen asked, looking round. There were three ewes in the field, each with a good-sized lamb.

'Oh, these are just the after-thoughts, born at the end of April. Yes, it's been all right, on the whole. Much as usual.' She spoke carelessly, as if it was of very little interest. 'Can I let him go now?' she asked Stephanie. Then, looking at Timmy, she added, 'He might turn into a crocodile if we say the right magic word.'

Karen laughed, doubtful that her little boy had understood the suggestion. By the way he gazed steadfastly at the lamb, it seemed that perhaps he had.

'Mizzlepop!' said Stephanie, obligingly, using the magic word that Drew had taught her. Nothing happened to the lamb, but a gunshot rang out almost immediately. Karen, to her eternal embarrassment, grabbed a child in each hand and flung all three of them to the ground, uttering wordless squawks of consternation.

'For heaven's sake,' Hilary chastised her. 'It's only Justin shooting pigeons or squirrels or something.' She hoisted Karen back to her feet without ceremony. 'Though I must admit it sounded rather close.'

The silence following the shot deepened, until Hilary said, 'Karen, is your little girl all right?'

Karen had been brushing at herself, struggling with a sense of embarrassment, unaware of her children. She jerked around, looking for Stephanie.

The child was standing rigidly, her eyes very wide, her mouth open. Karen's heart stopped. 'Stephanie!' she shrieked, grabbing wildly at the child. The small shoulders under her hands were unresponsive. Karen shook her. 'Steph! Come on, sweetheart,' she said in a calmer voice. 'It's nothing to worry about.'

Timmy was once more occupied with the lamb, apparently unconcerned by the crisis going on beside him. He was walking slowly sideways, chuckling as the lamb eagerly followed him.

'She's just shocked,' Hilary said. 'She'll be OK in a minute.'

'She's had too many shocks lately,' Karen muttered. 'That's what it is.'

'Did he die?' Stephanie whispered, her eyes fixed straight ahead, as if afraid to look around her. 'Did I make him die?'

'What, darling? What do you mean?' The child shook her head dumbly.

'She thinks she made the gun go off with her magic word,' Hilary realised. 'She's talking about the lamb.'

'The lamb's perfectly all right,' Karen said, with a relieved laugh. 'Look, Timmy's playing with it.'

'Not *the lamb*,' Stephanie hissed. 'The *man*. Like when the window broke. The man – did he die?' She stared urgently at her mother, vitality returning, only to bring a rush of distress.

Karen knelt down, and cuddled her daughter to her. 'I don't understand, sweetheart. What are you talking about?'

Stephanie just shook her head again and thrust her thumb in her mouth. Karen reproached herself for her stupid panic reaction to the gunshot. That, she was sure, had frightened the child. It seemed crucial to understand what Stephanie was thinking.

'When the window broke?' she repeated. 'You mean when we went to the supermarket?'

'There was a man. He fell over, when I was looking at him. That lady, she was looking at him as well, and then, she made the window break and the man fell over. And then Della fell over. And then *you* fell over – and there's a man. He's dead. I heard you say he was, to Della.'

Hilary cleared her throat and caught Karen's eye. 'Let's go and have some drink and biscuits,' she said. 'This is all getting a bit complicated.' She rubbed a friendly hand over Stephanie's head. 'Guns *are* scary things. I'm going to shout at Justin and tell him he shouldn't shoot things near the house.'

Karen released Stephanie reluctantly, still completely bewildered as to what was going on in the infant mind. Some strange confusion between the supermarket bomb, Della's faint and the incident just now. In vain, she tried to remember exactly where Stephanie had been, and what she'd been looking at, when the bomb had gone off. And who was 'the lady' she'd seen? Presumably it must be Mary Thomas. And if so, Karen realised, there was a second witness to Mary's presence at the scene. It wasn't simply Karen's word against Mary's. And at the same time, she realised she couldn't possibly enlist her little girl as backup. It wouldn't be fair, and what she said wouldn't be reliable.

'Come on then,' she said. 'Everything's all right now.'

The morning passed quickly, with Karen feeling more like a tourist than a visiting friend. Timmy wore himself out exploring and almost fell asleep on his feet. Karen put him in the car, under a shady tree, with the door left open, and sat with Stephanie on a grassy bank close by, making daisy chains. Hilary brought out a bowl of semi-solid beeswax, which she was kneading into small tablets. 'It's wonderful furniture polish,' she said. 'I don't bother with all the fancy moulds and stuff; it works just as well like this. I'll give you some to take home.'

'I'm not much of a one for polishing,' Karen laughed.

'Never mind. You might get the urge one day. Just smear it on and then give it a good rub with a cloth, and you'll be amazed. It makes things smell nice, as well.'

Karen smiled ruefully. She didn't think she'd ever seen the effect of beeswax polish. Her mother hadn't been into housework, either.

It was a relaxed day, after the initial shock. Hilary's son Justin had shown up some time later, and been told off by his mother.

'Sorry,' he'd shrugged. 'It was a bloody great crow. I couldn't resist taking a pot at it. Missed it, though. I'm a rotten shot.'

He was nineteen, strongly built and tanned – the sort of boy, Karen thought, that you'd expect to see on a farm, but somehow seldom did. He seemed to be a figure from a bygone age.

'What sort of gun have you got?' she asked, merely to make conversation. He no longer had the weapon with him.

'It's a Brocock,' he said, clearly with no expectation that she'd be much enlightened.

'Oh? Is that a shotgun?'

'No, just an airgun. Pretty harmless. You don't need a licence for them.'

'But they can kill a crow, can they?'

'Well, just about.'

'It didn't *sound* like an airgun,' Karen said thoughtfully. 'It was much louder than that, surely?'

Justin turned away, as if he hadn't heard her. 'They're coming in for lunch in a minute, Mum,' he threw over his shoulder at Hilary.

'As if I didn't know,' she sighed. 'Every day, I have to feed five grown workers, strictly at one o'clock. Would you believe it? It's like feudal times.'

'Five?' Karen queried.

'Husband, brother-in-law, son, tractor driver and a casual chap who comes on Wednesdays.'

'Not counting yourself, then?'

'Too busy to eat,' Hilary laughed. 'Though I suppose I pick so much through the day that I end up eating more than they do. I'm certainly not *thin,* am I?'

'Not fat, either,' said Karen. 'But . . . the farm can support you all, can it? I thought things were at crisis point these days. How do you manage?'

Hilary shrugged. 'Hand to mouth. We don't buy much, don't pay proper wages.'

Karen looked at the venerable farmhouse with a feeling of foreboding. On the face of it, it was indestructible, the surrounding land faithfully producing lush grass and whatever crops were profitable this year, but she knew it was much less secure than that. The economics of agriculture were on the brink of collapse. Despair prevailed and families like the Hendersons were hanging on by a thread.

And yet Hilary seemed genuinely contented with her life. She was busy, cheerful, sociable, unworried by events swirling around her, and the probable future her children could expect.

Lunch presented Karen with a difficulty that Hilary did not appear to have noticed. 'Er – should we go now?' she faltered. 'If you've got to feed the family.'

'Oh, no. Don't be daft. I've got a special picnic prepared for us. We'll have it out here, once I've sorted the hordes. There's a shepherd's pie in the Aga for them, and I'll do some frozen peas to go with it. It'll only take a few minutes, then I'll be with you.'

The effortless organisation made Karen feel weak. 'Shall I come and help?' she said.

'Of course not. Stay here and keep an eye on

these little ones. I'll bring it all out soon. Will Timmy wake up, do you think?'

'He'll probably be quite hungry soon. That usually gets him moving.'

They ate on the grass, like day trippers in a bygone age. Hilary provided cold sausages, hard-boiled eggs, mixed salad and home-baked bread rolls. They drank apple juice, and finished with yoghurt that was clearly homemade. It came in white china pots and had lumps of banana in it.

Stephanie ate slowly and minimally. Timmy had to be woken up and was groggily half-asleep throughout the meal. Karen found herself eating to excess, in an effort to make up for the children's poor efforts. Hilary ate even more than Karen, despite seeming somewhat distracted.

Karen found herself wondering just what she was doing there. It felt like an invasion, notwithstanding Hilary's relaxed hospitality. The children had evidently had enough, and were, in their own ways, also wondering about the visit.

'I'd better be going soon,' Karen said. 'It's been really lovely. Thanks. The kids really need to see some proper farms now and then. It's not always easy to organise.'

'No,' agreed Hilary absently.

'Funny, when you think about it – how cut off and remote farms are. I've got no real idea about what goes on here, on a daily basis.'

'Karen,' Hilary interrupted. 'Do you have any theories about who killed Peter Grafton?'

Karen shot a worried glance at her daughter, but Stephanie was being bossy with Timmy, trying to force him to eat some yoghurt, and did not seem to be listening.

'Absolutely none,' she said frankly. 'Have you?'

'Not at all. It seems crazy. Here we are, more than a week later, and it all seems to have gone cold. What are we supposed to make of it?'

'I suppose it's most likely to have to do with this supermarket contract. You know about that? He was going to supply fresh apple juice to SuperFare.'

'Yes, I knew that,' Hilary nodded. 'I think we all did, one way or another.'

'I didn't.' Karen felt fleetingly resentful.

'Ah. Well, he didn't exactly broadcast it, knowing how we felt about it all. But somehow we all got to know about it.'

'Drew and Den are both interested in solving it,' Karen laughed self-consciously. 'That sounds odd, I suppose. Drew's been involved in murders before, one way and another, and Den was a police detective, so he takes a professional interest. Or, rather . . .' she paused in confusion.

'The interest of an ex-professional?' Hilary

suggested. 'I suppose that makes sense. He must be feeling a bit left out.'

'You know him, do you?'

'Sort of. I know he's with your Maggs. I haven't ever spoken to him, as far as I can remember. He came to the market an hour or two before Peter was killed. I noticed him.'

'People do, with him being so tall,' Karen nodded. 'Anyway, there's not much teamwork going on,' she continued. 'Drew's busy, and Maggs seems a bit distracted these days. We all seem to know different bits of the story, and never get together to pool it all. Basically, I think we're just playing at it this time. And yet, I *knew* Peter. I feel I ought to be making a lot more effort.'

'And Drew's doing his funeral,' Hilary put in quietly.

'Yes. Tomorrow. He's seen Julie, and Sally. Geraldine had a word with him, too.' She munched on yet another bread roll. 'It's all arranged, I think. At least it means the cause of death was straightforward.'

'Pardon?'

'Oh, letting them have the body for burial. They wouldn't do that if they thought there was any risk of somebody's defence lawyer wanting another post-mortem.'

Hilary held up both hands to stop her. 'Defence lawyer?' she queried.

'When the murder comes to trial,' Karen explained. 'When they catch who did it.'

'You think they'll catch him, do you?'

Karen nodded, scarcely pausing to think. 'Oh, yes,' she said. 'They're sure to catch him in the end.'

'I admire your confidence in the forces of law and order,' said Hilary.

Karen heard the irony. 'No you don't,' she smiled. 'But let's not worry about it.'

'We really do have to get together, all four of us, and pool our findings,' said Maggs. She was with Den in the car, on Thursday morning. 'I'm going to tell Drew the same thing.'

And she did. 'Can we have a proper meeting this evening?' she persisted. 'Is Karen going to be in?'

'I think so,' he agreed. 'But she might not feel very cooperative. I get the impression she's rather sick of the whole business.'

'Well, then, the sooner we clear it up the better,' said Maggs.

'We've got the funeral before that,' he reminded her. 'Busy, busy.'

'Right boss,' she said.

Elsie Watkins was buried that morning, at ten thirty, with minimal ceremony. Despite their best efforts, Drew and Maggs could not prevent their attention from returning repeatedly to the oncoming funeral that afternoon. Peter Grafton was going to be their most famous interment so far. His murder had made the national press, albeit not as headline news. There would be reporters, police, curious onlookers and shell-shocked relatives. There would be Sally Dabb, Julie Grafton and even Della Gray. All the women – as far as they knew – who had harboured fond feelings for him. There would be Geraldine Beech and Hilary Henderson, and perhaps Mary Thomas to complete the threesome of local witch-women.

Maggs chattered animatedly to Drew over their snatched lunch. 'We haven't really been very good in keeping our promise to Sally Dabb, have we?' she said. 'We told her we'd try and scotch the rumours about her, and I for one haven't mentioned it to a soul. What about you?'

He shook his head. 'I haven't really seen anybody,' he said.

'It's a lonely life you lead,' she sighed unsympathetically.

'Shut up,' he said.

But Maggs was irrepressible. 'Who else do you think will come? Is the vicar going to say the right things? Is it the usual organist? I hope he doesn't *leak*.'

Leaking was a particular hazard with natural burials. The conventional undertakers used endless quantities of white plastic sheeting to line coffins and wrap bodies, to prevent just such an eventuality. Peaceful Repose Burials were environmentally sensitive, and that meant not using plastic. Instead they made the best of hessian, shredded paper and in extreme circumstances, wood shavings. Anything absorbent and lightweight.

'He won't leak,' said Drew. 'And the organist is Eileen Hopworthy, as always. Why are you so agitated?'

She crossed her arms over her front as if cold. 'I don't know,' she shivered. 'Premonition?'

Drew gave a melodramatic sigh. 'Don't get into that,' he said. 'It's bad enough as it is, without you seeing into the future.'

They had a checklist of details in the run-up to the funeral. The two of them, plus Peter Grafton's brother and a neighbour, were carrying the coffin in and out of the church. They had decided against using any vehicles, as was often the case. The church was three hundred yards up the road, so the entire gathering would follow it from Drew's office to church for the service, and back again for burial. It worked well enough, although rain made for complications, and Drew could never quite reconcile himself to the inclusion of a church service at all. His ideal was a pagan or humanist ceremony at the graveside, where everybody who wanted to freely expressed their thoughts and feelings, saying goodbye in their own ways. The intervention of a minister of religion never failed to offend him.

But Maggs persistently reminded him that some people were actually Christian as well as environmentally sensitive. And for a Christian, the presence of a vicar was essential. So it seemed was the case with Peter Grafton.

CHAPTER FIFTEEN

The service was due to begin at three. Fifteen minutes beforehand, Julie Grafton arrived, in a small blue car driven by a man who Drew recognised as the brother who was to be a bearer. He went out to meet them.

'I'm sorry I didn't come again to view him,' she said composedly. 'I decided against it. I hope you weren't waiting for me?'

'We were ready for you, but it's not a problem,' Drew assured her. 'Do you want to wait out here? I'm afraid we don't really have a waiting room.'

'I thought I should be a bit early. Then I can welcome people as they arrive.' She wore a pair of smart black trousers, and a long black tunic, making her seem much taller and slimmer than Drew would have thought possible. Her face was pale, but she was carefully made-up and her hair looked as if it had just been freshly washed and styled. A woman acting the part of a new widow for all it was worth, he judged. Some women seemed to confuse funerals with weddings, which he supposed was not too hard to understand.

Somewhat to his surprise, the next to arrive, on foot, were Della and Bill Gray. Mentally, he checked the day, and whose turn it was with the kids. Thursday – Karen. Right.

Della almost threw herself at Julie, her face crumpling. 'Oh, Jules! How on earth are you coping? How can you *bear* it?'

Drew watched in trepidation for Julie's reaction. Almost anybody would give way under such an approach, he thought. But the widow was serene. She pushed Della away slightly, with a flicker of distaste around the mouth. 'I'm surviving,' she said. Then she looked past Della to Bill, as if asking him to remove his annoying wife. He appeared to get the message, and took hold of Della's arm.

'It's good of you to come,' Julie said to him.

'Peter and I were old mates,' Bill said. 'I'm going to miss him.'

Cars began to draw up along the lane outside Drew's hedge. Maggs always put a sign out to indicate where people should park.

'Looks like quite a turnout,' she reported, at

five to three. 'Some members of the press, as well. I'm going to tell them to move their cars further down, to leave room for the proper mourners.'

Drew watched in admiration as she marched off, in her smart black funeral outfit, to issue her instructions. It seemed she was sufficiently authoritative: three cars moved jerkily down the lane in reverse to the spot she indicated.

Drew mobilised the bearers, and they carried the cardboard coffin at a respectable pace down the leafy country lane. Overhead were larks and rooks, chaffinchs and even a distant curlew. The bright green leaves of early summer filtered the sunlight onto the procession, and a sense of timelessness descended for a moment. Mixed as his feelings were towards the undue ritualisation of death, Drew enjoyed a pang of satisfaction at the way it was going.

The church service lasted a brief twenty minutes, with one hymn and a eulogy. Julie had elected not to speak, and nobody else had come forward. The vicar had at least known Peter, and much of what he said was apposite. A man of strong ideals, a go-ahead innovator, a pillar of the community and popular with everyone. That just about covers it, thought Drew.

Then they shouldered the coffin and retraced their steps. The procession behind seemed to straggle a little more this time, and the coffin felt considerably heavier. The people from the media were behaving well, hanging back and refraining from taking premature photographs or questioning the mourners. They'd probably get a bit more pushy when it came to the actual interment, Drew supposed. His natural burials still attracted considerable interest.

As they rounded the bend, Drew saw Karen and the four children in her care standing in the garden, watching their approach. His first reaction was to sigh inwardly with irritation. He'd *told* her he didn't want the children in evidence during a funeral. But then he remembered that Karen would have liked to attend the service, and had been prevented by Della's firm insistence that her boys were not to be in the main part of the action. Della would probably be considerably more irritated to see them there now, witnessing the latter part of the funeral.

If anything, the sun seemed even brighter as it began its slow decline to the west. They were sideways on to it, and Drew felt his arm and leg getting warm in the dark clothes, on that side. He heard again a lark over a grass field close by.

He glanced at Maggs sharing the front end of the coffin with him, wondering whether she was struggling with the weight. She seemed to have a knack of perching the corner on her shoulder in such a way that she could walk freely and balance it with only the lightest hold. She met his eye and winked. Behind them, the two volunteers were rocking the coffin slightly, as they fell out of step for a moment. Drew often thought it would be much safer for him and Maggs to take the rear, since there was less chance of the whole thing being dropped that way – but he also felt he should lead the procession, which meant being at the front.

It was impossible to look back. Sally Dabb had arrived late, and sat at the back of the church. Geraldine Beech had gathered her friends about her, and sung loudly. Drew could hear her voice now, three or four people back in the procession, but didn't know who she was talking to.

They were nearly there. Karen had come forward, almost hanging over the small gate from their front garden to the road. Stephanie was perched precariously on the garden wall, her head slightly lower than Karen's, and only two or three inches distant from it. Timmy was peering through the bars of the gate, but Finian and Todd were nowhere to be seen.

And then, without any ceremony or warning or fanfare, it happened. There was an explosive crack, from somewhere very close, and Karen gracefully keeled over backwards, releasing the gate as she did so. A silence that seemed to last forever was finally broken by Stephanie's scream.

'*Mummy!!*'

Ridiculously, Drew found himself unable to move. He couldn't just let go of the coffin. He couldn't put it down without the cooperation of the other three. He couldn't go to his wife, and yet it was the most absolutely necessary thing he had ever had to do.

Maggs took over. She twisted round to address the two men at the rear corners. 'Put it down!' she ordered. 'Now.'

Somehow they did it without turning the whole thing upside down. All around was a babble of confusion, but the only sound that Drew could hear was his daughter, wailing over and over, '*Mummy!*'

Karen could hear her child's screams, as if from a very long way off. She seemed to have somehow condensed into one small point of awareness, in which the image of one person's eyes was still before her, as well as Stephanie's frantic voice. The person who had shot her had first made eye contact with her, cool and unemotional and utterly treacherous.

There was no pain, no light or dark, no fear. She couldn't think or feel. She didn't say to herself, I must be dead, or even, I must go to

Stephanie. It was a place beyond reach, beyond all control, that she had retreated to. But she could still see those eyes and hear the screams.

Drew was almost as detached, in his own way. He folded Stephanie tightly into his arms, letting her cling to him, but wanting terribly to be with Karen. He still had no clear idea what had happened. All around people swirled and chattered, calling out and asking questions. He looked briefly for Timmy but soon gave up when the child was not immediately visible. The sky seemed to have gone dark, and he was cold. He hugged his little girl for warmth, and tried to force his mind to function.

Someone had shot Karen, but where was that person? Where was the gun? How could they not be standing there, unmistakable, in a cloud of black smoke, evil grin on their face? And yet nobody stood out. They just milled and pushed. Somebody took a flash photograph, which Drew felt as a searing blow both physically and emotionally.

Maggs seemed to be everywhere. She shouted at the photographer, who lowered his camera but didn't move away. Then she was kneeling beside Karen, and speaking loudly to someone. She pushed a woman away, and reached a hand to a different person.

'It's a head wound,' he heard her say. 'She's been shot in the head.'

And then, very strangely, there was a loud noise in the sky, and a sudden wind. Stephanie stiffened in his arms, turning her head this way and that. 'Helicopter!' she whispered.

Drew looked, then. 'Yes, helicopter,' he confirmed automatically. He still didn't know quite why, or how, but he felt something click into place inside him. He knew he wasn't to be allowed the luxury of paralysis. He was needed too urgently for that. He stood up with Stephanie still in his arms.

'Is she alive?' he asked Maggs.

'Oh yes,' came the sturdy reply. 'Breathing quite normally, and pulse not too bad.'

'But she's unconscious.'

'Yes.'

The crowd straggling along the lane and circling the abandoned coffin came to his notice. 'Oh, God – the funeral!' said Drew. Stephanie wrapped her arms around his head in consolation.

'That can wait,' Maggs asserted. 'They have to get Karen to hospital first. Lucky there was a helicopter on standby. Lucky we had somewhere for them to land.' She flashed him a reassuring smile and showed him her mobile phone, tucked into the waistband of her smart black trousers.

Even in the midst of catastrophe, Drew knew she'd scored a point.

'What happened, Maggs?' He had moved to stand beside Karen, but couldn't touch her because of his daughter. 'Wasn't there a shot?'

Maggs nodded again and swept the onlookers with a single gaze. 'One of them must have done it,' she said unemotionally.

'But they'd have to have had a gun on them. They'd be easy to spot.' It sounded completely foolish in his own ears.

'So you'd think,' she nodded. 'But it probably isn't as simple as that.'

Some of the crowd were in easy earshot. Julie Grafton was squatting beside her husband's coffin, one hand resting on it protectively. Della and her Bill had retrieved their children already. Drew thought he remembered seeing them both running from his back garden where Karen must have sent them to play. Almost absently, he saw that his own Timmy was holding Della's hand, as if content to let her be his mother in Karen's absence. Geraldine Beech was alongside Julie, as was the brother-in-law and the neighbour. Hilary Henderson and Mary Thomas were both in the same general area. The volunteer bearers seemed to think their role had been transposed into guardians of the coffin. Another twelve or fifteen people had retreated slightly, as if to differentiate themselves from the main players. Staring at them all, Drew focused again on Mary Thomas, with her long skirt. Something clicked inside him.

'Mary Thomas!' he gasped. 'It's her! It must be.' He looked at Maggs, eager to have her understand, but she'd gone.

Two men in odd uniforms were kneeling beside Karen, and Maggs had withdrawn to give them space. 'Husband?' one asked.

'That's me,' Drew supplied.

'What happened?'

'Someone shot her. Maggs said it was in the head.'

'Mummy,' Stephanie whimpered, heartbroken. Drew thought he'd preferred her screams.

'Mummy's going to be all right,' he assured her. 'They'll take her to hospital in the helicopter and make her better.' He almost believed it himself as he said it.

Deftly the paramedics produced a stretcher and lifted Karen onto it. Then they trotted briskly back to their air ambulance. Drew stared after them. 'Where will they take her?' he asked nobody in particular.

'I'll ask,' said Maggs, setting off in pursuit. The helicopter's engine was still idling, the rotor blades now motionless, but Maggs bent over, just the same. People always bent over when they were near a helicopter, thought Drew inconsequentially.

'What about the funeral?' came Julie Grafton's voice, the words bursting out as if no longer content to wait.

Drew turned to her. 'I don't know,' he said. 'I don't know what to do.'

'Can we do it ourselves?' asked the brother-in-law. 'I mean – you're not going to be in any state, are you.'

'Where are the police?' Drew demanded, then. 'There's just been an attempted murder. We ought not to touch anything. Everybody should stay where they are.' A sudden surge of rage swept through him. He wanted the person who'd done this to be caught and tortured and reviled and then executed very painfully. 'Who was it?' he shouted. 'Who did this to my wife?'

The sound of a car door slamming was followed quickly by two more. As if conjured by his words, uniformed police officers materialised from along the lane. And then another car engine became audible: one that Drew thought he recognised. Two minutes later, the tall figure of Den Cooper came into view.

'Den!' called Drew, thankfully. 'Oh, Den, it's good to see you.'

Maggs came stumbling back over the field and garden from the helicopter, evidently feeling exactly the same. Neither she nor Drew paid any attention to the policemen trying to make sense of the scene before them.

Den eyed the air ambulance, as it noisily lifted into the air, and then the coffin on the ground at his feet.

'Somebody shot Karen,' said Maggs. 'Somebody here. One of these people did it.'

'Hey! Steady on,' said Peter Grafton's brother. 'You don't know that. It could have been someone hiding behind the hedge, or one of the cars. With this crowd, you can't possibly know exactly what happened.'

'And where's the gun?' said the neighbour. 'There hasn't been time for anyone to dispose of a gun. We'd have seen them if they'd thrown it over a hedge. How could anybody do that without being *seen?*'

'Well, somebody did,' said Maggs flatly. 'Because Karen's got a bullet hole in her head. Unless you think it somehow fell out of an aeroplane up in the sky, or came from a gun with a range of half a mile.'

'Everybody's still here, I assume,' said Den. The two police officers were moving deftly from person to person, taking down names and addresses and brief statements. 'You'd have seen if anybody drove away.'

'Yes, I suppose they are,' Maggs agreed. 'Except

they could easily have *walked* away, back towards the church, then across fields, to a waiting car.'

'Do you know exactly who came to the funeral? Did you make a list?'

She shook her head. 'We hardly ever do that. I would think Julie knows who they all are. She was early, and watched everybody arrive. I counted thirty-eight, not including small children.'

Den's attention was mainly on the policemen. Another two cars arrived, parking ostentatiously in the middle of the road. The men who got out quickly began to run tape across the thoroughfare, preventing any through traffic. 'Good God, they can't do that!' said Maggs. 'Nobody's going to want to go the long way round, in and out of the village.'

Den just shrugged. 'They're going to have to,' he said.

Maggs was jigging on the spot, worrying about Karen, terrified for Drew and the children, angry at what had happened and embarrassed at the sudden abandonment of the funeral. It felt as if she ought to be in six places at once. Drew, she supposed, must be in an even worse state of indecision.

'I have to follow them to the hospital,' he was saying loudly to Della. 'Can you look after the kids for me? I ought to have gone with her in the helicopter.' He was holding himself tight, hands

269

on elbows, shoulders hunched, as if trying to cope with a sharp abdominal pain. He'd somehow managed to remove the clinging Stephanie and pass her to Della. He looked round. 'Maggs!' he called, as if she was much further away, 'Can you deal with things here?'

'Course I can,' she assured him.

'Just a moment, sir,' one of the policemen intercepted his jerky progress towards Karen's car. 'I need to speak to you for a few minutes first.'

'But . . .' Drew's eyes grew wilder. 'What if she *dies?* What if she dies when I'm not there?'

'Just two or three minutes, sir, and then we'll provide a vehicle for you. You might not be too safe to drive just now.'

'But then I wouldn't be able to get back. And the children will need me. And the funeral . . . oh God, the funeral.' He let go of his elbows and clutched both sides of his head instead. 'I keep forgetting the funeral.'

'That can wait, sir,' the policeman said calmly. 'It's unfortunate, but true, all the same. The lady . . .' he nodded towards Julie Grafton. 'She's being very understanding. Don't worry about that.'

'They'll do it themselves, Drew,' Maggs said. 'We've already got it sorted. They don't need us, really.'

Another wail from Stephanie distracted Drew

yet again. 'Wait a minute,' he said curtly to the policeman, and went to his daughter, where she was standing next to Della, the woman's arm around her shoulders, with the three little boys all clustered silently beside her. She looked like a symbolic statue of Motherhood. Her husband Bill was also part of the tableau, holding the hand of his son Finian. All the faces were white and expressionless. Except for Stephanie's which was red and enraged.

'Where's Mummy gone?' she demanded of Drew. 'What did they do to her?'

It occurred to Drew and Maggs simultaneously that the little girl might have actually seen who shot Karen. She had been level with Karen when it happened, facing the same way. If the person had been visible at all, then surely Stephanie must have witnessed the shooting. But if she had, wouldn't she have said? Wouldn't she have at least pointed to the individual in accusation?

Maggs acted first. She knelt down beside the child, and pulled her gently towards her. 'Steph, we'll have to let Daddy go and talk to these policemen, then they'll take him to be with your mummy. You and Timmy can stay here with Den. He'll play with you until Daddy gets back.' She glanced over her shoulder at her startled boyfriend. 'Isn't that right, Den?'

'Well . . .' he began, with a frustrated glance at the scene in the lane. 'I thought Della . . .'

'It's probably best if they stay at home,' Maggs said firmly. 'Della's going to have her hands full with her own boys. They look fairly shell-shocked to me.'

'Oh, well.' Den knew when he was beaten. 'I'll do my best.'

'Sir,' interrupted Drew's would-be interviewer. 'I really think we need to have a talk.'

But there was no real urgency in his tone. All the impatience was on Drew's side. So long as nobody left the vicinity, the questions and examinations could go on all day and all night, for all the police officers cared. They were, in any case, awaiting the arrival of a more senior officer, to make decisions and give instructions. Plus a photographer, although nobody believed there would be anything useful to record now. They had already exchanged muttered remarks, to the effect that they had to find the gun, prevent people disappearing and try to dispose of the obtrusive cardboard coffin – preferably in that order.

Maggs heaved a long steadying breath. The first shock was abating now. Things were beginning to settle down. She gave the crowd a hard look, examining the people one by one.

The first thing she noticed was the group of

three women, all oddly alike, standing together a little way removed from the rest. She knew their names: Geraldine Beech, Mary Thomas and Hilary Henderson. They were of a similar age, and there was an odd air of intimacy encircling the little tableau they made. Den followed her gaze.

'The three witches,' he murmured. 'Now I can see why they call them that.'

CHAPTER SIXTEEN

The police did not find the gun that had been used to shoot Karen. The bullet was removed from her head in an operation that lasted three hours, and which left the surgeons trembling and sweating. They had expected her to die under their probing forceps at any moment.

It was a .22 bullet, and although cautious about making premature assumptions, it was suggested that it came from a converted Brocock airgun. This is what Detective Superintendent Hemsley told Den Cooper on Thursday evening. 'There are quite a few of them around these days,' Danny said. 'It's not terribly difficult to convert, if you've got access to the machinery. It makes a legal airgun into a powerful weapon. And it makes life very hard for us: they're almost impossible to trace.'

'Well, I can't say I know anyone with a Brocock, converted or otherwise,' admitted Den. 'Not being very helpful, am I?'

'You were pretty prompt getting to the scene this afternoon,' Danny said.

'I was on my way anyhow. I dithered about whether to go to Grafton's funeral. You could say I was disgracefully late, in actual fact. I thought I'd hang back until it was mostly over, and then have a word with Maggs and Drew.'

'I dare say they were pleased to see you.'

Den heaved a sigh. 'I don't think they'd have been *pleased* about anything,' he said.

Investigations at the scene made little progress. It was always difficult when the victim hadn't died immediately, and therefore had to be whisked away to hospital. Not only was there no certain evidence as to how the body had fallen, where the direction of fire had come from, who had been in what position – there was also massive disturbance of potential forensic evidence. In this case, as with the murder of Peter Grafton, there had been milling people, jostling and shuffling, coming and going, leaving almost nothing to reveal precisely what had happened.

But this time, the mystery was even deeper. How could a person surrounded by others have drawn a weapon from a bag or pocket or waistband and directed it at Karen, fired it and subsequently hidden it, without being observed?

'Must have been more than one person involved,' was Detective Inspector Danny Hemsley's conclusion. 'Someone shielded the killer, and then took the gun and disposed of it in the confusion.'

'It wasn't in the ditch or the hedge,' came the definite report. Both had been exhaustively searched. So had the mourners, and their cars, before they'd finally been allowed to go home. But all the police officers knew that there had been many minutes before they'd arrived, in which the weapon could have been concealed. Anyone who wanted to could have walked away, come to that. If the shooting had been planned, then the opportunities for concealment and escape were plentiful. And if the killer had been someone uninvolved in the funeral, hiding in a field opposite the Slocombes' premises, he could have run off long before anybody could notice or apprehend him.

'Except it must have made quite a noise,' Hemsley remarked. 'Wouldn't you expect everyone to turn to the source of the sound? Wouldn't you think they'd know more or less where it came from? Why are they all so vague about that?'

One of his officers had relocated from

Birmingham, where shootings were more frequent. 'It echoes around, sir,' he said helpfully. 'And seems to come from all sides at once. Different people will tell you it came from entirely different directions, depending on where they were standing in relation to the shooter.'

'Like when you hear a car backfire,' added another. 'You can never be sure which vehicle it is, even if you're looking right at it. Funny, that.'

'Bloody frustrating,' grumbled Danny, thinking of the whole confused case.

But Den Cooper wasn't feeling frustrated. It was a collection of far hotter emotions. Rage, passionate anxiety for Karen, and an inescapable excitement at this startling new turn of events. Being with Danny gave a further twist – the warm sense of being part of a team, the throb of a headache from all the hard thinking, the fear of failure: it all came flooding back.

'Two different people to look for?' he suggested. 'Two different weapons used for the attacks, after all.'

Hemsley nodded, but he wore a dubious frown. 'Not so different,' he judged. 'But I still don't get how a person could fire a gun in a crowd without being seen. They certainly couldn't have sighted it properly. Not unless they were behind the hedge.'

'It's all about angles again, isn't it,' Den said.

'Have we got a report on that? The point of entry, I mean?'

Hemsley overlooked the *we,* but Den had heard it as soon as it left his mouth.

'It wasn't fully head on, as far as they can tell. But of course she could have turned her head to look down the road, and been hit in the middle of her forehead by someone standing at ninety degrees to her. Do you follow?'

'Perfectly. I don't suppose anybody was watching her when it happened?'

'Not with any degree of attention. Nobody's come up with anything so far, anyway. They're all too gobsmacked at how it could have happened.'

'If the gunman fired from the hip, or even chest, the angle would be upwards,' Den realised. 'Wouldn't it?'

'Yeah. But she was standing at the top of a few steps, already above the road. So we have to factor that in. It's all horribly imprecise.'

'Poor Drew,' Den sighed. 'He must be going through hell.'

Maggs would never have believed the strength of her feelings for Drew, until forced to face them. His grief and fear were ravaging her, making words like *sympathy* and *concern* laughably inadequate. And although she worked heroically to save him from having to think about the job or the house or the children, nothing could protect him from the terror he felt at the prospect of losing his wife.

Den in his turn was also afraid. Not for Drew, or even Maggs, but for himself. He knew himself to be lacking in some way, to be falling short of expectations. *If he can't make Karen better,* he could almost hear Maggs thinking, *then he should at least be able to locate her attacker. There should be* something *useful he can do.*

And so he understood where his main role lay. He had to continue to conduct his own investigation, either together with the police or independently, and never rest until the job was done.

Den knew a little about motives for murder, from repeated experience, and top of his list came 'Jealousy'. People could be jealous of a number of things: a preferred sibling, a good name, money, health – and it often made them mad enough to kill. It could spark a sudden rage, or creep up on you in a long slow burn. It could be mixed with pride or hatred or greed. It could disguise itself as something else. It could arouse a desire for revenge. Whatever form it might take, Den had learnt that it was an excellent place to begin when searching for a motivation in a killing.

Logically, it seemed right to begin with the

death of Peter Grafton. He and Maggs had agreed that Karen had most likely been shot because she had discovered the identity of Grafton's killer, whether wittingly or not. And he also agreed with Maggs that they'd both been dilatory in consulting Karen about the whole business. They'd given it less attention than they ought to have done, leaving her to carry the burden of witnessing the man's death as well as some aggravation afterwards from people like Mary Thomas. Along with all the other feelings, there was a simmering guilt on both their parts.

'She wanted to talk about it,' Maggs had said sadly. 'She knew the people involved. She wanted us to help her work out what was going on.'

'I went to see Mary Thomas,' he defended himself half-heartedly. 'But I let her sidetrack me into a lot of stuff about her sons. I don't think she was taking me very seriously.'

'So what now?' Maggs had wondered.

'We find the killer,' Den had said emphatically. 'Before anybody else has to go through what Drew's going through.' The depth of Maggs's gratitude was painful when he said that.

They'd drawn up a list of potential suspects. Everyone at the farmers' market, for a start. Maggie Withington, Joe Richards and Oswald Kelly were no more than names, gleaned only after Den had dropped into the Incident Room and cribbed from the notes on one of the whiteboards. 'Maggie sells bread, and Kelly sells ostrich meat,' he told Maggs. 'And Richards must be the man I bought our chops from. Very organic and very expensive.' Sally Dabb was in a category on her own. She had been too close to Grafton to be on a list of suspects for that killing, but she had as much opportunity as anybody else, when it came to the attack on Karen.

The list of those in the frame for killing Grafton had seven names on it: Geraldine Beech, Hilary Henderson, Mary Thomas, Sally Dabb's husband, Julie Grafton, Humphrey Thomas (son of Mary) and – because Den knew the police could not entirely rule this out – Karen Slocombe. Plus, of course, an unspecified number of people, who might have had unfathomed reasons to want Peter Grafton dead, and who could have lurked in the public lavatories with a crossbow.

'I know it's crazy,' Den agreed, when Maggs gave a shout of protest at the inclusion of Karen on the list. 'But they don't know her like we do. They only have her word for it that she was where she said, and saw the bolt strike. They're sure to think it at least possible that she invented it all as a cover for herself.'

'But *we* know she didn't,' Maggs insisted. 'Why is she on *our* list?'

'Just in the interests of completeness,'

he assured her. 'And because she was at the supermarket when that bomb went off.'

He should not have added this last remark. He knew he'd blundered as soon as the words were out. Maggs stared at him through narrowed eyes.

'You think there's a chance she shot Grafton!' she accused. 'Don't you?'

Den shook his head. 'No, really I don't. But there is a logical possibility. I was trained never to make assumptions, always keep an open mind. That's all I'm doing here.'

'But hardly any of these people could have popped into the loos and out again without someone noticing,' Maggs objected, realising as she said it that it was feeble. People were coming and going all the time, inevitably, and it would be hard to pin down witnesses who would swear to precisely who was where at the exact moment the bolt struck home.

A second perusal of the list confirmed that everybody on it, except for Sally's husband, Archie Dabb, had been at the funeral. 'And he might have been hiding behind the hedge,' Maggs pointed out. 'If we're aiming for a process of elimination, there's an awfully long way to go.'

Den had retained enough of his police training to know that close attention to the murder weapon would repay the time and trouble spent. He recalled Hemsley's cautious remarks about a 'Brocock conversion'. This was a new one on Den, and he was conscious of the deficiency in his understanding. As far as he could remember, a Brocock was a relatively harmless airgun, beloved by hobby shooters. He was very hazy about what a 'conversion' might entail.

'Look it up on the Internet,' Maggs suggested.

'They're not going to describe the whole process, in detail, are they?' he scoffed.

'You might be surprised.'

But when he'd logged on and done a search of the Web, he'd found nothing more than some plaintive statistics from a shooting webpage, claiming that Brococks were seldom converted, rarely implicated in criminal activity and undeserving of their bad reputation with the police.

'They would say that,' he muttered to himself, but he did wonder just how sure forensics could be that this was what they were dealing with. The bullet in Karen's brain was a .22, as Danny had already revealed. It would normally have been fired from a rifle, rather than an airgun. The conversion, he suspected, was not as simple as Hemsley had implied. If his assumptions were correct, it would need someone with a metal lathe to make and then insert some sort of sleeve, which could deal with the explosive 'rimfire' method of expulsion used for a .22 bullet, rather that the airgun which employed a gas. One practical consequence of this conversion was that firing the thing would produce a far louder noise than it would have done as an airgun.

But Den knew from experience that the entire community was full of people with very handy practical skills. They probably did have metal lathes, some of them, tucked away in their workshops or garages. They recycled as much as they could, turning unwanted objects into something useful. Karen took her lawnmower just down the road somewhere to be overhauled; Drew knew a chap who could provide metal nameplates occasionally for the coffins if the family demanded it. And wasn't Sally Dabb's husband some sort of mechanic? Den jotted a brief note beside the man's entry on his lists.

Den had phoned the Social Services office and told them he wouldn't be back until Monday at the earliest. They hadn't seemed concerned. That gave him three days to pursue his enquiries. Or two and a half now: already it was the middle of Friday and all he'd done so far was talk to Maggs and sit over his notepad, deep in thought.

Unfortunately, concentrated thought proved elusive. Images kept intruding of Karen undergoing brain surgery to remove a bullet, combined with Drew's ravaged expression and Stephanie's desolate wails. It was a calamity almost too huge to grasp. Like a boxer's punchbag, it kept swinging back and bashing him in the head. How was it *possible*? How could their own Karen have fallen victim in that way? What – what – *what* – had she seen or heard that made the killer strike her down so ruthlessly?

She'd spoken to Geraldine Beech and Hilary Henderson, according to Maggs. And had tried to visit Mary Thomas, to argue the point about the woman's presence at the supermarket. Den recalled his own session with the last-named, and came to a decision: he was going back to Cherry Blossoms in Ferngate, to speak to Mary Thomas again.

It was as if she'd been expecting him. Before he could reach the front door, she had thrown it open and was standing waiting for him, unsmiling and pale. Her small eyes had shrunk even further into her head, and her hair was wild. Her clothes looked strange, too. In place of the long skirt there were tight jeans, which he could see were not properly fastened at the waistband. A wedge of flabby beige flesh protruded, clearly visible beneath the incompletely buttoned shirt she wore over the jeans. She seemed entirely unaware of the figure she presented.

'Hello,' she said. 'Come in, will you?'

He ducked through the doorway and followed

her down the spacious hall. They went into a large square room, with a high ceiling and polished antique furniture. Who, he wondered, did the polishing? It didn't strike him as something Mary Thomas would do herself.

She made him sit down in a leather armchair, and then perched tensely on the edge of a sofa opposite.

'How's Karen?' she asked. 'That poor girl! Her poor husband!'

Den shook his head. 'I haven't heard anything since early this morning. She was still unconscious then.'

'Have they caught anybody?'

This, he felt, did not do her justice. It was obviously a silly question, for several reasons.

'I doubt it,' he said with a brief lift of one eyebrow.

'You're not working with the police, are you?'

Another daft remark. What was the matter with the woman? 'No,' he said. 'Of course I'm not.'

'So what *are* you doing?'

'Trying to help my friends. Drew Slocombe is my girlfriend's business partner. It's almost like family. I need to know why Karen was singled out, why it happened.' He stopped himself, hearing the edge of violence in his own voice. He discovered that his fists were tightly clenched, and forced them to loosen.

'We all need to know that,' said Mary Thomas quietly.

'Have the police interviewed you?'

'Again, you mean? Oh yes. But they didn't take me in for questioning this time. They searched me for a gun in the road yesterday, and asked me exactly where I was standing, where I thought the shot came from, whether I knew who might wish to harm Karen, how this might connect to the killing of Peter Grafton. They asked everybody the same things. I thought you were there? They presumably asked you, as well?'

He frowned at her. 'Not really. I didn't arrive until it was all over.'

'Didn't you? Well, well. It just shows how unobservant I am, doesn't it.'

'Drew's a very good bloke,' Den said softly. 'He didn't deserve this.'

'You think I'd argue with that?' She leant towards him. 'You think I don't admire him, wish him well, regard him as one of the best people I know? I promise you, that's how I feel towards the Slocombes.' She heaved a deep sigh, and he thought her close to tears. 'Drew Slocombe sets the sort of example we've been dreaming of for years. Most of what's good about this community is exemplified in what he's doing. We *rejoice* in him.'

'We?' Den asked, feeling rather overwhelmed.

'Geraldine and Hilary and me, and the others. We've been trying to show people how to live for years now, struggling the whole time against the tide of commercialism and greed and sheer stupidity. We were gaining ground, in spite of everything. Trying to keep the wretched farmers afloat, through the horrors of foot and mouth, and government apathy and consumer blindness. Trying to get people to stop wasting so much, and to understand what it means to live more simply. We were getting there. The tide was beginning to turn. And then . . .'

'Yes? Then what?' he prompted her.

'Then it all started to go wrong.' She looked away, rubbing one ear. 'Starting with Peter Grafton.'

Den knew better than to hope she was about to tell him chapter and verse of who and why and how, but he couldn't avoid a sudden lift in his expectations.

'Tell me about it,' he invited.

She told him quite a lot over the next half hour, concerning the establishment of the farmers' markets, the ideological enthusiasm of the participants, the sense of being involved in something important and promising. And then the slow onset of disappointment and disillusion. One by one the stallholders came to accept that they were playing at the very fringes of real food provision. Nobody, absolutely *nobody* relied on their wares for their staple shopping.

But the individuals concerned were not the type to give up. They were determined to change the way people thought about food. In various ways they diversified, and promoted their point of view.

'We go into schools, you know, and get ourselves into the media. We criticise the intensive farms, battery hen units, use of pesticides. We never rest.'

Den nodded ruefully. 'I know,' he said. 'Drew and Maggs talk about it all the time, too.'

'And still it never feels as if we're getting anywhere. So, a few months ago, things began to crack. Compromises, fighting talk, just a general impatience to win through. The language changed. I remember Hilary saying "It's war" and thinking she was right. It was time we stopped trying to be sweet and cuddly and kind, because that wasn't working.'

'So you put a bomb in SuperFare?' Den asked, unable to believe it possible.

'No, no,' she waved a dismissive hand.

But Den noticed she didn't meet his eye as she made her denial. 'So who did?'

'I really don't know. Someone from outside. It couldn't have been one of our Food Chain group.'

'And you still say you weren't there when it happened?'

'I was not there.' She shook her head regretfully. 'That was such a disaster, Karen practically bumping into . . . my sister.'

Den guffawed rudely. 'Don't tell me; your *twin* sister?'

Mary Thomas widened her eyes offendedly. 'Yes, as it happens. She's called Simone Baxter, and lives in Bristol. Twins run in the family.'

'Does anybody around here know about her?' He was still deeply suspicious.

'Hardly anybody. It's a long and rather sad story, as they usually are, I suppose. My mother had three children already, when she was expecting us. There wasn't much money, my father was in poor health, my older brother was getting into trouble for lack of attention. She never dreamt she was having twins, and the shock was terrible. As it happened, she had a friend who knew a couple who were desperate for a child. These things happened fairly commonly in those days. A private adoption was arranged, and Simone was taken to live in Vancouver. She had a happy childhood, on the whole, despite a constant sense of something missing. I had that same feeling.' She gazed at the floor for a long moment.

'Then Simone found us again. When she was about thirty-five, shortly before Mother died.

It was all quite awkward, and we never could make up for all the lost time, but gradually she and I became good friends. She moved to Bristol three years ago, and – in the way these things often happen – she became very involved and active in food politics. We discovered we shared an outlook on life, moving along much the same tracks. She's extremely good at organisation and motivating people.'

'And your friends – Geraldine and Hilary – have they met her?'

Mary smiled. 'Oh, yes,' she said. 'They've met her all right. It's funny – people never really believed me at school, when I said I'd had a twin. It was no secret in the family, you see. But neither did my parents broadcast it. So when she reappeared I wasted no time in introducing her to them.'

Den had nothing to say to that. The sudden introduction of a twin sister felt like playing dirty. It was cheating, and he found himself chafing at it. Besides, he suddenly realised, a woman raised in Vancouver was unlikely to be mistaken for Mary Thomas, the moment she opened her mouth.

CHAPTER SEVENTEEN

Maggs was learning more than she could ever have guessed about living through a crisis. Drew's anguish was like a heavy chainmail garment weighing down on her shoulders, making everything she did ten times slower and more complicated. She wanted to assure him that everything would be all right – but didn't dare in case it wasn't. It occurred to her that it would have been easier if Karen had been killed outright, and then upbraded herself for the terrible thought. People telephoned, to the house and the office, asking for news, offering condolences, wanting to help. Drew spoke to a few of them, but in a daze. Maggs took most of the calls, when she wasn't trying to produce food for the children or keep them amused. The business was put on hold, though fortunately no new funerals presented themselves.

Della had not suggested she take the children, which seemed a bit off to Maggs. She said as much to Drew. 'I wouldn't have let them go to her, anyway,' he said vaguely. 'I want them here with me. And we were a bit churlish with her yesterday, when she did offer to have them. She might feel disgruntled.'

'But you might have to rush off – to the hospital, I mean.'

'So? You can stay with them, can't you?' Neither of them was really thinking about what they were saying. Maggs would normally have told him to get a grip, but under these circumstances, she hadn't the heart.

The hospital had sent him home late the previous evening, and told him they'd be doing tests next morning. 'Leave it until later in the day,' they told him. 'Bring the children if you want to.'

'They said I could take the kids,' he remembered. 'So nobody needs to mind them. I'm going after lunch.'

'Will you take them both?'

He let his unfocused gaze rest on his children, first one, then the other. 'I don't know. What will it do to them? I don't know. There's a policeman stationed outside her room, you know. That would seem strange to the kids.'

'They're worried somebody will have another go?' The thought was chilling.

'Well, they have to cover themselves,' he said, as vaguely as before.

Maggs hated his empty eyes, his drifting gaze. 'Drew, you do look awful. Shouldn't you go and lie down or something? You've probably got traumatic stress, or whatever it's called. Pretend you're one of your own patients, from when you were a nurse.'

He shook his head. 'It doesn't work. You'd think I could deal with it, wouldn't you? I've seen the worst things that can happen – but then I think, there can't be anything worse than this. If she'd died, it wouldn't be as bad.'

Stephanie looked up at him, her face pinched and pale. 'Is Mummy dead?' she asked.

Drew groaned. 'No, sweetheart. But she's very poorly, and she can't wake up. She's asleep all the time.'

Stephanie pushed a thumb into her mouth and frowned. 'Same as being dead,' she decided, indistinctly. Maggs was tempted to agree with her. Dead without the funeral, she thought wryly.

'They might have the results of some of the tests,' Maggs suggested. 'It might be good news.'

'I keep seeing it, over and over again. The

coffin on my shoulder, the shot, Steph's screams. All night, it just kept on replaying, the whole thing. I've never had that happen before. I couldn't stop it. I can't think about anything else. Poor Karen!' He ran his fingers through his hair in a parody of distractedness.

Maggs went to him, and laid a hand on his shoulder. 'Phone them first, see how she is, before you decide about taking the kids,' she advised.

He shuddered. 'I'm scared of what they might say,' he mumbled. 'Will you do it?'

So she did, and was told they would only disclose information to the next of kin. Drew listened shakily for less than a minute, and replaced the receiver. 'Nothing conclusive, they said,' he reported. 'No significant change. Why do they use such horrible language?'

Maggs could feel a headache beginning. She who never had headaches was succumbing now. It throbbed. She wanted to go away and lie down. She wanted Den, because he was tall and strong and familiar. But she also wanted to wrap her arms round Drew and cradle him better, to let him cry if he wanted to, and be weak and small and miserable. The two men in her life had their similarities – a shared outlook on the world, a core of decency – but in personality they were very different. Drew had chosen to work with death because the dead were no trouble.

They were the safest kind of people you could find, and their grieving families were usually straightforward, too. The dying might have been messy or shocking or agonising, but by the time they reached Drew they were past all that. And Drew needed things to be safe, Maggs had realised early on. He coped badly with the contradictions and misbehaviours of ordinary life. He needed approval and affection and gratitude.

Den wasn't like that at all. He was dogged in the face of hostility, seldom taking it personally as Drew would. He let people's troubles wash over him, and stood there like a pillar of stone until the turmoil subsided. He knew that life was rarely tidy, that good intentions were not enough, that anybody was capable of dreadful deeds. He knew it, and accepted it as the way things were. He had joined the police out of a wish to keep things as straight as possible. To prevent crime where he could, to identify criminals and apprehend them. He was kind and patient and sometimes slow. His brain was not given to flashes of insight or intuition, as Maggs believed hers to be. He thought carefully before coming to any conclusion. Maggs sometimes wondered whether he would ever have managed to leave the police if Drew hadn't made him see how much he wanted to.

Except that now she wasn't so sure that he *had*

really wanted to at all. He'd been in a period of gloom, shared by much of the rural population, lonely, pessimistic and stagnant. Something had had to change, and with unprecedented decisiveness, he'd given in his notice.

And in amongst all the pain and panic of the previous day, Maggs had permitted a question to enter her head: was Den now wishing he'd never left?

'I love Drew, you know,' Maggs said. There was something exhilarating in uttering the words, knowing Den would want her to be frank, whatever the effect on him.

'I know you do,' he said. 'I do too.'

'We're all quite special, aren't we? The four of us. We've got a bond.'

'Definitely.' They were snuggled together on the shabby sofa they'd bought in an auction sale. Den had told her some of his conversation with Mary Thomas, and she was obsessing about Drew and Karen.

'I don't think I should have left them,' she worried. 'He's not really in any state to be in charge of those kids.'

'They'll be OK,' he assured her. 'And he can call Della if there's a problem.'

'There doesn't seem to be much sign of Della. She's probably one of those people who hates to be around when there's trouble. She scooted off fast enough yesterday, flapping about the effect on her boys.'

'They did seem quite upset, I noticed.'

'They were more worried about Stephanie than Karen, I think. Steph was making such a noise.'

'Poor little thing. It's going to take a lot of committed TLC to get her back on track.'

'You sound like a social worker,' she accused. 'Which reminds me—' she hesitated.

'What?'

'Well, I was wondering . . . you know how you've got into this murder investigation, talking to Mary Thomas and people?'

'Ye-e-es.'

'Well, I was wondering whether you're sorry you ever left the police. I mean, you seem to be wishing you were still doing it – still a detective, trying to solve the crime.'

'Maggs,' he took her chin gently in his long fingers, 'police work isn't all murder investigations. It's sitting all day staring at a computer screen, or slogging round hundreds of houses asking the same questions over and over. Or letting a known criminal go because you know you'll never find enough hard evidence against him. Loads and loads of grotty stuff like that, which grinds you down, wears you out –

and still nobody likes you at the end of it.'

'But you do like it when there's a murder, don't you?' she grinned.

'Yes,' he admitted. 'I like it when there's a murder. I want the killer caught, because they've committed the ultimate wicked deed. Oddly enough, they often seem to *want* to be caught, in a way. The guilt's too much to carry for some of them.'

'Maybe they get flashbacks, like Drew. Do you think they do?'

'Is Drew getting flashbacks?'

'Something like that. Seeing Karen falling over, hearing the shot, again and again.'

'Poor chap. Well, yes, I expect murderers do get them, as well. The decent ones, anyway. The ones who only do it once.'

'How about twice?'

'Well,' he cuddled her up closer, 'I expect they find it easier the second time. Much less traumatic.'

'Are we thinking the same person shot Peter Grafton and Karen?'

'We're keeping an open mind.'

'What does Danny think about you meddling in his investigation?'

'He's not particularly happy about it, but I've made a few promises, which helped. Obvious things like telling him everything I think is 'relevant, and not putting myself in danger.'

'So you told him about Mary T's twin, did you?'

'I did. I'll tell you more about that in a minute.'

'Ooh! Is it exciting?'

'Mildly. But let me tell you everything in the right order. Starting with this afternoon.'

'As you like,' she dimpled compliantly. 'And what did you do this afternoon?'

'This afternoon I went to talk to Mrs Geraldine Beech,' he disclosed. 'And after that I went to have a word with Hilary Henderson, the honey lady.'

Maggs sighed contentedly. 'Tell me all about it,' she said.

Geraldine Beech had been difficult. 'You're not with the police, are you?' she'd challenged, on the doorstep. 'What right do you have to come and cross-examine me, when you're just an ordinary member of the public?' Her scowl would have made King Kong quail.

'I'm not planning to cross-examine you. I've just come for a chat, as someone very much concerned about what's been happening. The investigating officer knows I'm here, if that makes you feel better. But in any case, I'm not contravening any laws. People are allowed to talk to each other, you know.' He'd deliberately kept his tone mild, as if it didn't much matter whether she talked to him or not.

She didn't respond verbally, but the frown relented slightly.

'Karen Slocombe is a friend,' he pressed on. 'I'm extremely upset at what happened to her yesterday. This is supposed to be a close supportive community. Doesn't that mean we ought to talk to each other?'

'She was my friend too,' the woman said. 'I mean *is*.' She opened the door wider to let him through.

The house was spare, with stone floors and neutral cream-painted walls. Pine furniture predominated in the room she led him to. It seemed to be part dining room, part study, with a big table and a desk strewn with papers. There was a large rug covering part of the stone-tiled floor. The temperature was the same as outdoors, with a window thrown wide open and obviously no heating turned on.

'So?' she challenged him, as they sat at right angles to each other at one corner of the table. 'What shall we talk about?'

'I've just come from Mary Thomas,' he said. 'She told me a lot of the background – how you and she have been friends for decades, and are both very committed to the Food Chain group, and the whole thing about local food being so important.'

'Right,' she nodded, with little sign of interest.

'And how it began to go wrong. People compromising, breaking rules, backsliding.' He was deliberately employing more emotive language than Mary had, trying to get a reaction.

'Human nature,' she said. 'There weren't any real problems.'

'But you haven't been making the headway you hoped for, have you? The farmers' markets are still just a sideline. They make good material for Radio 4 programmes, and that's about it. They're not having any real impact on anybody's shopping habits.'

'It isn't just the markets. It's the boxes and the educational stuff, and the networking. We've come an *enormously* long way, if you think back just five or six years. Every town has a farmers' market now. Everybody knows, even if they don't translate it into action, that the supermarkets are a disgrace. They know their town centres have become mausoleums, zombified by the out of town shopping centres . . .' She stopped, and smiled wryly. 'Well done, lad. You pressed the button there, didn't you.'

Den laughed. 'Bingo!' he said gently. 'It wasn't very difficult.'

'But what's it got to do with Karen and Peter Grafton? That's the next question, isn't it?'

'There's something about Grafton selling his apple juice to a supermarket group – is that right?'

She clenched her jaw for a fleeting moment, and her hands tightened where they lay on the table. 'How did you know about that?'

'His wife said something to Drew and Maggs. Is that why he was shot?'

She gave a weak smile. 'I have absolutely no idea,' she said flatly. 'I don't know who killed him, or how, or why. I was as horrified as everybody else. If you think about it, it was extremely bad news for me, and for everything I feel passionate about. The markets are tainted by it, the whole community losing confidence in its way of life, suspicion and mistrust growing up like weeds. It's a horrible, awful thing. And I do not know who did it.' She fixed glittering eyes on his, and he believed her.

It was three o'clock when he drove up the track to the Hendersons' farm. He had given them no advance warning, and was not sure what to expect in terms of their reaction. But he had visited many a farm in his time, and knew that the workers were likely to be in for some tea within the next hour or so. There was a milking herd, and most people started afternoon milking at around four, though he'd known some who left it till six or later. The farmer's wife, the matriarch, the provider of tea, was a dying breed, rather like vicars' wives, but Hilary had struck him as a good old-fashioned example of the stereotype. She worked her socks off, both on and off the farm, another active member of Geraldine's Food Chain. But she was almost certain to be around at this time of day.

And she was. As he pulled into the farmyard, he glimpsed her going into a barn, wearing a red-checked man's shirt and tight jeans in a glaring imitation of Mary Thomas. Did they agree each morning on what to wear, or was it some sort of female telepathy? He didn't know Mrs Henderson well; couldn't even remember speaking to her, but he knew her by sight. He waited for her to notice his arrival, knowing she must have heard the car and was deliberately ignoring it until she'd done whatever she wanted to in the barn.

He sat patiently until she came back, two minutes later. Then he unfolded his considerable length from the driver's seat and stood waiting for her.

'You're the ex-policeman,' she told him, rubbing something yellow off her hands. 'What can I do for you?'

'Den Cooper,' he said, proffering his hand.

She looked down at hers and grinned. 'Better not,' she said. 'This is fairly poisonous stuff. Some patent herbal concoction to prevent fly strike in sheep. You have to mix it up yourself. I don't suppose it'll work.'

'Are you organic here?' he asked doubtfully.

'No, no. We've no patience with all that. But I'll try anything once. I remember my grandad used to say linseed oil was about the best thing for fly strike. That's one ingredient of this potion. Come on in, and I'll give myself a wash.'

He followed her into a huge farm kitchen that was as different as possible from Geraldine's stark room. There were four or five ancient hairy armchairs, some with sagging seats, prolapsing onto the floor beneath. Crocheted blankets were thrown over them, all colourless with mud and hair. Three shaggy farm dogs lay on makeshift beds around the room. The small window was closed and the Aga was obviously going full blast, even in mid May. The only similarity with Geraldine's place was the big table. A colossal old table dominated the room. Mountains of papers had accumulated at one end, leaving about two thirds available for eating. It was covered with a flower-patterned oilcloth. Along one worktop were massed about a hundred empty glass jars. Den remembered that Hilary sold honey at the farmers' markets. 'Taking your honey off soon?' he asked.

'I'm hoping for some in a week or two,' she nodded. 'They've had a mild winter, so I think there'll be some. It's always extra good this time of year, provided they haven't found any oilseed rape, of course. I *hate* it when they bring that back. Revolting stuff. It should be banned.'

'They're testing some GM versions, I gather?' he said. 'Up in Scotland, I think. Protesters have been tearing it out.'

'So I hear,' she said noncommittally, before adding, 'Bloody fools.'

'Who? The protesters or the people who grow it?'

'The idiots who invented it in the first place. Monsanto and their friends. People think they've stopped, because the media haven't been following up the story – as usual. But they're at it as much as ever. Trying to destroy us all for the sake of a bit of money. It makes me so *sick*.'

Den pondered the way these women were all so easily prompted to reveal their ardent feelings about food. It was as if they thought of nothing else, as if they were overflowing with zeal and commitment, and could never resist talking about it. Where, he wondered, had it all begun?

'You obviously feel as strongly as the others do about it,' he remarked.

'Others?' She was pouring boiling water into a big brown teapot, without checking whether he'd like a drink.

'Geraldine Beech and Mary Thomas, to name two,' he said.

She turned towards him, her expression hard to read. 'They're not just any two, though. They're *the* two. With me, they're the core of the whole thing. We started it all. We've known each other forever, you see.'

'So I understand.'

'Mary went away for a while, in her twenties. And Geraldine went to university, clever thing. But we've been back here together for thirty years or so now. Funny how time works.' She gazed dreamily out of the grimy window. 'It's not really a continuum, you know. It's a *package*. That's how it feels. Everything that's happened is still right *here*.' She smacked herself on the chest. 'It all still matters just as much as it ever did, and it's all remembered. At least, between us we remember everything.'

'And you've never fallen out? Three can be a very awkward number.'

'We've argued – passionately at times. We've taken breaks from each other. But we never really fell out, no. We made the pact, you see, in 1960.

307

We were eighteen. We all loved the village – villages, I should say. The five villages, we called them. Anyway, we had this ideal of preserving what we loved about this whole area. Very old-fashioned we must have been back then. Country girls, in love with the fields and rivers and hills. We knew the wild flowers and birds and trees. We read Laurie Lee and Thomas Hardy and Agatha Christie. We didn't hanker for the city life at all. We despised girls who wore make-up and got excited about clothes and pop music. We were above all that.'

Den tried to imagine it, and failed. 'You were lucky to have each other,' he realised.

'Yes!' She almost applauded him. 'That's *absolutely* right. If there'd only been one of us, it would never have stuck. But three is a powerful number anyway, and we gave each other strength. And it wasn't really so difficult. We had all enjoyed happy childhoods, with freedom and good schooling and security. We were golden girls. We were really only unusual in realising our good fortune. And, of course, the world just confirmed our opinions, more and more, as time went by. The whole direction that society took was opposite to what we wanted. So it was easy to feel like campaigners and martyrs to the cause. We were lone voices in a great wilderness, and that's a thrilling feeling.'

'And now it's turning back your way,' he suggested.

'Well, not really. Or only in small pockets. For most people, the powers of darkness are completely in control. They are ignorant, materialistic, miserable, city-bound morons. But locally – *here* – we prevailed. We deliberately set out to do what we did, and now, in the year we all reach sixty, we feel we can congratulate ourselves.'

'Except that there's been a murder. Possibly two murders,' he said.

'Yes.' She plonked the heavy teapot down in front of him, as if suddenly unable to hold it. 'Yes. And it might have wrecked the whole thing. We might yet find everything we've worked for crashing down.' She blinked rapidly. 'And we might be too old to build it all back up again.'

Den sipped the tea, and patted one of the dogs that had ambled over to him. There was something enormous in what Hilary Henderson had just told him. Something heroic, almost cosmic. Three women fighting to maintain values and attitudes from the fifties in the face of twenty-first century ways. What did they think about computers, he wondered. And there must be other modern gadgets that would cause them to feel threatened. Probably, though, they would have answers for everything. The crime rate would be due to working mothers, and the typical

309

family's greed for material possessions. Pollution and levels of waste were due to ignorant and lazy lifestyles, where the connection between the source and the consumption of goods was lost. Institutions failing to provide effective services in terms of health, law enforcement, education, transport – all could be traced, he supposed, to the increased desire to acquire wealth. Everything seemed to come back to that, if you looked at life through Hilary's spectacles.

Except Hilary didn't wear spectacles. At sixty she looked to be in her late forties. Good skin, straight back, strong wiry hair. She could obviously see and hear and move as well as she ever could. If she was well-covered with flesh, that seemed to be all part of a general air of well-being.

'So you don't know who killed him?' he said.

'No, I don't know who killed him. And I don't know why. And I don't know whether it was a friend or a foe.'

Den raised his eyebrows.

'I mean, someone who thought they were doing us a favour in some way. We do attract a few oddballs, you see. Inevitably, these days, when the only groups who embrace the values we've been upholding are young hotheads, very inclined to take the violent path. Direct action, they call it, and in many ways I completely approve of them. But there's an unpredictable element. Some of them aren't very stable, or very bright. They don't think through what they're doing. Still, they're probably our best hope, so I wouldn't dismiss them.'

'But you think someone like that could have shot Peter?'

'It's the only thing I can think,' she said.

He called in on Detective Inspector Hemsley on his way to collect Maggs from North Staverton, and tried to convey everything he felt was relevant.

'Ah! Here comes my friendly local informant!' Danny greeted him jovially. 'What priceless leads have you brought me?'

Den waited until they were settled into one corner of the Incident Room, with screens on two sides. Then he summarised his day. Hemsley kept an eye on his computer, which seemed to be searching or collating. Hemsley made pencilled notes on a pad in front of him, but on the whole, Den had the impression that he was not producing anything new in his account of his day.

Except for the mention of Mary Thomas's twin sister Simone. Hemsley narrowed his eyes at that. 'Let's see, then,' he muttered, tapping at his keyboard. 'What's her surname, do you know?'

'Baxter,' Den said, trying to remain casual.

'Good. Let's see then . . . Hmmm.' He tapped

and waited, tapped again repeatedly at the Down arrow, until the screen produced something of interest. 'Oh, look! Mrs Simone Baxter, born 1942, Royal Victoria Hospital, Garnstone, original name of Marianne Simone Weston. Conviction in 1994 for riotous behaviour, suspended sentence. Arrested again the next year, but released for lack of evidence. Criminal damage to a grocery outlet. Retained on list of potential troublemakers regarding damage to GM crops, foodstores and similar. Well, there you are!'

Den chewed his lip. 'Marianne?' he queried. 'Isn't that a bit odd? Calling your twins Marianne and Mary?'

'People do odd things like that,' Danny shrugged. 'And maybe the adopting parents named her, anyway. Can't see any grounds for concern there, myself.'

'See if there's anything for Mary Weston, then. Born the same day and place.'

'There won't be. She hasn't got a record. We already ran a check on her. Like we did on Mrs Beech, and the Henderson woman. And all the other stallholders.'

'Including Karen?' Den already knew the answer to that.

'Including your Karen Slocombe,' the Inspector confirmed.

* * *

Wearily, Den regaled Maggs with the whole of the day's events. She listened with impressive attention, prompting him when he seemed to be falling asleep.

'So you don't think any of those three did it?' she summed up when he finally finished.

'I can't see it. They all seemed so straight. Very different from each other in most ways, but with this burning *mission*. You have to admire them.'

'And what does your friend Danny think?'

'I don't know,' he admitted. 'I don't think he found me of much use really.'

'But the best bit is the twins,' Maggs enthused. 'That's wonderful.'

'Why?'

'Because it's obviously not true,' she laughed. 'There's no such person as Simone Baxter. Mary Thomas made her up. *She's* the one who got picked up for rioting and smashing shop windows. I bet you anything.'

Den shook his head. 'She's on Danny's computer as a separate person,' he said.

Maggs raised her eyebrows. 'Is she? I thought you told me there wasn't anything for Mary?'

Den rubbed the side of his face, long fingers resting on the long cheek. 'So I did,' he said. 'Well – I wonder . . .'

CHAPTER EIGHTEEN

Drew awoke on the Saturday morning to a small voice in his ear, whispering, 'Daddy? Daddy! Wake up.'

Frantically, as if electrocuted, he hurled himself out of bed, almost landing on top of his little daughter. 'What? What?' he croaked.

Stephanie laughed at him. 'You fell out of bed,' she mocked. 'Silly you.'

He sat on the floor comically for a moment, enjoying her amusement. 'Why did you wake me up? What time is it?'

She gazed at him patiently, without reply.

'Let's see. Quarter past eight. Goodness, that's quite late, isn't it? Are you hungry?'

'Timmy is. He's crying.' Drew realised there was a background sound of grizzling from the children's room.

'We'd better sort him out then,' Drew said, noticing that now his heart rate was slowing slightly, he seemed to be feeling rather better than he had the previous day. The wakening flood of terror about Karen was yielding to a more normal concern for his children. They had to be fed and dressed and reassured and amused. He had to phone the hospital, and plan the day. And there'd be people phoning him. Karen's mother was threatening to come and help, which considering she'd only visited them three times in two years was a bit rich. Numerous friends and relations were making persistent offers of various kinds. Responding to them yesterday had been too much, and Maggs had done most of it. Today he felt much more ready to enlist all the support he could find.

Soon all three were dressed and making toast. 'Is Mummy coming home today?' Stephanie asked carefully. Drew could see the conflict going on inside her. The need to have an answer fighting with the knowledge that Drew did not like questions about Karen.

'No, not today,' he said. 'I don't know when. We'll just have to wait and see.'

Timmy, who the day before had remained remarkably unperturbed by events, now seemed to have realised something was badly wrong. He continued to grizzle, acting like a baby, turning his face away from all offers of food. Although irritated, Drew felt a sort of relief at the normality of the behaviour. 'Come on, Tim,' he urged. 'Be a good boy.'

He knew he should phone the hospital for a report of Karen's condition. But the fact that they had not phoned him did at least mean she was still alive, and also that no miraculous recovery had taken place. He was in no hurry to hear the flat unemotional phrase, 'No change'.

The doorbell rang just before nine. Stephanie turned wide eyes towards the hall, and Drew understood how nervous she was, after so many shocks.

'I wonder who that can be,' he said cheerfully. 'Somebody nice, I expect.'

It was, greatly to his surprise, Julie Grafton. The widow whose husband's funeral he had so utterly abandoned halfway through. The widow who had in the end been forced to oversee the burial herself – and who had done it with total dignity, according to Maggs afterwards.

'Drew,' she said, her voice full of feelings, rich with emotion. 'How are you?'

She looked composed, even strong. Clothes all straight and clean, hair nicely brushed, face free of tears or shadows.

'I'm just about surviving,' he said, wishing he could lean his head on her shoulder.

'Let me come in and give you a hand,' she ordered. 'It must be awful for you. Is there any news about Karen?'

'I haven't called them yet. They'd have been in touch if there was any change.'

'I feel terrible about it, you know,' she said, again surprising him.

'You do? But why?'

'Because it seems obvious that she was shot because of Peter. I mean, she has to have known something, seen something, which the killer wanted to stop her from reporting. That is obvious, isn't it?'

Drew blinked. 'I don't know,' he said. 'I hadn't thought about it.'

'But whoever it is must be ever so clever. How did they hide the gun? How did they manage it, in the middle of a crowd of people, and nobody saw them?'

'You didn't see anything?'

She shook her head. 'I was right behind the coffin. All I could see was my brother-in-law's back, and Steve, next to him. I had my head bent, mostly, just watching the ground as I walked along. I think probably most people were the same. You do, don't you? I mean, I've never done it before, but I'm sure most people fold their hands in front of them and walk with bowed heads in a funeral procession. At least they don't stare all around them or watch each other. It's not the way it's done.'

She was speaking breathlessly as if pent-up thoughts were tumbling out almost faster than she could voice them.

'So it seemed to me that the person with the gun must have been right at the back of the line. And we should be able to work out who that was.'

'Did you say that to the police?'

'No, no. I hadn't thought it through at all then. And they weren't really listening to me, because it was Peter's funeral. They were very embarrassed, poor things.'

'Well, who do you think was at the back?' His flickering attention was caught, if only for a few moments.

'I have no idea,' she admitted. 'Not family. Probably not the Food Chain people. Someone who felt they were only peripheral; there were one or two I didn't know. Hangers-on, or friends of his that I hadn't met. But between us you and I could surely come up with a complete list. We'll have to for the police, anyway.'

'OK.' He ran a hand through his hair. 'I'll have to think.'

'I don't mean now,' she assured him. 'I've come to see if I can help you with the children. I could stay with them if you wanted to go and see

Karen. If you haven't got somebody already?'

'Well . . .' He stared helplessly at her. 'They don't *know* you. I was thinking, probably Della would have them. They go to her twice a week, you see. They'd feel comfortable with her. Except it's Saturday, and I think she usually goes off to see her mother or somebody most weekends. The whole family goes. We see them driving past at about midday on Saturdays.'

'Routines,' Julie scoffed. 'Surely they could give it a rest in an emergency like this. But it doesn't matter – I'm here now. They'll soon get to know me. I'm good with kids.'

Drew's natural curiosity flickered into life. 'You never had any?'

Her smile was twisted. 'We were trying,' she said bleakly. 'Been trying for seven years, on and off. But I was sure it was going to work this summer. I've been much more relaxed about it, much healthier and . . . well, too late for all that now. It's a relief in a way. I wouldn't want to bring up a child without Peter there to help.'

'Well come and talk to them, anyway. I'm not rushing off, if I can help it. Not unless . . .'

'Not unless they phone,' she supplied.

'You're being wonderfully kind,' he blurted. 'I don't know what to say. I never expected . . .'

'It's a distraction for me,' she smiled. 'Good

therapy. But tell me to go away if I'm a nuisance.'

He looked at her, standing patiently waiting for him to assemble his thoughts. Something was too good to be true, some eagerness just below the surface, something close to hunger in her eyes. Mistrust was not a natural feeling for Drew, but he felt it now. Julie Grafton was there for some reason of her own, and he didn't think it was anything to do with the welfare of the Slocombe children, or Drew himself.

Stephanie came out of the kitchen to where Drew and Julie were still in the hall. 'Is it somebody nice?' she asked Drew, as if the visitor couldn't hear her.

'It's Mrs Grafton,' he told her. Timmy had stopped grizzling, he noticed. 'Is Timmy OK?' he asked Stephanie.

She moved her head in an ambiguous half-nod. Drew went to check. 'Hey, Tim,' he called. 'Finished your breakfast, have you?'

The little boy was playing glumly with some toast crusts and ignored his father. Julie squeezed past Drew and went to the child.

'Tim? Is that your name?' she asked, squatting down beside him. 'I'm Julie.'

Drew closed his eyes, trying to settle the thoughts and feelings seething inside him. It was like being in the middle of a howling gale – it scrambled all your thoughts and took away most of your autonomy. He didn't feel capable of controlling or deciding anything. He was at anybody's mercy.

Stephanie seemed to be feeling rather the same. She clutched his hand and gave a little tug. 'Are we going to see Mummy?' she asked.

'In a little while.' When he opened his eyes, he seemed unable to look at anything but Julie Grafton. What had she been saying, about the procession and the reason someone had shot Karen? It had all slipped his mind, in the two minutes since she'd uttered it.

He made a great effort. 'No,' he said. It sounded very loud in his own ears. 'No, thanks. I think we'll all go. Karen might respond when she hears the children's voices. I think they need to see her.' The realisation that he'd made a decision drained him of any further energy. He quailed at the thought of driving through the town. But there was no way he could leave his children with this woman.

She gave him a frowning stare of disbelief. 'But . . .' she began.

'Thanks for the offer,' he repeated. 'It's really kind. But they don't know you.' She should understand that this was all-important. Stephanie clutched his hand more tightly, giving him strength.

Of course Julie Grafton couldn't have shot

Karen. But the thought shaped itself in his head unbidden: *Well, yes she could.* If she'd been walking alone behind the coffin, nobody would have seen if she'd directed a gun, concealed in her clothes somehow, at the garden gate as Karen stood looking over it. Nobody would have watched what she did next, as the coffin was dumped and chaos reigned. And, he admitted to himself, she might quite easily have killed her husband, jealous of his affair with Sally Dabb. Was this why he so suddenly mistrusted her? Why he knew there was no question at all of letting her watch over his children?

His mangled brain was not making rational connections. He wasn't even trying to follow a logical thread. It was all gut feeling and an all-consuming need to evade any further trauma. He had to keep himself and the kids safe, for Karen's sake. But there was a thought, nudging away somewhere on the edge. Something to do with Stephanie. He didn't try to capture it, but it meant he was certainly not going to let the child out of his sight until things settled down again.

And that might be never, he acknowledged miserably to himself.

Den knew, if he thought about it, that he was likely to be a lot more objective than either

Drew or Maggs, because of their deep emotional involvement in what had happened. They had scarcely even started to wonder about the reasons for Karen's shooting, while he felt he was moving steadily towards an answer to that question. He felt himself uniquely placed to produce an explanation, with his personal knowledge and professional expertise. He allowed himself some moments of complacency as a result.

He spent an hour on Saturday morning filling in several pages of a new reporter's notebook with everything he could think of to do with the two murderous attacks. There was a separate page headed 'Theories' where he noted anything for which there was no actual evidence, but which might fit the known facts. This was the page Maggs found most interesting, and to which she had mainly contributed.

• Grafton killed because of selling out to supermarket
• Karen saw the killer without realising it
• Karen also saw supermarket bomber
• Connection with Mary Thomas/twin/police arresting her while Karen present
• Karen has information that would lead to the killer
• Grafton and Karen both present threats to the 3 witches' plans

• Killer concealed gun in garment, bag, box while doing the shooting. Is this possible?

• Mary Thomas has no twin. It's her all the time.

Maggs sucked the end of her pen as she scanned the page again. 'This is all obvious stuff,' she complained. 'We haven't really thought *laterally,* have we?'

'Except for the twin, which I still think you've got wrong,' he agreed.

'So let's see.' She closed her eyes and tilted her head back, as if awaiting divine inspiration. 'I know: what if Grafton was shot by mistake for Karen? So it was just another attempt at her on Thursday?'

Den winced. 'Surely not?' he spluttered.

'Or even *worse,* but still not impossible – what if *Stephanie* saw something at the supermarket? And she was the intended victim on Thursday.'

'Maggs, you worry me,' Den said. 'What a terrible idea. And daft, because Stephanie wasn't at the farmers' market, was she?'

'True. But I could be right about Karen. Now, the gun. Where could it have been hidden? Where's the last place anyone would look?' Her eyes widened. 'Hey! Maybe they hid it in Grafton's coffin! Nobody looked there.'

'I know I've said this before, but you really

do watch too many second rate movies, you know.'

'No, but listen. It could be right. They haven't found it, have they? And it would be a huge risk for somebody to carry it away with them. The police did search people once they'd got the idea of what was going on. They could have stuffed it in if they'd lifted one corner of the lid.'

'Are you sure? Don't you seal them down?'

'Well, we do, yes, but not as securely when it's cardboard. We actually run parcel tape around it. The colourless stuff. It doesn't show too badly. And it's better than the lid accidentally coming off. So if someone had a sharp knife, they could easily cut a section.'

'They would have been seen, Maggs,' he objected. 'Surely there was never a moment when the coffin was unattended.'

'Well, no, there wasn't,' she admitted. 'But everyone was looking the other way, in the first few minutes. It's like conjurors – they distract attention from what they're doing. If it was all part of a plan, it would be possible. I'm sure it would.'

'A gun's quite a big thing,' he said. 'I think it would be much too risky. What a giveaway if they were caught.'

'Hmm. So where else? The other place they

use in movies is a pram. There weren't any prams, so that can't be right.'

'Thank heaven for that,' Den said fervently.

'Now who do we have on the suspect list, again? It's quite a number, because everyone was at both places. Nobody has an alibi.'

'Except Sally Dabb's husband,' Den reminded her. 'He was at work both times.'

'Pity. He's quite a likely suspect otherwise.'

'Why would he shoot Karen?'

'Um . . . well, maybe he thought she'd been encouraging Grafton and Sally's affair. Actually, he isn't so likely, now I come to think about it.'

'So we've got the three witches, Mary, Geraldine and Hilary; Julie Grafton; the other stallholders – Joe Richards, Maggie Withington and the ostrich man. Some villagers, maybe, though I can't imagine why. They were at the funeral and could have been at the farmers' market. People like Della and the Westlake woman.'

'Who?'

'Della. The one who looks after Drew's kids.'

'Yes, I know her. Who's the Westlake woman?'

'Oh, she lives at the farm down the lane from Drew and Karen. Towards the village – that nice big farmyard.'

'How do you know her?'

He smiled patiently. 'Sometimes, if I get to you

early, I leave the car and go for a little walk. She's often in the yard, and we have a little chat.'

'Shit! You've got another woman. How old is she?'

'Sixty-ish. Maybe a bit less. Nice brown eyes.'

'Was she at the funeral?'

'Oh yes. Hanging back, on the fringes, but there. She gave me a friendly nod when I arrived.'

'Well, add her to the list then. She might have designs on Drew's field. Or want to put them out of business for some reason.'

He puffed out his cheeks in admiration of her inventiveness.

'Or,' she added, 'if she's sixty, that puts her in the same age group as the witches. Yet another one from that little gang. What a time it must have been when that lot were at school together. I wonder what made it so special.'

'Hilary said it was 1960, the year they left. I suppose that must have been some sort of turning point. Wasn't that when Kennedy got to be president? And youth culture was born. And according to Hilary, the first signs of the rot setting in.'

Maggs was thoughtful. 'All a bit vague,' she judged. 'I wonder if something a bit more definite happened – a bit closer to home. Don't they say that most motives for murder go back well into the past?'

'That's true,' he said. 'We could have a look at the newspaper archives. See if there was some big local crisis.'

'That's an Internet job,' she decided. 'Whose computer can we use?'

'Danny's. Though he might have already thought of it. He usually gets one of the DCs onto that job, in the first day or two.'

'How do they know what to look for?'

'They don't. They just trawl through local papers for background. They learn to spot familiar names cropping up over the years. Plus big local events like protests against new developments. The sort of things that make people hate each other.'

'I'm impressed.'

'You didn't think the police were that clever?'

'You said it.'

'So it would really be quicker to check with Danny first.' A renewed eagerness caught his attention.

'You haven't met him, have you?' Den realised. 'You want to see what he's like.'

'I did see him, I think. When we first met. But I don't remember much about him.'

'Come on, then,' he said. 'He'll probably be there today, after what happened to Karen. The whole thing's going to be ratcheted up quite a bit now. No rest for the SIO.'

'The what?'

'Senior Investigating Officer. Keep up, woman.'

Karen knew she was awake. She could hear and think, and feel something cool and smooth under her hands. But she couldn't open her eyes, and certainly couldn't speak. It alternated between being worse than the worst imaginable nightmare and being oddly restful. The complete removal of control should have been terrifying – and was at intervals – but it was also very liberating. Then as time went on, and her thought processes seemed to clear a little, stark terror began to filter in. What if she was going to be like this forever?

She found she could only think in short childlike phrases. Little ribbons of unjoined-up musings flickered through her mind. 'Drew-and-the-children' was a recurring one, because she could hear their voices close by. 'I-can't-move' and 'My-head-hurts' came up quite often, too. Everything quite unemotional, except for the fear that lurked on the sidelines. The fear she knew would pounce as soon as she managed to understand what was going on. So she stopped trying to make sense of it. It could do no good, and only increased the pain behind her eyes.

Something was touching her hand, pressing warmly against her skin. It felt good, a contact that went much deeper than words. But it was frightening, too. An insistence went with it, a demand that she make some kind of effort. And making an effort was so terribly risky. Something inside her gave up and she sank into a comforting greyness which was quite a lot like sleep.

Drew tried to convince himself that Karen had responded to his touch. A tiny frown, a flicker under the eyelids. A nurse had been watching from the other side of the bed, and had silently nodded at him, sharing his hopes. But there'd been nothing further, and Timmy began to wriggle and complain, so they left the room.

A young doctor had been watching out for them. He ushered Drew and the children into a small room, and began to talk about different levels of unconsciousness and the difficulty of making meaningful predictions.

'What usually happens?' Drew asked clumsily.

'There isn't really a *usually,*' the man explained. 'Each case is different. There are too many variables, you see. The extent of the damage, the age and health of the patient – and something that looks like the desire to get better. It sounds a bit new agey, I suppose, but patients do differ in the amount of effort they'll put in. It can be so tantalising, watching them. Some just give up without much of a struggle at all. I'd give anything to know what goes on inside.'

Drew chafed at this, especially as Stephanie was paying close attention to the doctor's words.

'Well, she'll be a fighter,' he said robustly. 'No doubt about that.'

'I'm sure she will. And, as I say, she's not as deeply unconscious as she might look. All the scans show a lot of brain activity. She could wake up at any time. Believe me, I'm not just saying that.'

'I believe you,' Drew assured him, with a smile at Stephanie. 'We believe him, don't we?' he said to her.

The child frowned. 'When will she wake up, then?' she asked. 'Why is she so tired?'

'She's not tired, Steph. She's hurt. She's poorly, and people always sleep a lot when they're poorly. It's nature's way of making us better. If we lie still, all the poorly parts can mend more quickly.'

'Mmm,' came the dubious reply.

Timmy was clearly puzzled by events, and clung round Drew's neck like a magnet.

'We'd better go,' Drew decided. 'We can come again tomorrow.'

It felt almost violent to be leaving Karen there alone with whatever strange dreams she might be having. His place was by her side, day and night, talking to her, urging her to emerge from the darkness back to her rightful life. But he had to consider the children, and instinct told him that they needed him more than Karen did.

The drive home seemed to shake him out of his dazed misery. Either the visit from Julie Grafton, or the sight of his injured wife, or simply a spontaneous recovery – whatever the explanation, by the time he pulled up outside the house, he was anxious to speak to people about the shooting. Maggs, Geraldine, the police, even Mrs Westlake from the nearby farm – they would all have vital information for him, or ideas and suggestions. He couldn't drift uselessly any longer.

But first there was the matter of survival. The freezer was well stocked with fruit and vegetables from their own garden, and meat and bread from other Food Chain people. Karen sometimes bartered her produce for that of other people, which always gave her and Drew a buzz. 'Wait till we do a funeral in return for a year's supply of clothes for us all,' Drew had joked. 'Hand-made, of course.'

Karen hadn't been very amused. 'We've already got the kids' clothes exchange,' she reminded him. 'And I never need anything, now I'm not working.'

'Well, something else, then,' he insisted. 'Surely you approve of money-free transactions?'

'I do, of course,' she nodded. 'But it's not as simple as you might think. When we explored the feasibility of a LETS scheme, we decided it wouldn't work.'

'LETS? Remind me.'

'Local Exchange Trading Scheme. It just means bartering, really, but with an organised structure.'

'Ah, yes. One of those things where you say the last word twice,' he'd teased, determined to avoid getting too serious about the whole issue. 'You said LETS scheme. The S stands for—'

'Yes, Drew, I know. For heaven's sake.' He hadn't really understood why she'd been so tetchy about it. Surely it was possible to live simply, and still be able to find some humour in it?

Now he winced as he remembered this and other occasions when he'd been irritating and deliberately derisive about Karen's new-found philosophy. It wasn't at all that he'd disagreed with her; he just wished she wouldn't be so *solemn* about it. And for the first time, it dawned on him that because he'd been glib and seemingly unimpressed, she might well have been thinking and doing things that he hadn't known about.

His thoughts flew back to the bomb at the supermarket, and how surprised he'd been that she'd been there at the time. Karen did not go to supermarkets. So why had she suddenly deviated from her own rock-solid stand? And how come she'd been there at the very moment that a bomb exploded?

It wasn't a clear thought, but a mere nudge at his awareness. As soon as he felt it, he wrapped it in a thick blanket and packed it away out of sight. But the nudge had been enough: what if Karen had known about the bomb? And if she had, then perhaps that would go some way towards explaining why she'd been shot.

CHAPTER NINETEEN

Stephanie and Timmy ate their lunch with no ructions, and Drew put his mind to how he should spend the remainder of the day. He couldn't go anywhere unless he took the children with him, but he could phone people. He could alternatively try to find someone to babysit. Della was the obvious first port of call, especially as he didn't know for sure that she'd gone with her family on the usual Saturday outing. The events of Thursday afternoon must have shaken her up, just as they had everyone else, and perhaps she and Bill wouldn't feel like going anywhere.

But, as with Julie Grafton, Drew felt an odd reluctance to leave his children with Della. Who, he asked himself, *could* he trust? Well, Maggs, of course, but she wouldn't want to be summoned back to North Staverton on a Saturday unless it was on a funeral call. Apart from her, he really couldn't think of anybody. All the obvious candidates had been there when Karen was shot, and any one of them could theoretically have done it. And that meant the same person might take it into their head to murder Stephanie and Timmy as well, unspeakable as the thought might be.

So he started telephoning, first having set the children up with a chaotic assortment of toys on the kitchen table. He supposed it was the strangeness of the situation that ensured that they played quietly, and with no visible enthusiasm.

'Maggs? Is Den there? Has he seen his Inspector friend today? Does he have any idea what's going on?'

'We're just back from seeing him, actually,' she said.

'We?'

'Yes, I went as well. I'm not going to be left out of this. You know how good I am at coming up with theories about what must have happened.' Then she seemed to remember something. 'Oh, Drew, listen to me. Are *you* all right? Have you seen Karen?'

'I'm much better than I was. And yes, we paid a quick visit this morning. No change, really. They think she'll be OK, though.'

'Really? Is that what they said?'

'They say she could wake up at any moment.'

'Thank goodness for that.'

'And I want to know who shot her,' he said emphatically. He told her about Julie Grafton's visit and her offer to look after the children.

'And you wouldn't let her?'

'No. I can't trust any of them. How can I? Any one of them could have shot Karen.'

'Not Julie, surely?'

'Yes, of course Julie. She was walking alone behind the coffin. Everybody had their heads bent . . .'

'How do you know? You couldn't see them.'

'Well, they probably did. Anyway, she could have hidden the gun in her jacket, whisked it out and back again before anybody noticed.'

'I can't really see it,' she said. 'I *like* Julie Grafton.'

'She's OK. But it was funny, her showing up like that. What did she *want?*'

Maggs snorted. 'Well, I know it won't have occurred to you, but I think she might possibly have her eye on you.'

'What?'

'Well she's on her own now, isn't she? Some women can't cope with that, even for five minutes. They're out trying to find a replacement before the first husband's body's cold.'

'But surely not *me*. I'm not available.'

Maggs's silence was eloquent. Drew's could feel trickles of ice right through his system. 'That's horrible,' he said faintly.

'I expect I'm wrong,' she said, sounding apologetic. 'Forget I said it. She's much too nice for that.'

He inhaled deeply, and tried to get back to the central issue.

'She talked about the shooting,' he said. 'Her suggestion was that it must have been someone at the very back of the crowd. Maybe they lagged behind on purpose, knowing nobody was going to turn round and look behind them.'

'They would when they heard the shot, though. How could anybody fire and then hide the gun in that tiny second before everyone turned to look?'

'Have it under a coat? Pretend to be turning and looking as well?' Drew felt himself become fully engaged in the conversation. He could visualise the scene as he spoke: the scene from another angle, for a change. His flashbacks and re-livings had so far all been an image of Karen falling, her head whipping back from the impact of the bullet. Now he mentally scanned it from all sides, trying to capture the entire scene.

Maggs waited a few seconds, then said, 'It's pretty unlikely, isn't it? I mean, that someone could do that, and nobody else notice? I think there must have been at least two of them. One to shoot and the other to stage some sort of diversion – make sure everybody looked the wrong way. Something so clever that we can't remember it now.'

'The obvious answer,' he said slowly, 'is that it was the three women. You know, Hilary, Geraldine and Mary.'

'The three witches.'

'What?'

'That's what the village people call them, apparently. Den's been to see all three, since Thursday. He's worked his little socks off, bless him. He knows all about them now.'

'And does he think they conspired to murder my wife?' His voice thickened. 'She thought they were her friends.'

'No, he doesn't. He told his Inspector Hemsley all about them, and he agrees. They do have strong feelings, but not that strong. They all genuinely liked Karen, he's convinced.'

'He can't know that for sure. They've got means and opportunity, for Grafton's killing as well. And some sort of motive to do with food politics, I suppose.'

'There's something odd about Mary,' Maggs remembered. 'She's the one he isn't really sure about.'

'The supermarket,' Drew said, with another wave of ice washing through his veins. 'Karen was there . . .'

'So?'

'So nothing, Maggs. It's just—'

She read his mind instantly. 'Drew, you don't believe she had anything to do with that, do you? I admit the thought did occur to me, and then I remembered she had Stephanie with her. That in itself should tell us she'd never have been involved with setting a bomb off.'

'You're right,' he said, feeling miserable and relieved at the same time. 'But I realise now that she hasn't been talking to me about the market stall and the whole food business for a long time. I'd rather lost interest in it, if I'm honest. I feel quite bad about that.'

'Has she been taking an interest in Peaceful Repose?' Maggs flashed back. 'Come on, you idiot. That's the way it goes. You and Karen are a great couple, with great kids and independent lives. You're beating yourself up for nothing. It's good that she's got something of her own to do.'

Drew sighed. Maggs was twelve years his junior, but she'd always felt it part of her duty to lecture him on life, relationships and feelings. He sometimes had a vision of her taking the same role with her long-suffering parents, from the moment they adopted her as a small child.

'I want to be doing something,' he said, gathering what scraps of dignity and energy he could manage. 'Have you any ideas?'

'You should get back to Julie Grafton,' she said without hesitation. 'Talk to her, but keep in mind that she could have done it. And Sally, too. She was at the funeral, and hanging back, as I recall. You could give her a ring.'

'But she couldn't have shot Peter Grafton. Karen said she was right next to him when it happened.'

Maggs made a cynical sound. 'Maybe she's just very clever,' she said. 'Or maybe she has an accomplice.'

'Which is where we began,' he reminded her. 'And all that theory does is make for a lot more very confusing permutations.'

'Well, now you're on the case, we'll unravel it in no time,' she said robustly.

Despite Maggs's advice, Drew did not phone Julie or Sally Dabb. The mere act of bracketing them together made him uncomfortable.

Peter Grafton's two women, in effect, in some kind of unwholesome relationship that he was not keen to explore. And if he was going to talk to them about the attack on Karen, then he would also have to ask about Grafton's shooting, and

341

that could lead down paths he'd prefer to avoid.

Settling down to watch a video with the children, he tried to create some mental order out of the scraps of knowledge concerning Karen's activities. She had taken her lead from Geraldine Beech, right from the start. Geraldine had advised her on what to grow, how to prepare it, what to charge for it, and what to say to her customers. She had encouraged Karen to attend the Food Chain meetings, and bullied her into showing up at a few local schools to talk about their initiatives. Karen had shown every appearance of wholeheartedly endorsing all the opinions, practices and ideologies of the people in the group. Drew could not long entertain any theory that involved Karen being a traitor to the cause.

There were, however, several uncomfortable ironies attached to Karen's evolution as an ecological proselytiser. Drew, after all, had been the one to establish Peaceful Repose Burial Ground, making the disposal of the dead as natural a procedure as he could. Drew had called for biodegradable containers, shallow graves and new trees. He and Maggs had given talks to groups across the region, sowing the seeds in receptive minds, to the effect that cremations were not merely lacking in spiritual content, but they were bad for the environment. When he arrived in North Staverton, it was to a deafening lack of reaction amongst the local people. They had continued with their own lives for quite a while before the significance of his service dawned on them.

And it had been Geraldine Beech who called in one day, with no other motive than curiosity. She who had eyed the burial field with favour, but who had become really excited when she noticed Karen's burgeoning vegetable plot. This, Drew felt, was where the ironies began. Suddenly it was Karen who joined the mainstream of village life, with her involvement in Geraldine's Food Chain organisation, and her awakening to the potential of her home-grown produce. Although people referred routinely to 'the Slocombes' as both being in the forefront of the newly energetic environmental initiatives, Drew could never avoid the suspicion that he'd been usurped in some way by his wife.

And this feeling, if he was honest with himself, went some way towards explaining why he took less of an interest in what Karen was doing than he could have done. He and Maggs were the true pioneers. They were the ones who had made people think, and who had struggled for years with minimal reward and numerous setbacks. They had endured the active hostility of Plant and Son, the undertaker in Bradbourne who stood to lose business to Peaceful Repose. They had been treated with mockery and suspicion at times, forced to defend the shallowness of the graves and the simplicity of their practices.

But Geraldine had clearly seen things differently. She had talked as if *she* was the driver of the bandwagon, the leader of the wagon train, and everyone else was falling in behind her. Pleased to have her support, Drew was nonetheless irritated by her.

Now, there was a sense again of being usurped – this time by Den Cooper. Maggs had implied that Den was now actively pursuing his own investigation into what had happened to Peter Grafton and Karen, and discovering leads and connections that Drew knew nothing about. Handicapped by the needs of his children, as well as having to keep the business going at least on a minimal basis, he wasn't going to have time to keep up. Even if Maggs related everything that Den told her, it would all be too pre-digested to make him feel directly involved.

And besides, his rightful place was with Karen. His stoical wife, who worked so hard, and seldom complained and tolerated his pathetic income and unsocial working hours. The mother of his children, the person he most enjoyed talking to. He conjured the image of her lying there in hospital, her face oddly unrecognisable on the white pillow. She never lay like that, flat on her back, chin up. She curled on her side, chin tucked down, hair all messy. The real Karen liked brightly coloured pillowcases, and a duvet that would wrap itself tightly round her by morning. The thought, that he had until now managed to keep at bay, finally thrust itself through, causing him to clutch both children tightly to his sides. What if she never woke up? What if that familiar Karen was lost forever?

'Daddy!' Timmy complained, wriggling crossly.

But Stephanie seemed to read his mind. She huddled herself closely to him, her thumb in her mouth, her eyes fixed unseeingly at the television screen.

Den was not thinking about Drew at all. He was aware of no competition between them, no reason why Drew should feel resentful. After all, any success that Den might achieve would only be good news for the husband of the injured Karen. Maggs, who might well have understood the sensitivities, was too excited to lend them her attention.

'It's *got* to be about the supermarket connection!' she insisted. 'Grafton signs a deal with SuperFare to sell his fruit juice to them. The Food Chain people get to know about it, and decide he has to be stopped. He'll undermine the whole shebang, if he goes on like that. Terrible publicity, dreadful betrayal of all they hold dear. Maybe someone talks to an activist – one of their sons, even. Haven't they got four or five sons, between them? So, he sneaks into the gents behind the farmers' market, sticks his crossbow out of the window and does the deed. But Karen sees too much, somehow. He knows she'll eventually twig, and go to the police. Can't risk it. So Karen has to be stopped.'

Den held up both hands, as if to arrest an oncoming juggernaut in full flight. 'Whoa!' he pleaded. 'Hold your horses.'

She laughed. 'Keep up,' she said. 'Where did you lose me?'

'Crossbow. Gents. Son. Karen.' He ticked them off, finger by finger. 'Who says anybody's sons would be interested?' Then he remembered. 'Ah! Mary Thomas's twins. Humphrey's an animal rights activist, or something. Did I tell you that?'

'More or less,' she confirmed. 'Except I thought he was against GM crops.'

'Right.' Den nodded. 'That's what I meant.'

'Didn't they teach you to get the details right? Surely accuracy was quite important for police work?'

'Shut up. I wasn't on a police investigation,

was I? I just chatted to the woman, and tried to remember all the stuff she told me.'

'But now you're supposed to get it right, because Inspector Hemsley wants to know everything you find out.'

'Only because he's short of men, as usual, and wants me to provide him with some free assistance. Not a lot of people fully grasp that the vast majority of police investigations are resolved thanks to information received from members of the public.'

'Come off it. Stop sounding so pompous. Anyway, of course people know that. It's obvious.'

'Only when you stop to think about it.'

'Maybe so, but don't forget *you* went to *him*. You're *dying* to be part of the whole thrilling business again.'

He shook his head in defeat. 'I can't see that it really matters, anyway.'

'No, it doesn't.' She waved an impatient hand. 'Let's get *on* with it. You said yourself the public loos were probably the place the killer fired from. Seems fairly obvious to me.'

'It isn't obvious at all. It's one of about ten possibilities.'

'But it fits really well. Windows at the back, all along that wall, facing the market stalls. Chap goes in, with the crossbow under his coat, shuts himself in a cubicle, fires out of the little window, replaces weapon under coat and walks away, in completely the other direction from where people will be looking.'

'What if there was someone else in the loo? They might have seen him.'

'Obviously, the killer would wait till there wasn't anybody.'

'They wouldn't know if someone was next door, in the Ladies.'

'But that wouldn't matter. A crossbow makes hardly any noise. That's the beauty of it. I wonder why they didn't use it again at the funeral?'

'Probably because it's even more difficult to hide than a gun.'

'Just as easy to aim from waist level, though. Or so I would think.'

'It might not have been the same person,' Den reminded her. 'Don't jump to conclusions.'

'I'm not. I know it could be two different people, with two different motives. Maybe it was Genevieve Slater, still after Drew and wanting Karen out of the way. You remember I told you about her? We buried her mother's old friend this week.'

'Yes I remember,' Den laughed. Despite himself, he was impressed by her endless inventive enthusiasm. Her mind moved so quickly and competently, it was like watching sunlight flickering over water. 'What we still don't have is proof – any sort of proof,' he reminded her.

'Well, we'd better try to find some then, hadn't we?'

Den didn't know quite how she proposed to accomplish that, but he acknowledged to himself that he was really looking forward to finding out.

Karen could feel herself emerging slowly from the gluey state she'd been in. So slow and fragile was the sense of return that she was afraid to give it her attention, in case it changed direction and plunged her back. There was a new touch on her hand, a dry firm grasp very different from Drew's gentle stroking. 'Karen?' came a low gentle voice. 'Can you hear me?'

Karen made no attempt to move or speak. It was far, far too soon for that. And besides, when she did re-emerge into the world of the living, she wanted it to be Drew who welcomed her.

But the person was insistent. She was doing something to Karen's hand, lifting it, and placing it inside her own. 'Wiggle your finger if you can hear me,' came a clear instruction. 'Just tickle my palm.'

She couldn't ignore the order. It was such an easy thing to do. Without noticeable thought, she let her forefinger flicker. It was as if it had wanted to, from the start.

'Good girl!' applauded her visitor. 'Very good indeed. You'll soon be better. Right as rain in no time, you'll see. But now, I want you to help me. Karen – did you see the person who shot you? Do you know who it was? Wiggle your finger if the answer's yes.'

Karen's finger twitched again, as the face returned to her inner eye. That face, staring at her, full of cold intent. Oh yes – Karen knew who her would-be killer had been.

'Excellent!' breathed her interrogator. 'Thank you, dear. Now, I could run through a list of names, and you'd probably reveal to me which was the right one, but I don't want to tire you, or upset you. You've told me all I want to know for now. I'll leave you to gather your strength.'

And it went quiet again, except for something ticking rhythmically somewhere in the room.

CHAPTER TWENTY

Sally Dabb was very much behind with her pickles. May was an awkward month at the best of times, with little or no fresh produce available for her usual range. Although she did have a few dozen jars remaining, she was worried that they'd all sell during the next few weeks. Geraldine had suggested some new lines – mint jelly, something with elderflower or even dandelion. 'Why not try something herbal, too?' the organiser had said. 'Feverfew grows like crazy around here. Can't you concoct some sort of headache remedy from it?'

Sally had not been keen. It felt like quackery to be selling folk medicines without proper testing. Besides, she wouldn't have the first idea how feverfew should be presented. She knew her mother had been in the habit of nibbling the leaves to assuage a migraine, now and then, but Sally had never really believed it worked.

She had planned to design some new labels and try them out on her computer, but Archie was doing his accounts and she couldn't get near the machine. Anything that risked upsetting Archie these days would be a very bad idea.

She knew, though, that she absolutely *had* to keep busy. If there wasn't something to occupy her mind, she'd go back to thinking about Peter, and that would lead to tears and Archie would notice and get angry again.

He had known all along that she was very fond of Peter. They'd all been at school together, and even now, fifteen years later, it was fresh in everyone's minds. Peter Grafton had been the most handsome boy in the school. Ridiculously handsome, at about sixteen. His skin always seemed tanned, his golden hair burnished. He walked with a rare grace and smiled indiscriminately. All the girls had adored him. One by one they had wangled dates with him, triumphing over their sisters during those brief weeks of glory. But somehow nobody ever managed to keep him for long. It was simply too much hard work, they agreed amongst themselves, afterwards.

He hardly spoke, he passively agreed to any

proposals as to where they might go, and seemed to forget just which girl he was supposed to be going out with, from one date to the next.

Julie Grainger, who he eventually married, had not been a local girl. Her family lived in Yorkshire, and Peter had met her during his time at university. He had married her and brought her back to Bradbourne a month after they graduated. As far as anybody could see, she suited him very well. Over the years he changed from the beautiful dumb schoolboy to an assured man, gradually losing his looks. The more ordinary he became in appearance, the nicer his character seemed to be. Sally and others observed this with mixed feelings.

And then there he'd been, a fellow stallholder at the farmers' markets, and such a very appealing person. He had been fulsome in his delight at meeting her again. He had admired the pickles and preserves, helped her arrange them, questioned her closely on what went into them. He was clearly converted to the whole business of local food production, zealously running off leaflets for Geraldine and showing up at all the meetings.

Then someone had killed him. Right there, inches away from Sally herself, so his blood splashed her and his dying gurgle echoed in her head. The police had wanted to know every tiny detail, making her describe it again and again. They had wanted the whole story of her relationship with him, obviously believing the gossip that she and Peter had been having an affair. And Sally wasn't daft enough to miss the implication that her husband was one of the very few people with an identifiable motive for the murder.

The police, Sally discovered, were very poor at grasping the complexities of human interactions. They seemed unable to deviate from the blinkered scenario: Married woman having affair with fellow stallholder; husband discovers this, is jealous and shoots lover. Simple. Happens all the time. Though Sally did wonder whether they regarded Julie Grafton with the same degree of suspicion. And if not, why not?

In any case, the police line was wrong on about a hundred details. Firstly, she and Peter were not in any official sense having an affair. They had not in fact had full penetrative sex together. They had kissed and cuddled a lot, in the back of Peter's van. There had been skin contact and much use of hands. But in a court of law, she was fairly certain she would be found innocent of adultery. Peter had insisted on this, from the start. 'We're just good friends, having a friendly cuddle,' he said, more than once. And indeed, Sally found it a relief to retain a clear conscience. What she most enjoyed was their conversations, anyway. He made her laugh, he understood her feelings, he inspired her with ambition and optimism, with his vaulting visions of the future.

Furthermore, the police had shown no curiosity as to the nature of Sally's own marriage. They had taken details of Archie's work, and where he was on the morning of the shooting. And they had been forced to conclude that his alibi was sound, and he could not have been the killer. At that point they drifted away, leaving Sally oddly frustrated and resentful. Didn't they owe it to her – and somehow to Peter, as well – to pay a bit more attention? Funny, she realised, how urgently she wished she could disclose the truth about her married life.

Finally, the threesome did get together for a long overdue comparison of findings and hypotheses. Maggs and Den drove to North Staverton at seven thirty that evening, and helped Drew put the children to bed. Stephanie had monopolised Den as soon as he arrived on the scene, and regularly complained that she didn't see him as often as she would like. Timmy seemed to have embarked on a campaign, almost from the moment of his birth, to seduce Maggs into adoring him. He seemed to think he was making progress, as time went on, albeit slowly. Den and he were thus in a kind of alliance, each seeking to discover the best way to please her, each basking in the moments of success. There were even times when they seemed to be teaching each other how best to achieve their goal.

The bedtime developed into a kind of muted party. The hospital had phoned Drew with their end-of-day bulletin, cautiously revealing that Karen was now in a far lighter coma, with a lot of flickering eye movement and healthier brain scan read-outs. He had agonised about whether to drive back to see for himself, but the sister had assured him it was still too soon for any real excitement, and they'd phone the moment anything substantially changed.

This came as a relief on a number of levels. Despite – or perhaps because of – his experience working as a nurse, Drew did not like hospital wards. His heartbeat accelerated and he felt itchy and hot, every time he walked into the building. Sometimes he felt sick, too. Good old-fashioned *fear,* he told himself. A perfectly rational response. But it was not something anybody would willingly put themselves through if they could avoid it.

So he threw himself into enjoying the company and good sense of his friends, encouraging the children to relax and be indulged. It was a warm evening, and Timmy was grubby from playing outside. Drew organised a complicated bath routine, with Stephanie's favourite Den given charge of water and bubbles, and her special story afterwards, while Maggs rolled up her sleeves and ensured that Timmy was entirely clean in all departments. It seemed, Drew noted, that everybody was more than happy with their allotted roles. Certainly the noise was all shrieks of laughter followed by murmurs of sleepy contentment in a surprisingly short time. He withdrew downstairs, and having already raided the freezer, slid three sirloin steaks under the grill and a quantity of chips into the deep fat fryer. A bottle of organic red wine was already on the table.

It was with a sense of defiance that he called upstairs, 'Ready in five minutes!' What if one of Karen's market friends came to the door now? They wouldn't be able to fault his choice of menu, but they might raise their eyebrows at the fact of a dinner party at all, with his wife struggling for life in a hospital bed.

But it wasn't really a dinner party. It was the gathering together of investigators into who and how and why – the history, motives, methods and intentions of whoever had shot Peter Grafton and Karen Slocombe. A gathering that they all knew should have taken place some days earlier.

The steaks were tender – local pure bred Hereford cattle, killed in their own field, hung for three weeks and expertly butchered. The chips were made from Karen's own potatoes, and the vegetables were last year's broccoli and french beans. 'It's a feast!' Den declared.

'I sometimes think our meals are a trifle repetitive,' Drew mused. 'We never have rice these days, or anything with noodles or even much in the ways of pies. Just plain meat and veg.'

'That's the simple life for you,' Maggs said. 'You never have chicken, either. And hardly any fish.'

'There's a whole pig just gone in the freezer,' Drew agreed. 'Masses and masses of chops.'

'Wonderful!' enthused Den. 'Don't knock it, you fool. Most people would change places with you like a shot.'

'And a head,' Drew continued, after a small wince at the metaphor. 'They make you have the head as well. In fact, there are now *three* pigs' heads in there, because Karen's not really sure what to do with them.'

There was no answer to that. Den and Maggs met each other's eyes, and silently agreed not to venture any suggestions as to how to deal with a pig's head. Neither had any recollections of mothers or grandmothers being called upon to resolve such a dilemma.

'You live well,' Maggs said, after the pause. 'Everybody around here lives well.'

'Thanks to the three witches,' Den added. Drew's stare of total incomprehension served to focus them all on the matter in hand. 'You don't know what we know about the three witches,' Den realised. 'Time I filled you in, then.'

Drew listened with complete attention as the former police detective lucidly recounted everything he'd learnt over the past week or so. The steaks disappeared magically, Den talking with his mouth full, and Maggs let him have the limelight while she enjoyed her meal. The wine was soon consumed, and Drew wished he'd provided a second bottle.

For afters, he produced a bowl of peaches, bottled in a heady syrup laced with brandy. 'Sally Dabb made these,' he said. 'We've had them since Christmas. I think you'll like them.'

Den's tale was told by this time and Drew was trying to digest it all. 'We still don't really know as much about these people as Karen does,' he worried. 'She's been working with them, going to meetings, dropping in for coffee, for a year or more now. She's the real expert.'

'Which is probably why she's also the victim,' said Maggs, with a sturdiness born only minimally of her alcohol intake. 'She knows something that would incriminate the person who shot Peter Grafton. That seems obvious.'

'It's an assumption,' Den corrected her.

'I know it is,' she frowned. 'Because I've already thought of at least one completely different scenario.'

'Which is?' Drew prompted.

'That Karen was the intended victim the first time, too.'

'What?' Drew's heart lurched at the idea. 'But why? What possible . . .'

'Maybe to do with the supermarket bomb,' Maggs interrupted. 'She was there. She saw Mary Thomas. She might have seen something else, without realising it.'

From nowhere, another idea hit Drew. It was like a barbed missile, smacking him in the face, attaching itself to his mind, making him desperate to shake free of it. He didn't think he could utter it aloud.

'What?' demanded Maggs, seeing it clear in his eyes.

'Stephanie was there, too. And she was right beside Karen on Friday morning.'

'No, Karen was *holding* her. She was in Karen's arms.' Maggs was keeping up magnificently. 'Their heads were almost level.'

'But she wasn't there on the Tuesday, when Grafton was shot,' said Cooper, wide-eyed. 'Nobody would deliberately shoot a little girl.'

'They missed her by inches when they shot Karen,' said Maggs. 'And if the gun was concealed under a coat or in a bag, the aim wasn't likely to be very accurate. It's hard to believe they really cared who got hit.'

'We've got it completely wrong,' Drew said. 'I'm all for some brainstorming, and looking at it from every angle, but this one makes no sense.' He put down his spoon without finishing the peaches. 'It's sickening.'

'Right,' agreed Cooper. 'But nobody's asked Stephanie for her view of what happened, have they? *She* knows some of these people, too. She's a witness.'

'You don't interview four-year-old children in a murder enquiry,' said Drew stiffly. 'It's been bad enough for her as it is.'

'Well, actually, sometimes they do,' Den corrected. 'Plain clothes WDCs, in special rooms, made to seem like home. Usually only when they're directly involved, though. Their evidence isn't usually admissable in court if they're only four.'

'I should hope not.' Drew was cold to his bones. 'You can't call her a witness. It's bad enough that she's been involved in the first place.'

'Relax,' Maggs ordered him. 'Nobody's going to upset her any more than she is already.

But she's a tough little thing. Always has been.'

Stephanie had spent much of her early life playing more or less contentedly in a corner of Peaceful Repose's office, while Karen continued working as a teacher. Only when Timmy's birth was imminent did Karen abandon work and become more available. Stephanie had somehow absorbed the realities of death and grief, just by being in its presence, or so Drew sometimes thought. He had seen her studying the faces of the newly bereaved, as they came to make arrangements for the burial of their loved one, and wondered how much she was understanding. It seemed now that she had learnt something of the deeper aspects of life and death, at that time. She was a serious child, compared to her brother. Stoical, in many ways, but alive to the emotional undercurrents, too. He found himself dreaming of how she would be at fifteen, or even twenty-five. What a friend and companion she might become. How proud he'd be of her, how uniquely understanding she was going to be, after the rich upbringing they were giving her. Stephanie, in short, was destined to grow up as somebody very special and infinitely cherished by her father.

'We're running ahead of ourselves,' Den reminded them. 'We should be sticking to facts, trying to see patterns. We should be assembling every scrap of information we have, between us, which the police might have missed. After all, they're completely dependent on what people tell them. They've interviewed all the stallholders, everyone who was at Grafton's funeral, shopkeepers close to the market site in Bradbourne. And I get the impression they're floundering. Sally Dabb's husband has a solid alibi, and no reason to shoot Karen. There's vague talk about past alliances and present politics, but nothing to warrant committing murder. Our only hope is that between us we've got a much more complete picture than we realise.'

'Past alliances, present politics,' Maggs echoed. 'That sounds very grand. What does it mean?'

'Back to the three witches,' Den said. 'I can't help thinking it's all tied up with them.'

'And they're the three women who were teenagers together,' Drew put in. 'But were there only three? I think Della – who minds our kids – had a mother who was at school with Geraldine. Presumably that means she was one of the gang as well? Or at least knew about them.'

'It was Della who first told me about the threesome,' Den said. 'I don't think she mentioned her mother.' He frowned, trying to remember.

'She's dead,' Drew said. 'Died a year before we came here. Della keeps saying she'd have loved a grave in our field, if only we'd arrived a bit sooner.'

'We need to list absolutely everybody, and check them all for means, motive and opportunity,' said Maggs. 'We need some sheets of paper. Then we can add everything we know about them.'

The two men both looked at her like children receiving instruction.

The exercise was duly carried out. In spite of Den's interviews and Drew remembering various encounters with the locals over the years, essential facts were hard to ascertain. 'I'm beginning to understand why the police find it so hard,' said Drew, ruefully. 'It's so difficult to force people's complicated lives into any sort of shape, when you know so little about them.'

'It's good, though,' Den insisted, rather to Drew's surprise. 'I'm getting a better feel for it all.'

'Are you?' The others both pushed their lips out in sceptical expressions.

'Look.' Den flourished a hand over Maggs's scribbles, which had acquired arrows and underlinings and question marks galore. 'There are two distinct strands. One – the Food Chain thing. People getting all ideological about where their cabbages come from. Supermarkets, secret deals, treachery. And two, there's the personal stuff. Adultery, jealousy, the usual things.'

'But it's *massively* more one than the other,'

Drew objected. 'The only personal stuff takes us back to Sally Dabb and her husband, and we already decided they're in the clear.'

'Not quite,' Den gazed at the jottings on the sheet of paper. 'I think we're missing something else along the same lines. All these women – they fall into two clear groups. One lot are sixty, known each other all their lives. And there's another lot, look – all early thirties, some with little kids. I'm not saying I can see the whole story, but I'm thinking we should look a bit more closely at the younger lot, and not get distracted by the three witches.'

Maggs blew out her cheeks. 'You're just saying that because they're almost all women. You think women are only capable of jealousy.'

'I don't think that at all.' Den was indignant. 'That's not what I'm saying.'

'I must admit I don't really follow your logic,' Drew put in quietly.

'I'm not saying there *is* any logic.' Den smiled. 'But I am saying I think we're looking for a woman here. None of the men in the story seem to feel very strongly about *anything*.'

When he woke on the Sunday morning, to the sound of Timmy laughing, and the sun streaming in through the window, for a second, Drew felt that all must be right with the world. But the empty bed beside him brought a rapid return to reality. *I should get up* he thought urgently, without moving a muscle. Slowly he turned onto his back and stared at the sunlit patterns on the ceiling. Timmy was still chuckling and Drew supposed that Stephanie was entertaining him. Good sweet Stephanie, so clever and independent already, such a source of pride. She'd been at close quarters to a bomb and a bullet in rapid succession, had seen her mother in a coma and suffered Drew's shameful state of numbness that immediately followed. Now she was keeping her little brother happy while her useless father lay in bed, apparently unable to summon the will to move.

'You're being too hard on yourself again.' He could almost hear Maggs saying it, as she had many times in the past few days. He had always been inclined to take the blame for anything going wrong, and when a child died under his care during his time as a nurse, the habit seemed more than justified. Despite an official ruling that there had been no negligence on his part, he knew he would never cease to feel responsible. In some part of him, he still expected retribution to fall, and now he had his own children, it seemed only logical that his punishment should fall via them. Although not obviously overprotective, he and Karen both knew how much he worried about their welfare and how easily he could slip into agonising about the dangers they would have to face.

Now it was Karen herself who'd been hurt. Karen who had faced the ultimate danger, in the shape of an unknown malice firing a gun. How was that possible? The realisation struck him as if for the first time, that somebody had deliberately made a decision to kill Karen. Someone who knew what was involved, since they had supposedly already killed Peter Grafton. It took a dedicated killer to perform the same deed twice. Was it, he wondered for the first time, perhaps a paid assassin, lurking behind the lane hedge, and not one of the mourners at the funeral after all? That would be easier to swallow. A stranger doing it for money. A cold heartless professional, who had done it so many times there were no finer feelings of remorse or pity left. But that was too easy. Even if true, then somebody they knew must have hired the killer, given instructions and paid over the cash. In the end, it wasn't so very important who actually pulled the trigger.

There had to be treachery involved. Everybody who had come to Grafton's funeral had been known to Julie, and almost all were known to Karen. She considered them her friends. She lived close to them, worked alongside them. They would all have smiled and greeted her if they met her in the post office. Drew experienced the bitter mixture of helplessness and outrage that the victims of treachery endure. Shock and loss of trust in the world at large were there, as well. And a lurking sense of being made a fool of, for missing the signs that must surely have been there.

And so he continued to lie in bed, savouring the many unpalatable emotions that this Sunday morning was dumping on him. Only the fierce pride of parenthood shone through the murk.

It was some time before Stephanie ventured into the room. 'Daddy?' she whispered, from the doorway. 'Are you awake?'

'Mmm,' he mumbled, pretending to be just rousing.

'We're hungry,' she went on, with a hint of apology. 'I think it's breakfast time.'

It was quarter past ten. Even for a Sunday, this was very late. 'Yes, it is,' he agreed. 'I'd better get up then, hadn't I?'

'Timmy wants to get dressed. I said he should wait for you. His shorts are muddy. I can't find any more.'

The system for clean clothes was haphazard at the best of times. Drew had a feeling there would be nothing clean available. Most of Timmy's clothes were almost certainly sitting in the laundry basket, awaiting attention. Karen's insistence on living an ecologically benign lifestyle extended to not using the washing machine more than once a week. Drew approved, in theory. It kept the electricity bills down, and seemed to present no serious difficulties.

'He can wear the muddy ones today,' Drew suggested. 'It is Sunday, after all. Nobody's going to see him.' Then he remembered that they were probably meant to go to see Karen in hospital that afternoon. How could they do otherwise? And how could he forgive himself for his deepening sense of reluctance?

CHAPTER TWENTY-ONE

Julie Grafton had been intending to make some phone calls, thanking people for letters and flowers, bringing them up to date with her state of mind, just making contact with other human beings. But she kept putting it off. It was Sunday, she remembered. People did family things on a Sunday. They didn't like to be bothered by the phone. But even so, there were two or three who wouldn't mind.

It was nearly two weeks now since Peter had died. She wondered if there was a rule or formula for how a new widow was supposed to be feeling after this length of time. It would be interesting to know. She tried to remember her grandmother, after Grandad had died. All she could recall was the elderly woman – actually not quite seventy – walking briskly down the main street of Wakefield, greeting friends and holding tight to a long shopping list, while Julie tagged along behind her, under strict instructions from her mother to make sure Granny was all right. As far as she'd been able to tell, Granny had been fine. If anything she'd seemed rather more cheerful than she had in the weeks prior to being widowed.

Of course, that had been different. Grandad had been ill, and a very cantankerous patient. It had obviously come as a relief when he did eventually die. With Peter, nobody could have expected it. She would be assumed to be still in shock, unable to believe the enormity of what had happened. Perhaps she *was* in shock. Perhaps that was the right word for this floaty feeling, this sense of irresponsibility and selfishness. Once she'd been told that Peter had made a will, so that everything came undisputedly to her, and that his sister had no intention of arguing about it, the worst immediate worry was removed. She wouldn't starve. But every time she permitted herself to glance to the future, she was gripped with a panic that left her gasping. How would she ever manage by herself? She'd married at twenty-one, had almost never spent a night alone, and couldn't begin to identify herself as a single woman.

But that was dealt with by a stern refusal to look ahead. There was enough going on in the here and now; enough emotions to distract her from her terrors. Emotions of sadness, frustration and puzzlement. Somebody had actually *shot* her husband. This simple fact swirled around and around, obscuring a lot of what she would be thinking otherwise.

It had to be because of his apple juice contract. She had warned him it would make him unpopular. 'And you know how you hate it when people dislike you,' she'd reminded him. 'What are you thinking of?'

'They'll understand,' he'd replied, with total confidence. 'I'll be a sort of third columnist. I'll show them how grand organic juice can be, and that it doesn't have to cost the earth. I'm doing this for the whole community. Forging links. It's time they all realised that we're never going to get rid of supermarkets. So we have to join forces with them. It's absolutely obvious. Common sense. They'll soon see it my way.'

Julie had doubted it, but he had gone ahead with the contract anyway. She hadn't realised that anybody else knew about it. Peter had sworn her to secrecy, and seemed intent on keeping it private until the very last moment. Presumably somebody at SuperFare had blabbed, and the whole thing had somehow leaked out. That, at least, had been her initial assumption when she heard he'd been shot. Strange, she thought now, how instantly she'd managed to explain it to herself. And how little she cared, then or now, about revenge.

Maggs and Den had driven home after their steaks and debates, each feeling slightly dissatisfied. 'We didn't really get very far, did we?' Maggs said. 'I was hoping a name would leap out at us, once we all three got together.'

'I'm not sure,' Den sounded vague. 'I need to have more of a think.'

Now, on Sunday morning, Maggs was impatient for his conclusions. 'Well?' she demanded. 'Any progress?'

'Not really,' he admitted. 'There is something about these three witches that's niggling.'

Maggs huffed impatiently. 'I don't think you should call them that. It's silly. They're not witches at all.'

He shook his head. 'I know. It was just the picture they painted. It seems to fit.'

'Well, don't get carried away. It sets the wrong tone, somehow. Gives the wrong idea. They're probably not in any kind of alliance, when it comes to it. Mary Thomas isn't directly involved in the farmers' markets, for a start. Geraldine is all organisation and hardly any actual hands-on farming. They live in three different villages. How often do you think they actually see each other?'

'OK. I get the point.' He took a slow mouthful of coffee, almost forgetting to swallow it. 'But they are important all the same,' he said at last. 'I think it all centres around them.'

'Well, let's find out then,' she said impatiently. 'I'm all for making things happen. We could sit around like this for months, with the trail getting cold, all the evidence washed away. People will forget and carry on as before. What proportion of murders go unsolved?' She stared at him challengingly. 'Just because everybody loses interest and wanders off.'

'Mostly it's obvious who did it,' he said. 'And mostly we get a lot of help from the public.'

'We?' she echoed. 'Listen to yourself! This time we're the public. Don't forget that.'

'No, I won't,' he said meekly. 'Now, let's hear the worst, then. How exactly are we going to make things happen?'

'Ah! Well . . .' She sat down facing him across the kitchen table. 'I haven't worked out the details yet. It can't be any sort of re-enactment, because we haven't got enough of an idea what happened. But I thought we might make some waves, and see what gets washed ashore. So to speak.' She dimpled her plump cheeks at him. 'Pretend we know more than we do. That sort of thing.'

Den's features crumpled in a grimace. 'It sounds dreadfully – well, *risky*,' he demurred.

'No, no,' she breezed. 'Not at all. Just listen to this.'

Drew took the children to see Karen that afternoon. A senior nurse met him at the door to the ward, and asked if she could have a word. A different policeman was positioned on sentry duty in the corridor.

'Your wife is beginning to regain consciousness,' the woman announced, with an air of someone bestowing a prize. 'She might even speak to you, if you're patient. She had a visitor yesterday evening who seems to have helped the process.'

Drew glanced at the policeman. 'Are you letting her have visitors, other than me?'

'Oh, well, yes. If it's somebody we know. And we were careful to keep an eye on her.'

'Who was it?'

'Mrs Beech. Constable Plover was here at the time, and he knows her quite well, apparently.'

'But—' Drew felt alarmed and helpless. How could they be so blind as to think Geraldine Beech above suspicion? He himself could see no reason to remove her from the list of suspects. 'But Karen's been all right since then? I mean, she's continued to improve?'

'Oh yes. I think we'll soon be able to say she's out of the woods.'

He had a fleeting image of his wife wandering blindly between great dark trees, lost and lonely, frightened and powerless. Oh yes, he thought, may she soon get out of the woods.

He ushered the children gently into the room. Karen lay exactly as before, flat on her back, still looking like somebody else. The dressing on the side of her head concealed most of the shaved area, and looked much less odd than might have been expected. It wasn't that so much as her stillness, and the waxiness of her skin. She looked, Drew could not deny, like a dead body in his own cool room.

With no warning, Timmy launched himself onto the bed in a flying leap, too fast for Drew to stand a chance of intercepting him. The child landed in a scrabbling muddle half on top of his mother, feet dangling as he struggled for a toehold amongst the framework of the bed.

'Timmy!' Drew hissed, afraid to shout. 'Get off, you stupid boy.'

But Timmy ignored him. He had one arm wrapped round Karen and was nuzzling into her chest. The sight made Drew shudder, and reach out to drag the child away. What if he'd killed her? It would be Drew's fault, for not keeping him under better control.

But it seemed there was no need to worry. 'Timmy,' came a low purring voice. 'Hello, baby.'

Stephanie and Drew were transfixed, rooted to the vinyl floor. Timmy burrowed harder. Karen opened her eyes.

As if aware of what was happening, the nurse came in behind Drew. 'Mrs Slocombe?' she said in a normal voice. 'Your family are here.'

'Yes, I know,' said Karen, her voice just as normal as the nurse's. 'Timmy's trying to crush me, I think.'

'How do you feel?' the nurse continued. Then, without waiting for an answer, she approached the bed and removed Timmy as casually as if he were a misplaced garment. 'Let your poor mother breathe,' she said easily, and stood him on a chair next to the bed.

'I feel sort of – hollow,' said Karen. 'Like a dry husk.'

'Any pain?'

'Not really. I think my head would hurt if I moved. What day is it?'

Drew finally managed to move and speak. 'Sunday,' he offered. 'Sunday afternoon.'

Karen exhaled, a little huff of laughter. 'Should I ask what *year* it is?' she said. 'For all I know, I've been here for decades. Except . . .' she swivelled her eyes to look at Timmy, who was leaning over her, 'Tim doesn't seem to have grown very much.'

The policeman came to the doorway. 'Has she woken up?' he asked, his face as eager as a small boy's expecting good news.

'Indeed she has,' the nurse told him, her voice all smiles.

He came into the room. 'Mrs Slocombe – I'll have to ask you some questions as soon as you feel well enough. You probably don't know what happened? It's just . . .' He squared his shoulders. 'It does seem to have been a – well, a murder attempt.'

'Yes,' Karen agreed.

Drew watched her in disbelief. Could she really be so completely normal, after having a bullet lodged in her brain, and surgery to remove it? After lying in a coma for almost three days?

'I know who it was,' she said now. Everyone in the room, Timmy included, held their breath. 'But I still can't really believe it,' she added. Drew wondered whether he was the only one who noticed her voice losing power. Like a torch with a failing battery, a light was dimming as he watched her face.

'Karen?' he said. 'Karen!'

Her eyes flickered shut: down . . . up . . . halfway down . . . up a millimetre . . . and then firmly down. They remained closed. She sighed.

'Oh!' said the nurse.

'Hmm,' moaned the policeman.

'Karen?' Drew repeated.

Keep calm came the silent command. *This is not what it seems.*

It wasn't, quite. Karen breathed, a shallow tentative breath. Drew clutched her warm unresponsive hand. Timmy pressed close to the bed, staring at his mother's face. Stephanie inched forward, her eyes large.

'She's relapsed,' said the nurse, unnecessarily. 'It does happen. I'll go and fetch the doctor. Don't worry.' This last she threw at Drew as she left the room.

'Ohhh,' the policeman murmured. 'Oh dear.'

'But she was *all right* a minute ago,' Drew said, to an uncaring cosmos. 'What's happening?'

'She'll wake up again, won't she, Daddy?' Stephanie said, her voice full of confidence. 'She didn't say anything to me. I want her to talk to *me*.'

'Her head is still poorly,' Drew explained. 'She needs to give it a lot of rest. I expect the doctor will come and tell us all about it in a minute.'

He heard again what Karen had said. *Timmy doesn't seem to have grown.* It was a joke. Her last words had been a joke. Like *Bugger Bognor,* only better.

But no, that hadn't been the last thing she said. She'd spoken to the policeman last. He shook himself angrily. What was this about *last,* anyway? She wasn't dead. She'd just gone back to the quiet still place she'd been in before. She'd emerged once; she could do it again. It was bound to be a slow process.

'Maybe we'd better get out of the way,' he said. 'The doctor won't want to find the room full of people.' The policeman had already retreated to his post by the door. Drew found himself blaming the wretched man. Why couldn't he have waited? Let Karen surface more gradually, speak to Stephanie – and him.

It was worse now. Much worse. He'd seen her conscious, amused, her old self, and then lost her again. Like someone struggling to free themselves from the tentacles of a giant octopus, he thought. They come bursting one last time to the surface, gasping and optimistic, only to disappear again, forever.

Last. The word would not go away. He couldn't get a grip on the slippery surface of hope. His insides felt heavy and thick with despair.

The doctor came, listened to the nurse's account of what had happened, lifted Karen's eyelids, checked her monitored readouts, and almost shrugged. 'We'll just have to wait and see,' he said.

'But . . .' Drew wanted much, much more than this.

'I'm very sorry, Mr Slocombe. The brain is a fragile, unpredictable thing. We don't know how much damage has been done. The effects of a bullet can be very wide-ranging. We know, clearly, that a good deal of it must be undamaged. Your wife recognised the people around her, remembered the moments before she was attacked, and could evidently see and hear normally. All this is extremely good news. But there is a lot more to it than that. The bullet was lodged in an area of the brain that seems to work as a kind of back-up. It's in the hindbrain, an area known as the "pons". Well,' the man smiled ruefully, and toyed with a lank strand of hair at the back of his own head, 'if you must have a brain injury, this is probably the best part to have it.'

'Why?' Drew felt intensely irritated, all of a sudden.

'Because it doesn't affect consciousness, memory, identity – the stuff that makes a person who they are, if you like. All that, as I say, appears to be intact.'

'So you're talking about the part that controls breathing, muscles, heartbeat,' Drew supplied angrily. 'The part that keeps a person alive.'

'Not exactly, no. She is obviously breathing on her own, for a start.'

'Thank you, doctor,' Drew interrupted. 'I think I understand. I was a nurse, you know. I've seen people in comas before.'

'Ah. Right,' said the doctor, and stood there, at a loss for words.

'We'd better go and find something for the children to drink. And I'll phone my colleague. She'll be wondering how things are.' He ushered the children out of the room, with a backward glance at Karen. Surely she'd wake up again in a minute?

Only when on the phone to Maggs did he properly remember what Karen had said. 'Geraldine Beech visited her,' he also recalled. 'The policeman knew her, so he let her in.'

Maggs wasn't interested in Mrs Beech. 'She said she saw who shot her?' she repeated. 'But didn't give you the name?'

'It's crazy, isn't it,' he admitted. 'But somehow that didn't seem very important. Not compared with giving Timmy a cuddle, and asking her how she felt.'

'Did she speak to the Beech woman?' Maggs's interest abruptly revived.

'No, I don't think so. She didn't wake up until Timmy climbed on her.'

'Poor you. It must have been terrible. But it's very hopeful, surely? If she can wake up once, she can do it again. It's bound to be fits and starts for a while.'

'Bound to be,' he agreed hollowly.

* * *

Geraldine Beech was trying to contact Maggs at the same moment as Drew phoned her. The engaged signal exasperated her. She'd waited more than twenty-four hours as it was, before deciding she had to do something. Now it seemed as if there wasn't a moment to spare.

She slammed the receiver down and paced her spartan living room, thinking hard. She'd been a fool to ask Karen that question, and then leave it at that. She now knew too much, and not enough, all at once. Karen had seen her attacker; she knew who it was. But Geraldine hadn't asked for identification. She could have whispered one name after another, until a responsive squeeze gave her the answer. It would have been easy. So why hadn't she done it?

Well, she consoled herself, it probably *wouldn't* have been so easy. Karen might have become agitated, causing her fragile brain further damage. She might have squeezed at the wrong name. She might not have wanted Geraldine to know. And the policeman on the door might have noticed something going on. The only certainty was that Geraldine could not now rest until she knew who it had been.

She would have to flush the killer out of hiding, she resolved. Because it was, surely, the same person who had murdered Peter Grafton. She had to pretend she knew who had done it, that Karen had confided in her. She would offer herself as bait, tempting the person to have another go at silencing those who presented a danger.

But would the killer cooperate? Was there a limit to the murder attempts a person would undertake? It seemed almost farcical, looked at like that. Better, perhaps, to creep away unobtrusively, to leave the country and hide somewhere. Would that be seen as an admission of guilt in itself?

And still, like everyone else, Geraldine could not understand precisely *how* Karen had been shot. Where had the gun been? Where had the shot come from? Geraldine couldn't recall anything useful about the direction of the sound. It had seemed to envelop them all, to come from the whole procession all at once. If she'd been forced to say, then she'd have plumped for the back of the group. Someone from the village, then? Someone who had not been amongst Peter's closest family and friends. But that was unreliable. Geraldine herself had been walking next to Hilary Henderson, with Hilary between her and Karen. In front of them had been Joe Richards and Maggie Withington. Others were straggling somewhat, whispered conversations erupting here and there. She remembered thinking Sally Dabb ought to have been close by, as another stallholder. Then she had wondered just where Sally might be, given the uneasy circumstances. Probably right at the back, she'd concluded, with a pang of sadness at poor Sally's grief, which presumably could not be openly expressed.

The shot had not been deafeningly close. It had been frightening, shocking, in a way more immediate than the killing of Peter Grafton had been. That had only dawned slowly, with Sally's cries and Karen's pushing progress to the place where Peter lay. The second time, Geraldine's mind had simply frozen for a few seconds. It hadn't even occurred to her that there might be another murder victim. It had taken more seconds to notice the skirmishing at the garden gate, the shrieking child, the abandoned coffin. Suddenly there had seemed to be ten times the original number of mourners, all clustering and talking. Geraldine had stepped slightly back, away from the focus of attention. Hilary had stepped with her, and Mary Thomas appeared beside them. There were people enough seeing to Karen, they silently agreed. This time, they would stand aside, mere observers, unless called for.

It hadn't been Hilary. Nor had it been Maggie or Joe. That much Geraldine could vouch for. She would have seen their arms and hands, if they'd been holding a gun. The noise would have been inescapable.

And so she had to make her list. Everyone she could think of who had been present, no matter how unlikely they might be as killers. And then she had to let them know, indirectly, that she'd been Karen's confidante. The logical problem glared at her: she couldn't speak directly to any of them, and say 'Karen tells me it was you who shot her.' Neither could she say, 'Karen told me *who* shot her,' in case it was the person she was addressing.

She paced the room again. She'd have to enlist some help – that much she'd already concluded. And her choice had been Maggs Beacon. Maggs who seemed so sensible and competent; who was clearly above suspicion and had that ex-policeman boyfriend who might be expected to assist.

But Maggs was on the phone, and Geraldine was in a hurry. Well, then, it would just have to be Hilary, after all.

Hilary had been her first thought. Lifelong friends, understanding each other, privy to each other's secrets, it had initially seemed obvious to recruit her. But then she thought again. Hilary had that son, Justin, who seemed to be going rapidly off the rails. He was involved with some unsavoury characters, it seemed to Geraldine, although Hilary wouldn't have a word said against him. It might be far-fetched to link him with the market murder, and he certainly hadn't been at the funeral – but Geraldine wanted to be careful. Whoever she confided in would be given the task of spreading the word that Geraldine knew who the killer was, and would be going to the police with the information when . . . Here she hit another logical difficulty. Why hadn't she *already* gone to the police? What was she waiting for? She paced again.

OK. She was waiting to see how Karen was, over the next day or two. If the actual victim woke up and told everybody around her who had shot her, then Geraldine would not need to get involved. That would be a lot more direct, infinitely preferable in every way. It wouldn't be mere hearsay evidence. The police would take note, but they might not act on the information.

But that might not happen, and Geraldine still needed to act. She tried Maggs's phone number again, with the same result. So she would call Hilary, and give her very careful instructions.

Hilary would have to pass the information on as if telling no one else. It was so sensitive, so alarming, that obviously she couldn't shout it from the rooftops. And, of course, she would be slightly worried about her own welfare.

On a sudden thought, she phoned the hospital,

persuading the ward sister to disclose the basic fact that Mrs Slocombe was still in a coma, but had rallied briefly, to speak to her husband and children just for a minute or two.

That gave Geraldine some pause. Had Karen told Drew who shot her? Would it make any difference if she had?

She realised she would be disappointed now if she couldn't enact her plan. She was excited, eager to get on with it.

She phoned Hilary Henderson.

CHAPTER TWENTY-TWO

Drew talked to Maggs again when he got home, for twenty minutes, repeating himself, describing what had happened, consulting her on what should be done. 'She knows who shot her,' he said, again and again. 'And she was just going to tell the policeman.'

'She'll wake up again at any time,' Maggs assured him. 'And when she does, the policeman's there to listen.'

'He'd better not let anybody else in to visit,' Drew grumbled. 'I still think it was wrong to let Geraldine Beech in.'

'Of course it was,' Maggs agreed vigorously. 'It could easily have been her who shot poor Karen.'

'I didn't mean to suggest that,' he objected.

'Not really. Didn't we decide she was unlikely, last night?'

'Oh, well, you can't be sure, can you? She ought to have checked with you first, and she should have told you afterwards, as well. At best, it's a bloody cheek.'

Drew sighed.

Maggs went on, energised by this new twist. 'I tell you what, though,' she said, suddenly conspiratorial. 'We could *pretend* that Karen told you who did it. I could get Den to mention it here and there, just say he thinks the police know who they want, but they need more evidence. That sort of thing. Flush the person out. What do you think?'

'I don't know.' Drew's head was feeling clogged again, as it had after Karen was shot. He couldn't seem to follow a logical thread. 'Why do I keep thinking about Julie Grafton?' he asked. 'Something she said. Was it her, do you think?'

'She's certainly on the list,' Maggs agreed.

They talked around it, Drew struggling to keep his thoughts in order. Even when in enthusiastic mode, Maggs was somehow soothing. She seemed so eternally confident, so sure that everything would eventually come right. Up to now, he supposed, it always had. When you worked as an undertaker, you accepted death as a normal part of experience – or at least you got closer to that state of mind than most people did. You knew it was the eventual outcome of any story; that it was probably the cleanest option in many situations. Sometimes Drew wondered whether he and Maggs both jumped ahead a trifle too readily, assuming death to be more imminent than it actually was. Hadn't he just done that, with his own sweet Karen? Hadn't he automatically preferred her death to a long lingering survival in a coma, or a helpless paralysed state? And didn't that make him horribly abnormal?

If it did, then Maggs shared his aberration. And that was soothing.

'I'll get Den onto it, then,' she eventually wound up. 'He can go and see Mary Thomas first, and make her think he's telling her a big secret. I could pay Julie Grafton a visit, maybe.'

'It does sound very *contrived*,' Drew worried. 'Shouldn't we just leave it to the police this time? It's *Karen* we're talking about.'

'Yes, Drew,' she said patiently. 'It is Karen, and we want to know who did this to her, don't we? We don't want it to happen to anybody else.'

'Don't pull that one,' he snapped. 'It's unworthy of you.'

'Sorry. You're right. Well, then – call it revenge,

if you like. Call it nosiness, even. But I for one need to know who's roaming the countryside shooting people we love. Right?'

'Right.'

The children ate toasted cheese and drank milk while Drew skittered around the kitchen trying to get them organised. The cheese was rather burnt, but edible. At least he'd got them through another day, he told himself. And Karen had made a joke. And Maggs was on the case in a big way. Perhaps it would all be OK in the end.

'Someone's at the door, Daddy,' Stephanie told him, her voice loud. He hadn't heard a knock.

'Hello?' The visitor had evidently let herself in. 'Anybody there?'

'Della!' Stephanie announced. 'It's Della.' She didn't get down from the table, but the half-eaten cheese toast remained in mid-air.

Drew frowned. Hadn't there been some reason for coolness towards Della? That seemed weeks ago now.

'Come in,' he invited. 'We're in the kitchen.'

She looked taller somehow, standing over the table, her head bent down towards the children. She seemed to fix her attention on Stephanie to the exclusion of Drew or Timmy. 'Everybody OK?' she asked brightly.

The children nodded. Drew indicated a chair. 'Cup of tea?' he asked.

Della sat down obediently. 'Lovely. Thanks. Sorry I haven't come over sooner. I didn't know whether you'd be at the hospital all day. How is she? What do the doctors say?'

'She woke up this afternoon, actually. Just for a few minutes. She was completely normal; even made a joke.'

'Timmy did it,' Stephanie said, without emotion. 'He climbed on top of her, and she woke up. Then she went to sleep again.'

'Made a joke?' Della echoed.

'Sort of. She was so *normal*.' He rubbed the side of his face. 'And then went right down into the coma again. Deeper than ever.'

'How awful! What do the doctors say?'

'I don't know, really. I mean, *they* don't know. They say her memory and awareness and all that part of the brain are undamaged – but it's the pons – do you know about these things?' She shook her head. 'Well, it's the hindbrain, where the motor controls are, if you like. And a bullet does a lot of collateral damage. Everything gets shaken up. Blood vessels rupture. It's all terribly unpredictable.'

'You poor things.' She smiled at Stephanie. 'Do you want to come to me tomorrow?'

'It's Monday tomorrow,' said Stephanie. 'That's not your day.'

Drew tutted. 'Hey Steph, things aren't really as usual now, are they? If Della wants you to go to her house, you should be grateful.'

'No, no,' Della corrected him. 'Don't say that. We all like our routines, don't we? It's just that I'm not going anywhere, and if you need some back-up, I'd be happy for them to come to me. Finian and Todd would be very pleased. I mean, we all feel as if they're all one big family, really, don't we?'

Drew forced a smile. Is that how they felt, he wondered? Stephanie seldom talked about Della's boys, and he had the impression she didn't expend much feeling on them, other than an apparent partiality for Finian's help with some activities. For the first time, he tried to understand what it was like for his daughter, expected to spend four days each week playing with three boys. Finian was older than her, but much less bright. Todd and Timmy had paired up fairly harmoniously, as far as Drew could tell, which left Stephanie somewhat isolated, he feared. How hard it was, he thought despairingly, to read the mind of a child.

'Thanks,' he said. 'Can you bear it if we don't decide anything now? It all depends, really . . .'

'Of course,' she beamed. 'That's not a problem. Will you be going back to the hospital again this evening?'

'I don't think so.' He noted the lurch of anxiety at the suggestion. His reluctance to visit Karen had not abated. If anything it seemed stronger than ever. Irrational, almost shameful, but nonetheless real for that. 'They'll phone if they think I need to be there.'

And anyway, he had to be with his children. He had to put them to bed, read to them, and then stand guard over them. There wasn't anybody who could perform that role for him – not for the whole night. And he knew how hard it was to leave Karen's bedside, once he got himself there. Maybe that was why he resisted going in the first place? He was a mess, and he knew it. And there didn't seem to be much he could do about it.

'I can babysit any time, you know,' Della pressed him. 'Bill can take care of our two. I could even stay the night, if that helped.'

He shook his head, trying to hide the irritation he felt. He never really liked being helped; refusal was automatic, even when the offer came from Karen or Maggs. 'No, no,' he said. 'Thanks, but I'd rather be here. I know Karen's being well looked after. They've even got a police guard on the door, just in case.'

Della blinked. 'Gosh,' she said. 'How boring for the poor chap.'

'He's waiting for her to say who shot her.' Stephanie spoke into a silence, her words echoing and important. It seemed to Drew almost as if some other entity had spoken through the child.

'Is he?' Della's voice was faint by comparison.

'She nearly told him today, you see. She remembers everything.'

Drew felt as if he was being forced to confront something he'd been very eager to avoid. The moment could no longer be side-stepped. 'Steph,' he said gently. '*You* didn't see who it was, did you?'

The child turned large eyes onto his. 'There were too many people,' she whispered. 'I *should* have seen.' She pounded a small fist on the table. 'I *should*.'

'No, no, sweetheart.' He went and wrapped his arms round her. 'It's good that you didn't. It's not a nice thing to see.' He visualised a cold-eyed killer, pointing the concealed barrel of a gun at his wife and child. His little girl meeting those eyes, and being haunted by them for the rest of her life. 'It's *really* good that you didn't see,' he repeated.

Sunday evening was unusually active. Visits, phone calls, conspiracies, all quietly coming to a crescendo. Maggs imagined it as a sort of underground eruption, hardly stirring the surface of the sleepy villages enjoying a long May evening. But just below ground, there were tunnels and rumblings, plans and secrets, terrors and determinations.

Den had gradually warmed to Maggs's idea. 'It can't do any harm,' he judged. 'Not so long as Karen's being properly protected by that PC at the hospital.'

'He let the Beech woman in,' she reminded him. 'Maybe you should tell Danny to tell him to be more careful.'

'I wasn't planning on speaking to Danny,' he demurred. 'Not until we've got something concrete for him.'

'Mmm.' Maggs gave this some consideration. 'I suppose that's OK.'

'It is,' he said firmly. 'At the moment there isn't anything to tell him. We obviously can't reveal what we're going to do. He'd feel obliged to try and stop us. So we get on with it, and with any luck by tomorrow morning, it'll all be sorted.'

'Um.' She frowned. 'Even I think that's rather optimistic. How can it possibly be sorted by then? We need somebody to have another go at Karen, don't we?'

'Maybe not,' he said mysteriously.

Maggs's image of subterranean tunnels was not far removed from the way Geraldine Beech was viewing things. She was still determined to see the whole matter through to a conclusion before another day was over.

'It can't go on like this,' she had said to Hilary. 'We have to cut through all this inertia and really *do* something.'

Hilary had seemed very slow to understand the logic. 'But – I still don't see.' she'd grumbled. 'Are you suggesting we confront Sally and Julie? And is there anybody else you have in mind?'

'We're not *confronting* anybody. I just want you to phone them both, all natural and chatty. Tell them you've just been talking to me, and I told you I'd been to see Karen and – big secret – I now know who it was who shot Karen. But I didn't tell *you* who it was. Now do you understand?'

Hilary had sighed. 'Not entirely. I mean – you don't *really* know who it was, do you?'

'No. But the list has got a bit shorter, once I started to really think about it. All we're trying to do is flush the person out. If my hunch is right, they'll find some pretext to go and see for themselves just how Karen is. If she's showing signs of waking up – well, they'll either do something stupid, or they'll run away.'

'Something stupid?'

'Well, something to stop her from talking to the police.' Geraldine felt her fragile patience crumbling. 'Just *do* it, Hills. Trust me. This business is causing all sorts of damage to our campaign.

We have to identify the person responsible, and make sure nothing else happens. Don't you see?'

'I suppose so. What about Mary?'

'What? What *about* Mary?'

'Does she know about this plan of yours? Is she one of your suspects as well?'

'No, you fool. She was right beside you and me, wasn't she? How could it possibly have been her?'

'Well, yes, I suppose she was – at the funeral. But what about Peter? I must admit I couldn't help wondering – the way she suddenly turned up like that. It seemed very *artificial* somehow.'

'Don't worry about Mary,' Geraldine instructed. 'She's got nothing to do with it.'

'Well, I'm pleased to hear it,' said Hilary stiffly.

'Come on,' Geraldine urged, refusing to let her friend have the last word. 'Bear with me, will you? I'm only asking you to do it because there isn't any way I can manage on my own. You do want to know who it is, don't you?'

'I suppose I do,' Hilary acknowledged. 'So long as it isn't someone I care about.'

Geraldine took a deep breath. It had to be faced. 'You're not thinking about Justin are you?'

'What? What do you mean?'

'Only that he's got that gun, and he's been

mixing with the yobs from Fallowfield, and you might be feeling rather worried about him.' She was almost shouting, trying to get through to Hilary, who did seem uncharacteristically obtuse.

'Why should I worry about him?' Hilary folded her arms across her chest. 'And anyway, someone stole his gun a few days ago.'

'What?'

'Yes. He's really upset about it. It was the day Karen came to see me with her kids. Justin showed her the gun. He'd been shooting birds with it, and frightened her. I did wonder whether *she* took it, but I don't see how she could have. Nor why she'd want to.' She tightened her arms, gripping herself hard. 'Christ, Gerry, you don't think that I think *he* shot Peter, do you?'

'I can't think why he would,' Geraldine said. 'But how could anybody steal his gun? Didn't he keep it locked up?'

Hilary shook her head. 'It's only an airgun,' she muttered.

'Is it?' Geraldine paused. 'If it's only an airgun, how come it scared Karen? They hardly make more than a little pop.'

'I don't know. He's been mucking about with it, making it a bit more powerful. I don't understand the technicalities. And I don't know who stole it. One of his yob friends, I s'pose.'

Geraldine abandoned the topic of Justin for

the time being. 'So you'll do as I ask, will you?'

Hilary was still grudging. 'All right, so long as you understand that I don't like meddling. We're trying to do the work of the police, and I'm quite sure it'll backfire. What if I do as you ask, and Julie or whoever it is decides to shut you up? Have you got someone to protect you? No. Not even a dog. Are you immune in some way? I don't see how. It's *you* I care about, you idiot. If I do what you want, and that leads to someone taking a shot at you, how d'you think that'd make me feel?'

Geraldine could feel herself smiling. 'Don't worry about *me*,' she said cheerfully. 'I'll be all right. In fact, that's rather what I'm *hoping* will happen. That's what I mean by flushing the killer out.'

'Oh, I see. So you'll be marching up and down the High Street wearing a bulletproof vest then, will you? And something to cover your head. And legs. That's all right then.'

'Something like that,' Geraldine laughed. 'Now you just make those phone calls, and leave the rest to me.'

Maggs gave herself what she considered to be the best job. She got her motorbike out of the garage, checked it for fuel, tinkered briefly with its workings, and fished her crash helmet

401

out from behind a cobwebby pile of cardboard boxes. 'Time I used the poor thing again,' she said to Den. 'It must be six months or more.'

'Will it still go? Is it taxed?'

'Course she'll go, and I'd rather you didn't ask me about the tax. Now listen. I'm going to call on Sally Dabb and her husband – what's his name? I'll feed them the story, same as you will to Julie Grafton. I did tell you you'll be going to see her, didn't I? Then we'll meet at the Three Crowns at Ferngate to compare findings, before dropping in on Mary Thomas. OK?'

'Sunday evening,' he worried. 'Funny time to drop in on people.'

'Not this time of year. It's light until half nine. Nice weather. We're just out for a bit of a jaunt, called in at the pub, then decided to see how she's doing. Perfectly natural.'

'Right,' he sighed. 'Why did I ever think this was a good idea?'

'Because it is,' she said firmly.

But almost from the start things went awry. As she pulled up outside the Dabbs's house, she had the definite feeling that it was empty. No car in the drive; all doors and windows closed; everything quiet. Knocking on the door produced no response. 'Darn,' she muttered. 'Now what?'

It was far too soon to head back to Ferngate,

so she decided it wouldn't be very much of a detour to go and call in on Drew. He could probably do with some more cheering up and there might be fresh news about Karen.

But she should first try to phone Den, and let him know she'd drawn a blank. Or better still, text him, in case he was in the middle of a delicate conversation and couldn't speak freely.

Nobdy at dabbs. Gng to c drew instd. Call if anything to reprt.

Den would hate the 'c'. Try as she might, Maggs couldn't convince him that texting was a language all of its own, and perfectly acceptable as such. He stubbornly sent his replies in conventional English, wasting characters in the process. He and Drew were united in their aversion to mobile phones in general. Maggs dismissed them both as dinosaurs.

As it happened, the quickest route to North Staverton was down a narrow one-track country lane, which approached via the little-used direction at the other end of the village from Drew's cottage. It had taken Maggs years to fully explore the network of hidden lanes, but gradually, as she and Drew were called out to collect bodies, she had developed a comprehensive inner geography of the entire area.

There were effectively five villages within a seven-mile radius, as well as the town of

Bradbourne itself. None of the connections were on good straight major roads, although there was an A road sweeping through the middle of them, which had to be crossed, and even used for a few miles here and there. The Dabbs lived at Lumstone, midway between North Staverton and Ferngate, and only about two miles from North Staverton. Peter and Julie Grafton had taken over the farmhouse originally occupied by his parents, a mile or two west of Ferngate.

The road ran in a gentle curve, hedges high on either side, and Maggs kept her speed modest. The light was good, the sun behind her, throwing strong patchy shadows onto the lane. Anything coming towards her would probably be dazzled, she realised, since they'd be driving into the sun.

She became aware of a car behind her, apparently eager to overtake. She slowed and pulled into a passing place, letting the car accelerate past. It was a green BMW, which she had seen before, but which she couldn't place. It had two men in it.

Entering North Staverton from the north-west, she had to slow down to pass two cars parked in the road. There was scarcely enough space for anything to get past them, Maggs judged. Although nobody much used this road, it still seemed rather cavalier to obstruct it in this way. She had a closer look, and recognised both vehicles.

As a child, Maggs had been an avid carspotter. She'd known all the different makes and models, their engine capacities and acceleration rates. Her mother had despaired of her, but her father had enjoyed and encouraged her interest. It had waned when she left school, but she could still effortlessly identify any car, and associate it with its owner.

Here, she noted, was a green Mondeo, last seen parked outside Peaceful Repose for the funeral of Peter Grafton. Parked in the prime spot, since it belonged to his widow. And beside it was a red Citroën ZX, owned, if Maggs was not mistaken, by the missing Sally Dabb. And the house outside which they were parked was that of Della Gray, part-time minder of Drew Slocombe's children.

Well, well.

Keeping her head averted, she sped past. There didn't seem to be anybody watching her. A minute later she was knocking on Drew's door, at the other end of the village.

He let her in, looking drawn and bleary-eyed. 'Maggs!' he said superfluously.

'Listen,' she began without ceremony. 'Something's happening. I need to phone Den.'

Den didn't answer for a long time. Maggs tapped the wall impatiently, hissing through her teeth. 'He's left it in his coat pocket,' she fumed. 'Or he thinks it's something else playing a tune. God, he can be hopeless sometimes.'

She was just about to give up, when he answered. 'Where were you?' she demanded. 'Where *are* you, I mean.'

'Julie isn't in,' he said. 'I've been knocking on her door. Now I'm back in the car.'

'She's here, that's why,' Maggs said. 'I mean, they're *all* at Della's house, here in North Staverton.'

'Who?'

'Julie Grafton, Sally Dabb and Della.'

'Well, Della would be,' he said. 'What about the husbands?'

Then the penny dropped. 'Ah – I think I just saw the husbands, in Bill Gray's BMW,' she said. 'Look, Den, why don't you call your friend Danny and suggest he keeps an eye out for them?'

'Why?'

'Just a hunch. I can't explain, and I'll be ever so sorry if I'm wrong – but it wouldn't hurt, would it? He can just put a message out to all their officers on the road. The number's T442 FDR.'

'I'm impressed.'

'So you should be,' she chuckled. 'Have you written it down?'

'Of course. So what are you proposing to do now?'

For the first time in ten minutes she took a proper breath. 'Oh . . . well, I'm not sure.' She caught Drew's eye, as he stood in the kitchen doorway. 'But I think I might be having a bit of an idea. Please come, Den. I want you to be here.'

Drew waited for her to replace the phone, then he approached her, face flushed. 'Maggs? What's going on? Why are you in such a state?'

She tried to explain the original plan. 'And now, you see, everything's changed, if they're already somehow ahead of us. Well, I don't know.' She tapped a finger against a front tooth. 'Drew, have you spoken to any of them today? Julie, Sally or Della?'

He nodded. 'Della called in this afternoon.'

'And what did you tell her?'

'That Karen woke up for a few minutes. The whole story, I suppose.'

'OK. So let's assume that *she* had the same idea as we did. That she thinks it must be either Julie or Sally who shot Karen. So she invites them round, to tell them Karen knows who it is, and see what their reaction is?'

'Why would she?'

'Well, she's fond of Karen, isn't she? She's your friend. She must care about what happened.'

'She knows Julie, I think. Bill worked with Peter Grafton, so they probably met.'

'And Sally?'

'I don't know.' He spread his hands. 'I have no idea.'

'Well, I'm going back there.' She crossed her arms defensively, as if waiting for him to stop her.

'Is that wise?' he asked mildly.

'Necessary,' she said.

'Well, you're on your own, I'm afraid. I can't leave the kids.'

'I know. But Den'll be along soon.'

'Maggs, this isn't the same as last time, you know. You're dealing with a deliberate killer, who hasn't a lot to lose. With a gun and a crossbow, at least. Perhaps they're all in it together. If they think you're a danger to them, you're in real trouble.'

She smiled widely at him. 'I love you too, Drew,' she said. 'I do really.'

CHAPTER TWENTY-THREE

Karen surfaced from the grey mist again, listening deliberately to the sounds in the room. This time, her thoughts crystallised almost immediately, and with some urgency. There were questions jostling and insisting, which she badly needed to answer.

The main one was *why?* This she thought about carefully for several minutes. She had to do it little by little, nibbling away at the shocking implications of what had happened, without letting herself get overcome. That would simply send her back into the fog, and she'd already spent far too much time there.

Gradually she had most of it clear. She rested, satisfied with a job well done. Still there were no sounds of another person in the room. She resisted the temptation to open her eyes for a look, however. The sentinel policeman might be watching; something might register on the monitor. And she did not want to attract any notice just yet. Not until she was ready.

But there was more still to do. More questions clamoured at her. What had been going on out there, while she'd been drifting so irresponsibly? What would happen next?

A ghastly answer came to this last question. An answer that caused her eyelids to fly open, and her mouth to form a seriously loud scream.

'Call Drew!' she ordered, as soon as a nurse appeared. 'Phone my husband. I have to speak to him – now!'

Geraldine was aware of the battered Metro following her along the main road. When she turned off towards North Staverton, it came too, and she began to feel a flicker of concern. Despite her cavalier words to Hilary, she knew only too well that she was taking a considerable risk by doing what she planned to do.

The change of plan whereby she directed her course to North Staverton, rather than to Julie's house, had come as the result of a brief visit to Mary Thomas in Ferngate. She reported having seen Julie's car driving towards the main road, only twenty minutes earlier. 'Thanks!' Geraldine had cried, before setting off in pursuit. It had occurred to her instantly that Julie was on her way to see Sally Dabb. Those two obviously had unfinished business between them, of one sort or another.

But the Dabbs's house was empty, as Maggs had already discovered. And from there, the easiest way for Geraldine to get home was along the same sun-dappled narrow lane that Maggs had pursued previously. After North Staverton, there was a lane off to the right, which would take her back to her own hamlet of Didleigh.

History repeated itself in almost every detail. Geraldine recognised both cars outside Della's house – but didn't know whose house it was. Then, diverging from Maggs's line of action, she decided to stop and intrude, with no prevarication. It seemed, indeed, like a heaven-sent opportunity. If they were having a party, then she didn't see why she shouldn't join in too. Besides, the road was obstructed, giving her the perfect reason for banging on the door.

Without pausing to rehearse her opening words, she left her car on the roadside and walked up the path to the front door. Sally was her friend and colleague, after all. And Julie, in her role of new widow, could expect people to be watching out for her welfare. The difficulty might be that the person who lived here took exception to a strange visitor.

As it turned out, Geraldine did recognise the young woman who opened the door to her. She had been at Peter's funeral, with a man and two small boys. She was Della, daughter of her schoolmate Celia, sadly dead in her fifties. Geraldine reproached herself for not knowing that this was Della's house.

'Yes?' the young woman said, her face pale and strained.

'Hello, there!' Geraldine breezed. 'I'm so sorry to bother you, but I saw Sally and Julie's cars outside. I've been looking for them, actually. Is this awfully rude of me?'

'Geraldine Beech,' said Della, her voice thick with resignation.

'That's right.' The girl had a look of her mother, Geraldine noticed. 'I think you know Karen Slocombe.'

'I look after Karen's children.' The voice was still low and toneless. It felt as if all this was very much beside the point, and that Geraldine had interrupted something important.

'So could I have a word with Julie?' she pressed on. The silence in the house behind Della was strange; a kind of breath-holding.

'She's a bit upset just now,' said Della, glancing back over her shoulder.

'Is your husband in?' Geraldine asked, suddenly apprehensive.

'Oh no. He's out. He's taken the boys to his mother's. We . . . well, that doesn't matter. It's just as well, really.'

Confronted with increasingly clear evidence of something wrong, Geraldine found herself wanting to take several steps backwards and retreat to her car. Even more than the killing of Peter and the attempt on Karen, this present moment frightened her. She had deliberately walked into it, and would have to carry it through – but she very badly didn't want to.

The sound of a motorbike engine scarcely registered until it materialised into an actual Suzuki with a female figure astride it. The figure dismounted, removed her crash helmet and became recognisable as the coloured girl who worked for Drew Slocombe. She stood, solidly planted, watching the doorstep tableau with interest.

'Maggs?' said Della, her eyes narrowed in puzzlement. 'What do you want?'

Maggs smiled faintly. 'I noticed the cars, and thought it might be useful to talk to all three of you together.'

'Three of us?'

'You, Sally and Julie.'

'Why?' The word emerged on a high note,

spiced with anger, defensiveness, frustration.

Maggs just maintained her smile.

Then Sally Dabb came to the door. One eye was swollen and red, with a spreading bruise darkening her temple. Her hair was in extreme disarray.

'Gosh!' said Maggs. 'Have you been fighting?'

Geraldine stepped forward instinctively. 'Sally!' she cried. 'You poor girl! Let me have a look.' She hadn't fully understood how much she cared for the girl until now. It flooded through her, the need to touch and soothe and assuage. This, her favourite of all the stallholders, the most promising of her generation. Sally stood still, neither retreating nor approaching, simply waiting.

'Who did it?' Maggs demanded. 'What's been happening? Where's Robin?'

Nobody answered.

'Where's Mrs Grafton?' Maggs went on. 'Is she hurt as well?'

Della stirred, pushing herself away from the doorpost, where she'd been leaning tiredly. 'She's all right,' she said. 'Everybody's all right now.'

'Except Karen,' said Sally, her voice unexpectedly strong. 'My friend Karen – remember? In hospital with a bullet in her brain. Remember?'

Geraldine became aware of her seniority. She also became aware that they were standing in the front garden of a house in a village and before long they would be observed by local residents. There were two cottages in sight, as well as the Westlakes' farm just around the bend. Any raised female voices in a summer evening would be likely to attract some attention. 'Perhaps we should go indoors,' she suggested.

Drew was reproaching himself sternly for feeling such relief that he didn't have to confront anybody. He had already forgotten exactly what Maggs had said about Della's house, and why it was so important to go there and get things sorted out. He had a confused image of several women all gathered together, with secrets to disclose and confessions to make. Most of it would concern things he knew nothing about – things that Karen had become involved in, without keeping him informed.

But Maggs had phoned Den, who had said he was on his way. Did *he* understand what was going on? As far as Drew could work out, the former police detective had focused his attentions onto a completely different group of women: Geraldine and Hilary and somebody else. Three witches, all over sixty, and pillars of the community, in one way or another. Not really witches at all. That was just Den's silly word for them.

It was shock, he told himself. He was still suffering from the shock of seeing his wife motionless in a hospital bed. Still unable to work out whether she would live or die, and how he was going to manage, either way. What if she was permanently disabled? What if she needed constant nursing, from here on? This, he finally admitted to himself, was the thing he feared most. Drew Slocombe, who had once been a nurse himself, did not want to spend the prime years of his life tending a helpless wife. Especially since a helpless wife would also mean having to take full responsibility for the children. It wouldn't be *fair*, he whined to himself. Surely that wouldn't happen to him? Surely he'd never done anything bad enough to deserve such a fate as that?

Den arrived then, in the familiar battered car. He unfolded his long legs from the driver's seat and came quickly to the front door, where Drew was waiting for him.

'Where is she?' he demanded. For a moment, Drew could only think he meant Karen, and that this was a very silly question.

He opened his mouth, then shut it again. 'Oh, *Maggs*,' he realised. 'She went to Della's.'

'Where is that, exactly?' The impatience was very carelessly concealed.

'Just up there. You know. Through the village.'

'I know that much. What's the house called?'

Drew stared at him blankly. 'Della's house? It's white. On the right hand side. You'll see the bike, I suppose. And cars. She said there were other people there.'

'Are you OK?' Den leant down slightly to examine Drew's face. 'You look a bit weird.'

'I should have gone with Maggs,' Drew said, a sudden moment of clarity restoring him to a brief normality. 'I was scared.' He looked at Den like a small boy. 'I don't really think I can take much more. That's pathetic, isn't it?'

'Not surprising,' said Den calmly. 'I don't expect Maggs wanted you along. She'd have been worried about you.'

'I'm worried about *her*,' said Drew, realising how true that was, as he spoke the words.

'Me too,' agreed Den, and strode back to his car without any further comment.

Drew was summoned back into the house by the sound of the telephone ringing. He knew, even before he picked it up, that it was the hospital.

Den had no difficulty finding Della's house. The light was rapidly fading, and a clump of tall white daisies in the verge outside Della's gate glowed luminous in the twilight. The two cars parked halfway across the narrow road were an annoyance. Den pulled in as tightly as he could, a short distance from them. He could see Maggs's motorbike leaning against the stone wall that encircled Della's front garden.

There was a light on in a front window, and before knocking on the door, he glanced in.

The scene was apparently peaceful, despite the fullness of the room. Geraldine Beech was squatting, low down beside a fireplace, staring up at two younger women sitting side by side on a sofa. Maggs was standing, with her back to the window. Della, looking taller and thinner than before, was beside the door, a hand on the knob, head up and chin thrust forward. The words *at bay* flitted into Den's head as he watched.

It was with some reluctance that he stepped away from the window and knocked on the door. He knew he was disturbing a situation full of intensity. Something was happening, a climax building, that ought to be allowed to run its natural course. But this very sense of climax made it impossible for him to hold back. The looks on the faces of Della and Geraldine had persuaded him that this was no friendly evening get-together.

Whatever Maggs had intended with her 'flushing out' strategy, this was undoubtedly the closest she would get to it. One of these women was presumably being 'flushed out' at this very moment, and Den thought he had discerned which one, from that brief glance through the window.

And yet, how could Maggs have had time to put her plan into action? He had come the moment she'd phoned him, taking less than twenty minutes to cover the distance to Drew's. Was it possible that she had said her piece and drawn the anticipated response in those few minutes? Or had she walked into something that had already been happening before she arrived?

Nobody responded to his knock for a long time. He considered stepping back to the window and rapping on it, making his identity clear. He knocked again, knowing there was no chance that he'd gone unheard. They were preparing what they would say to him, or concluding their conversation – or deliberately excluding him from their all-female assembly. So he grasped the door handle, turned it, and pushed open the door, knowing all along it was very unlikely to be locked.

He was met by Sally Dabb, with a vividly bruised face and wild expression. She said nothing, but barged past him and out onto the garden path. He turned, as if to follow her, but was stopped by the voice of Maggs. 'Let her go,' she instructed him. 'We don't need her any more.'

Den entertained a brief image of a flock of

sheep, needing to be herded into a compound for shearing or worming. He'd helped various friends and relatives over the years with such tasks. He knew that when you let one escape, you were doomed. Somehow, all the others would manage to follow. With sheep, it was definitely all or nothing. 'Are you sure?' he asked.

'Yes,' she affirmed. 'Quite sure.'

Della then appeared, moving stiffly, chin still defiant, skin still pale. 'Hello,' she said. 'Join the party.'

He nodded to her, but his attention was all on Maggs. 'Are you OK?' he asked her.

'Of course I am.' She was obviously cross. Was it because he'd interrupted, he wondered. That would be unreasonable, after she'd summoned him so unequivocally.

Somehow they all returned to the living room, where Julie Grafton remained on the sofa, and Geraldine slumped onto a fragile-looking footstool near the fireplace.

Geraldine, Den realised, was the odd one out – the one he hadn't been expecting to encounter. In his mind she was inextricably connected with Hilary Henderson and Mary Thomas; it seemed wrong, somehow, to see her here with the younger women.

'Mrs Beech,' he said, acknowledging her. She looked up at him, and he became acutely aware of the strangeness of the situation. He had no right to be there. He wasn't a police officer, he barely knew anyone present, apart from Maggs, who had probably intruded as shamelessly as he had himself. Geraldine Beech seemed to read his thoughts.

'We all seem to have barged in on something,' she said. 'Poor Sally, it's all been too much for her, I'm afraid.'

'Don't go feeling sorry for *Sally*,' said Julie Grafton. 'What about *me?*'

Geraldine sighed noisily. 'It's terrible for all of us, I suppose,' she said. 'The whole thing is dreadful.'

Den kept his gaze on Maggs. 'Are you going to explain?' he demanded, with a sinking sense of having arrived either too soon or too late.

'It's not really . . .' she looked around the room, and shrugged elaborately. 'Geraldine was saying she went to see Karen. Julie was upset because she'd lost her temper with Sally. And Sally was already in a state because Archie's been talking to Bill Gray, about Peter. And he hit her.'

'Slow down,' Den ordered her. 'You're not making any sense at all.'

Geraldine shifted on her footstool. Maggs stopped talking and seemed to droop.

'But why is everybody *here?*' Den wondered, turning to look at Della.

The question seemed to cause the room's temperature to drop dramatically. Everyone froze. Maggs was apparently about to embark on an explanation when the sound of another car engine, racing impossibly fast along the village street, distracted her.

'Drew!' she said, a moment later.

Maggs went out to meet him, with the others straggling behind her. He came through the gate, his face red, the car engine still running.

'It's Karen!' he announced. 'She's woken up again and is desperate to talk to me. I've got to get there as fast as I can. I've sent Mrs Westlake to sit with the children, but she says she can't stay long. Maggs . . . Della . . . someone – will you go and take over from her?'

Without even waiting for a reply, he reversed the car into a narrow gateway across the road from the house, and somehow turned it around.

'He'll have an accident if he drives like that,' said Den severely.

'Karen must want to tell him who shot her,' said Maggs, in a clear voice. 'And there's a policeman there, as well. He'll be sitting there, listening. We'll soon have an answer to the whole business.'

Geraldine, Julie and Della all heard her, as she had intended.

Without warning, Della began running

towards the garden gate. Unbidden, the image of another escaping sheep came into Den's mind. He threw an all-embracing glance over the remaining flock, wondering who was going to make a dash for it next. 'I'll go and sit with Drew's kids,' Della said. 'Poor little things.'

Stupid with relief, Den stood aside to let her go. Maggs, on the other side of the gate, made a similar move. 'Where's your car?' she asked.

Della hesitated. 'Bill's got it,' she remembered. 'But I'll walk. It's only five minutes. Mrs Westlake'll wait. She hasn't got anything urgent to do; she just likes to get to bed early.'

Something about her tone made Den blink. She was too calm. It was as if she'd thought this through in advance and knew just what her moves were going to be. But he didn't know her at all. Maybe she was always like this, seeing right through to the central task in hand and dealing with it. Some people were.

'We'd better drive you, all the same,' he offered.

'No, no. I don't want you to. You'll need to talk to Julie and Geraldine. They've both got plenty to say to you.' She gave a bitter smirk, before setting off at a trot towards the other end of the village. Den watched her, feeling he'd just lost some sort of match. She was carrying a shoulderbag, and wearing sturdy shoes. The impression returned that she'd been intending to make an escape in any case.

'How could she have known . . . ?' he murmured aloud. Only Maggs heard him.

'What? Known what?'

'That Drew would turn up when he did. That the kids would need minding. She seemed *ready* for it, don't you think?'

'She's just quick, that's all.' Maggs was dismissive. 'Let's get back to the others.'

The living room seemed just as full without Della, although considerably less tense. Julie had gone back to her sofa, but Geraldine was now comfortably deep in an armchair.

Den had no idea what to do. He was not, he reminded himself sternly, an investigating officer. He was a local chap, interested in the local people, and concerned at what had been happening. He simply wanted to *help*, he told himself.

'I think we have to talk about who killed your husband,' he told Julie, almost regretfully. 'Isn't that why we're all here, anyway?'

'I know who it was,' said Julie, her pale blue eyes turning towards him where he stood so tall over her.

'No, Julie, you don't,' Geraldine corrected. 'You've got it wrong. I *know* it wasn't Bill.'

Bill? Den rummaged through the collection of names in his head.

'What? Della's husband?' said Maggs. 'Why did you think it was him?'

'Because he and Peter worked together on a project connected with genetically modified fruit.'

'OK,' said Maggs slowly. 'When?'

'Four years ago. It was very secret. Peter never liked it. He began to realise the implications, and talked to other people about it. People like Geraldine.' She flipped a hand towards the older woman. 'Until most people in the Food Chain group knew about it. Then SuperFare got wind of it, and decided to run a trial on the shelves.'

'But they're not allowed to do that!' Maggs was horrified.

'They were then. They were very careful. Everybody assured them it was perfectly safe. And I suppose it was. They hadn't done anything too ghastly to the apples, as far as I could work out. I thought Peter was being a bit daft about it, to be honest.'

'It's *you* who was daft,' said Geraldine crossly.

'Anyway, it was vitally important that Bill thought Peter was still entirely on his side. He'd have lost his job if the secret came out before the trials were completed. It was all incredibly cloak and dagger; everybody acting as if they were in MI6. But it just felt like a game, until last year.' She heaved a deep sigh, and dashed a finger beneath one eyelid.

'Which one would have lost his job?' queried Maggs. 'I think I got confused at that bit.'

'Bill, of course. He'd stuck his neck out with the supermarket people, as well as various growers and exporters. There was a huge amount of money to be made, but everyone knew how precarious it was. And then Peter just blew it, the idiot.'

'How?' Den and Maggs uttered the word simultaneously.

'He sent a letter to SuperFare, threatening to tell the media what was going on. He wanted them to withdraw the contract for the GM fruit. Then he offered to supply them himself, with the same quantities of organic fruit, as a sort of sweetener.'

'And they accepted! Amazing!' Maggs was stunned.

'Not quite. It took a year of negotiations, but eventually they said they'd buy juice from him. And they never really promised to stop their involvement with GM stuff. They just put it on hold.'

'No great hardship, the way the public started acting up,' said Geraldine sourly. 'Peter had much less influence than he thought.'

'But he meant well,' Julie insisted. 'And he put everything into the juice business. Left the laboratory job and concentrated everything we had into the new venture. That was very brave.'

'So his stuff was completely GM-free?' Maggs checked.

'Of *course* it was.' Julie's expression was outraged. 'That's the whole *point*.'

'And Bill lost his job?'

'Sort of. It all fell apart, anyway, a year or so ago. He blamed Peter for that.'

'And you think he waited a year and then killed him at the farmers' market?' Den was sceptical.

'He had reason. And he's got a crossbow.' She presented this final shot with a flourish.

Den and Maggs exchanged a look. 'Has he?' said Den.

'I saw it ages ago, when we were here for a meal. Della and Bill invited me and Peter. I went up to the loo, and had a bit of a snoop round, like you do. It was hanging on the wall in their spare room.'

'Didn't you tell the police when Peter was killed?'

Julie shook her head. 'I was going to, but then Bill seemed to have an alibi, and it was quite a while ago. And I thought – well, what *good* would it do? I always quite liked Bill, you see.'

Maggs leant towards her. 'Liked?' she echoed.

'Oh, nothing ever came of it. You could say it

was just a way of evening things up. Della always had a big thing for Peter, after all.'

Den and Maggs exchanged another look. She blinked and he frowned. Geraldine seemed to have been struck speechless.

'So what about Sally?' Maggs asked after a moment's pause. The question seemed to rip through a carefully constructed barrier. Julie's face registered shock.

'Sally?' she breathed.

'She seems to have been terribly fond of your husband, too.'

'That was a smoke screen,' said Julie, matter-of-factly. 'They've always been good friends, but nothing sexual in it. Peter was using Sally as a cover up.'

'Whoa!' Maggs pleaded. 'Is this for real?'

'No, it isn't,' put in Geraldine. 'You have to trust me on this, Julie. Peter really was in love with Sally. I'm sorry to have to say it; I know it's going to hurt you. But they were truly besotted with each other. I saw it growing and deepening. Whatever he told you, it wasn't true.'

'But he said it was all intended to get Bill and Della off his back. He said they were always after him, blaming him for the failure of the project, sniping and sabotaging.'

'But how would an affair with Sally change any of that?'

'He said Della had always had a thing for him, and she was giving out signals that he needed to deflect. He thought that if she could be discouraged, Bill would leave him alone as well.'

The room hummed with muddled thoughts and scrambled bits of mental jigsaw.

'I remember Peter Grafton when he was seventeen,' said Geraldine. 'He was absolutely gorgeous. Not just girls of your generation were chasing him – most of their mothers had private fantasies involving him, as well.'

'Which does sort of confirm what Julie's just been saying,' said Maggs. 'I suppose.'

Den was approaching it quite methodically, sifting and eliminating. He held up a hand. 'Bill didn't do it,' he said to Julie. 'His alibi is solid.'

'But he did have a crossbow,' said Maggs. 'And a motive.' The collective penny dropped. 'I think we'd all better go quickly to Drew's house,' said Den.

For Maggs the penny rolled down a further chute or two. 'We have to save Stephanie!' she yelled.

CHAPTER TWENTY-FOUR

Karen was still awake when Drew arrived. The sentinel policeman was by her bedside, with notebook open. 'She wouldn't tell me anything until you got here,' he grumbled to Drew.

'I'm obstructing the course of justice,' she said proudly, the bandage on her head looking loose and lopsided.

'I want you to know who shot me,' she said to Drew. 'Because it sounds so bizarre, the police will think I'm crazy.'

'Go on, then,' he encouraged, taking hold of her hand. 'Put us out of our suspense.' He felt light-headed, carefree. Somewhere, the situation was almost funny. Perhaps that was an occupational hazard – funerals could so readily slip into farce; someone almost always managed to say the wrong thing at a moment of high tension. It got so that you expected hysteria to erupt, whenever things got strained.

'It was Della,' she said, her voice low. Drew felt a thud of anti-climax, almost disappointment. Karen *was* crazy, after all.

'No, darling,' he corrected. 'Of course it wasn't Della.'

'Yes, it was,' she insisted, wide-eyed. 'She stood there, in front of everyone else, looking right at me and Steph, and pushed a gun barrel out from under her anorak. She must have been holding it under her arm, somehow. I never heard the bang, but I saw it. And I saw the look on her face.'

'But why? Why in a million years would she do that?'

'I think – and this is the truly awful part – I think she took Stephanie and Timmy with her when she went to kill Peter. I think she left them in the car, went into the public loos with the crossbow and shot him through the window overlooking the square. And I think Stephanie either saw the crossbow, or noticed something – I don't know – and Della got more and more worried that she'd say something.'

'But . . .' Drew's mind was working slowly.

'Yes, I know. It's awful to think of. Maybe she just wanted to add some new trauma, which would make Steph forget. I still can't really believe she'd deliberately try to shoot a little girl – a child she's looked after for over a year. But then, the more I thought about it, the more I decided she'd never liked Steph. And she's always wanted a girl of her own.'

'But why would she kill Grafton?'

'That I don't know,' Karen admitted. 'But Drew – you have to go now, and make sure Stephanie's all right.' She closed her eyes for a moment, inhaling deeply through her nose.

Horror flooded through him as he remembered. 'Oh, no!' he cried, getting to his feet. 'I've just asked Della to go and look after them.'

'What?' Even in his haste, he noted her colour fading.

'Don't worry, Kaz. I'll go and make sure she's OK. You just leave it to me. And don't get worked up. It's not good for you.'

She smiled wanly and he tore himself away. The nurse was already hurrying to the bedside. 'Will she be all right?' he asked, from the doorway.

'I'm sure she will,' came the reply.

He paused in agony. 'Maybe I could phone someone?' he said, to the policeman and the nurse together. 'And stay here.'

The policeman was already heading for the phone that had been dedicated to his use. 'As you like, sir. I'll get our people onto it, anyway.'

Drew dithered. Wife – child; child – wife. How in the world could he choose? Karen made it easier for him.

'Go!' she repeated. 'They need you, Drew. Go and bring them back safely. I want to see them when I wake up again.'

Den drove the short distance with the three women chattering like starlings in the car, trying to explain everything to each other. Nobody listened, and little sense was made, beyond the utter conviction that they had identified the killer, and that the Slocombe children were therefore in jeopardy.

They arrived to find the house quiet, and Karen's car missing from the parking area beside the house.

'Wait there,' Den ordered them all. 'I'll go and see what's what.'

Mrs Westlake, rosy-cheeked farmer's wife, met him at the door, eyebrows raised.

'Hello?' she said slowly. 'It's my lover boy who walks down the lane.'

'That's right,' he agreed, trying to control his impatience.

'Might I ask what's going on, then? Why has Della Gray gone off with little Stephanie the way she has? Nobody said anything about that, when I was asked to come and babysit.'

'She's taken Stephanie?'

'Said you told her her mother wanted her at the hospital, and she'd got to borrow Karen's car, since her husband had hers. Seemed all right, I s'pose.' Her tone was doubtful and resentful. 'Wasn't too sure about the insurance, mind.'

Den almost howled his alarm and frustration, but controlled himself, knowing he must keep the woman's goodwill and cooperation. 'Mrs Westlake – would you be able to carry on here for a while longer, keeping an eye on Timmy? Is he asleep?'

'He was, until Della showed up. Then he kicked up a fuss and said he wanted to go as well. Fact is, *he* wanted to go a darn sight more than his sister did. Della ended up carrying her to the car, with all sorts of trouble. Didn't seem fair, I thought – poor little man, left behind.'

Only then did Den notice a small face peering out from behind Mrs Westlake's broad hips. 'Hi, Timmy,' he said. 'Are you being a good boy?'

Timmy did not reply.

'I'll go and fetch Stephanie back, shall I? And your dad might be home again soon, as well. Best go back to bed, and in the morning it'll all be just as usual.'

He marvelled at his own facile untruths. But they seemed to have some effect. 'Come on then, Timothy,' said Mrs Westlake, turning and shooing him back into the house. 'Let's get nice and comfy, shall we?'

Den didn't wait for any more. He hurried back to the car, and opened the rear door on the driver's side. 'Sorry, ladies, but this is just Maggs and me from here on,' he said firmly. 'You're going to have to walk back to your cars. I'll catch up with you another time.'

Maggs was making her brain work double time. 'So, is this what happened? Della and Bill are in a foursome with Julie and Peter Grafton. Everybody fancies everybody else, and a bit of wife-swapping might not be out of the question. The men work together, and Peter betrays Bill bigtime. Then he betrays Della, who thinks if he's going to have a girlfriend, then it's definitely going to be her, not Sally Dabb. Everybody's talking about them. Julie's fobbed off with some garbage. Della flips, and shoots the bloke before he can do any more damage.'

'A woman scorned,' Den agreed.

'But *how?* She was looking after the four kids that morning. Nobody even considered her as a possible, because of that.'

'She must have taken them with her. Left them in the car, probably.'

'And Stephanie saw something. Or heard something. Enough for Della to worry that she'd give the game away.'

'Right.'

'Because we know – don't we – that she wasn't aiming that gun at Karen at all. It was *Stephanie* she meant to shoot.'

'Assuming that was Della as well,' he cautioned. 'That's a bit of a leap.'

Maggs shook her head. 'It was her,' she said. 'And I bet I know where the weapon is, too.'

'Weapon?'

'Sorry – weapons. Call Danny again, and see if they've stopped that BMW yet.'

'Where are we going?' she asked a minute later.

'Nowhere in particular. We're just keeping a lookout for her.'

'We should be able to work it out,' Maggs sighed. 'There has to be some clue we've missed.'

They each puzzled silently, while Den drove along the main road for a few miles, in a westerly direction. A sign pointing to the left saying FERNGATE seemed to trigger a thought in Den's mind.

'Mary Thomas!' he said. 'The glaring loose end in this whole mess.'

'Hmmm?' Maggs only half attended. 'Why Mary Thomas?'

'Because she's been much too quiet and invisible these past few days. And nobody mentions her. As if there's a conspiracy to make us forget all about her.'

'OK,' Maggs shrugged. 'Any hunch is better than none.'

Den swerved recklessly into the small road, with little time to slow down before doing so.

'Yes!' he crowed, as they entered the pretty compact little village. Karen's car was clearly parked outside 'Cherry Blossoms'.

'Call Danny,' Maggs ordered him. 'This is no time for heroics. And I'm going to call Drew. Let's hope he's not still in the hospital, or the mobile won't be switched on.'

Den was more successful than Maggs in making his call. Drew's phone rang, but he didn't respond. 'I bet he's left it at home,' she tutted irritably. 'I'll do him a text message – though I doubt if he'll see it.'

Steph with della and mary thomas. Frngate. Will keep u posted.

Den was too late to stop her sending it. 'What good's that going to do?' he demanded. 'It'll drive him even more frantic.'

'I just thought he should be kept up to date,' she pouted. 'It's his kid, after all.'

'So what now?' he asked. 'Do we just sit here?'

'We do,' she said firmly. 'And hope they don't notice us.'

'Until the cavalry arrive?'

'Something like that.'

He let her think she was making the important decisions. Den had developed a knack of allowing Maggs to assume control. It oiled their relationship miraculously.

'This is fun, isn't it,' she said after a minute or two. 'You and I haven't done this before – not really. Though I must admit that this time there isn't the same adrenalin rush. I just can't believe Della would do anything to actually harm Stephanie.'

'I wish I had your confidence,' he said. 'I'm only staying out here because I think it would make things worse to rush her. I'm not at all sure about her mental state.'

'And Mary Thomas? Is she going to be a calming influence?' Den gave this some consideration. 'Probably,' he concluded.

The police arrived with the most admirable circumspection. No sirens, nothing to indicate the sudden presence of six officers, two of them armed. They were just *there*, from one moment to the next. Maggs gave a stifled squawk as they loomed out of the dark and surrounded the car.

'Two women and a kiddie in there, is

that right?' Danny asked Den, with perfect professionalism.

'As far as we know,' Den confirmed. 'We haven't actually seen anybody.'

'And we have the strong suspicion that one of the women is the killer of Mr Grafton, and is the same person who attempted to kill Mrs Slocombe?'

'That's right,' said Den. 'A very strong suspicion.'

'Right.'

'I don't think she has a firearm with her. I'm almost certain she hasn't,' Den added. 'And we believe the second woman will be entirely cooperative. She's on our side.'

'Or so we think,' interjected Maggs. 'That might be wrong.'

'OK.'

Detective Superintendent Hemsley mobilised his team. They moved on the house, back and front simultaneously. Den listened for sounds of doors being kicked in, shouts, screams, even shots. There was nothing. He and Maggs stood beside their car and strained their ears.

Then a group of people came out of the front door, as if assembling for a funeral party. A woman police detective was carrying Stephanie. Maggs ran up to her. 'Hey, Steph,' she greeted the child. 'Are you OK?'

Stephanie wriggled in the woman's arms. 'Put me down,' she said.

'I think she'd be best coming with me,' Maggs said. The policewoman looked dubious. The threat of conflict was averted by the arrival of Drew in the Peaceful Repose van. Maggs recognised the engine sound before anyone else even noticed. 'Here's her Daddy, anyhow,' she said.

Den was standing in front of Della. 'You killed Peter Grafton,' he said.

'Hey, steady on!' Hemsley cautioned him. 'That's not the way to do it. Surely you haven't forgotten?'

Della said nothing, but Mary Thomas stepped forward. 'I'm afraid she did,' she said. 'It's all most dreadfully sad.'

'And you? Where do *you* fit into the story?' Den demanded.

'I don't think this is quite the time or place, do you?' she replied, with some gentleness. 'Let's just say I've followed developments fairly closely.'

'Just tell me this,' he insisted, with a glance at Maggs to ensure she could hear. 'Have you or haven't you really got a twin sister?'

For reply, another woman stepped from out of the shadowy porch of the house. She was a greyer, plumper version of Mary, the facial features identical. 'I'm Simone,' she said, in a voice lacking any trace of an accent. 'I think that answers your question, doesn't it?'

Den realised that it did no more than unleash a further long list of enquiries, but he merely nodded and turned to where Drew and Stephanie were enjoying a happy reunion.

Della was inserted into the back seat of a police car and driven away. Hemsley led Den to a point below the one and only village street lamp, and gave him a severe look. 'I don't believe you kept me very well informed on all this,' he accused. 'If it hadn't been for DC Plover at the hospital confirming that Mrs Slocombe had clearly accused Mrs Gray, I don't know that I'd have believed you when you called this evening.'

'I'm glad you did,' said Den. 'For Stephanie's sake.'

'Would she really have hurt Steph?' Maggs asked in a low voice. Drew and the child were not far away.

'Who can say?' shrugged Hemsley. 'But I might just mention that she was relieved of a rather nasty knife just now. The sort of knife you'd expect to find in the pocket of a mugger or a street gang member. It suggests she meant business.'

Maggs winced. 'Why did she come to Mary Thomas's, then? Surely Mary would never have allowed her to harm Stephanie?'

Den cleared his throat. 'I think I know the answer to that,' he said. 'Mary Thomas was Della's mother's best friend. They've always been special to each other. The story about the twin sister being the person Karen saw at the supermarket was pure fabrication. Karen did see Mary there – and she had just set that bomb to explode. What's more, Stephanie had seen her as well. I think you'll find they were checking on whether the child recognised her. If so, then Mary would have reason to collude in her disposal.'

Maggs winced again, and Hemsley uttered a low moan. 'An innocent witness – one of the most dangerous situations to be in,' he said thoughtfully. 'Thank God it never happened.'

'You can say that again,' chimed Maggs, watching Drew clasping his daughter tightly to him, while telling her that her Mummy would be fine, and very soon everything was going to be all right.

Karen took a whole day to resurface again. In the meantime the hospital had scanned and tested and concluded that there was some permanent damage to her brain, which was likely to lead to some dispraxia, at least for the foreseeable future.

'Dispraxia?' Drew echoed. 'You mean she won't be able to walk?'

'She will walk, but probably jerkily. Carrying things will be difficult. Writing, sewing, small movements – they'll all be compromised.'

'Gardening?' Drew asked faintly.

'Probably that will be possible,' came the wary response.

When she did finally start talking again, the first thing she said was, 'It must have had something to do with Timmy's knee.'

'That's right!' Drew said. 'It seems that he actually knelt on the crossbow, and Della went mad. Shouted at him, and pulled the thing away so violently, he fell over. Then she was all apologies, kissing and cuddling him. Stephanie and Tim both found the whole business bewildering. They didn't know what the crossbow was, and Della quickly packed it away in a big blue canvas bag.'

'Steph knew it was canvas?' Karen's woozy brain seemed intent on picking up minor details. Drew struggled to remain patient.

'No, no. The police found it last night. As well as the gun. It was Justin Henderson's converted Brocock.'

'Uh-h-h?'

'Sorry. You don't need to know about that.'

'Justin? Hilary's boy? But I saw the gun. He fired it when I was there.'

'So I gather. Hilary told me. She also admitted that she was so angry with him, afterwards, that she took the gun away from him. Then she left it in the back of the car when she went to Grafton's funeral. She never dreamt it was loaded, or so she claims. Just snatched it and then never got around to doing anything with it. When she realised what had happened she thought Justin had crept up at the funeral and shot Karen. So she pretended the gun had been stolen.'

'Hilary?' Karen was barely keeping up.

'I don't think Della really intended to do anything at the funeral. But she saw the gun, sticking out from under a blanket, and just took it, as we were all going down to the church. She had it under her coat when we processed back. The thing is, Bill saw her shoot you. He grabbed Della, and rushed her along to get their boys. Afterwards, she admitted the whole thing, and he decided to dump both weapons, yesterday.'

Karen sighed. 'So that's the whole story, is it?'

'Except for Archie and Sally,' he remembered.

'Tell me.'

'For much of yesterday, Sally was crying about Peter Grafton, and Archie was getting more and more angry with her. In the end he hit her. She ran out of the house, saying she never wanted to live with him again. I don't know where she was going, but she took the car and headed down towards us. He didn't try to follow her, but sat down to try and think it all through.

'He's a builder, you know. He never bothered much with the Food Chain or any of that – but he was well up with all the local gossip. He knew what people were saying about Sally and Peter. But they didn't know that he and Sally hadn't been living as husband and wife for ages – or so she told Julie and Della.'

Karen flapped a feeble hand, trying to encourage him to get to the point.

He smiled. 'It's not such a big thing, really. Just that Archie phoned Bill Gray, after Sally had gone. Asked him to come round for a chat. I don't know the details, but the two of them were in the car together when the police caught up with it. They were parked in a lay-by, not really bothering to keep out of sight. The gun and crossbow were in the hedge, right next to the car. And the men were kissing.'

'Goodness me,' Karen murmured. 'Goodness gracious me.'

If you enjoyed *A Market for Murder*, you'll
love our other books by Rebecca Tope . . .

Grave
Concerns
Rebecca Tope

The Sting
of Death
Rebecca Tope

'One of the most intelligent and thought
provoking of today's crime writers'
Mystery Women

'The classic English village mystery
is alive and well'
Sherlock Magazine

'Exciting, humorous and topical'
Crime Time

'Rich in psychological insight . . . Tope is
particularly skilled in creating interesting
and unique characters'
Deadly Pleasures

THE COTSWOLD SERIES

A Cotswold Killing
Rebecca Tope
Murder in the heart of the Cotswolds...

A Cotswold Ordeal
Rebecca Tope
A beautiful setting ...for a sinister death

Death in the Cotswolds
Rebecca Tope

A Cotswold Mystery
Rebecca Tope
There's trouble brewing in the Cotswolds...

Blood in the Cotswolds
Rebecca Tope

Slaughter in the Cotswolds
Rebecca Tope

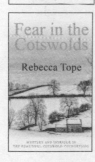

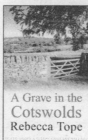

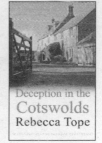

Fear in the Cotswolds
Rebecca Tope

A Grave in the Cotswolds
Rebecca Tope

Deception in the Cotswolds
Rebecca Tope

To order visit our website at
www.allisonandbusby.com
or call us on
020 7580 1080